The Carborundum Conundrum

Other books by Robin C.M. Duncan

The Quirk and Moth series:
The Mandroid Murders
The Carborundum Conundrum

Anthologies:
Distant Gardens
Farther Reefs
Lofty Mountains
The World of Juno

The Carborundum Conundrum

A QUIRK AND MOTH FIASCO

Robin C.M. Duncan

Space Wizard Science Fantasy
Raleigh, NC
www.spacewizardsciencefantasy.com

Publisher's Note: This is a work of fiction. Names, characters, places, and incidents are a product of the author's imagination. Locales and public names are sometimes used for atmospheric purposes. Any resemblance to actual people, living or dead, or to businesses, companies, events, institutions, or locales is completely coincidental.

Cover art by MoorBooks
Editing by Heather Tracy
Quirk & Moth logo by Paul Harris
Book Layout © 2015 BookDesignTemplates.com

The Carborundum Conundrum /Robin C.M. Duncan.—1st ed.
ISBN 978-1-960247-07-0

Author's website: https://robincmduncan.com/

Warning: This book contains character dialogue containing derogatory terms used against lesbians and other queer people.

This book is dedicated to two men, both great in my eyes: Maurice Taylor Duncan and Dr. Erik T. Paterson, who never faltered.

My father, Maurice, introduced me to Science Fiction at an impressionable age by giving me a copy of Larry Niven's anthology *The Year of the Horse*. I never looked back and doubt I ever would have been a writer without him. He tutored me in Physics, and in life.
I love you, Dad, and wish I'd said that more when I had the chance.
I hope your rest is a peaceful one.

My father-in-law, Erik Paterson—when not tending to the sick—wrote galaxy-spanning adventures, penned papers about medicine in space, and gazed at the stars through his telescope. Erik was the first to show me that writers were just people, people with something that they could not exist but to say.

Also, this book is dedicated to Canada: Yes, all of it. That nation—perhaps unsurprisingly given its deserved global reputation—has been incredibly kind to me. Not only has it provided me with a wife, and therefore by extension a daughter, but also a son-in-law and, by further extension two of the coolest co-parents ever; any number of warm welcomes; true inspiration from its trees, mountains and lakes; and a whole host of poignant, tender, heartfelt memories.
Go Canucks!

"There is no honour among consultants."
—Constable Moore
(*The Diamond Age*, by Neal Stephenson)

CONTENTS

00

"BEATRIX'S ROMAN ENCOUNTER"

FADE IN:

EXT. ROME—DAY—BRIGHT SUN IN A CLOUDLESS SKY

A person with soft, Mediterranean features—who will, in under forty-eight hours, earn the soubriquet 'Beatrix Potter'— approaches a tall man, bearded, of dark countenance, who stands in the shadow of a towering historical monument. Roman ruins form the backdrop to this anonymous meeting.

> DARK BEARD
> A new assignment. The one you wanted, I think.
> (he proffers a handset)

> BEATRIX POTTER
> I'm in the middle of something. This better be him.
> (taking the handset, Beatrix speaks into it)
> Pronto? (pause) Ah, it's you.

> CALLER
> This is about our common acquaintance. He has things to do first, but stay close. His time is coming. Not on Hygeia, nor in Milan, but soon. You'll be advised when. For now, just keep an eye on him. Details to follow.
> (coughs three times)

> BEATRIX POTTER
> Are you unwell? Nothing trivial, I hope. Anyway, I need to hear the words, for insurance purposes.

>   CALLER
> When the instruction comes, you will terminate
> Quinton Kirby with immediate effect. Do you
> understand? Please acknowledge.
> (pause, during which two coughs)
>
>   BEATRIX POTTER
> I understand.
> What about the Rigel people?
>
>   CALLER
> (cough)
> Nobody needs to worry about Toni di Fantano
> anymore.

DISSOLVE TO:

EXT. MILAN—DAY—48 HOURS LATER—THE SKY IS AZURE

Quinton Kirby, sporting his indigo suit with dark green pinstripes, walks away across the Piazza del Duomo towards the Galleria Vittorio Emanuele. The person now labelled Beatrix watches him go, a welter of emotions broiling within, which, for an accomplished assassin, is not a good thing. Only two days before xis biggest client called with the assignment xe had long anticipated. Not-Beatrix had known it would come, and that it would come to xim, having been there in Toni di Fantano's house five years ago, having seen this strutting rake skulking around, having watched helplessly as Quinton Kirby literally dodged the bullet that killed xis partner and lover Pascal.

Not-Beatrix's breath catches. This pain will never leave xim, hopefully. The pain of losing a partner in life and love, and in such farcical circumstances. This pain feeds xim, fuels this personal quest, brings a succulent satisfaction to the whole thing, knowing that xe holds Quirk's life in these hands, and can—in any one moment—preserve it, or end it.

In a sense, the handsome, elegant, conceited, self-righteous shit is already dead.

01

3 months later...
21:03, 16 November 2099
200m off Lakeview-Arrowcreek Road, Creston,
British Columbia, Canada, North American Federation, Earth

The last vestige of day had departed, and the sky was a clear midnight blue. The stars winked at Moth as she plodded with uneven steps down the snowy bank between looming, half-seen trees. The crescent moon gave her light to choose a path as she picked her way slowly through the woods towards the house.

She took another awkward step, tugging her booted foot free of the creeping cold, only to sink it back in as she descended the forty-degree slope from the road above. She paused again, concerned about straining her reconstructed leg even though it felt totally normal. She shivered. The self-warming gloves Quirk bought her in town were fine, but they didn't do her toes any good, or her nose. Earth's 9.81 metres per second squared gravity circumvented her better judgement and dragged her, arms windmilling, downslope to the foot of the bank. She let herself stumble the last few metres and clutched the thick trunk of the last tree; a paper birch, she thought, from the way its bark crinkled under her gloves.

Lines of black, spectral fruit trees, outlined by the light from the house, stretched across the level ground towards a timber slat fence. Thirty-three metres away that fence, according to Kodak PlanetView, which whispered to her earbud in the voice of her handset, zipped up in a slightly illegal scan-proof bag in her pocket. All because the target hated anyone else's technology so very much that he'd installed scanners all around his property.

Asshole, thought Moth. *Stealing other people's shit is not cool. But we're gonna take you down.*

She puffed out her cheeks and refocused. All she could see of her path ahead through the orchard was the black barrier of the fence, but beyond it she knew was the pool and then the back door. Lighted top floor windows glowed gold in the darkness, beckoning her out of her wintry hell. Even from here, she could see a grey-haired man with a glass in his hand, talking to someone, presumably Quirk, over his shoulder.

It started to snow again.

This was no place for a good Milanese girl—a convent girl at that—who always said her prayers and brushed her teeth. Moth shivered again. *All because Quirk's finely chiselled face fit the fucking story, he gets the easy end of the deal, again!* "Oh no, Moth dear, I need to arrive in the car to look the part of the art dealer, and Eighty needs to be my android chauffeur. I'm the only one who can play the part, Moth, dear. And you're so young and athletic; you'll be able to vault over the concrete road barrier; scamper down the snow-covered, forested bank; skip through the frozen orchard; hop over the fence; tip-toe around the winterised pool; creep up the back stairs to the deck and record the conversation. I'll be scanned at the door, and Eighty will have to stay in the car, drive away in fact, because alleged art thief Greiner is very suspicious, and trusts no technology but his own."

Another case where she ended up with the donkey work and Quirk would glad-hand the client and make some offhand remark about her invaluable assistance.

Assistance! Cheeky bastardo.

She started forward slowly, pushing off the paper birch. A low branch raked her arm, somehow finding the gap between glove and parka sleeve. "Fuck," Moth hissed as the jutting twig tore her skin. She stopped in her tracks, sucking in chill air. Her breath caught in her throat then came out in a white puff that she failed to conceal, was blown back onto her face to freeze there. Her arm stung. She pulled her woollen scarf up to cover her nose. Hot, damp breath was trapped against her face.

She fucking hated Canada, bloody hellhole. Even the Moon was warmer. She looked up at the glowing lunar crescent as she tramped across the open strip of glistening, fairy-dust snow to the first apple tree. She struggled to believe that she had been there six weeks ago, struggled to process her feelings about the dozens of deaths caused by Gregor Callan, engineer of the Lunaville dome disaster.

She stopped as her breath caught again, this time from a surge of unwanted emotion. She brought a big Snowtex glove to her mouth, stifling a grunt, the fabric crackling as it folded. She still had nightmares about being trapped in the collapsed Androicon building, smothered in rubble and bodies as the air leaked away until being dragged out by NAF marines. She'd been sure everyone was dead, including Quirk out there on the lunar surface, or in the building, where his body was. It was hard to admit she had prayed for him to live, despite her uncle conning Quirk into becoming her guardian. And now her guardian and employer was comfy in the splendid surroundings of Louis Greiner's plush, Kootenay Valley super-rich retreat, while she was stuck doing the leg work, and with a rebuilt leg!

After three more deep breaths, she started forward through the dormant orchard. She made it a whole ten metres before stopping again. There was something...moving. There, beyond the trees. A low shape, a dark grey smudge against the brown darkness of the wooden fence. She shuddered like someone had tickled her grave with a feather. There was a gentle sighing *behind* her. It sounded for all the world like breathing. Slowly, Moth looked over her shoulder, back through the first few spindly trees, which were *not* closing in and reaching towards her. They weren't! There were three more low, pacing shapes behind her. *Oh, shit.* The lovely-but-nosey lady in the Canyon Street outdoor store where they'd bought Moth's parka had said something about wolves. "Have a great day. Don't go up in the mountains at night, eh." *Fuck.* And yet this was wrong. She recalled Natural Science, Module 12, Lecture 7: "*Homo sapiens* as Lunch," which was very clear that wolves did *not* behave this way. And yet the shapes moved with that slinky, lupine grace, their silhouettes appearing soft, as with fur, pointed ears pronounced against the moonlit snow. So, were they some kind of genetic hybrid? Big dogs with brainboxes?

She wished she had a knife, or even a stick. Maybe a SIG Sauer P777-J semi-auto pistol with the fifteen-degree grip. But she didn't, she only had stupid NEMP tech. *Neuro-Electromagnetic Pulse: Zapping-the-fuck out of android operating systems since 2043. Strictly law enforcement issue only. Strictly not for the use of Milanese convent girls, and fuck all use against flesh and blood.* She really hoped they were androids, preferably programmed to scare. She started backing towards the fence, because one behind her was better than three, right? She darted a glance over her shoulder to see a second grey-dark shape skirting the fence. *Great, but two is better than three. It is.*

Running left would take her back to the forested bank. They would be on her in a flash. To the right was another bank down to the same public road that enclosed Greiner's property in a tight loop, but it was twenty metres away and the waiting canines were fifteen metres ahead and behind her. She wouldn't make it.

The low shapes encircled her and began a threatening chorus of deep growls. Moth fumbled for her pockets. Shouting for Quirk would be useless, he'd never get down here, even if he was inclined to break cover. Maybe her faithful android syRen® S-0778a—Eighty for short—would come crashing in and unleash the full fury of the Laws of Robotics. Any, second, now! Like...now! Maybe, now?

Nope.

She edged toward the fence again. The growling became louder. Moth's heart hammered in her chest and her breath came in quick puffs of alarm-system-visible white, but it hardly mattered now. She was more worried about being savaged by a cyborg lupine killer, because an android couldn't, the laws prevented it. So, either these were dumb, walking man traps, prowling animals angered by her incursion, or scary but impotent android warning signs. Time to find out.

She had maybe ten metres to spare front and back. Five pairs of eyes glowed in the dark. One of the wolf-things snapped its jaws. Moth's smartlenses fed infrared data to her cLife, which whispered that the fence was 200cm high, and she was 160cm in her boots with a 31cm reach: she'd have to jump. *No surprise there then.*

She turned and ran at the fence.

The pair of wolf-things ahead growled and crouched, teeth flashing in the moonlight. Her snowbound steps were so slow. A chorus of angry barks erupted all around her, shredding the night's silence. Moonlight picked out the teeth in front, and those glowing eyes. *Glowing? Flashing? Not meat. Droids!*

She dropped into a baseball slide. The beasts sprang forwards. She flung off her $479.99 super-gloves and pulled her hood up hard, tucking into a crinkly Snowtex ball, ripping Velcro, she grabbed at her inside pocket. She found the NEMP and jammed her thumb down on the big, red button then shuddered against the expectation of jagged teeth ripping at her—even though they couldn't, shouldn't—powerful, urgent snouts seeking weak spots. Hot breath steamed inside her synthetic cocoon, but it was hers. There was no attack. The barking had stopped. The only sensation was the chill seeping into her limbs.

She risked raising her head. Through a crack between the snow and the furry edge of her hood she saw two grey-dark mounds lying on the snow beneath the canopy of gnarled branches. A third shape remained standing, but its eyes were dark, inert, deactivated. She squirmed around towards the fence making a panicked snow-angel, and saw another prone wolf shape almost within snapping reach of her, also still and silent. The final wolf stood statuesque by the fence.

Moth gasped as she uncurled, sitting up in the snow, a broad smile plastered across her face. *Eat NEMP, android mofos!* She struggled up, kicking the nearest wolf-thing, then walked to the fence.

Her handset's velvet tones whispered in her ear. *"Message from Eighty: Alarm system deactivated."* With a grin, Moth stepped up on the standing wolf's back, pulled herself over the fence and dropped down into the snow-blanketed pool area.

* * *

Quirk smoothed the olive-green pinstriped indigo fabric of his Merrion suit from the top of his thigh to his right knee, which was crossed over his left. His hand took off slowly from his thigh, mimicking a GA-13 atmospheric shuttle leaving Dinklage Field spaceport in New Jersey, describing a lazy arc back to the arm of the chair. *Is that wool? Maybe worsted.* He glanced languidly around the beautifully appointed living room. It was warmly lit, decorated in alpine chic, lots of wood, but pale cream walls on which hung a small sample of Greiner's collection. It was magnificent. *Roses* by Samuel Peploe, circa 1920; Henri Manguin's *Woman Bather*; *La jetée à L'Estaque* by André Derain from the same year, 1906.

Quirk looked up at the grey-haired Greiner, whose back was to him as the man fixed their drinks. He disliked looking up at people. It was the worst kind of pantomime one-upmanship. When the host stood, it weakened a seated guest. That was Greiner's intention, of course, this was a negotiation after all. Well, Greiner thought it was. Quirk's slender host turned away from the glass-topped cabinet holding two cut crystal glasses. He moved with an easy, efficient gait, regarding Quirk down his slightly hooked nose.

"Ungava and tonic," said Greiner. "Are you trying to ingratiate yourself by choosing a Canadian gin?"

Quirk smiled slightly, a filtered *Rictus of Insincerity*, watching the swirl of the clear, slightly yellow liquid, listening to the tinkle of ice cubes, wondering if Greiner might try to drug him.

"Je m'en fous de m'attirer les bonnes grâces, Monsieur Greiner," which was entirely true: Quirk never *had* given a damn about ingratiating himself to anyone, apart from the fairer sexes, of course. And maybe a dwindling cadre of men he would deign to consider friendship with. For some reason, his mind went unbidden to that strange encounter in the Piazza del Duomo in Milan.

"I'm just here to see the Modigliani. Anyway, I enjoy the complexity of the Northern Canadian botanicals. The Inuit know how to respect a herb."

"Not an *'erb*?" Greiner smiled.

Quirk clamped his jaw against a grammatical tirade. "I was born in Scotland," was all he said, and curtly at that, as Greiner handed him the drink. *"Merci."*

"I have told you already, Monsieur Jefferson, the painting is not for sale," Greiner's lips pinched, answering pique with pique.

"And yet here I am"—Quirk sipped his drink anyway, then raised the scintillating glass towards the older man—"at your invitation."

Greiner nodded, repeatedly, but made no move towards either of the other burnt sienna armchairs in this part of the open-plan lounge. He brushed imaginary dust from his tweed waistcoat then sipped his Tom Collins.

"The truth is, Jefferson, that I like to have people come and admire my collection. This is a fruit farming community, largely. Oh sure, there are musicians, artists of many and varied stripe, but as far as sophisticates like you and me, the population is...limited. We've corresponded for so long, to be honest I wasn't sure you were going to come."

Is he flirting with me? Good grief, the man has no sense of timing. And anyway, elitist isn't my type, ironically. Quirk smoothed the ends of his fake moustache with thumb and forefinger. He hated the stupid soup-strainer, but Moth thought he should have a disguise. She was such a child sometimes. Only now he realised that she might have been winding him up. Oh well, too late.

"What little I can see certainly is very impressive." Quirk's hand waved vaguely towards the Derain in its dim corner, picked out by a gentle spotlight. "Although I don't care for the Peploe. Still-life is anathema to me, the worst contradiction in terms."

Passion illuminated Greiner's steel blue gaze. "But, my dear Jefferson, that is the very *heart* of what painting is, to craft life from inanimate materials. To imbue oil and pigment with the vital force of existence." The banker took a deep breath to reinforce his plea to Quirk's better judgement then stopped, reaching for his pocket. He retrieved a real leather-cased cLife handset, pushing out his lower lip as he looked at a message.

"Problem?" Quirk's tone was unconcerned, but he was certain this was a notification of a certain someone interacting with Greiner's security system.

He had done his research, or rather the increasingly capable Moth had, a month of it. The French-Canadian banker and art collector prized portraiture above landscape and still-life, it was his weakness, and it would be his downfall. But then the silly old sod should not have resorted to fraud to capture Amedeo Modigliani's *Draped Nude*, oil on canvas, 1917 from the Koninklijk Museum voor Schone Kunsten, the Royal Museum of Fine Arts in Antwerp. This was the museum's view at least, and so they had engaged The Quirk Agency. *Great art always seemed to need rescuing from something or other.*

"A technicality," said Greiner, although it seemed an important one from the furrowing of his brow.

Quirk wondered if Moth had deployed the NEMP. Whatever the case, it seemed that her entry onto the property had not gone undetected. Still, she was a better bet than Eighty, since the android would have pinged the security system at a hundred paces. For a foul-mouthed fourteen-year-old, his recently acquired ward and assistant was remarkably focused and committed when she wanted to be. Then there were the other times, of course.

"I'm not here to drink your gin, Greiner," Quirk countered, hoping to deflect the man from his handset. "Show me the Modigliani please, or I'll call my driver back and be on my way."

The older man held up a hand without looking away from his cLife, which he was tapping at. "But that would require me to release your handset from my door safe, would it not? Anyway, I'm done. I just needed to call up a security sweep. My androids will take care of it." Greiner looked up, smiling, and suddenly seemed like a hook-beaked hawk, regarding its prey. His eyes narrowed. "You must think I'm stupid, Mister Quirk, and for God's sake take off that stupid moustache, you look like Magnum P.I."

Quirk shrugged nonchalantly. There were worse comparisons, he supposed: those shorts...dear lord. "So, the game's up?"

"It is." Greiner took a long draw on his Tom Collins then smiled with complete satisfaction. "You probably think you're going to waltz out of here and confirm to that bespectacled little Dutchman Van der Poom that you've traced the picture, but I would remind you that you haven't seen it. I've said nothing to imply that I have the particular Modigliani that you are engaged to find."

Finally, Quirk stood, dusting a hand across the Merrion's lap. He drained his drink, smacking his lips at the big kiss of alcohol and quinine, then placed the glass on the chair's wide arm.

"The thing is, Greiner, I get to do the expositing this time." Quirk reached up, peeled the nasty-assed painter's brush off his top lip and threw it on the carpet at the banker's feet. "You see"—he pushed his hands into his pockets and paced to the full-length picture window—"I'm not just engaged by Martin van der Poom at the MvSK, I'm also here on behalf of Mademoiselle Matilde Perrot. I'm not just here for the Modigliani, I'll take the Derain too." Quirk nodded towards the painting that hung behind Greiner. "And I'll wager you've got the Maltese Cultural Institute's Caravaggio stashed around here as well. I guess you could call this a classy action." Quirk smirked at his own joke.

He had Greiner's attention now. The man's eyes narrowed even further, and his lips tightened. He moved back to the drinks cabinet, much less elegantly than before.

"That stupid girl." Greiner sighed deeply and turned towards the painting in the corner of the room. "It was wasted on her. Did you see her gallery? Anarchists and heretics, stuffing fish and painting hubcaps: idiots and conmen." The older man lifted his tall glass to his lips, his back to Quirk now, seeming to savour both the painting and the drink as if thinking they might be his last.

"All very well, monsieur, but she released the painting on the understanding that your agents were acting for the Musée d'Orsay. They issued her with a receipt, a forgery, while acting under your instruction. I'm no lawyer, but that smells like fraud to me. And now the picture is hanging on your wall."

"For all you know, it's a copy, or maybe I'm borrowing it."

A likely story, a desperate one. Quirk had him. "And borrowing is the sincerest form of daylight robbery, Monsieur Greiner."

The grey-haired man turned back towards him, levelling an ugly-looking black pistol at Quirk's gut. "I dare say in your line of work you know what this is."

Quirk cocked his head to one side, slowly removing his hands from his pockets and spreading them wide. "Actually, I don't. That's more my young colleague's side of things."

Greiner smirked. "Too bad you didn't bring him along, he could have told you this is a Heckler & Koch 56M-3 laser pistol, the most effective, publicly available laser pistol on Earth. It will give you the biggest shock of your life, Mister Quirk. If I turn this dial..."—Greiner turned the dial—"this pistol will shoot you with two hundred Watts, double the power of a surgical laser and enough to stop you caring about anything very much."

While Quirk did not want to die, he could not help but be distracted by how monumentally stupid Greiner was being. Expounding like a time like this? Ridiculous. "And what then?" Quirk enquired.

"Dispose of your body, of course," Greiner smiled.

"My *young colleague* will be very unhappy about that."

"I'll just need to put him out of his misery then."

Quirk sensed a shadow moving on the deck outside the window. The handle of the plass door rattled, turning back and forth uselessly. How many times would he have to explain legerdemain to Moth?

"I doubt my *YOUNG COLLEAGUE* would put up with that." *Damn it, Moth, get in here!*

Greiner raised the weapon then flinched as a hollow thunk left the plass of the picture window wobbling.

"What—?" asked Greiner.

Thunk, again. A little white star appeared in the centre of the plass. The dark shadow flickered again, darkness against darkness.

"My androids, I don't..." Greiner was properly confused, but sufficiently aware to shoot when his guest moved.

Quirk twitched, Greiner's Heckler whined, and Quirk threw himself headlong behind an armchair, followed by a sizzling crackle. He dragged his legs in as another impact made the plass window thrum again, this time followed by a loud crack.

There were footsteps on the Persian rug. Greiner was coming.

Quirk twisted around behind the chair, crouched, and gripped the chair's bottom edge. As the laser whined again, he caught a pungent whiff of burning carpet. He surged forward, pushing the armchair like a defensive tackle in training, using it as a battering ram.

It is *worsted. Nice weave: beautiful combing.*

The laser whined once more. Greiner called out. *Must be on target.* Quirk stopped pushing and heaved the edge of the chair up with all his might. Greiner's bright blue laser beam scythed towards Quirk as the chair spun up off the floor and tumbled into Greiner.

Quirk dived sideways as Greiner fell backwards into the drinks cabinet. The laser beam raked the ceiling and winked out. Greiner's impact smashed the antique cabinet's doors to shards and splinters. Quirk's shoulder hammered into the floor. The dark window shattered, and a big solar barbecue plunged into the living room with Moth behind it leaping through the shower of shattered plass.

The barbecue lurched and crashed onto its side as Moth planted her feet apart, unzipped her parka dramatically to reveal a white-on-black T-shirt emblazoned with the moto "People Make Shit" then scooped up Greiner's fallen pistol. She levelled the gun at the groaning banker who lay bleeding from his forehead in the wreckage of the drinks cabinet.

"You're busted, fuck-face!"

Quirk groaned and slumped back onto the carpet as— almost apologetically—the upturned armchair burst into flames.

02

09:07, 18 November 2099
The Real Time Cafe, 1417 Canyon St,
Creston, BC, Canada, NAF

...and that's KCJH local radio, Creston Valley's sign of the times. Morning headlines, and more snow due this lunchtime. Two centimetres just to keep us topped up, eh. But it won't slow down our parliamentarians as they pound the pavements and the virtual byways in search of your precious votes. Thirteen days from D-Day—that's D for democracy, folks—and the polls still look bleak for our premier and NAF president during Canada's rotation, Peter Liano.
Meanwhile on KCJH, the hits keep coming. This oldie gets my vote: it's Queens of the Stone Age...

Quirk tried to tune out the grungy music issuing from the restaurant's speakers. "I still say you were cutting it fine, young lady," he sipped his Americano, staring at Moth over the edge of the steaming mug. She flicked her black bob at him, scowled and said nothing, slouching on her side of the booth in the back of the restaurant, nodding her head to the chugging guitars.

"At sixty-eight point four decibels, the music is somewhat louder than the average human is likely to find comfortable," said the android, Eighty, its quietly handsome features unperturbed.

Moth's latest model syRen® had replaced the wrecked original, Eight, the remains of which must now be buried in moon dust. The 2100 edition retained the tall, subtly muscular physique, but the Pantone 266C violet eyes were an update from the previous model's 267. The hair remained light brown, verging on blond, but the lips were slightly darker. Most importantly however, Eighty was as well-spoken as ever.

The tan bench seat squeaked as Moth slouched down further.

Real leather...this place is so quaint.

Quirk still struggled to accept he had a fourteen-year-old ex-convent orphan as his sole employee (androids not being on payroll), but he'd brought it on himself consorting with the capo. Toni di Fantano had a lot to answer for, and he had, by getting assassinated. Quirk sighed and sipped again. He'd come so close to extracting himself, but no. Toni had to rope the irrepressible Miss Angelika Moratti, his bratty niece (hereinafter called Moth, or else) to some poor, unsuspecting sap. Enter Quinton Ignatius Richmond Kirby: age 33, I.Q. 149, sole proprietor of The Quirk Agency, married once, divorced twice (just to be sure), father of...none. He would never accept what Jennifer had done. Cloning a son without asking was just vile.

And the rest, as they say, is misery. Or is it history? Same difference.

"Hey, cloth ears, I'm talking here."

"Pardon?"

"I *said*, I told you packing two NEMPs was smart; that's my insurance policy. Boom! I lay out five wolf-oids then I'm over the fence and upstairs to the deck. Then two syRen®, wham, bam: 'Not today, metal-heads!' I lured them in and put them *both* down. Thank fuck for that BBQ though, or I'd never have got through the window."

"'Lupinoid' or 'caninoid' would be a more appropriate term, Miss Moth," said the syRen®. "As you know, 'android' comes from the Greek 'aner' meaning man, and 'oeides' from which 'oid' derives through modern Latin to mean 'form.' Combining this derivation with the Latin 'canis' for dog, logically leads to—"

"Zip it, Eighty." Moth held up her hand, palm out. The droid stopped talking. "School's out today, *capiche*?"

The syRen® sat back impassively, factory default almost-smile playing on its lips, because androids staring at walls weirded people out. Quirk still felt the tug of déjà vu when he met those violet eyes, almost comforting now he was not dangling two thousand metres above the lunar surface on the end of an android's arm.

Damn. His hand was shaking. He blew out a breath. He needed a new distraction, to be busy with a new case. Already he had options. The peculiar thing was he felt a compulsion to consult his assistant, an alien concept for a long-time sole trader, accounting for the views of another. He'd forgotten how fragile independence could be.

Moth snapped her fingers. "Boy, you're really out of it today. Stay with the programme, will you? We need to make tracks, remember? Calgary tomorrow, Friday Toronto, Cayambe by Saturday: Six days to Geostation One and home to Aldiss Station. Fuck, I hate travelling." Her face fell and she scowled at the table.

Quirk shrugged and sipped his coffee. "It is an intrinsic part of your chosen career path, an opportunity for contemplation. Anyway, I've decided to stay here. We need a new case, and we have a prospect here in Canada." In fact, he was enjoying being Earth-side again, and was in no rush to leave.

Moth held out her hands palms up as if testing for rain, hunched her shoulders, dark-shadowed eyes wide. "What, the actual, fuck? We're booked all the way through! You know the only thing I hate more than travelling is—"

"Surprise!" Quirk smiled broadly. He took his cLife handset from his pocket and slid it across the table towards his quietly fuming assistant.

"Who's Barry Rowland?" she asked, reading the screen.

"No idea, but I received that message two days ago."

He observed as Moth opened Rowland's message, tucking her bobbed hair behind her ear in that way she did when she was concentrating. The hair fell out almost immediately, in that way it did because it was hair, and it didn't give a damn, being dead already. She had been concentrating a lot lately at home on Hygeia with her Grade Eleven lessons in full swing. He couldn't possibly tell her how impressed he was with her being skipped ahead two years; she was insufferable enough as it was. In truth, he marvelled at her adaptability. She would rant about being messed around, but this Rowland thing looked easy. Quick too. Probably, they could wrap it up in a couple of days before going on to one of the more exotic options in his inbox.

Quirk scanned Rowland's message again upside down as Moth read.

> Mister Quirk,
> Mohinder Singh at Legal Associates gave me your name. He said you tracked his pedigree Staffordshire from Brooklyn all the way to Newark and the cops broke up a dog fighting racket into the bargain. Mo praised you highly and that'll do for me.
> I'm Security Manager for Hygen Resources in Yellowknife. I found something strange, but the police aren't interested. I've been told to let it go but I can't do that. It's important this package gets to where it should be.
> Can we meet? Let me know.
> I need your help.
> Regards, B.R.

She would take all of five minutes to worm her way into this he was sure, picking at details, pushing questions and theories before he got a chance to air his thoughts. He sighed, recalling five glorious years working as a man alone. He had enjoyed the solitude. Nothing was more liberating than doing whatever you wanted, especially after the debacle of his marriage. But, oh no, solitude was too good for him. Yet his internal protests were becoming vague, his external remonstrations muted, right up until Moth yanked his chain of course, and he was swept away for another ride on the bitchy-go-round. But they had reached an equilibrium, of sorts.

And it *was* different. Moth was completely unlike Jennifer with her duplicity. Moth was open, painfully so, and expected him to reciprocate, to speak about his ex-wife. Nowadays, he defended his privacy by asking about the origin of her nickname. That set her off every time. Moth abhorred discussing her dead parents, and her soubriquet brought those memories back somehow, yet she demanded its use. Children were strange. Even La Madre Superiora at Moth's former convent home in Biella would not reveal why Angelika had to be called Moth. All he knew was that using her given name was a one-way ticket to Snitsville.

She looked up from his handset, brushing croissant flakes from the front of her H.P. Lovecraft T-shirt. Red letters dripping like blood on a yellow background proclaimed that the Lurker at the Threshold would get him. Quirk didn't doubt it for a moment, knowing his luck.

"I would suffer Canada a bit longer for a slam-dunk like this," she nodded. "I could use a longer break from the Belt, the gravity's weird, and Creston's growing on me, even though it's small, quiet. Why d'you have to live in the Belt anyway? It was to get away from your wife, wasn't it?"

"Ex-wife. Yes"—he sighed at the energy of her questioning—"and because it was small and quiet."

She frowned. "But in the Belt, it's really hard to get all that prissy stuff you like. Bo Concept this and Naoto Fukasawa that. And if I hear another word about that fucking Phillipe Starck table, I'll scream. So yeah, let's do this"—she waved his cLife around as if trying to swat a fly before handing it back—"or d'you have something more exciting in mind? Let's invade Iceland!"

"I'm pleased you know where that is," said Quirk as he tagged the messages in his "Jobs, Incoming" folder and slid a finger off the top of the cLife's screen towards Moth's handset. "Use your initiative: what's your assessment?"

"Well, I aced the crap out of Earth Geography 101," she said, but her tone was distracted, attention already locked on the screen of her blingy, actual gold handset. "But then I am European. I'm surprised *you* can find Earth with both hands."

"Comic effect would be maximised by referring to Uranus," offered S-0778a.

Moth scowled and the android clearly deduced that silence was preferable. She read the seven other job offers Quirk had received this week. Four were missing persons and of little interest to him. It was sad that souls got lost sometimes, and he was not immune to the emotions that drove people to search for them, but, in his experience, forty-eight percent of missing persons wanted to be missing and did not appreciate it when you found them. Not only that, seventy-two percent of clients only wanted to find the missing person so they could kill them, figuratively or otherwise.

One job was on Mars, where a settlement of five hundred souls under the domes on the Aurorae Planum had a thief amongst them. The Sheriff of Mars needed a new face to go undercover, hence her appeal to Quirk.

"Well, straight nix on this Mars thing," Moth announced. She poked a finger at him in a most aggressive manner. "They've got domes. I'm done with domes. No fucking domes. Domes are out."

"Fine," he held up his hands in defence. "Mars is a bit on the rustic side anyway." Truthfully, he did not have the appetite to rough it to that degree. Hygeia was one thing, but Mars was entirely another.

He thought Moth might jump at the next case. The Grand Floridian Hotel at Disney Planet on Australia's Gold Coast offered a year-long security adviser contract. Surely that was the kind of stability he ought to be providing Moth at her age. It was good money, as if that mattered given the millions Toni had bequeathed to ensure Moth wanted for nothing. Maybe she would deride him for taking it, perceiving a sell-out. That did not mean it was the wrong choice. But there he was verging on the parental again. Where was his tried-and-tested selfish streak when he needed it? He remembered counting the seemingly endless days until he would be rid of Moth, now his emotions were less clear cut. *Damn it.*

Anyway, there was a clear winner. The Ladies Cricket Federation of Sweden was departing on a tour of Asia and required the assistance of a skilled and resourceful individual to chaperone the players when off duty. Tasks included escorting shopping trips, acting as dinner companion, and attending a plethora of social events, official and unofficial. It had Quirk's name filigreed all over it. He could even hear a voice in his head, calling to him plaintively in English accented with a seductive Scandinavian lilt. *"Help us, Quirk, please help us. Protect us from evil and the temptations of distant lands. Only you can safeguard our virtue."*

If only Moth might—

"Not this cricket one." And there it was. "Christ, you and a bunch of scantily clad Scandis on a tour bus? All we need is for their coach to be Kurt von Muscle-Ripped and that's the cherry on your cake right there."

"Moth, again, not gay, or bi, or omni, or pan, although if I was, what would it matter to you?"

"It wouldn't," she deadpanned. "Just be honest with yourself."

"Look, I just enjoy the company of cultured, sensitive men with a strong sense of their own identity. That does not mean..."

Her small hand patted the table. "Hey, I'm just stating the fucking obvious. Anyway, what about this new case?"

"Hmm?"

"You sent me eight."

"Oh," Quirk glanced down at his handset. There *was* a new message, only six minutes old. He tapped. The Berlin

State Library needed support repatriating material from various cities around Europe. Quirk would assist Fräulein Professor Cassandra Streich, act as courier and confidante on the week-long tour of the Old World's great capitals. All expenses paid. There was even a childminding allowance. It was perfect.

"You just wet yourself, didn't you?" Moth was smirking. "I see Rome is on the list. It's only two hours to Milan by train. I could visit Aunt Giulia."

Quirk's lips compressed. *Too* perfect. "They ran us out of Milan, remember?" That and he had been nervous enough seeing Giulia di Fantano at the convent. Or, more accurately, nervous about her seeing him *again*, although she had not called him out.

"I bet things have chilled. Don't be a scum-sucker, Quirk. Take the Berlin job."

Goodness knew he wanted to. Not least due to Professor Streich's reputation as a scholar and intellectual, of course, but also for her severe and decidedly androgynous beauty, to which he was an enthusiastic subscriber. Add in her proclivity for attending social events in men's dinner suits. *Oh, think of the fun we could have.* And the timing was remarkable. Stranger still, Moth was angling to go back...as if she had a reason.

He blew out his cheeks. "I think my contract with Uncle Toni precludes it."

Eighty began, "The contract does not—" Quirk held up a hand.

"Look, we *will* go back to Milan sometime. Once I've scouted the lay of the land. Or maybe we could meet Giulia somewhere else: Grenoble, for some skiing."

"Shit, Quirk, she's a nun, not a fucking winter Olympian. And you know she was a mess when Toni died, still ragged round the edges when I called last week."

He nodded. "No doubt she needs more time."

"Nuh-uh," Moth's bob danced as she shook her head. "What she *needs* is her vivacious, fun-loving niece who brings sunshine to every life she touches. The Berlin job doesn't start till December. We can wrap this Rowland thing in two, three days, *easy*. Plus, it says you get to leave me in a condo with my android babysitter for the duration. You'd enjoy *that*."

What Quirk thought was, *how like a German librarian to think of everything*. But what he did was snap. "Don't tell me what I'd enjoy." That was Jennifer's schtick, always pushing and pulling him into the shape she wanted. "I'm still counting the days to your twenty-first birthday when I will happily burn Toni's contract and synthesise a diamond from the ashes. We work well enough together when you keep your attitude under your hat. Let's concentrate on that, shall we?"

Surprisingly, Moth did not explode or take a monumental huff, but simply nodded curtly. "But you'll take the Berlin job, right?"

"Of course," he sniffed. "It would be rude to refuse such a gracious invitation."

Moth just smiled.

Quirk messaged the professor's secretary, nodding when he hit "Send."

Moth flicked her hair idly. "And we could check out Rowland's package to fill the time before Berlin."

"That was my thought," said Quirk, refusing to acknowledge her innuendo.

"So, let's call the man," said Moth, "tell him the dynamic trio is on the case."

Quirk spoke the number, swallowing his irritation at Moth having learned so quickly how to boss him around. Rowland did not answer his handset and so the call went in search of him through the Hygen Resources phonebook, displaying the message "Call for Barry Rowland" on any devices it bounced to, locating him on his deputy's handset.

Their Phoneface conversation was as brief as Rowland's note. Quirk accepted the job with his corporate smile,

Quality Assured. The grizzled man looked pleased—as if a weighty problem had just been halved.

"I'll jump on the solar prop tomorrow; be in Creston in jig time." Rowland chewed through words like he was worrying a porkchop. "Thanks, Mr. Quirk."

Quirk extended their booking at the Ramada then they took in the sights: the town museum, the candle factory, the brewery tour and the wildlife centre. The wineries were closed for the winter. They lunched at Smitty's Diner and Quirk spent most of the meal contemplating the wooden grain elevators across the road next to the rail track. He wondered at the effort involved in preserving these ancient monuments from the Honduran cellulose worm.

They walked Canyon Street again, its footways cleared and de-iced by a squad of robots the size of shoeboxes. Quirk savoured the crisp air. Clouds rolled over the mountains, the clear, blue sky darkening as they strolled. He engaged with the campaigners stumping on street corners. The opposition had clubbed together against the incumbent, a position reflected nationally, they said.

Meanwhile, Moth peppered Eighty with questions about Yellowknife and Hygen Resources. She had the android dig into Rowland's virtual footprint. Undoubtedly, she invested time feeding her brain. He admired that, but her unpredictability remained brutal. Still, in six years, two months and four days she would be twenty-one, but sometimes he wondered why he was still counting. He'd become accustomed to her face—hers and Eighty's—and the "vibrant" dynamic forged in the last six months.

Oh, God, we're a team. I'm in a bloody team.

They crossed between snowbanks and started back from where they'd come. The politeness of Canadian political campaigning impressed him. Most shops displayed all four candidates' posters, while the front of one old man's mobility scooter bore the Neo-Liberal poster but had the Conservative's glued to its rear.

They dined again at The Real Time Café, eating in silence as they thawed after too long in the icy wind, even with self-heating jackets, microwaveable boots and furry hats. Only after pushing away a plate now empty of avocado black bean quesadillas did Quirk feel comfortable. Moth had scarfed down her bison burger and yam fries with barely a pause for breath. Eighty sat and watched them, sipping water that it then vaporised and vented (invisibly) from its nose, because research showed that such humanising touches aided the customer in assimilating the presence of an android in their life.

Their waitress appeared and stacked their plates on her arm. She could have been Moth's good twin, slight of stature and build, very dark hair (braided in the waitress's case), but with a disposition as sunny as Moth's was cloudy with a chance of Armageddon. Her nametag read *"Hello, I'm Terra. Here to help!!"*

"Everything okay for you folks?" Terra beamed.

"For sure," said Moth, smiling too brightly.

It irked him how easily his assistant slipped into mockery. Another reminder of Jennifer. He gave Terra one of his best smiles, *Getting to Know You, Getting to Know All About You, Act 1.* Perhaps a bit much for a casual meeting, but the poor girl didn't deserve Moth's thinly veiled scorn.

Terra seemed unperturbed by either of them. "Can I tempt you with our homemade cheesecake? It's served with blueberry-chocolate compote for $29.95."

"No, thanks." said Quirk, rubbing at the ache in his shoulder which the cold had exacerbated.

"I'll have some vanilla ice-cream with a slug of that sauce, please," said Moth, straying towards pleasant, presumably having taken a wrong turn at the outskirts of acerbic.

"Coming right up, honey." Terra departed.

Moth flipped the bird at her back. "Pleasant sucks," she grumbled.

Quirk hmphed. "You"—he pointed—"are mean. Not a good look."

Moth shrugged. "Terra? Like the planet?" She smiled with off-the-chart faux perkiness. Quirk shook his head. The sooner Rowland arrived the better. They could solve his problem and be on the way to Germany, and his well-earned respite.

"Let's brainstorm the Rowland case." Moth extended her gold cLife's screen to the touch pad format and pulled up live satellite mapping of Yellowknife. The terrain was almost entirely white, including the lakes. She rolled back to August and a mottled green and grey landscape emerged, slashed with blotches of midnight blue water and the massive, brooding presence of Great Slave Lake, which dwarfed the city. "He didn't give us much."

Quirk tutted. "More to the point, have you finished your homework? This is a school night."

"Fuck, why do you two always burst my bubble with that shit! We just closed a case. I was with the police for two hours yesterday, you were interviewed for three. It's the school of life." She crossed her arms and jerked back causing the booth to shudder.

"As a dutiful guardian, Quirk is quite entitled to inquire," said Eighty.

Quirk blew out his cheeks, preparing for battle as Terra returned.

"There you go. Enjoy." He shot Moth a warning glance.

She gave the waitress the most unconvincing smile he had ever seen, leaving him to say "Thank you" on her behalf, another thing he bridled at. He was no Uncle Toni rent-a-suit, and she was a brat sometimes. Most of the time. All the time.

"Eighty, Moth's homework status, please."

"Miss Moth's homework is up to date. Monsieur Afobe has graded her submissions across twelve subjects with an average of A minus. Miss Moth's continuing grade in English is C plus," the syRen® added with a note of earnest concern.

"Tha's fawking boo' shit!" Moth forced out around a mouthful of ice-cream, then swallowed. "Why do I need Shakespeare? Guy's five hundred years old and wrote fucking gibberish."

Quirk essayed a rueful smile. "'There is nothing either good or bad, but thinking makes it so.'" He winced and moved his arm off the table.

S-0778a turned to Quirk. "*Hamlet*, Act Two, Scene Two featuring Rosencrantz and Guildenstern. Quite apposite. In relation to Miss Moth's English grade, one also might have quoted *Love's Labours Lost*. 'They have been at a great feast of languages, and stol'n the scraps.'"

Quirk chuckled. So often the android was the peacekeeper. And it spoke when spoken to! Luxury. "Moth certainly has been chewing on colloquial scraps all the time I've known her. Has it never occurred to you, Moth, that your foul language pushes people away?"

"Now you're getting it," she winked.

Quirk retreated into a silence which lasted five seconds, when one of Eighty's algorithms must have triggered. "My quotation is more appropriate than you might think, sir," the android said. "That line is spoken by the character named Moth."

In unison, Quirk and Moth turned to look at the syRen®.

"You're joking," said Quirk. His Shakespeare was quite comprehensive.

"Are you shitting me?" Moth enquired.

With inimitable android equanimity, Eighty educated them both. "In *Love's Labours Lost*, the character of Moth is Don Armado's page. Young and quick-witted, Moth often betters Don Armado, who is something of an effete braggart and prone to flowery language."

Moth spluttered, failing to contain her laughter, spraying ice-cream droplets over the laminate tabletop. "That's totally you, Quirk." She tried to giggle and swallow ice-cream at the same time, nearly choking.

Quirk hoped she would. "There is no substitute for good manners," he muttered.

"I should add," the syRen® added, "that Shakespeare's Moth is a boy."

Quirk was still chuckling when Terra placed the check in his outstretched hand. He was positively jovial in that moment, full of the joy of life, literature and companionship. Moth's un-twin anti-sister slipped away, no doubt unsure how to share their laughter. Finally, his good humour turned Moth's frown upside down. Even Eighty dialled into its library to deploy a pre-programmed chortle.

Quirk's handset vibrated. Languidly, he retrieved the cLife from his pocket.

[Number unavailable]

Damn.

"Hello?"

The voice was cold, but somehow softer, smoother than he remembered. *"I'll keep it short, Quinton. Rowland needs your help, I'm serious. He's in a real bind. Do it for me, or the memory of the good times we had, would you?"*

Shit.

Quirk's ex-father-in-law, The Old Man, Joshua Simister hung up.

"Who was that?" asked Moth.

"My ex-wife's father," he hesitated, puzzled by the voice not exactly matching his recollection. But then, the man was older. "Urging me to help Rowland."

Moth frowned. "He's the asshole, right? My *zio* Toni's arch nemesis, and manipulative ballsack?" Her eyes narrowed. "So, job's a bluff, a setup? We nix it?"

Quirk's throat tightened. He licked dry lips, thoughts racing like chickens as a fox stalks the coop. "Maybe a bluff, maybe double bluff, or maybe he was being straight," he hissed. "He does that sometimes just to toy with people. But his mistake was calling at all. He must have some interest in this, so no"—Quirk spat—"we don't drop Rowland's case. Maybe that's what TOM wants, but I'm onto him, and we're going to comprehensively dismantle whatever web he's weaving."

"Okay, boss." Moth nodded. "You know you split an infinitive there, right?"

"Oh, I know," said Quirk. "That's just how angry I am."

The decision to defy TOM felt good, but already doubts floated like scum on the surface of a familiar, roiling dread.

03

"Polls are polls are polls, that's all I'm saying," Canadian Prime Minister and serving North American Federation President Peter Liano turned away from the tall, rain-spotted window and the view of umbrellas bobbling along the tree-lined street below. "We've beaten these odds before two weeks out. We can do it again. Increase the ad buy and the break-in spots in cinemas, handset home-screens, Autocar TV and pitch-side flicker. We can do it. I'll get Jim in here and—"

Forsythe shook his head. He clasped his hands in front of his chest as Liano returned to the desk co-opted that morning from BC's premier. "It's a big sample, Peter, and it's the third drop in a week. You need something bigger. Jim's a career man." Forsythe hardened his tone. "He's not going to do what's necessary."

"What do you mean?"

Forsythe's gaze swept the oak-panelled wall. "You're the incumbent, Peter. You have stature." Leaning forward, he placed a fist in front of him on the highly polished maple desk. "Arnold's got good writers, but her platform's all policy, she lacks gravitas. You have power, Peter. Use it." He leaned in further still, almost growling. "You just need the right kind of...crisis. Leave that to me."

Liano's lips compressed into a thin line. "What are you suggesting?"

Forsythe held the president's gaze. "I'm not suggesting anything. I'm saying you would know how to save the people if you had to."

The president's eyes narrowed. "From what, exactly?"

Forsythe sat back, folding his arms across his chest. "Who knows?"

Liano glanced toward the window again, where rain from a darkening sky swept across the crystal clear plassteel, spattering against the big panes. He cocked his head to the right, taking in the glowing monitor and the graphs of polling and approval ratings, then turned back to Forsythe and nodded.

* * *

11:17, 14 November 2099
Genextric Headquarters,
747 Fort Street, Victoria, BC, Canada

"*It's me,*" the political agent's flat voice was clear, even from a cheap burner handset. The software confirmed Forsythe's identity.

"You're late," said Glenda Marshe.

"*It's government, not business, everything takes longer, but we're where we need to be. You can go ahead.*"

"You're sure? The potential for—"

"*This is cleared from on high. It'll be uncomfortable for a couple of days then the authorities will come in and mop things up. No harm done. So, get on with it, yes?*"

Marshe let out a slow breath. "Yes."

"*Good.*" Forsythe hung up.

Glenda took a scrap of paper from her pocket and unfolded it. The ultimate in modern anonymity, paper-and-pencil. She snorted then tapped in the number and raised the handset to her ear. The device purred back, mimicking a contentment she did not feel. Again, she wondered when and how she had lost her independence, her ethics, her pride. It was increasingly hard to remember the point at which she'd left her career track and stepped onto the road to hell. The challenge had been to get out with a pension. Now, she suspected it would be a struggle to retain her liberty.

It was ridiculous, but that was business, that was politics. "Bolitics," Chakraborty had jibed at the last board meeting. A poisonous endeavour if ever there was one. She hung up. The number of rings she'd allowed dictated the number of minutes for the call-back. Did it matter, when each party would vaporise their burner when they were done? Of course it did, because there was enough computing power in the human worlds now that absolutely everything could be analysed. Everything was traceable, locatable, decipherable and decodable. But the thoughts in her head were her own, for now. Just as well too. Increasingly, the human mind was the only haven, and a scrap of paper with fifteen scribbled numbers in the wrong order was the most private of records, a sacred, inviolable communion between her mind, eyes and fingers.

Thinking of board meetings made her think of Eve Meyer. *Bitch.*

Glenda sighed. This was going to have seriously shitty repercussions for Eve, and she liked Eve. She *really* liked her, hoped one day to repeat the breathless, energetic sex they had shared in the executive washroom. Perhaps they could. Coming events could not go unpunished, but she could reassign Eve, maybe find her a job somewhere beyond C Corp's reach, if there was such a place. How ironic that Yellowknife was Eve's big step up, when it sounded about as appealing as exile to Siberia. Such was the nature of the industry. If people hated genetic research a hundred years ago, they absolutely loathed genetic modification now. Unless they needed it, of course, to optimise their precious foetus, slow their aging, or breed specialised terra-fauna to render their new homeworld safe for settlement. *Damn hypocrites.*

The Porsche 885 Luxe handset glowed. Glenda picked it up. "Yes?"

"He'll speak to you."

Deep breath. "Thank you." There was a pause.

"This should not have been your next call. There better be something wrong."

"It's about Eve Mey—"

"Enough. Timing is everything, and you're mooning over some girl in a suit. If you're not capable of making the call, I'll do it myself."

The line went dead, cutting off a cough.

* * *

11:25, 14 November 2099
Ground Floor Cafeteria, Genextric Gamma Laboratory,
Ingraham Trail, Yellowknife, Northwest Territories, Canada

Derek Morton sat on his own in the company café, his bento box finished, sipping cranberry-infused water and watching Eve Meyer's ass as she progressed along the counter towards the pay-point in her nicely snug, dark business suit. It was a pity she was a dyke. He would have enjoyed boning her, he was sure of it. And no conflict of interest, as he was C Corp's security advisor, not employed by Genextric at all.

A soft tone pinged in his ear, and he reached up to squeeze his right lobe in answer.

<Morton,> he subvocalised, the biocall interface linked to subdermal sensors around his mouth translating muscle movement into words that went to a satellite, but not the room.

"Derek." The Old Man's voice was unmistakable, his replacement vocal cords making him sound much younger than his one-fifty plus, although they were still a little rough, still bedding in. *"That piece of research we discussed.*

*It's been approved. Fully funded. A successful outcome will
lead to that re-posting you want."*

So like TOM, offering the Holy Grail if you sold your
soul to get it. He watched Eve shrug off her suit jacket and
tuck a napkin into her unbuttoned collar to protect her silk
shirt. She leant forward and the strap of her bra made a
line on her shoulder.

<Noted.> Morton projected bland disinterest to the café.
<I'll see to it.>

* * *

16:17, 14 November 2099
Corridor A14, Genextric Gamma Laboratory

Eve Meyer stepped out of the office into the bare, strip-
lit corridor, tugging down the hem of her dark blue jacket.
She knew the staffers thought she was deranged wearing
Wall Street chic within spitting distance of the Arctic
Circle, but she didn't give two hoots. It was another seal of
her authority, the trappings she utilised to keep her staff in
line, and keep this billion-dollar operation running
smoothly. Better than smoothly, in fact. Genextric's
Gamma Lab was running hot, months ahead of programme,
and that was down to her direction.

How her former fellow assistant directors had shuffled
and mumbled when the CSO gave her the Yellowknife
position. How mock surprised she was. There had been no
luck involved, of course: (A) she had aced the research and
knew for her interview exactly how Yellowknife ticked;
(B) she had broken rules and spoken to staff here,
inveigling from them info on YK's development curves,
displaying exemplary knowledge in her presentation; and
(C) she had gone down on the CSO in the executive
washroom an hour before the interview. Glenda Marshe
was still a bit flushed announcing Eve as the YK lab
director. Later, Marshe told her the decision had been

made the day before. Oh well, no harm in being thorough. Eve smiled.

The barely audible hum of the ground-source aircon marred the corridor's silence. Eve crossed to the framed image of some Norwegian fjord on the wall opposite Doctor Tania Terjesen's door. She used her reflection to straighten the collar of her white shirt, then ran her fingers through her short blond hair, flipping her fringe into place. Tania had a habit of mussing it up when they...negotiated over energy allocations. The power requirements of keeping the complex's subterranean habitats at their respective median temperatures would have horrified Eve if she'd given a shit about the Niflheim programme's resource cost. But she didn't, she gave a shit about succeeding, which was exactly what she was doing. That and solar, hydro and wind were free.

Satisfied with her hair, she rolled her lips together to even out her Lipsync Platinum Peach No. 3. It was time to inspect the troops. She sighed. There were other things more pressing than this daily ritual. She wanted to re-run the staff profiling and review the satisfaction surveys, she wanted to reschedule the section head meetings and recap the minutes, she wanted to revise revenue projections, and she wanted Tania. She wanted lovely, funny, geeky, married Tania again, as soon as possible.

Eve had decided to use sex to progress her career at university, where she discovered women still had to fight for their goals. She had deployed her tools, against other women too. Because she *had to* escape where she had been, and talent wasn't enough in this or any other business. Discovering she liked women more than men had been an unexpected bonus. Her career strategy was how she knew her feelings for Tania were real, because there was no professional advantage in their relationship, only lust—perhaps love—and risk, but she wanted it anyway.

And yet it wouldn't do; it affected Eve's work now. Yes, Tania was an expert in her field, but she was not the only geneticist in the world, or even the lab. While counted among the world's best, she was a powerful distraction, and they were attracting the wrong kind of attention. Eve relegated her heart and loins to the backseat. Tania should be reassigned, and soon, before their relationship *did* start to impact Eve's career.

She turned around and knocked officiously on Tania's door. It opened a second later, Gamma Lab's chief scientist pulling on her white lab coat. The taller woman had tied back her long, blond hair again. She smiled sheepishly at Eve—*Damn those Nordic cheekbones!*—and they walked to the elevator in silence. The door slid open and they stepped inside.

"Five," said Eve.

The elevators all had cameras, of course—as did Tania's office, as did all the others—but Eve had the keys to this kingdom. She used her handset to erase the record of their most recent assignation, as she had those previous. No one would question the gap in the record. Well, Morton might, but C Corp's stooge had made gaps of his own. Gaps that her clearance did not enable her to investigate. Not that she cared what he got up to as long as it didn't affect her.

"Do we need to do this every day?" Tania asked in her clipped European tones. "You can see all the subjects remotely."

Did she shiver just now? Many of them are her creations!

"Tania, Tania, Tania. Screens can't convey the nature of these creatures. I know they're just projects for you, but it's too easy to forget what they are, their purpose."

The ritual had started as a ruse, a way to spend a little more time with Tania. Damn, but she hated how weak she felt when they were together. She was becoming like Glenda. Oh well, the perspective would help when she took Glenda's job as Genextric CSO.

Doctor Terjesen nodded at Eve's words, gaze downcast as if chastised. Or maybe it was fear, the fear of the scientist who, in pursuing lofty goals for Humanity's progress had manufactured a monster. Twelve monsters in fact, between her and her colleagues, and now they descended into a deep hole in Canada's Northwest Territories to confront them.

"Is it so bad?" Eve whispered. "Are you scared, really? You did encode a clearly defined purpose, and I requisitioned forty-eight security androids." Eve smiled encouragingly.

The elevator door slid open and two syRen® guards stepped aside to permit them entrance to basement Level Five. In the floor, glowing strips of ULEDs pointed the way down the hundred-metre-long corridor, floor-to-ceiling plassteel windows forming its sides. It was wide too, fully eight metres of highly polished, pale grey plascrete, but two railings down the middle corralled visitors into the corridor's centre, holding them back from the windows. Even with the opacity of the decimetre thick plass at one hundred percent—the default setting—some of these things could still "see" you.

Eve strode forward between the railings right to the end of the corridor, past the five wide, opaque windows on either side. She stopped at the last railing-mounted control panel on the right and waited for Tania. The androids flanked Doctor Terjesen, walking behind her, mean-looking black laser carbines pointed down, but available.

Eve and Tania faced the first window. Eve turned the opacity down to zero and the dark blue, smoky texture of the plassteel clarified, revealing a mass of tropical vegetation. She sensed rustling in a stand of tall leaves then a gaping, pink maw smashed into the clear surface, smearing saliva as it whipped back and forth trying to reach her, desperate to taste her flesh.

Tania jumped and squealed. Eve twitched despite her earlier bravado. The dark, hump-backed beast dropped to four legs then sprang again. Thumping into the window with less momentum, it stayed glommed onto the clear surface, jaws working at trying to bite them, to eat them. Eve could see down its dripping, pink gullet through double rings of teeth—the inner a dog's, the outer a shark's—gnashing against the plassteel.

As she leant forward for a better look, another of the beasts slammed into the window then another, their heads scything from side to side as they tried to reach her. She felt that jerk in her stomach again, her intestines, which she'd seen these things rooting for in a kill, unless they dragged it away for later.

"Where's the fourth?" she asked Tania, who leaned back against the other rail.

"They ate it yesterday. At twenty-one-oh-eight hours, one of the *Crocuta (Carcharhinus leucas) crocuta* made an aggressive gesture towards one of the alpha pair. The alpha pair attacked the aggressor. The second beta joined the attack against its partner when it became certain the alphas would prevail."

The three remaining examples of the spotted hyena/bull shark concoction had calmed. They sulked behind the plassteel, snapping idly in the humans' direction. Their matted hides were mottled like disease; their ugly, black eyes sunken in dark pits. So pronounced were their spines that the bony ridge stretched the sick-looking hide. Eve thought it looked like a fin trying to burst through. The staff called these things "mangetouts." They all thought the epithet was funny, because it sounded like the skin disease mange, so appropriate for this hybrid. Corporate protocol dictated abbreviation to MT.

Eve maximised the opacity. These things were no laughing matter. They were the shock troops of terraforming and colonisation, because the Laws of Robotics might prevent androids from doing what was necessary, and why put humans in harm's way when you could reproduce purpose-bred animals at a fraction of an android's cost? If mankind did stumble on any dangerous indigenous species, Genextric's terra-fauna would "manage" them to pieces. All part of C Corp's terra-forming toolkit.

"You'll replace the lost unit?" she asked.

Tania nodded, still a little green around the gills. *LOL.* "There are ten in the vats. We're bringing three up to maturity tomorrow. I'll naturalise the optimal candidate."

Eve nodded. It always puzzled her that the scientist was the squeamish one in this scenario. She glanced at the androids—impassive, implacable tools. Tools for use in Genextric's advancement and therefore her own. She straightened her jacket and watched Tania smooth her lab coat.

"I'm already sorry for the first planet these things are deployed on," said Eve.

Tania stiffened. "They'll do their job."

"I know." Eve hoped her tone was placatory. She wanted to touch Tania's arm, but it would just be more footage to delete, or more unwanted questions. The decision to reassign Tania still felt right. It would be hard to let go, but it would free her from this compulsive desire.

They turned to the window opposite the mangetout enclosure. Eve made an opened-handed gesture towards the control box, and Tania obliged. Unlike the mangetouts, this enclosure did not frighten the good doctor, even though its inhabitants were just as deadly. Perhaps it was their ruthless efficiency the scientist admired. Eve considered it a mirror of her own, which Tania admitted had attracted her to Eve. Did Tania have authority issues then? Perhaps, but they never discussed such weighty subjects. They talked about nice things, silly things, easy things. Not people.

The wide, plassteel window clarified to reveal a jungle environment that seemed very similar to the last, unless one knew enough about the painstaking accumulation of species to spot the subtle differences. Eve moved to stand beside the scientist. The enclosures were the same size, twenty metres by thirty, but these creatures appreciated their space, and so had the run of two habitats, this jungle and the neighbouring veldt. Tania pampered them, but Eve went along with it. These were Doctor Terjesen's pride and joy, the subject of her University of Oslo thesis, the work of over a decade, and the reason Tania had joined Genextric in the first place. Because what did you do if you didn't possess a handy piece of amber holding a Cretaceous mosquito conveniently imbued with the velociraptor DNA? Why you made your own, of course.

A visitor would say that the gentle shifting of fern fronds ten metres back from the plassteel was just the synthetic breeze, but Eve knew better. She tilted her gaze down to the status screen, seeing wind set to zero. She felt their eyes on her before she saw that reptilian head poke bird-like through the vegetation. The svelte, grey body glided between the foliage, slowly, steadily, moving directly towards them.

When the creature was a metre from the barrier, the second velociraptor materialised from the side. Eve caught the movement in the corner of her eye only as the closest vegetation parted. And yet the creature, almost of a height with her, did not strike. It knew that plassteel separated them. In the wild, she would be dead already.

"They're playing with us," said Tania with a smile.

"Hunting," Eve agreed.

"Exactly," said Tania.

Like the creatures of classic monster cinema, Tania's velociraptors were twice the size of the Cretaceous beasts, but Tania's—*no, Genextric's*—had been hard won over many years of sequencing, synthesis and breeding. Eve always wondered at the scale and intricacy of the task. Vulture and crocodile, shrike and Komodo dragon, cassowary and kangaroo: all had contributed genetic material to Tania's quest, birds donating the vast majority, of course. And her efforts would have been useless without the company's resources and its proprietary acceleration chambers. A prodigious achievement. Had she been allowed to publish her work, Tania might have won a Nobel nomination, but it was clear in the doctor's adoring eyes that her reward was right here, twenty metres underground in the enclosure before her. Her babies.

Tania practically swayed in time with the velociraptors' measured movements as they regarded her and Eve, and yet not the syRen® that accompanied them. Eve grunted. All she saw were two killers considering how best to get at the live food before them. At least the mangetouts dealt with their prey quickly. Eve had seen the raptors on the hunting ground—the final level below their feet—prolong the chase for their own cold-eyed enjoyment. Or so she imagined while watching on-screen due to the heavy access restrictions on Level Six and the hidden service corridors and ramps leading down to the hunting ground. Because even in envsuit or armour, humans left something behind, a trail, a scent, the litter of dead skin. Humans left tracks, they left hair, they left DNA. So, despite the lowest level of Gamma Lab being a huge open space, twenty metres tall and two hundred metres on a side—a full four hectares of forest, scrub and dusty plain—any human presence would contaminate it.

"You know they don't love you, right?" Eve asked.

They couldn't risk any of these beasts getting a taste for human, hence their injection with the UN-mandated Demon Seed, thousands of nanomachines—nanocytes—carrying microscopic loads of C4X that would rush to the subject's neck to combine in a fatal payload, decapitating with extreme prejudice any terra-fauna that outlived its usefulness. As it had on many nights here in the frozen north, the thought gave Eve comfort.

Tania turned away from the now-opaque window and they moved to the next enclosure. Ho-hum, just the common-or-garden duster, eagle blended with condor and albatross genes. An elegant and cost-effective solution to the problem of depositing Earthly spores and seeds over vast distances while droids and machines were deployed on more immediate tasks. These were not elegant creatures though. Despite some of their forebears, they looked almost tattered, as if their feathers didn't fit.

"Thinking of flying the coop, Meyer?"

Shit.

The voice made her start. She clamped her jaw down on a stutter, hating how easily she'd been blindsided again, this time by the reptile that was Derek Morton. Genextric parent company C Corp's security advisor moved away from the elevator, radiating square-jawed, magazine-cover masculinity from his stubbled chin to his chiselled cheek bones and noble fucking brow, his slicked-back dark hair and his dirty grey eyes. Eve saw through every offensive line of the gym-pumped quarterback package. She had too much experience of the man. They liked too many of the same things, like seeing rivals fail, manipulating mediocre staff or watching them mess up on their own, and being the top dog.

"What is it? I'm busy." It took no effort to convey disinterest.

Morton shrugged. "Random spot-check." He tried a nonchalant half-smile, but only managed serial-killer feigned amiability. "Can't let you ladies have all the fun."

He loved to taunt her with her widely suspected proclivities. *Asshole.* She hated that the same old jock shit still got to her. *Can't work with him, can't fire him, can't drop him into Level Six and release the hounds.* Morton was a C Corp lacky with a roving brief. She wished he'd rove the hell away from Yellowknife. He had her security chief running around looking for leaks and holes in the fence while Morton spent his time getting in people's faces, trying to rattle them into making mistakes.

"I'm done here anyway, seen enough," he nodded to Tania and turned, walking back to the elevator, hands in pockets.

She and Tania rolled their eyes at each other, but thanks to Morton's interjection the sense of two intimate friends surveying the products of their shared endeavours had evaporated. He had disrupted Tania's equilibrium as much as he had Eve's, although for different reasons. Tania's new hesitation revealed a fear of Morton, whereas Eve just wanted to pound his smug, handsome features to a bloody pulp. Best shut those thoughts away. She reaffixed her professional demeanour and they continued their tour.

They checked the spider-hunters, the munchers and the stomach-bombs, and Eve's nagging annoyance at the scientists' nicknames for the creatures multiplied as they went. They were descriptive, but too simplistic, too graphic for her tastes. Tania hated that they called her velociraptors "snapping assassins." The labels given to Niflheim's products aped the nicknames assigned to Japanese warplanes in the Pacific Campaign over a hundred and fifty years ago. They were called codenames, but surely it was the more straightforward inability of the Allies to pronounce names alien to them. Unconscious bias or straight prejudice? Well, if you couldn't be prejudiced in a war, when could you?

She would miss sharing their interest in history when Tania was reassigned. Correction: when *she* reassigned Tania. The subject was declining in the outside world now that it wasn't taught in grade school, a thought that came with a hollow, melancholic feeling in her gut that she liked to contemplate with a glass of tequila and Tania curled up against her, their ice cubes tinkling in time.

The inspection was almost done. If they skipped the tenth habitat they could leave for dinner, separately, of course. But Tania had moved ahead to stop at the tenth window. This one wasn't opaque, it was silvered, mirrored on both sides. Eve came to stand at Tania's shoulder.

"We shouldn't stop here. Let's go."

Tania shook her head. "I have to," she whispered.

Eve did place a hand on Tania's arm now and damn the watchers to hell if anyone bothered to look.

No control console here: no data stream from inside this habitat. Neither was there any door to the rear, nor opening in the floor that allowed the...inhabitant to descend to the killing field of Level Six. Only two openings breached the immaculate enclosure of this cell, twin half-decimetre pipes, triple locked. Fresh air and slop went in, stale air and waste came out. She didn't understand the logistics and didn't try to. Tania *did* understand. Tania had treated...him, but Eve had learned not to ask.

"It wasn't your fault, Tania."

The scientist covered Eve's hand with her own, her touch delicate and cool. "Tell that to my guilt. Some of my research was used."

Eve stared at the huge mirror, seeing two women standing together, but trying to imagine what lay beyond, a being she had never seen, but Tania had. She felt Tania's whole body shiver and again cursed their C Corp masters for vetoing its destruction. *No,* his *destruction.* The corollary of the decision was that C Corp had a purpose for him.

She felt the same chill as Tania then. Perhaps reassigning her would be a favour. Tania might not hate her too much for being separated from her biggest regret. Either way, with her focus firmly on business, perhaps Eve could discover C Corp's purpose for the occupant of Habitat Ten, and get him the hell out of her lab.

God rest his tormented soul.

04

The knock on the door made Tania start. For one thing, it had been dark for—she looked at the illuminated digits on her wrist—ninety-four minutes. Secondly, she was relaxing in front of the multivision watching the last season of *McDouglas* before the new one landed, and there had just been a murder. Thirdly, her long, narrow house had arrived in Yellowknife on the back of a semi over a hundred years ago, so it was thin walled, giving the knock a heavy quality. She hoped it was Eve, but her friend hadn't messaged. Who wouldn't message at this time in the evening? Maybe Eve was just passing, except nobody just passed in November in Yellowknife.

Stretching up from the sofa, Tania moved to the door, brushing crumbs from the front of the baggy, cable-knit sweater that hung to her thighs. She pressed her hand flat on the cold wood between her and the night and looked through the peephole.

The view didn't make sense. All she could see were dark, blurred, amorphous shapes. Someone with their back to her standing very close to the door.

"Eve? Who's there?"

Shapes moved, a figure receding, turning, leaning in again. Swollen at the centre of a fish-eye picture of a night-time street were the rugged features of Derek Morton. He smiled broadly, but then the smile faded. He said nothing.

"Morton, what do you want?"

"A chat, if it's not too late."

His breath puffed out in big, white gouts. It must be minus twenty out there. Tania knew she should send him away, that Eve would scream at her to send him away. She hesitated then opened the door.

Five minutes later she was slumped on her sofa sobbing, her breath catching in her throat as she tried to suck in enough air to sob again. Her face was damp, the front of her sweater too, and her fingernails—short though they were—had drawn blood across her soft palms. Morton had taken just two steps into her home, folded his arms nonchalantly across his chest, not even unbuttoning his coat before tearing her life apart in front of her clouding eyes.

Now he was done, and Tania wanted to die. She considered all the ways to escape: throwing herself into Kam Lake if she could find a fishing hole in the ice, opening her wrists with her father's cut-throat razor that she used for her legs. Oh, God, how had this happened, what had she done to deserve this horrific bullying, this blackmail? And what he wanted...it was madness. She wouldn't do it, she couldn't, she would fight him, she'd call...

She thought she would vomit. She rubbed at her face with the woollen sleeves balled in her hands. She wanted to scratch Morton's eyes out, or her own, but mostly she wanted to die so he couldn't make her do it.

"It...it's insane. What's...the point?" She sucked air, tasting copper.

Morton just stood there. "You don't need to worry about that. Focus, Tania. Focus on what I told you. I know about you and Eve; I've got pictures. *I* don't care you're a dyke, and I know company policy forbids discrimination against dykes or fags and the rest of the rainbow. But I guess you're scared of the reaction of your husband and son in Stavanger, or maybe your parents? Or it could be Eve you're broken up about, her being dismissed for gross misconduct. Maybe it's the scientific community backlash when they learn how you behave on assignment. But, in case you think you can ride out professional embarrassment and corporate blackballing, I know you applied to the UN settler programme: and you will *not* reach the stars with the cloud I will hang over your head."

He stepped forward. Tania shied away, pushing at the cushions with her stocking feet, but she was trapped on the sofa. She swallowed a whimper as Morton's hard features came close. "I don't care," he growled, and placed a memory stick on the glass coffee table.

"Wh...what's that?"

He straightened and turned towards the door. "Surveillance footage. All the bits starring you and Eve. I bet you think it's not the only copy, and you're right. This is the only other," he produced a twin stick from his pocket. "File authentication stamp confirms it, you can check. No one's going to stumble over it. It's between you and me, which might have been fun." He shook his head. "So, we've established I don't give a shit about you, you're a means to an end." He turned back, arms still folded. Tania looked up at him, her chin still trembling. "Do as I say, and you get the other stick."

She was unsure how much time passed after Morton left, but she spent it crying on the sofa. She felt a flicker of rage in her chest, but the deluge of her anguish extinguished it. No way out. She saw the faces of her family, heard their astonishment, their disapproval, their disappointment. Somehow—dazed as she was—she found her Book and accessed the stick, confirming Morton's words. Would he give her the other stick, truly? Why would he not? Actually, exposing her bore some risk for him. And being pansexual was in no way illegal. The scientific community respected her work. Maybe she could weather it, but...she had been unfaithful. Even if she somehow managed to keep her job, her career, their family dream to see the worlds would be destroyed because of her mistakes. Fear tore through her thoughts like a wildfire.

It was 23:42 by the time Tania pulled herself together sufficiently to dress. She stood before the bathroom mirror wiping fresh tears away then washed her face. She plucked her parka from its peg and pulled it on, fastening every tab, button and tie before wrapping her longest scarf around her neck and tucking it in. She wondered if hanging was as horrible as it looked on screen, whether a scarf would do the job. *Oh, God, please help me. I'll be good. I'll pray every night, I promise.* Maybe this would not be so bad. She tucked the stick in her pocket, glanced back at her empty-seeming living room then opened the door.

Face-sucking cold assaulted her, the snow all around the crescent of narrow, prefab houses like hers reflecting streetlight glow. Turning out her living room light felt like an ending. She closed the door, it locked, and she walked to her truck. The vehicle's beep as it recognised her hand on its door handle was gunshot loud around the circle of darkened homes. A short night journey on spot-lit streets. Only seventeen minutes through the city of Yellowknife. Some shops and bars remained illuminated, serving mine workers on shifts. Along Range Lake Road and Old Airport Road. She turned onto the Mackenzie Highway without remembering how she got there, off it again onto Ingraham Trail. The truck's winter mode adjusted throttle, gears, tyre pressure, spikes. She doubted its safety systems would allow her to steer off the road into a tree. She crossed the Yellowknife River Bridge and turned left into the access road bisecting the tall trees. The sudden appearance of the gate and the illuminated security post shocked her. She dabbed her eyes quickly as she pulled up to the glowing, plass box.

"Evening, Doctor Terjesen. Kinda late for you, isn't it?"

She couldn't remember the nightguard's name.

"Stupidest thing, I left my handset in the lab. I...got a bit worked up about it. I was supposed to call..." Her words trailed off as the barrier opened.

"No problem, doc. Gimme a wave on the way out."

...my husband. But what could Tomas do? What could anyone else do? She could phone Eve, *should* phone Eve. Eve would know what to do, but she would not drag her into this mess, ruin Eve's life too. This was *her* problem, the solution within her gift.

She passed three smaller buildings, each hunched in its own forest clearing, before turning off the tree-lined, snow-packed drive into the main building's parking lot. She opened the door and stepped down. *Shit.* She had left the house in such a daze that she was still wearing her slippers. *Idiot!* She took short, awkward steps across the snowy car park to the lighted entrance, reached into her pocket for her pass, but the door clicked open. Morton was watching! Of course he was, he didn't trust her. She pushed the plass panel inwards, shuffled across the foyer and padded up the stairs.

Blank moments later she sat at her desk staring at the wall. She regarded her not-at-all-forgotten handset, picked it up then put it down again. She pulled open her drawer, reached inside. Her fingers closed on the antique paperknife Tomas had given her for their eleventh anniversary. She turned the steel blade over. It caught the light from her desk lamp, reflecting it into her eyes. Could she do it? It was a way out, but the cost... She examined the balance between her pros and cons, sighing heavily. *No.*

If Morton got what he wanted he'd let her go, right? Why would he complicate things further, drawing attention to Genextric and Gamma Lab's operations? Of course he wouldn't. But what he demanded surely would. Was that the idea? So confusing, but what did it matter that she couldn't fathom his reasons? There were controls, protocols, a whole emergency infrastructure tested and tested again. She had to believe in that, and Morton's statement that no one would get hurt. She held her family's dream to start anew, their absolute trust and belief. She must do everything she could not to lose it.

Tania took out her pass and went to the elevator. The presence of an android shocked her, but it should not have. They attended this building every minute of the day. She hesitated, but kept walking, only seeing as she approached that the syRen® was deactivated, its eyes closed. Morton's doing, surely, clearing the way for her. What other security or safety systems had he shut down to hamper any consequent investigation? For there must be one, but that did not help her now.

She rode down in silence, dropping below ground, barely hearing the elevator's low hum. She got out on Four to be greeted by more inactive androids. She put her fingers to her chest where a weight pressed, as if that would help. The softness of her woollen sweater almost shocked her, like reality smacking her in the face. How could anything soft exist, now? She kept moving forward. The control room door slid open. *Why doesn't Morton just do it himself?* For the sheer pleasure of tormenting her, no doubt. And to have a distraught victim to throw under the wheels of the company juggernaut, the same company that—along with the UN resettlement panel—would assess her family's application.

It all became clear as she stepped into the control room with its dim lighting, banked monitors and array of fan-cooled processing towers, dark pillars with strings of tiny lights like a night-time cityscape. She would be alright, because Morton needed her to face the music at first, but then could allow her to disappear to the stars to be forgotten. Giving her what her family wanted made sense for him too. It would work.

Tania removed her parka and sat at the main desk, tapped the unrolled keypad and brought the screen to life, smiling grimly. She was not quite the helpless doe everyone thought she was. She had a trick or two. Like the log-in for that intern Patel she hadn't deleted from the secure list. She opened the maintenance screen. The intern didn't have access to the feeding controls, of course, but using his log-in would muddy the waters. She paused, rubbed her lip, then input her assistant's details to access the cameras on Level Five. More mud, right? He would have an alibi, surely.

She viewed the corridor, empty but for another motionless android, the image clear, like streaming a show. But this was no episode she could watch and forget. The watercooler critique of this show would be harsh indeed. It was all so painfully real. With a start she realised using others' codes revealed intent, so she used her own to view the enclosures. She would say she had tried to combat a cyber incursion.

Switching one screen to Level Six, she turned up the "daylight," setting the environment to early morning with a light north-easterly wind. She soaked in the sight of the expansive artificial veldt that covered the vast area of the lowest basement. Not only was the space massively tall, but walls and ceiling were active surfaces, emitting the image and light required to model an even wider vista, terrestrial or alien.

On another screen she saw a male mangetout nosing through their enclosure's undergrowth towards a female. She'd done this a hundred times, but her hand twitched as she disabled the warning system then opened the enclosure's rear door accessing the ramp down to Level Six. Then she activated the olfactory spray nozzles to attract the creatures into the tunnel and down to the feeding ground. Three hungry beasts needed no second invitation. They bucked up at the smells, stiff necks jerking, hairy spines straining. Clearly, they were barking, goading each other, but Tania kept the sound off. Always the sound off, to shut out those horrible, vacant yelps. It was bad enough watching the beasts snap and butt and fight to pursue the promising whiff of carrion.

After minutes off-camera, the humped-back killers lolloped from the tunnel onto the wide expanse of Level Six, sniffing the air for blood. Tania blew out a breath, then dropped the pre-loaded kill from Feeding Chute C. Three vile beasts reacted as one, darting with abandon towards the food, indecently fast, despite their shambolic gait, squat and packed with muscle. So destructive. They fell on their target in unison, ripping into the goat carcass with those twinned rows of teeth, black-eyed heads burrowing into the ribcage, seeking juicy organs. Their heads popped out, one after another, blood-smeared, snorting to clear their nostrils as they gorged on raw flesh.

With relief, she turned away to the control screen and deleted the tracking software from the beasts' on-board units. She gave them ten minutes, then opened the Level Six goods lift, activating the scent of a fresh kill with added dying deer noises. The mangetouts scrabbled after the promise of fresher meat, although one dragged a goat leg with it. She closed the lift door and sent the beasts up to the ground floor loading bay and its caged enclosure.

She paused, fingers steepled on the desk, head down as doubts assailed her fragile resolve, but she was committed now and anyway, in her logical assessment it would be alright. She zipped up her parka, logged off her various users and left the control room. Her walk to the elevator afforded too much time to think. Doubt redoubled its attack, but she pushed away imaginings of dirty shame and cringing apology. She would try to be more like Eve, hard and determined, forceful. She was almost there. Her colleagues were only people. Poor Eve, though. This would hurt her.

Emerging on Level A, Tania refocused herself on Morton's task. There was no room for carelessness. She walked empty corridors to the rear of the building, going from pale walls and framed splashes of amorphous colour to the dark grey, utilitarian chic of the operations and maintenance area. Deactivated androids marked the junctions en route. She slid past them self-consciously, terrified one would wake and challenge her, but no android stirred. Morton's control was complete. She hoped that some record of this day would remain, somewhere, some way to prove what Morton had done.

The maintenance office had more equipment racks than desks and terminals. Despite the air scrubbers and scent of spring morning deployed by the environmental system, the room bore an underlying aroma of grease, solder and strong coffee. A wide plassteel observation window dominated the room's far wall affording a view of the service and loading bay where rugged, yellow vehicles slumbered. Equipment decked the walls, many cables and ropes, reinforced metal crates stacked in corners ready to transport sedated terra-fauna to Edmonton Spaceport.

As Tania took in the brightly lit space the goods lift arrived from Level Six. Amber warning signals above its door began to splash orange light over the vehicles, the walls and the polished floor. All that remained was to release those ravening beasts into the wild, then she would get the second stick. Morton would trigger the Demon Seed nanocytes and her family's dream would be safe. Her heart thumped wildly in her chest. The goods lift doors and the heavy cage enclosing the space in front of it opened from here in the logistics office, but the control for the service bay roller shutter was attached to the far wall, beside that external opening. She had to go out there.

Tania drew in several deep breaths as she walked to the half-plass door into the service bay, unlocked the adjacent key safe and removed the roller shutter key. Her hand shook on the door handle. She turned it, and the door cracked open, the sound echoing in the high-ceilinged, plascrete-floored space. She walked out, slippered feet scuffing the hard surface, breath clouding the cold air that pervaded the unheated bay. The goods lift warning lights rotated, flickering like flares. She couldn't help picturing the beasts on the other side of the door. She heard them now, scrabbling at the bottom of that door, still slavering from their recent meal, but not sated, never sated.

She placed the key in the external roller shutter control box, gave it a half turn, then thumbed the green button. The metal shutter juddered raucously into life, its bands clacking loudly as it scrolled upwards. Freezing wind licked at her barely covered feet, frosted her calves, chilled her thighs.

"That's enough," called Morton.

Tania almost peed herself. She jerked around, the roller shutter crunching to a halt near head height. Cold air clawed at her, blowing snow around her pink slippers.

He was all in black, standing in the logistics office doorway. The orange warning lights splashed fire at his feet as if in tribute. Although the lift remained closed, the cage doors now gaped open.

Oh God. Oh God. Oh God. It's not okay. It's not okay!

Without explanation, Morton stepped back inside the office and closed the door. The goods lift shutter began to slide up. Twelve hairy legs and muzzles snuffled thirty metres away, thick necks—still bloody—straining to get out.

The car!

The thought burst through Tania's panic, and she turned and ran as the first scrabbling mangetout squeezed under the rising goods lift door.

She wished she'd opened her wrists in the office. *The paperknife!* She grasped at her pockets and felt the hard metal she'd put there absently on leaving her desk.

She managed ten metres out into the biting cold and blowing snow when her foot slid out of her slipper, and she fell. She threw out her hands and landed hard on the frozen ground, skin scraping on ice and gravel, ripping and tearing.

"Help me! Help me!"

She'd almost managed up to her hands and knees when searing pain lanced along her right leg, then her left thigh. She was jerked roughly backwards, then dragged onto her front, twisted, her left hand's frantic fingers grasping the ground, right hand gripping the paperknife for dear life. Massive pressure clamped her side, and her head swam as her body lurched again, away from the building. She heard incoherent screaming. Her right hand rose and fell. She could have been stabbing anything, even herself. The last thing Tania saw as she was dragged away into the freezing brush, surrounded by growling and slavering, enveloped in awful pain, was the dwindling light of the open loading bay door, and a black figure outlined in gold.

Darkness, whipping branches and animal stench closed around her, overwhelming agony blotted her senses, but her right hand rose and fell, rose and fell.

Rose, and fell.

* * *

00:43, 15 November 2099
Genextric Gamma Laboratory, Ingraham Trail, Yellowknife

Morton slipped through the undergrowth, trying to calm his temper, letting the night goggles and his training do the work while he cursed himself for being so fucking stupid. Careful planning, details reviewed, timeframe studied, but still it had gone to shit in two minutes flat. What did they say, never work with children and animals? Fucking right. The galling thing was he knew exactly what had gone wrong, the little detail he should have spotted but hadn't, and now Terjesen might still be alive.

He'd reviewed mangetout behaviour, asked researchers an idle question or two, listened to techs, but the real expert was the one he couldn't ask, Terjesen herself. She'd have told him, after one feed as scheduled then a second luring them to Level Six, that a third offer of food in the form of the scientist herself might be deferred. With only three mangetouts in play, each had eaten more at both sittings. The beasts had dragged Terjesen away to feed on her later. This outcome had been predictable.

Morton bared his teeth and growled, rechecking the safety on his Pretty Polly. Maybe the fence had stopped them; it was designed to hold a charging rhino, allegedly. The beasts might get frustrated and kill Terjesen in a rage at being thwarted, he might find them in a feeding torpor. That would do. Terjesen would be dead at the scene, he could kill and hide the mangetout, make a hole in the fence as if they'd escaped into town to wreak havoc. President Liano would deploy the National Guard and fly in to take the plaudits when the beasts were caught, once Earth's press had arrived en masse. Poor Doctor Terjesen, tragic victim of her own creations. If only she hadn't tried to smuggle them out to Genextric's rivals, ParaGen.

He ducked under a broken branch. Even meddling in politics, The Old Man managed a swipe at his rivals. All this mess and disruption, and ParaGen would take the blame. Priceless. But Morton needed all the bodies to make it work.

He eased his pace; eagerness led to mistakes. His training burned off any lingering fear, that and the weight of his Polyakov AR-97—also nicknamed "Crowd-killer"—providing complete confidence in his ability to lay waste to a handful of test-tube nightmares. They were just flesh and blood. It was the cost of failing that ate at him. The Old Man stamped on sources of failure within C Corp, but knew that death was no threat to Derek Morton. TOM's threat to him was the systematic erasure of his entire existence. Financial rating, military record, education, pension funds, and the poisoning of his family's web footprint to the third generation. The Old Man played for keeps.

Morton moved steadily through scrub and trees. This was nothing like the Kamchatka police action, or the "tactical consolidation" in Panama, but training was training, skills were skills. His thermal imager showed the blood on the ground was still warm, glowing orange on the landscape's chill purple. He scanned the ground and undergrowth ahead with his ethereal gaze as the muzzle-mic relayed night sounds to his earpiece. He raised the automatic rifle to his shoulder and edged forward. The beasts were oblivious to the signs they left, not because they had no predators, but because they didn't know what a fucking predator was. These vat-bred monsters worked just the way the scientists wanted, but that made them as vulnerable as any of Earth's once-great beasts.

Morton emerged from the undergrowth, vision flaring and compensating. Gamma Lab's woodland stopped here. He had reached the fence. Three metres high, topped with laser wire, formed of heavy chain link, the barbed kind. He flicked a tooth switch with his tongue, deactivating the goggles' thermal and infra-red layers. The fence was lit up like a night game, as was a ten-metre clear-cut strip on either side. Beyond the fence were scattered fir trees, tufts of scrappy yellow grass poking up through the snow and the odd silver birch, stark in its leafless state. In front of him a gaping hole the mangetouts had torn at the bottom to get out, a red-mottled trail of crushed snow and scraped dirt stretched away from the fence. The stupid smart wire—designed to differentiate between human and beast—hadn't fried the MTs because they had taken Tania with them. *Her body tricked the system.* Lucky MTs, unlucky DM.

Morton swore and rethought. Terjesen could be discovered elsewhere. They didn't even need to find all of her, but she had to be killed by the beasts. Having switched off the mangetout's safety system—disguising it as an external hack—he had bought more time to find them, aided by Genextric's emergency resources. As planned, there would have been no risk to the public, but that boat had sailed. Now, he must ensure that only he killed the beasts before the Guard arrived. Only after the mangetouts killed Terjesen though. And in that gap lay significant risk to the people of Yellowknife, and to him. He could not reactivate the Demon Seed to blow off the mangetouts' heads until Terjesen was out of the picture, unable to accuse him, and thereby, TOM.

He dropped to the bloodied snow and crawled through the opening, muzzle leading, because hunters everywhere loved a prone target. If the beasts fell on him in that moment he might as well roll over to get his belly tickled.

Through and up again, he moved easily into the darkened woods, resumed full recon mode and headed for the river. The mangetouts liked to drink after hunting, and they'd been observed dragging uneaten "kills" to depressions on the killing floor. There was more blood now, looked like multiple sources. Stupid fucking animals probably had ripped their hides open on the edges of the mangled fence.

The blood was a slick now, smeared over the patchwork of snow and pine needles like the remains of a seal cull in full swing, proper carnage. He increased his pace, abandoning stealth. This was a race now. If somehow Terjesen was still alive... If they left her on the road... He might have to finish her himself and deal with the consequences after.

He heard distant sirens through the muzzle-mic first, tore the buds from his ears to hear them naturally, although muffled by snow and vegetation. The trail was taking him back to the road, close enough to the river that open water carried the sound.

Morton accelerated, jogging. He flicked the safety off. *Hustle now, hustle, hustle.*

He came out of the trees onto gravel, the dark expanse of the river on his right. A ramp carried him up to the road. Streetlights dominated. He tongued the IR off and crouched. Gravel on the shoulder crunched under his boots. Vivid, twirling red and blue lights approached from town in a flock, closing fast. He tweaked the sensors, suffering the brief flare in his vision. Four-hundred-twenty metres at twenty-four metres per second average. ETA, twenty-two seconds, but who had called them? There was no time. With two flicks of his upper five molar, he turned up the zoom on the goggles and a sideways push triggered the motion sensor link to the AR-97. He played the sight along the bridge, the railing, down onto the water and quickly over the banks. A few trick readings from the lapping water.

He crossed to the far rail, sighting along the banks downstream.

There. Motion on the rocks on the far bank. The rock formation, a finger separating a large eddy pool from the main flow. A man crouched over a body.

Morton flicked off all enhancements. He had to know, risk be damned. He triggered his weapon's high-intensity ALP lamp. For a second it bathed the rocks in sharply focused light, and he saw Hygen's security officer Barry Rowland turn and shield his eyes. Below him lay Terjesen's battered body. As Morton watched—near death as she must be—her head turned away from the light.

He almost pulled the trigger, but it was too late.

Morton killed the lamp and ducked away, running low back to the trees. He silenced the muzzle-mic as the sirens blared. Cars skidded to a stop behind him as he hustled back down the snow-covered earthen ramp.

Back in the undergrowth, he slowed. There were still mangetouts abroad after all. He squeezed his earlobe, the call untraceable because the satellite's owner said so. He kept moving as he subvocalised.

<It's me.>

"Go ahead."

<There's a problem. The subjects took the source with them.>

"It was a risk, but the plan's not broken." The Old Man cleared his throat. *"Don't call again until everything's fixed. I mean everything."*

<How?>

"Sometimes the best way to cover up a mess is to make a bigger one."

05

Quirk bemoaned his poor sleep. The adrenaline from the showdown with Greiner was long gone and his shoulder ached solidly now. Eighty had downloaded a massage module and worked the muscles with technique approaching tenderness—leading Quirk to some unsettling thoughts while flat on the table—but his shoulder still ached, suggesting he had pulled something, in a bad way.

Furthermore, he was nervous. His pain must have made him look shifty during Sheriff Kreski's questioning the morning after Greiner. Enough to add an hour to his interrogation, specifically the hour of hologram interview with RCMP Serious Crimes in Vancouver. It was an excellent system that allowed the bigwigs to ask him all the same questions Kreski had without putting in the mileage. By the end he had a full-on throb in his shoulder regardless of where he leant, hung or rested his arm.

This morning brought little relief for Quirk's arm, but it was The Old Man's call that had disturbed his sleep. It was a dark, Mephistophelian presence risen again to stalk his nightmares. And there were plenty nowadays. In that way some people just got to you, TOM made him feel like the hopeless, loveless, emotional car crash he probably was. He shook now as if drugged, again. Yet there was nothing else for it but to persevere. Rowland arrived today, and he must dispel these newly-risen doubts—for the meeting at least. Because TOM was a lot of things, and a liar most definitely was one of them.

Quirk decided bacon would ease his pain and misgivings, maybe kick up his enthusiasm for Rowland's case. He, Moth and Eighty strolled to the hotel's adjoining diner and demolished over-easy eggs and dark, streaky rashers by the half dozen. After rye toast and glasses of blitzed whole oranges, Quirk considered his third cup of coffee, toasting success in swamping his negative energy with salt and saturated fat. Eighty sat charging at the table, violet eyes illuminated. Some considered that rude, but not Quirk. Androids had to sustain themselves too. Moth didn't give a monkey's, concentrating on pouring just the right amount of maple syrup on her waffle. Despite her four-scoop-a-day habit, even she didn't take ice-cream at breakfast.

"You have a rare appetite, Moth."

She shrugged. "I'm hyperactive. I'll flame it off by lunch."

"Mm," mused Quirk. "I don't know how you're not taller. Was your mother petite like you, or was it your father?"

A high-risk strategy mentioning the parents, but mealtimes presented a good opportunity to discuss the girl's past. He'd established early on that she was marginally less likely to explode in public, and both La Madre Superiora and Aunt Giulia—in response to queries about Moth's pseudonym and parentage—had stated she was entitled to her privacy. Moth's dark eyes flashed as her gaze flicked up to meet his. He almost flinched, but she didn't snap his head off, for once.

"You're not going to let it go, are you, even after four months?"

He shrugged, wincing as pain pierced his shoulder. "To work together effectively we should get to know each other better, don't you think? If I know what makes you tick, I'll be less likely to aggravate you in a sensitive situation. That sort of personal knowledge can be an advantage."

"Know how to charm a girl, don't you? Why should I spill my secrets when you tell me squat about your wife, kid, or yourself? I mean, I can see you're a dandy and a braggart, LOLs, but past that...not a fucking bean. And what was all that drama yesterday with the call? You looked like Count Alucard sucked you dry."

He nodded. "That's fair." Maybe it was a price worth paying. Goodness knew she gave him enough lip already. Still, there were parts of his past that he was not proud of, like leaving Jennifer. *Damn, but she made me do it. Growing a son and presenting a five-year-old like a present. "Look what I got you!" Controlling harpy. But sometimes, the control had been so sweet.*

Quirk tried to smooth the Merrion's lapel, but he wasn't wearing his favourite suit—Jennifer's special present—only his real leather belt. Eighty insisted on undertaking running repairs as November in Canada took its toll. The syRen® was right, of course. Instead of his urban armour, Quirk wore a plain T-shirt, black polo neck, active thermals and jeans, because November, in Canada. The half-metre of compacted snow outside seemed to be replenished by the hour. But he was avoiding the subject. Moth needed placation before they left for the airport.

"Okay"—he spread his hands on the table—"each day during this case I'll reveal something about my life before I became a detective of interstellar renown, provided that you reciprocate."

"Deal," said Moth, wiping strawberry juice from the corner of her mouth with the back of her hand. "When you dish the personal, I'll do likewise. I'll even go first." The girl's lips were tight, like her courage need screwing up, like it was costing her something. "My dad's name was Paulo Roberto Moratti. What's your son's?"

Quirk sighed heavily as fingers of familiar guilt began gouging the pit of his stomach. He reached for his Maurice Benisti high utility binylon puffer jacket, lined with faux rabbit fur, faux Eider down filled, in a bomber style with faux lamb's leather hood and trimmed with faux silver fox fur. It sounded like a really good dinner—maybe barring the fox—and was so warm that he daren't wear it inside.

"I don't know, and I don't want to know."

"Tell me about Jennifer then. You better give me something," said Moth dryly. "Or I'll start screaming just to liven this place up." She stood, pulled on her shocking pink ski jacket and stared expectantly, hands on hips.

"What have you been watching?"

"Whytube, why?"

Quirk shook his head. How could he tell her such close, personal details when he wasn't ready to consider them himself? The Old Man, Morton, Jennifer, their...son. Even five years later it remained raw. He had not moved on at all.

After an awkward silence Moth blew out her breath, lips flapping like an angry little pony. "Booooored. I knew you'd bail. I'm calling Rowland, check he's on time."

"Moth, we can check the..." but she had already placed the call, because she had Rowland's number, because all company traffic now synched between their accounts, because Quirk had been weak that *one* time. "Damnation, Moth."

Rowland's deep, gravel-bottomed drawl rolled over the diner's clinking chatter.

"That you, Mister Quirk? I'm on time. Just on approach."

"It's Angelika Moratti, Mister Rowland, Quirk's associate. I just called to say how positive we are that we'll be able to help. Can you tell us more, so we can formulate our inquiries? The first two days of any case often are the most important."

Good grief. She was developing business-speak faster than he could tie a double Windsor, and she was good at fabrication, too. The first two days indeed.

There was a pause. *"It's a missing person."*

Quirk rolled his eyes.

"That's helpful," Moth replied as she beamed at him in that I-told-you-so-mofo way she had. "Who's missing?"

"I can't say." He lowered his voice. The handset compensated, but the whisper was unmistakable. *"There's two others on the plane. I can't talk. Be real glad to see you though. It's a strain on Meriwa, she's worried. We're descending. Need to go. It's a woman. Speak soon."*

"But..." butted Moth.

The line was dead.

"Hah, see? I used my feminine wiles to get more info."

Quirk sighed. "You're too young to have wiles. Your wiles don't come in for another couple of years."

"How would you know, *Dad*?"

Little sh— Wiles or not, she knew how to hurt someone, specifically someone with family issues. And, another missing person. Perhaps he shied away from such cases because—like it or not—he had his own missing person. Two, in fact.

Rowland had sounded almost wistful, as clients often did when desperate to share the predicament they had placed themselves in, and their family. Quirk wondered if Meriwa was a sister, friend or wife. One of these was likely, but she wasn't the missing person, and you didn't look for a person who's name you didn't know so... Could Rowland have *found* the person, but not know who she was? *Damn, hooked again.*

He considered his missing people. Where might Jennifer be? He tried to imagine being able to think about her without feeling a pain in his throat. There was no avoiding this. He'd guessed being Moth's guardian would challenge him, just not like this, forcing him to confront a past he tried constantly to overwrite with new experience.

"Not long after Jennifer...presented me with the child; not long after I left, a man called Morton took the boy away from her at The Old Man's—that's my ex-father-in-law—at TOM's behest. He giveth and he taketh away. Jennifer was institutionalised." His voice had run down to a mumble.

Moth's eyes grew wide. "Wow. Is she out now?"

The girl's concern was genuine. "I...don't know."

"Jesus, Quirk." That was all she said. No judgement, no moral superiority. She just zipped up her jacket and walked to the door.

Completely unnecessarily, Quirk nodded a parting to Eighty—whose software update was due—and followed Moth, stepping out into the bright white, albedo-charged sunlight, and the skin-shrinking cold of the morning. His cheeks tightened and his eyes squinted in the milliseconds before his Ray Bans darkened. He thumbed his cLife and booked out one of the hotel's cars.

"It's the cerulean blue one," he pointed at a sleek VAG Wave with narrow, black sensor slits and dark auto-tint windows. The Ramada system had linked his cLife to the car and its lights flashed when he waved at it, hence the name. He clicked his heels together and Moth mirrored him. Thus deploying the metal studs in their soles, they started across the snowy forecourt.

Pre-warmed air welcomed them, and Quirk had only to thumb the scanner (now cloned to his handset) for the seat and mirrors to adjust to his height and reach. Eighty could have driven them, but Quirk liked to keep his hand in, and Creston was good practise as many people out here still leased U-drive cars.

He pulled onto Crowsnest Highway 3 heading south, on-board cameras monitoring his cautious turn. Driving felt unusual, like pulling on an old pair of shoes to find they no longer fit. Some manufacturers advertised their vehicles as uncrashable, leading to a regrettable fad among young hooligans attempting to disprove the claim. Naturally, they succeeded, thanks to human ingenuity. It served the NAF right for dispensing with driving licenses.

Quirk followed the strip into town, passing a cornucopia of businesses, outlets, workshops and eateries lining the die-straight road. To the left—behind the buildings—snow-decked, conifer-clad mountains rose up. The peaks to the right were distant, across the flat-bottomed, farm-patchwork valley through which a river wound. He admired such self-sustaining working towns, not unlike his home, Aldiss Station, buried in the heart of the asteroid Hygiea.

A mosaic of brightly coloured signs cluttered the road verge. Entering town a week ago to set up Greiner, Quirk had thought a winter festival was coming before recognising the names of electoral candidates. In Canada, Liano, Arnold, Benítez and the Co-op party pushed their agendas for all they were worth. With a week to go, campaigning teams tramped along the verge resetting signs after the latest snowfall.

Highway 3 bent east, paralleling the rail tracks, and became Northwest Boulevard. They passed a mall and a motel before entering town proper. Now neat picket-fenced lawns proclaimed candidates and parties in big black letters on bright boards. Quirk turned right, bumping over the tracks. The road wound downhill onto a straight pointing at the mountains across the valley. The VAG's mandatory hum changed as the vehicle switched modes. They headed downslope between wooden houses and snow-piled driveways, sentinel firs framing the bright blue sky.

At the bottom of the hill Quirk decelerated to the big, red "Stop" sign before the vehicle could intercede. He turned left on 21, toward the airport. Snow, sky, trees and techmac; snow, sky, trees and techmac. He had consulted Planetview while still under the duvet and now—not even looking at the VAG's screen—blithely turned left onto Mallory Road at the little Church of Earth's Children. Such freedom, intoxicating.

Snow, sky, trees, techmac; snow, sky, trees, techmac.

"Damn, Canada's boring," opined Moth, slumping further down in her seat.

"I thought you liked the simplicity?" He tried to rotate his shoulder and regretted it as his body stabbed him in the back.

"Simplicity was the town, this is rustic. When you've lived in a convent, rustic gets old *really* fucking quickly."

Just past the golf club, Quirk turned right onto Airport Road, narrower, enclosed by dark firs which cut out most of the sky. Then the outlook opened up, revealing distant, snow-covered mountains and a column of dark smoke rising above white-blanketed fields.

"Funny time to be burning," he mused.

"Big burn pile," said Moth.

They reached the airport access, a crossroads. Flashing blue and red lights caught Quirk's eye as he turned right, and again in the rear-view as he straightened the VAG. He stopped the car and craned around in the seat, shoulder protesting, jeans squeaking on the pseudo-leather seat. Moth turned too, their heads close together.

"Must be five or six vehicles down there," she observed in her business voice.

"Easily," Quirk murmured.

The red and blue chiaroscuro flickered like a fire near the base of the dissipating smoke column, but a more powerful, orange glow splashed the vehicles that was not from any warning light.

"I'll get Eighty onto this," Moth said, raising her handset.

"Good plan."

Quirk turned forwards and drove into the airport parking lot. The timing of this stunk like five-day-old socks. Maybe it was a barn, or an illicit trash burn out of control. He knew that ancient, real rubber tyres burned hot and black. Either way it was a big pile of something. He hoped that they were not about to stand in it.

Creston Airport comprised a cluster of pale grey sheds and a strip of techmac just wide enough to warrant a white line down the middle. The techmac lay stark black against the surrounding snow. Response vehicles sat on the apron, lights flashing yellow, anticipating a landing.

He pulled the VAG up carelessly, braking sharply enough to make Moth glare.

"He's not due for ten minutes. The flight'll keep schedule, right?"

"Come on," he said, climbing out.

He clicked his heels and started across the parking lot towards the control tower. This was a grey, pitched-roof prefab shed like all the rest, but for the big black letters that read "Control Tower," useful in case the control tower was mistaken for a shed. The air conveyed a harsh chill, but Quirk's blood was up, heart pounding. Halfway across the lot the door swung open, and a woman burst out, thudding down the steps.

"What happened?" he jerked his good arm towards the smoke.

"Solar prop from Yellowknife came down," the woman barked, barely glancing at him. She made straight for a brutish, red GMC truck which roared into life as she approached it. Her red ponytail bounced as she bounded onto the running-board and swung into the vehicle.

Quirk strode forward and stepped up on the passenger side, hauling the big door open. "How?"

"Get off my truck," the woman snapped, dragging the shift into reverse. "Now."

"We're meeting a passenger."

The cab's back door slammed as Moth plopped onto the big bench seat, buckling up. "You're going to the crash site, right?"

The woman threw her a glare then skewered Quirk with a scowl. "Is she with you? I'm tryin' to do my job here."

"So am I. My client's on that plane."

"Well, shit." She actually slapped the steering wheel. "Get in if you're comin'."

Quirk's knees were still bent when the truck leapt forward, turning in a tight circle, throwing his arse into the worn leather seat.

"This is a bit of a relic. Is that an IC engine?"

"Ethanol conversion, reclaimed in the valley."

He was still battling the seatbelt, even with its mag-assist, as they burst across the public road. The redhead's foot didn't even twitch towards the brake as the GMC ploughed onto the farm road towards the column of smoke and the lights.

"Goes like stink," he observed, grasping the overhead handle and looking sideways at the driver.

"That's the way I like it," she said flatly.

They were close enough now that the emergency lights reflected off the woman's pale skin. Quirk turned forward reluctantly. They were rattling down the farm road, post-and-wire on one side, three-bar wooden fence on the other. His eyes were glued ahead however, on the bright orange flames at the base of pillar of dark grey smoke. He jammed both feet down at a hundred metres. By eighty metres he was pressing the carpet hard enough to break the floor, but still they sped towards the conflagration, bouncing over the rutted surface. Quirk's teeth rattled.

Moth loved it. She grinned wildly. "*Mio papà* took me riding when I was little," she paused at one big bump. "When we galloped, it was just like this!" From sorrow or glee, he did not know, but her eyes shone. "That's a reveal you owe me! No, two."

Quirk could only stare ahead, blood draining from his face.

"Are you going to—"

At thirty metres the redhead planted her boot on the brake and the big truck slewed to a halt, grinding onto the road's rough verge as she tweaked the wheel. She gave no thought to her passengers, worked the zip on her well-worn jean jacket, and threw the door open, jumping down.

"She's feisty; I like her," Moth announced as she clambered out.

Quirk snorted and jumped down. His legs wobbled slightly on landing. The smoke's thick stench clawed at his throat, and the blaze's heat made his face ache, incongruous in the snowy landscape. Many figures moved around the fire, each about their job. Two fire engines blocked the road, one crew jetted water over surrounding buildings while the other sprayed suppressant foam on the blaze. Three police cars huddled on the verge opposite, shadowed by the towering plume. Fire crew wielding bulky, rubber-cased Books directed hooded fire-fighting syRen® in thick overalls how to direct the hoses. Melted snow and foam slicked muddily around the androids' ankles.

The small plane had gouged a furrow through the neighbouring field—a dark scar in the white snow—before plunging across the farm road and smashing into the barn, now massively ablaze along with the two buildings adjacent. The plane's striped tail projected from the burning barn at a crazy angle. Things didn't look good for Rowland.

The redhead stood with the strapping sheriff—Kreski—who had questioned Quirk about Greiner. Kreski had been ready to run him out of town, right or not. Quirk followed Moth toward them, skin stinging from the heat, the inferno roaring in his ears.

Kreski was shouting, brow furrowed, "—haven't found anyone who saw it, Natalie. I can't help you. Investigators'll be here in their time. Right now, you gotta bide yours and stay the hell back." He waved her away then noticed Quirk and Moth. "You again? You got no reason to be here, though I'm puzzled as heck why you are. Devan, get these three back and block the road like I told you!"

One of the deputies turned and started waving his arms, trying to herd them away. He lacked the sheriff's commanding presence. Quirk ignored him. "Is the passenger pod intact?" he called over the roar. "My client is aboard, Barry Rowland."

Kreski rounded on Quirk, strong hands on broad hips made to buckle a gun belt on. "Are you chasing ambulances in my town? I already dislike your fancy tone, *Mister* Quirk, and you ruined my week dropping Greiner on me. If you're still here in five seconds, I *will* ticket you for obstructing emergency responders."

Moth tugged Quirk's sleeve, which made him twitch, but he was having none of Kreski's musclebound parochialism. He did not respond well to bullying, no matter how well-intentioned; it was a matter of fairness. Although, the sheriff's office might be the best place to learn what happened.

"A simple question deserves a courteous answer, Sheriff." Quirk cocked an eyebrow at the big, rugged dope and that seemed to do it.

Kreski bristled. "Okay, I'm tagging you for impeding an incident. Book him, Devan."

The deputy moved, grin lopsided, reaching for the tracking cuff on his belt.

Moth went at him in a blur, kicked him hard in the shin. "Fascist pig!"

Two minutes later—both sporting electronic tags—he and Moth sat in Natalie's truck with a date to attend the sheriff's office. Being cut off from the smell and the heat was blessed relief. Natalie fired up the GMC and threw it around. His stomach tried to exit via the window. By now, ambulances were turning onto the farm road. Apparently, there was room to pass because nothing exploded when the vehicles met. Natalie hurtled across the junction, pulling up hard in the airport lot. This woman was crazy.

"Problem?" Quirk asked. "Apart from the obvious, of course."

She turned, elbow on the steering wheel, and seemed to see him for the first time. Fine features and opal eyes appraised him.

"Big fire, don't you think?"

"Big for a solar prop," Quirk agreed.

"There could've been propellant in the barn," Moth piped up.

"Not on Clifford's place," said Natalie not looking away from Quirk.

"What are you saying?" he prodded, unwilling to stick his neck out again today.

"How'd you know it was the solar prop?" Countering with a question, she was as closemouthed as him. Perhaps she was scared of something, like being right.

"Easy," said Moth brightly. "Although there was only one tailpiece sticking out barn, you could see where the connecting spar joined a twin tailpiece with a keying slot long enough to make it a Lear-Piccard VS334R." She winked. "I get bored at airports."

"How'd *you* know?" Natalie jerked her head at Quirk, ponytail bobbing.

"I listen to what she tells me," he said, eliciting a derisive snort from Moth. "That, and we were meeting the Yellowknife flight."

"You're both right. Lear's approach was pitch perfect. Prob'ly a droid at the stick, so it sure wasn't a heart attack or pilot error that dumped it in the barn. Something about this besides burning batteries stinks to high heaven."

"Deliberate then, potentially," said Quirk.

Protected passenger capsule or no, there remained a good chance Barry Rowland was dead, but a woman still was missing, or had been found, and this Meriwa person Rowland mentioned presumably still had a problem that needed solving. Could the crash—by some twisted design— be an elaborate murder? Where a call from TOM was involved, nothing could be discounted, so said Quirk's bitter experience. One way or another, there was work to be done. Less than a day into this Rowland affair, and everything had gone to excrement. That might be a new record. The first creeping tendrils of a migraine crept into Quirk's awareness.

Why go to the trouble of killing Rowland? Because you didn't want the missing person found? Because you were trying to eradicate a trail? And how in Dante's nine circles could Rowland not know who was missing? Intellectually stimulating questions, but The Old Man's call remained the one thing that made his nerves jangle. That alone was reason to proceed, to stick their noses into what now was an official investigation. The Old Man *may* have intended to bluff him into rejecting Rowland, but he would carry on simply to spite him. Because Quirk had a bottomless well of spite reserved for his ex-father-in-law and was only too happy to dip into it.

"Moth," he turned to her. "I pay my debts. He's called The Old Man because he is one hundred and sixty-three years old. Joshua Simister was born in nineteen thirty-six. He's a truly despicable human being, and my fear of him and what he's capable of is limitless."

Quirk met Natalie's clear mountain blue gaze again and shook the tag around his wrist. "Natalie, if I buy you dinner, will you come to Kreski's office and explain why you think someone may have killed my client?"

Her scowl eased, and she nodded. "Okay, I'll have words with the big, dumb jock, no dinner required."

Moth was right. He admired Natalie's directness.

"Good," he nodded to Moth. "Then let's roll up our sleeves."

06

"Well done, genius," Moth hissed at him as Deputy Devan Becker led her up the sheriff's office steps. His hold on her arm looked none too gentle. Quirk wished she'd kicked him harder. "We could've been halfway to Calgary, en route to Berlin, but oh, no, we'll just take this really *easy* case first."

She didn't get it. "We have a client now. We took the case, remember? If he's dead, we still owe someone an explanation. We need information." He tried to shrug Kreski's firm grip off the epaulette of his Benisti jacket, but the sheriff wasn't having it and steered him towards the plass door. Quirk might as well have been caught in the crush for Michael Bublé tickets. He was going nowhere but where Kreski steered him.

His words did not placate Moth, of course, because the day ended in "y." She continued to twist in Becker's grip. "At best it's attempted murder," she snapped. "Police matter: explanation over! We could have picked up Eighty and been long gone. But *oh no*, Quirk's chivalrous to the last. He wouldn't *dream* of putting himself and his assistant—who he's totally fucking responsible for—before a bloody corpse!"

Becker shook Moth again as he hauled her through the sliding door into reception. She'd kicked him to ensure they detained her too. *Good girl, but perhaps the situation could be destabilised just a little more.*

"Angelika, I wish you would behave more like a proper Milanese lady."

"Lady? *Lady?* Since when have you associated with ladies, you fucking kerb-crawler?!" She struggled so hard against Becker's grip that Quirk thought she would break free and come at him. "If Rowland's dead, we can leave!"

"There is a *verbal* contract." Over his five words, Quirk's growl swelled to a bellow, loud in the confines of the office. "There's such a thing as trust, you know."

They had the close attention of Kreski, Becker, two deputies behind the desk, and another who appeared from the corridor leading into the back.

Moth continued to struggle. "Time for the old lead pipe massage, is it? I guess assholes never take the day off."

"Impound their tech," Kreski barked, "then get these miscreants out of my sight!"

* * *

Clearly, the sheriff worked out, regularly. That or the municipality of Creston issued only one size uniform to their officers. The man's khaki shirt bulged at his biceps and triceps, and serious cords in his neck strained as he leaned forward across the table in the, by now, frustratingly familiar slate-grey interview room. Quirk didn't care for the musclebound look, not in men anyway, but he understood why some did. He thought the sheriff might possess a decent package between his ears though. That was what drew him to the man.

His strategy with Moth might have backfired a little though. They were in the right place to get information about the crash, and discover what had happened to Rowland, the thorny issue was getting out again.

"I didn't enjoy your last visit, Mister Quirk. A citizen is in my jail because of you. Now this plane thing." Kreski's lips pressed together so tightly his goatee looked like he was almost done swallowing a gopher.

Quirk was not going to sit still for such heinous accusations. He leaned forward, invading Kreski's personal space. "Your illustrious citizen is a French national and an art thief. I expect he'll be deported, but maybe you'll have time to give him the freedom of Creston before they cart him off. And what exactly do you think I had to do with the crash, aside from watching my client cook?"

The sheriff puffed out his breath. "Fast work taking a new case right after closing one. Did you have Rowland in your sights? Have him lined up in the crosshairs?"

Quirk smiled, *Bite My Ass, Mofo: Season 1, Episode 3.* "The thing is, Sheriff, I've been genetically modified by millions of years of evolution to be able to do two things at once. I'm very well organised, and outrageously popular."

Silence simmered between them. The sheriff seemed to be restraining himself. "So," Kreski rumbled, "Rowland—what's his beef? And he's still alive, by the way. The Lear had a capture foam passenger shell and passively safe furniture."

Ah, good. "I can't tell you that, Sheriff; client confidentiality." *And I have barely a clue about his "beef," but he's a very lucky man.*

It would be easy to walk away from Rowland at this point—assisting with the sheriff's inquiries and his earlier words with Moth notwithstanding—but that wasn't his style. Although he had walked away from problems before, one in particular.

Old regret like once-sweet fruit withering on the vine fluttered in the pit of his stomach, only the ghost of a smile where happiness had been. *Damn but Jennifer did it to me, and yet she paid the price, emotionally.* And what had The Old Man done with the...boy, when Morton delivered Jennifer's progeny to his master? Quirk realised he feared the answer. But why? What did that fear mean? Remembering the call from TOM set his stomach jangling. Maybe he needed to learn what had happened to them. Certainly, he would not walk away again, not from Rowland or Meriwa—whoever she was. The Old Man's earlier appeal was a red rag. *And it's time for this bull to charge into another china shop.*

Kreski banged the table. "Confidentiality horseshit."

Quirk shrugged. "At least he's alive. Amazing, considering the heat of that blaze. I presume the syRen® pilot is a pile of slag."

Kreski huffed. "Okay, you can have that one. Rowland is in the Valley Medical Centre."

"I'd like to see Barry."

Kreski shook his head. "He can't tell you anything at this time."

"As a licensed investigator I'm entitled to see my client and his possessions. That model Lear-Piccard has no cargo space, I believe, so everything *my client* had with him must have survived the crash."

The sheriff sighed. "Natalie tell you that?"

Quirk leaned back, content that they were in amicable conversation now instead of a testosterone-secreting competition. "Maybe she did. She's a red-blooded woman. You can't blame her for opening up to an urbane individual such as myself."

The big sheriff scowled. "She's prone to sticking her nose where it isn't needed."

Quirk smirked. "Sounds like my kinda gal."

"And picking losers," Kreski huffed. "So, you're clamming up about Rowland?"

"Let me peruse his possessions and we'll talk, but I'm not going to sit here and spitball with you. That's a thing you jocks do, right?"

The sheriff stood and moved to the door, turning back to accuse Quirk with his finger. "I'm not finished with you, Squirtle. You're still assisting with my enquiries."

Quirk raised his arm and shook the cuff that attached him to the table. "Well, clearly I'm not going anywhere."

* * *

Moth sat in the blank, boring room, swinging her legs from the chair. She yawned and stuck out her tongue at the two-way mirror, because nobody put a one-way mirror in a holding room. Why the fuck would you? For the prisoner to admire their police brutality bruises? Bullshit. She hoped Kreski would come back soon; he was fun. He must have girls, as he was unwilling to rile her beyond the mild suggestion of some vague threat. And then there was Quirk, with his go-go-gadget sense of ethics. Sure, he was a perfect gentleman until a trim backside walked by. She bit back an expletive because there was no one to fire it at, expect perhaps the chump behind the mirror.

"Fucktarts," she said to her reflection. "Piss junky, wank wranglers." She raised her middle finger at the mirror and scowled. "Fucking shit burglar," she complained at her own, pink-cheeked angry face.

The door opened. Not Kreski, but the girlhandler-in-chief, Becker. He sidled into the room, thumb hooked into his belt, removed his hat and dropped it on the table, putting his palms down flat in a terrible impersonation of a cop.

"Chief's in with your boss. So, I get to deal with you. Why don't you make it easy on yourself and just tell me everything?"

Moth giggled then covered her mouth with her hand.

"You think it's funny, little girl? You could end up in jail for obstructing emergency services. Juvenile detention's no joke," Becker sneered. "The big kids'll beat you up, lock you in the shower, toss you in a bath full of piss or some such."

Moth giggled again, shoulders clenching as she tried to restrain her laughter. This was just *too* much fun. "Oh, please, Officer"—she brought her fingernails to her teeth—"can't you help me? What can I do?"

Becker scowled. "You wanna play shitting the shitter?"

Moth frowned. "Huh? You've gotta work on your swears, man. That's just *merda completa*." Becker was weird, but weird was a game she could play. She hunched her shoulders. "I'm so scared, Officer. I'll do just anything to stay out of trouble."

Becker snatched up his hat, but didn't put it on. He leaned in close, and Moth leaned back, tipping the chair on its rear legs. Becker smelled of stale sweat and smoke. "Maybe what you need is a slap to loosen your tongue. Now, tell me about Rowland."

Moth pushed her chair back and stood up, moving to the far wall, and shrugged off her pink puffer jacket.

"What you doing?" Becker's eyes narrowed. "Sit down, dammit."

She threw the jacket onto the empty chair then pulled her dark blue sweater over her head, revealing her vintage Metallica Fiftieth Anniversary tour shirt. Her black bob flipped as she threw the sweater on the floor. She reached up and mussed her hair.

"Aw, Christ. What the fuck are you playing at? There's video in here. They'll know I didn't touch you."

"Don't bring Christ into it. He takes a pretty dim view of knuckleheads molesting his brides," she said in a stage whisper. According to cosmo.life, you had to establish dominance over this kind of man-child. "I haven't even met this Rowland guy. I bet you already got more from his Book than I could tell you, didn't you?"

"Let's pretend he wasn't carrying the Book. Assume I don't know anything."

"Okey-doke." She nodded. "So, you crapped out trying to break his handset too?"

Becker sneered. "Hah, as if. But forget that." He slapped the table. "Tell me what *you* know."

Dick. He really was unencumbered by a brain. She started counting on her fingers. "Well, he's a Chicago White Cubs fan, he loves his wife, his mother and his baby sister Babs, although she's twenty-five and pregnant, *again*. He likes ethical salmon fishing and only shoots the deer marked for culling. How am I doing?"

"Terrible," Becker snapped. "You're just making shit up. Cut the crap. Tell me about the missing passenger."

"The—" *Huh?* "Missing passenger, yes. Well, Rowland said there were two people with him on the plane." Educated guess required. "The local...man." She edged forward, toying with the hem of her Metallica shirt, tugging it up enough that he could see her navel. *Full of shit, Quirk. Totally bringing the wiles now, bitch.*

"Yeah, Elneny, we know about him." Becker made a chopping, hurry-up motion.

"Oh, Deputy, I don't think I should tell you." She fluttered her Latin lashes.

Sweat beaded Becker's brow. "What about Weiss?" he demanded.

Too easy. "Yes," she said, trying to sound authoritative. "The one that was...gone when you got the passenger pod open."

"Yeah," said Becker tightly.

Dio, men are such blabbermouths when you rile them up. But now she needed to talk to Quirk. Time to smack the man-child down. She came within a metre of him, looking up into the cop's surprisingly innocent, doe brown eyes and let her shirt drop.

"No idea." She threw her arms out wide. "Who's 'shitting-the-shitter' now, shithead? You've got nothing on me; nothing, ya hear? I. Want. My. Lawyer!" She banged her hand on the table to punctuate each word then threw her head back and yelled, "Get me Mary Quon!"

"Shit." Becker backed up to the door, reaching behind him, groping for the handle, pulling it open. "You're balls-out crazy!"

"Just as well one of us got some, you fucking pussy!"

The door slammed hard.

Sorted.

* * *

Eighty would have sent them a report by now, but Quirk's cLife languished in an evidence bag, maybe opened by now using police override powers. Perhaps he should get a 16G implant after all, but he hated the thought of a machine using his chemical energy to power itself, no matter how small the amounts. Most disquieting. And anyway, sensitive locations like hospitals, courts and cinemas used signal dampers.

He tapped his fingers on the tinny table to the seven-four-time beat of Dave Brubeck's *Unsquare Dance*, humming the counterpoint baseline until Kreski came in and sat down. Quirk stopped tapping.

"Looks like no one's talking. Maybe I'll bang you up for a few days and see if Rowland tells me anything."

Quirk just stared at him, showing no sign of giving the slightest shit, Moth style. What he *thought* was that the sheriff was the best option for actually meeting Rowland, the trick being to remain on the right side of the bars. Moth's rant on the steps—even though fake—did lead him to question the wisdom of pursuing the case, for a moment. But Rowland was alive, injured, and counting on them now.

The Old Man egging him on seemed anomalous, would have appeared coincidental had Quirk not visited Yellowknife before, a decade ago. C Corp's Genextric operation. He knew it neighboured Rowland's employer, Hygen. Coincidence? Of course not. TOM did nothing that wasn't out of self-interest. If there was the least chance to sabotage a scheme of TOM's, Quirk owed it to what he'd shared with Jennifer to do just that, with speaking to Barry Rowland being the first step. *Retribution, thy name is Quinton.*

The sheriff slid a cLife from his pocket and placed it on the table. The scuffed screen showed a weathered-looking man in his fifties propped up in a hospital bed. By his expression he'd been through the proverbial ringer. It was Rowland and he was awake. The view turned and Quirk met the gaze of a female deputy exhibiting all the forgiveness and understanding of a librarian at a state-sponsored book burning.

"Thing is though," said Kreski, "someone *is* talking. Your client is keen to see you. I can't hold you beyond two days—at a stretch—but I will hold you just to slow you down unless I sit in when you meet Rowland."

Kreski unlocked Quirk's cuff, stood and gestured politely towards the door. Quirk needed no second invitation. He gave his jeans a cursory brush as he stood then made for the corridor. He almost made it, but Kreski's brawny arm came up to bar his way. To Quirk's surprise— in addition to a moment of déjà vu—he received a whiff of Armani *Homme Plus*. He shook his head, refusing to accept that any man so ripped also could be blessed with good taste in cologne. Maybe there was hope for the big lug.

"Do you know any of the other passengers?" Kreski's gaze searched.

"No," said Quirk. "Can we go see Rowland now?"

* * *

Morton couldn't have bailed out of the solar prop if it hadn't been a Lear—a C Corp product—and therefore hackable for him. He couldn't have deactivated the droid pilot without his D-work digital backdoor into the syRen® processing core, provided by Androicon, a C Corp company. Accessing the hospital when he discovered Rowland hadn't died in the crash was just plain easy. He waited for visiting time then walked into the loading bay carrying a box from a nearby alley on his shoulder. This hid him from the cameras while he hacked the security door. Then he found a store cupboard, put on orderly scrubs (never pose as a doctor), and walked into the elevator. Killing Rowland with a lethal injection of EV7 should have been just as easy, but the local yokel deputy— Parks—had refused to be lured away from her post by his cloned call to her porous, government-issue handset. Who had won that contract again? Oh, yes, FKN, the C Corp-owned comms company. So, now he must wait for an organic opportunity to enter Rowland's room, time he spent checking and rechecking his spec-ops kitbag. That and contemplating the ridiculously good fortune that had brought Quirk back into his orbit. He could not remember the last time a message from TOM had held so much pleasure. All he had to do now was wait.

* * *

Moth fumed beside him as they sat cuffed in the back of the squad car. He had to smile. Looking past her aggressive manner, she had—very noisily and obtrusively over several months—become a quite effective assistant. The handcuffs deflected her ire—temporarily, no doubt—onto Becker, who had taken great relish in restraining them based on Kreski's flight risk assessment. Nonsense, but Quirk did not try to assert his rights this time in the interest of seeing Rowland as soon as possible. Anyway, he was not unfamiliar with the wearing of handcuffs—both professionally and at leisure—and the town burghers of Creston clearly took detention seriously, funding the latest stress-sensing auto-cuffs. He wondered if they had the low voltage shock option, and whether Natalie might be partial to a little dominance and submission.

He shook his head, trying to dislodge the flitting distractions infecting his mind since the Greiner case. His thoughts settled on The Old Man's call. The more it festered in his head the stronger the realisation that TOM had known exactly the reaction his appeal would have, that it would set Quirk full square in the direction of Yellowknife. *Double bluff, damnation!* That was its beauty, of course: twice as likely to work, provided the bluffer knew the bluffee inside out, as TOM did him.

Moth slammed her fist against the plastec finish of the squad car door.

"Don't make me come back there," Kreski grumbled affably over his shoulder through the cage that separated front and back.

She turned on Quirk. "This is *your* fault."

"Mine?"

"Don't fight it," Kreski's deep tones rumbled. "She's right."

Moth's hands—moving together due to being cuffed—grabbed Quirk's collar. She shook him—her black hair flying—then hauled him towards her. Was she going to bite him?! Her whisper was urgent. "There's a passenger missing. Name's Weiss." Then she let out a growl of frustration and plumped back on the seat.

The awkward silence in the vehicle reasserted itself then Moth began tapping on Quirk's foot. *Morse code. Clever cookie.*

What...does...it...mean?

The name tickled Quirk's memory. Perhaps it was the call from TOM sending his thoughts back to Quirk's time at C Corp. He'd only had one fleeting association with a man called Weiss, but it couldn't be. I...don't...know, he replied. But...stay...sharp.

They pulled into the hospital, Becker parking in a disabled bay. Kreski grunted, but didn't admonish his junior. Instead, he swung his tall frame out and pulled open the back door, taking Quirk's elbow in a heavy grip. Becker helped Moth out, grabbing her arm like he enjoyed it.

"Get off me, pervert! Where's my lawyer?"

"Can it," he ordered. "You've been detained. We say 'dance,' you say 'how high.'"

Kreski shook his head. Quirk smiled, meeting the sheriff's calm gaze.

"You can't hold us, you fucking letch!"

"Shut up," said Kreski and Quirk in unison. "Jinx," said Quirk, winking.

The sheriff scowled. "What are you, twelve?"

"Thirty-four," said Quirk. "Yesterday was my birthday; nobody remembered."

"Seriously?" asked Moth. "There's another thing you haven't told me, and you know mine. Closed—fucking—book. We have a deal."

"And now you know my birthday. So, can we please step off the crazy-go-round for a minute and speak to our client?"

They entered the hospital under a thunderstorm of grumpy. Nurses and orderlies paused as Kreski led his motley band into the quiet, pastel-painted reception. Becker went to the desk, but the sheriff waved Quirk and Moth to the elevator where Becker joined them. They rode up one floor in silence then walked down a wide corridor lined with doors and curtained windows, bright paintings by school kids hung between them.

Rowland's room would be the one with the khaki-clad deputy outside. *Does everyone in this town work out, but me?* Parks nodded to Kreski then stared at Quirk like she hated him in all sorts of ways from which he was free to pick his favourite.

"Any developments?" she asked Kreski, her sceptical gaze not leaving Quirk.

A missing passenger, apparently. Very curious. Well enough to walk away? Possible, but how did they walk through the fire, unless they left inflight. Tricky to do unless one possessed a tactical wingsuit, or iChute, but more importantly, a security override. Then there was the name Moth acquired by her growing tradecraft smarts. Weiss. A cold dread had settled in his stomach when she whispered that name, a name from five or more years ago, a pseudonym used by a sometime C Corp associate. Derek Morton.

"Not sure, Joan." The sheriff faced Parks, arms akimbo. "These two're involved. Court-ordered scan says their droid's been researching Rowland which supports him being their client." He waved a hand at the curtained room. "We'll have a talk and see what comes of it." Kreski removed their handcuffs and clipped them to his belt.

Parks nodded earnestly and reached for the door handle, scanning the corridor before she pushed the door open. Kreski motioned them inside. Quirk invited Moth to precede him, and his pint-sized assistant strolled through.

Quirk followed with the big sheriff at his back. The room smelled of hospital. There were four beds, but only one was occupied. The haggard-looking man sat up. Quirk recognised Barry Rowland from his profile: full features, weather-worn, salt-and-pepper stubble. The pelican-patterned gown was anachronistic on this outdoorsman, maternity surplus, presumably.

Time to go to work.

"The others?" asked Quirk.

"Elneny's a local, moved from Democratic Republic of Egypt in the fifties," said Kreski. "Known him for years."

"And you're missing one, I gather," said Quirk, innocently. Kreski did not reply.

"Mister Rowland, I'm Quirk." The man nodded warily. "My associate, Moth—"

"Ace detectives," she butted in, yet her expression remained professional.

Quirk smiled, turning to the sheriff. "Chances of getting ten minutes alone with my client?"

"Zee-ro."

Quirk nodded, reordering his questions. "Mister Rowland..."

"Barry."

"Barry, I don't want to talk about the crash. You said you had a problem in Yellowknife. Our android has researched your background. Tell us what you're comfortable with the sheriff hearing, and be aware you have rights. At this point, you are not assisting in any official capacity." He glanced sideways at Kreski. The big man didn't contradict him, just watched Rowland.

Rowland looked sceptical, his lips making a flat line. His monitor beeped twice before he spoke. "Hygen's site is across the river from Genextric's lab." Quirk tensed involuntarily at the name, but shoved his memories down. "Four days ago, I was out on our perimeter. Motion sensor tripped. We run a lot of monitoring against contaminants reaching the river, from over-ground flow or groundwater infiltration. Our UNEC limits are tighter than a polecat's asshole—begging your pardon, miss." Moth shrugged. Quirk suspected she was memorising the expression. "We mine all sorts up there, but the principal load is moissanite." Rowland looked from Moth's blank face to Quirk's to Kreski's. "Silicon carbide. Carborundum in old money."

"I'm studying Cantonese in school, if that helps," said Moth.

"It's chemistry," said Rowland patiently, scratching near his chest bandage. "Used in chips and other tech. They've been growing moissanite crystals for decades and synthesising powder, but mining is cheaper, if you can find it. Our load's very pure."

"Why were you on the plane?" growled Kreski. "Please," he added.

Quirk resisted scowling. *Because of a foundling he doesn't know who someone tried to kill him over, if Natalie's right. And now a missing passenger called Weiss.*

Rowland nodded and winced. "It's down to a tripped motion sensor. Usually, it's a snowshoe hare gotten in past the buzz-wire. It's after eleven, pitch black, cold as hell, but what's new? I hear a scream, kind of distant, I head for the shore. I'm down there with my torch. There's this spit of rock in the river near the bridge, inlet formed by eddies. The monitor under the bridge is clear, but I see a body on the spit. She's been savaged by...something, a bear." Moth twitched. "But she's alive, somehow."

Rowland paused, wiping a hand across his paling, stubbled chin.

"I call it in—sheriff and medics, fire and rescue—the whole nine yards. And I'm sitting with her, holding her hand. She's gripping like I'm God Almighty, like she's clinging to life. Says she's done a terrible thing, but someone made her do it, and she's sorry, and the droids'll fix it. Then there's a bright light, I..." Rowland shook his head. "Anyway, sirens are coming, and I try to calm her. I run up to the road to flag them down. There's a whole cavalcade of lights on the highway from town. We get back down there and...she's gone. Scoured both banks for half a mile up and down, and there's animal signs, but the trackers can't place them, and there's blood, which they sample. Sent dogs and droids up and down. Nothing.

"Two days later, still no news. I'm chasing the sheriff. Nothing. Another day and they've put it down to bears killing a hobo. It's bullshit. Sorry, miss. It's a cover-up."

"Shit," Moth scowled, dropping into that distracted contemplation she entered when wrestling with perplexing information.

Quirk pondered Rowland's story. The monitor beeped. Quirk shook his head. Nothing implicated Genextric or C Corp, so why had his ex-father-in-law called? Reluctantly, he dredged unwanted memories. The monitor beeped. The Old Man's form suggested a powerplay of some kind. Surely, he wasn't being set up as a patsy, *again*? His shoulder ached, but a headache was catching it on the rails. The monitor beeped. Moth sighed then the burgeoning howl of the fire alarm ruptured the silence.

The lights went out. Rowland's monitor darkened and fell silent. The alarm continued its insistent woorp, woorp, woorp.

Kreski moved first. The door opened, and Quirk saw Deputy Joan's compact form outlined by the emergency lights, as the sheriff pushed out.

Moth moved too, pushing the door closed behind the cops, but leaving a gap to peer through. "You think there's a fire?"

"Not the way our luck runs." He sat on Rowland's bed. "Let's tough it out for a minute." He squeezed his eyes shut against the strident blaring pounding at his temples.

"Barry, I don't think we can help you. We can't be standing on the cops' flat feet, that won't turn out well for anyone. Tell us the rest, quickly, but without the damsel—"

"She's alive. She's with my wife, Meriwa, hidden."

Rowland darted a glance towards the door. "Someone's threatening me, drinking on the job, misconduct, all sorts. I can ride that out, but that woman wasn't attacked by any bear. I don't know what's going on, but something's badly wrong. The crash..."

Quirk bowed his head. Already this was a conundrum wrapped in a fiasco lashed by a shitstorm, and each passing hour made things worse. Could Genextric be involved? TOM owning the company next door to Rowland's employer stretched coincidence to the limit. Quirk didn't doubt there was a rat, and Barry had smelled it, but was Rowland's missing person a whistle-blower, a thief, an animal welfare crusader? Quirk knew what Genextric did. In that building, a rat was never just a rat.

"We can't solve the world's woes, Barry. You should take her to the police."

Rowland's blue-grey eyes shone sharply in his furrowed face. "Big business runs my town now, Mr. Quirk. Everyone knows what Genextric does, and I think she fell afoul of them. She won't have any chance out in the open. Look what happened to me."

The piercing alarm and semi-darkness made thinking straight impossible. Regardless of the nature of TOM's game, to subvert it he must follow the trail.

From the door Moth snapped, "They're coming back."

Without preamble, the lights came on. Looking around, blinking, Quirk saw the air in the corner of the room shimmer. A tall figure appeared from behind a zero-viz cloak. Clad all in black, he wore a surgical mask, his pistol sporting a silencer. The man shot Moth and she crumpled backwards, her body slamming the door closed.

"No!" Quirk sprang up. *Engage, distract.* "You—"

Again, the gun spat angrily but Quirk was moving sideways round the bed. *Missed!* He kept moving. The gunman swung the pistol after him as Quirk grabbed Rowland's sheet and whipped it up to billow in the air between them. Gun spat, sheet twitched but wafted in space for a breath as Quirk charged, glimpsing Rowland swinging out of bed. The sheet fell, revealing the gunman.

Quirk was so close, but the man pulled his gun back to his stomach as he aimed, firing as Quirk reached out, fingers clawing as the assassin shied backwards.

Something slammed into Quirk just as his grasping fingers snagged the man's mask and tugged it down. Briefly, as Quirk collapsed, he saw Derek Morton's chiselled features spinning past, before hitting the polished floor, when the lights went out again.

07

Disinfectant stink filled Quirk's nostrils. His cheek was cold. He discovered he had arms and that they moved, somewhat. He lifted his head off the floor.

Moth!

Hauling himself around, hands scrabbling, head spinning, he saw her slumped against the door. Someone was pushing into the room and that damned siren was wailing like hell was disgorging its dead. *The man in black. Morton!*

The door edged open. Moth's body slumped aside.

"What the hell?" Kreski's head poked through the gap. "Oh, shit." The sheriff's pistol preceded him into the room.

"Moth!" Quirk practically screamed to compete with the insufferable siren. He jerked towards Moth, his legs pushing against nothing. The motion tipped his balance and he vomited onto the smooth floor. He felt like a walrus was trying to hatch his brain from his skull. "Moth," he spluttered.

Kreski crouched beside her, fingers on her neck. "She's alive." Then he howled, "Medic! Medic here!" He patted her cheek.

"Core-ssss I fuckn' all-live." Quirk barely heard the words from her pale lips.

Her head lolled onto the sheriff's forearm as he sat down to support her, gun in hand, strong jaw clenched. Quirk hung his head in relief. He lifted a fold of Rowland's fallen bedsheet and wiped the puke from his chin. That was when he saw the body on the floor. Barry Rowland was dead, open eyes vacant. He sprawled with pillows tumbled around him, yellowish saliva leaking from his mouth onto his stubbled cheek.

Definitely Morton, not a tranq-fuelled hallucination. Hell. Quirk thought he might heave again and reached for his handkerchief. His hand found something hard in his pocket. He hauled out a plastic vial the size of his little finger. The cap was missing, the vial empty but for a viscous, yellowish residue. *Ah.* Closing his fingers around the vial, he pushed up to his knees then stood. Then he decided against it, and sat on the edge of Rowland's bed, turning his head to ease the hard tension in his neck.

The siren stopped.

Quirk thanked whatever lord was current. A doctor and a nurse hurried into the room followed by Deputy Joan—blood running from a gash on her forehead. She glared at Quirk then reviewed the scene as the medics tended to Moth. Parks moved across the room and knelt by Rowland. She confirmed he was dead. Procedure at all times. Parks seemed to be a highly effective officer. That was good. She'd see straight through this mess. Morton must have followed Rowland from Yellowknife, possibly even caused the crash somehow. This was bad, Derek Morton bad. Old Man bad.

"You'll want to test the contents of this," he proffered the empty vial to Parks. "I've seen Morton use it before. Here—"

Smoothly, Parks pulled her gun on him, arms rock steady, not the slightest waver. "Hands on your head. Now."

"Wait, Parks." He spread the fingers of his empty hand, nodded urgently to the corner of the room. "There was a man in this room the whole time we spoke to Rowland. He was cloaked, clad in black, and armed. He shot us with riot control darts. There's probably some kind of..." Slowly, Quirk patted his chest searching for the evidence where Morton—*Derek bloody Morton!*—had shot him. Nothing.

Moth was sitting up now, shaking her head and accepting water from the nurse.

"Come on, Parks, Kreski. I've no gun. You turned me over already. There was an assassin. Derek Morton, ex-marine, very bad news. We used to...work for the same company. It's a long story, but be assured he's deadly, and his employer is merciless."

Kreski stood, pistol held casually at his side. "I've been all around this place, no sign of any man in black. I think I'll hold you 'til we see what's in that vial of yours."

"It's not *my* vial, it was in..."—*Oh, damn*—"the corner. I just..." *Double damn.* "Come on, Kreski, why would I kill my own client, a man I hadn't met until today?"

"No idea. Maybe you're in cahoots with this man in black. Maybe you're a quick-change artist. Whatever. I'm gonna tie you down 'til we sort out this mess."

Quirk wanted to shake his head, but didn't dare risk it. Had Morton acted on impulse in framing him? Unlikely, as TOM knew Quirk was here. So why hadn't Morton killed him given their very voluble and public falling out as acolytes of The Old Man five years ago? Morton who had requisitioned Jennifer's child for TOM, and who Quirk suspected harboured feelings for her, although his loyalty to The Old Man came first, it seemed. For this very reason, of course, to confuse the police, and to set Quirk up. Maybe Morton had planned to frame some other poor sap before Quirk fell into his lap. Oh, how Derek must be loving this, the scary, deadly bastard.

Morton would have an exit strategy, of course. The frame would be solid. He'd be arrested for Rowland's murder unless he could prove Morton's presence. And where was Derek going? Rowland's foundling must be Morton's target, the key to something big, and she was with Rowland's wife. Morton knew that now, and he would kill them. Quirk had to pursue him, find them first. Maybe he could lead the police to Morton, find his proof in the process. But how could they get out of Creston?

The medics helped Moth to her feet. As he watched, she went from woozy to wide-eyed, gaze darting from Parks to Kreski to Kreski's holster. He could see her mind racing down all the same alleys as his, but Moth was incapable of biding her time. *No, no, no, Moth! Not the gun, not the gun!* He glared at her. *Read my bloody mind!*

Too late.

Kreski thumbed the scan-pad on his holster and dropped his chunky pistol in, reaching for his cuffs. Moth pushed off the doctor's shoulder and swayed around Kreski's bulk, scooping the pistol from his holster by the big, meaty grip before the locking strap could engage.

Cue chaos.

Moth lurched past Kreski, who grabbed at air and shouted. Moth ran at the window. Parks raised her hands toward Moth's back, one hand pointing a finger at her, the other aiming her weapon. "Hands on head! Drop to the floor! Last warning!!"

Quirk didn't risk moving his hands. He shouted, "Moth, desist!" but flicked a fallen pillow with his foot, kicking it into the air to distract Parks.

BOOMMM!!

The howl of Parks' pistol in the small room made the previous alarm sound like a whisper. The slug ripped through the pillow which twitched in the air while Moth continued barrelling unsteadily towards the window.

Parks aimed for the fleeing Moth's legs. Quirk dodged the careening girl—just—and threw himself at Parks, bearing her to the floor, knocking the weapon from her hand, not failing to notice when he landed on top of her the contrast between hard equipment and softer deputy. He pushed up from the stunned lawperson, jumping upright. Moth approached the plass window, but she couldn't shoot it out with Kreski's coded gun. The sheriff pursued her, reaching out.

"Window!" Quirk shouted.

Moth cranked her arm and hurled Kreski's pistol at the panel of winter sunlight. The ugly, black weapon spun through the air and hit the window square on the "Break Here for Escape" point, cracking the window just as Moth dove forward, arm folded over her head. The plass bent under her momentum, looked for a nanosecond like bouncing her onto the floor, then snapped.

Teenager and pistol disappeared through the broken window.

"Shit and fuck," Kreski pulled up short, big hands slamming into the wall on either side of the opening to stop himself going through.

When the sheriff pursued Moth to the window, Quirk had started for the door—shaking Parks' grip off his ankle—dodging past the stunned medics. Becker appeared in the doorway at exactly the wrong time.

"Sorry, Devan." Quirk sucker-punched him in the gut with a right, following it with a short left jab to the jaw as Becker crumpled. Then—after stooping to tear the badge from Becker's khaki chest—Quirk sprinted away down the corridor. Running in a hospital was not entirely unexpected. They had emergencies here. The sheriff chasing you down a corridor was less typical, and people turned to watch. Quirk had seen too many shows in which people hammered on elevator call buttons, and so made for the stairs. He clattered through the door and half-leapt down each flight, grasping the rail tightly, slinging himself round the corners wishing that Moth had not panicked, hoping she had not broken her neck. He burst onto the ground floor. Moth had exited a second-floor window. *Not clever.*

"Stop that man!"

An orderly at the reception desk tried, but Quirk's still slightly woozy momentum was enough to bowl the stocky woman over, and he shot out the front door into the lot.

Madness. He would remonstrate with Moth quite severely, regardless of her facilitating their ability to pursue Morton. He barely paused to click his heels, dashing across the lot, caution to the icy wind, crisp air biting his skin. He started towards the corner of the building, then saw black hair whipping by above a line of shrubs and veered to the exit, turning downhill, clicking off his spikes for the cleared footway. Kreski must only be seconds behind. Up ahead, Moth approached the main street, running with panic-fuelled energy. *Oh, to be young again.* He decided against shouting then Kreski did it for him. Moth veered across the street with no regard for traffic, making for the 7-Eleven on the corner. It had pumps still, advertising Biofuel, SpryntCharge, ZipCharge, InstaCharge, and distilled water. This meant stationary cars, possibly unlocked. *She's just the right kind of mad.* With Eighty's help they still might get onto Morton's tail, even drag Kreski after them. With Quirk's knowledge and the sheriff's resources they could bring the bastard down, maybe put a big, bloody spike in TOM's machinations.

He risked a backward glance, saw Kreski turn the corner forty metres back, features twisted either with rage or a muscle strain. Quirk forced his pace, freezing air chilling his ears. Moth was right. They'd never talk their way out of Morton's frame in time to protect Meriwa. Moth was slowing now, deciding on a vehicle. Quirk ran to a car just pulling up at a pump.

"Moth!" She turned then doubled back.

They reached the car together, an aubergine Dyson hydrogen model. No charging for this guy, just a top up at the tap.

"We'll park it for you, sir," said Moth as Quirk pushed the emerging driver to the ground, snatching the man's spilled handset from the air while jumping in to prevent the driver immobilising his car. Moth dropped in beside him. Quirk pressed "Start" and they were moving.

Kreski smacked into Quirk's window, trying to put his elbow through it. The big cop's arm bounced off as the car surged forward, leaving the sheriff on the ground.

Quirk described a tight arc, bouncing over the kerb onto the main street. Moth struggled to pull her seatbelt close enough for the contacts to engage.

"Woohoo! Grand theft auto, baby!"

"What were you thinking?! The sheriff's gun? A second-floor window?!"

She grinned. "There was a veranda below and planting beneath that. We detectives pay attention to that detailed shit. Remember the little points for that critical moment. I'm surprised you didn't notice. Too busy ogling nurses, I guess. Anyhow, recently I've had more experience than you at running through the freezing cold."

Quirk smacked the wheel. Damn this speed limiter! Some getaway. "Are you *still* angry about that? Let it go, for goodness' sake. We are now officially on the run, you know?" The car slowed. He looked up to see a red light and queuing traffic ahead.

"Damn."

In the mirror Kreski and Becker ran down the centre of the street, guns out.

"Hot rod it," Moth insisted. "Let's go. We need Eighty. Side street." She pointed, seeming much calmer than he felt.

"Madness," he grumbled and hauled on the wheel, pedal down, turning onto the wrong side of the road, but the car was having none of that.

"Transgression of traffic law," it said and the wheel kept turning in his hands until they completed a sloppy U-turn to point directly at the descending officers. Both men stopped, braced and fired. Quirk yanked the wheel down again, completing the four-fifty-degree turn, almost took the nose off a pick-up, and sent their car lurching sloppily up 14th Avenue as the back window blew out.

"Damn!"

"Fuck!"

He took a chance and hit the power, veering sedately into an alley. It paralleled the main street. They were heading west again, towards their hotel, but that seemed terribly distant at this speed. They pootled down the alley, following redundant overhead power lines, eased through a parking lot then "burst" safely onto 12th at a carefully regulated thirty-five kilometres per hour. The Dyson's nose dipped and bucked as they crossed the street in a jerking stop-start to a chorus of blaring horns, although the vehicles would not have permitted a collision. It was pure chagrin on the part of the locals.

"What's up with this Morton guy?" asked Moth, gripping the grab handle.

"Can we outrun your mess first before we discuss that bastard?" Quirk snapped.

The Dyson bumped over the sidewalk into the next lot. Up ahead, Kreski stepped from a service door onto the alley's uneven surface, levelling a big, brutal-looking handgun. "Stop and get out!" he yelled. The vehicle recognised a human and slowed significantly. Moth pulled out the sheriff's pistol.

"You can't fire—" Quirk's protest began, but instead she laid into a panel on the dash labelled "Autopilot Unit" vigorously and without restraint, hammering the pistol butt into the dash to the sound of cracking plastec and splintering screen.

Kreski stalked forward. In the mirror, Becker puffed down the previous alley, catching them steadily. His weapon came up and bullets pinged the Dyson's bodywork.

"Go," Moth shouted. "Now, and hard!"

The car was still running despite her assault. Quirk jammed his foot down and the wheels spun before the vehicle shot at Kreski. *Big, athletic man; he'll be fine. Just let him have good—*The sheriff threw himself sideways—*reflexes.* Quirk saw the disgust in Kreski's eyes in the split second they passed as he tumbled into a pile of garbage.

The Dyson behaved completely differently now. Without the intervention of its pseudo-AI, it pitched and yawed over the uneven surface. Quirk sawed at the wheel trying to keep them out of trash compactors and badly parked vehicles.

"How do people do this!" He got them to the end of the alley, out onto the street and up to the traffic lights at the grain elevators. He thanked the traffic gods their signal was green, turning right as the cop car haring along the main street almost took their nose off. Quirk veered left, shooting down the hill they'd taken to the airport.

"That was Parks," said Moth, head twisting back to him. "She'll cut us off from the hotel. You need to loop around. We gotta get Eighty!"

Quirk drove downhill way too fast and braked early to avoid going through the window of the pizza joint at the bottom. A siren shrilled loud behind them. He sensed the blue lights in the mirror, turned left, south, away from the hotel.

"Fushit, what the crap are you doing?"

More spinning lights converged from the north, joining the pursuit.

"Airport," Quirk grunted, his concentration focused intently on the road ahead and keeping the unaided vehicle between the kerbs.

"What?! You can fucking fly now?"

"I always could, actually. And before you start bleating about Eighty, we're going back for him."

"Not it?" she smirked.

"Yes, it," he said. "Look, if I know Morton, which I do, he'll make a beeline for his target, now Meriwa and the not-missing woman. Aircraft is the quickest mode. He might buy a plane, he might steal one, but he will not prevaricate. Now that we're running, we should at least run in the right direction."

Moth sat back and crossed her arms. "You've got to keep ahead of the blue-and-whites," she snapped. "Don't let them get too close."

"You're in a snit? You're in a damned snit *now*? This better not be about me not opening up. I think I'm doing well so far."

"It's not that," she scowled. "I just don't know how we're still going."

"What do you mean?" A bad line into the next junction left the cop cars closer in the mirror, spinning lights almost blinding, wailing sirens deafening, but they had reached the junction, crash site ahead on the left, airport on the right. A blue-and-white SUV loomed large in the rear-view.

Moth spread her hands. "Well, duh. The cops will have remote immobilisers. How is it we haven't stopped? And don't make that divine intervention crack again."

Quirk managed to ignore that particular logic puzzle long enough to throw the purple Dyson sideways to block the airport access.

"Get out. Run!" He followed Moth out her door, clambering over the centre console away from the cops as the girl dashed toward the grey buildings. Police cars skidded up behind the stranded Dyson. Quirk snatched Kreski's gun from the footwell and sprinted away. Moth had a twenty-metre lead on him due to his inferior clambering. A gunshot boomed and he ducked but kept going. He hoped it was Kreski with his spare, being fairly sure the sheriff wouldn't shoot him dead. Parks or Becker he was less certain of.

Moth stopped at the control tower steps, looking back. At that moment, the door opened, and Natalie emerged. Two guns barked close together, one shot kicking up ice a metre to Quirk's left. He brought up Kreski's surprisingly heavy weapon. *This is madness.* A whole bullpen of emotions tussled for his attention. The victor—surprisingly—was rage. *I will not let Derek Bloody Morton do this to me again. He dismantled my first family. I guess I was The Old Man's stooge in that, but you do NOT get to shoot my ward, Derek. Knock-out darts or no; there WILL be consequences, you terrible waste of chiselled cheekbones.*

Shoving thought aside, he pointed Kreski's gun at Natalie with all the conviction he could muster, as if it would go off if he pulled the trigger. The redhead's expression was bemused as she descended the steps, watching the cops converging.

"Plane keys, Natalie. Now. Something nimble. Don't think, move." He was delighted when she scowled and reached into her pocket, removing an iFob which she dangled in his face. He kept the useless gun on her, flicking the barrel towards the techmac apron, moving to keep her body between his gun and the cops. If Kreski thought he was a killer, the sheriff surely would not chance that he might have another weapon. Out of sheer hubris, Quirk pointed the gun in the air and pulled the trigger—BANG!— he almost shat himself at the loud and completely unexpected crack.

"Fuck!" said Moth with total conviction.

Quirk moved forward, hesitated, then turned the gun over, pressing the handle into the small of Natalie's back, barrel most definitely pointing downwards because a coded weapon should *not* have fired, and what was up with that? "Sorry. We'll be gone soon. I won't hurt you."

Parks, Becker and three other deputies crouched behind vehicles in the airport lot. Kreski stood out front, hands on hips.

"Don't worry, Nat. He won't shoot you. Will you, Quirk? I mean what the hell are you doing? You weren't even arrested. We were just talking."

Quirk shouted, "Derek Morton set me up."

"So come in, tell all. Unless you killed Rowland you've nothing to worry about."

"Sure," called Quirk, prodding Natalie to keep her walking towards the parked planes, taking a handful of her collar and T-shirt in case she considered running.

"Secure the killer who framed me for murder, and we'll all be pals again."

"Quirk, I know you're upset, but don't make it worse than it is. That you're armed in my town doesn't play well."

"And you'll discover that very quickly if you take a single step in this direction," Quirk called. "We're taking a plane north. It won't be a big plane, so Natalie will be staying right here. There are two women in Yellowknife at serious risk of death from Derek Morton. I recommend inquiring into that, Sheriff."

Kreski stared at them, but came no closer.

Gently, Quirk tugged Natalie by her collar away from the cops, Moth behind him now. The officers stood, coming out from behind the vehicles, and watched them go.

Kreski's shout came just before they backed around the edge of a hangar.

"You messed up my town, Quirk. I *will* pursue you, jurisdiction or no. You are going to do time in my jail, and lots of it."

Out of Kreski's sight, Quirk pulled Natalie by the arm into a jog towards the aircraft ranked on the apron. She fumed, but ran without coercion, Moth alongside.

"As niece of a crime boss, can I just note this plan sucks? What are we doing?"

"We're going after Morton," Quirk puffed. "I owe him a bullet."

"Whoa! Bloody murder isn't your style, boss," she protested. "We were stitched up, sure as Becker's forehead-mounted dick, but what's with the righteous wrath?"

Natalie slowed, pointing to a fast-looking Nissan-Beechcraft in pastel yellow with shiny gold prop covers. He waved her to the plane. He did not want to talk about this, but he owed Moth an explanation, was about to owe Natalie a whole lot more.

"Well, our client is dead, TOM is playing me, and his henchman is cleaning house." They stopped at the Beechcraft. Quirk grabbed Natalie's arm as she reached for the Beechcraft's door handle. "Morton took Jennifer's...my ex-wife's...our son away at The Old Man's behest. It broke her, the last of too many straws. I was one of them. I cannot walk away again." He looked down at the gun that should not have fired.

Moth crossed her arms, clearly unconvinced. "I thought you hated her."

Quirk blew out a breath. This was *so* not the time. "I hate what she did to me, to us, but maybe I don't hate why she did it." He smiled ruefully. "You'll learn one day Moth that love is complicated. In summary, I hate Derek Morton more. He heard our discussion with Rowland. I'll bet he needs Barry's foundling for some reason. Now he knows she's with Rowland's wife. I think he's going straight back north to kill them.

"The Old Man doesn't pick up the phone unless the stakes are global. This is something big, something connected to Yellowknife." He gripped Moth's shoulder and, for once, she didn't shake his hand off. "It isn't your mess, Moth. My history seems intent on fouling up my present. You should stay here with Eighty, study, take your exams. Kreski won't pin this on you, it's me he wants."

"I'll make sure he doesn't," said Natalie, and Quirk's eyebrows rose. She shrugged. "Sounds like there's more to it, and Sheriff Shrek can be an ass sometimes. I've got strings to pull. I'll talk to him. Now, this is *my* bird," she bit back a swear and patted the plane's skin. "I'm not trusting you with any o' my customers' wings. So, believe that I *will* kill you in custody if you so much as scuff a tyre."

He nodded, but Natalie still made him show his pilot's license, which he accessed via her handset. Still not content, she checked his record, publicly available courtesy of the Association of Terrestrial Pilots, while he and Moth glanced nervously towards the hangar. The cops were fanning out across the apron, but kept their distance.

"Your plane's in safe hands." He gave her the best he could muster under the circumstances: *Simple Smile No. 2—open, honest, heartfelt.* "I'm not sure why you're trusting me, but I certainly appreciate it. Maybe if I'd stayed—"

Natalie sighed. "Jesus Quirk, this isn't a romance, get in the plane and fly away. Avoid the electrical storm over the Rockies: fly north."

"And as for benching me, fuck that," spat Moth. "I'm a card-carrying member of this shit-show. 'All for one.' 'The greater good.' 'Once more unto the breach.' 'The needs of the many,' yadda-yadda. And you'll just shoot yourself in the ass. So, like the lady said, get on the fuzking plane, boss, we're outta here."

Rumbling down Creston's runway at the stick of a four-seater with AI-assist switched off was the furthest thing from breakfast at the Ramada Quirk could imagine. Then again—murder (suspected of); resisting arrest (guilty); grand theft auto (guilty); damage to private property (accessory only there); damage to public property (again, accessory); possession of a firearm sans licence (might beat that one on a technicality); assault (guilty); reckless driving (guilty); kidnapping (guilty?)—none of those had made his to-do list either. Damn though, he would not let Morton trample all over his life again, and certainly not on Moth's. She looked nervous, yet exhilarated, like she actually trusted him to fly this thing, which was nice. *Concentrate, Quirk. You haven't done this in a while.* He checked ground speed, trim, etcetera as the acceleration pressed them into their seats then eased the stick back, lifting them into the air. The aircraft swooped eagerly upwards into a blue winter sky. He banked east, tipped the starboard wing down to give Moth a view of the airport, felt the reassuring tug of gravity.

Two cop cars sat on the runway now, lights spinning like a firefly formation team, doubtless collecting Natalie for interview. The rest would be on their trail. Kreski knew where they were staying, having given them the "Don't leave town" speech at Greiner's house while the fire department removed the armchair.

"So, what now, Einstein?" Moth raised her voice over the aircraft noise, which wasn't bad for an ethanol turbine, not enough to risk headset chatter being overheard. "This thing don't VTOL and you need to rescue my robot, and my T-shirts, not to mention your precious Merrion, blessed be the name."

"Firstly"—he fished out the Dyson driver's aging handset—"please message Eighty to be ready. But use code, for goodness sake. They'll be all over the comms in the valley, encrypted ones too."

He levelled out and pointed them north-east, didn't want to make straight for the hotel, although he doubted Kreski would guess what he was contemplating. Still, this heading looked like striking a course for Yellowknife, but allowed him to cut back at the last moment. With luck, the sheriff would send his blue-and-whites east on Highway 3. "Damn. I forgot to ask Natalie what airborne resources the police have."

"Hush up," Moth snapped, bringing the headset to her lips. "Rosencrantz, Rosencrantz, this is Guildenstern, Guildenstern. The geese are flying home."

"Seriously?" Quirk interjected. "Code, damn it, not melodrama!"

"If you're going to be a smartass, you do it!"

"I would be a smartarse, but I'm busy flying a plane. Just tell it to be ready."

"Rosencrantz, Rosencrantz, prepare to fly the coop, over."

"*Nest*, fly the nest! Chickens can't fly."

"Will you fucking shut up? He's not replying."

"Give it a chance, it will."

Sure enough, Moth received a time-check ping fourteen seconds later. That could have come from anywhere, but a second ping thirty-five seconds after that confirmed it. "Your age followed by mine," Quirk smiled. "I told you. And, Eighty remembered my birthday."

He checked their position, scanned the display and surveyed the sprawling river valley below. Almost time to make the turn, another minute. "Right, listen. Things are about to get uncomfortable: (a) I haven't flown in a while—standard take-off and regulation turns are fine—but the next bit won't be that, and it's been a decade since I did any stunts; (b) we must assume the cops are on their way, that they're monitoring Eighty, maybe impounded him—*it!*; (c) landing on a road is tricky at the best of times due to vestigial poles and wires, even in this time of astounding scientific advancement; (d) depending on how (a) to (c) go, I can't guarantee getting us off the ground again."

By now, Moth had crossed her arms angrily on her chest. "You're shitting me. Land on a road? As a pilot, you're meant to inspire confidence, shithead."

He nodded, keeping his eyes on the display and forward view. "Okay," he sighed, "more background. You're going to owe me after today. My C Corp job title was Executive Pilot. I flew the top brass in and out of many interesting places, Morton too, sometimes." He wished he could say he never knew why.

"Wow," said Moth. "So, all my chatter about planes, you know all that stuff?" She remained silent for a good ten seconds before speaking again. "So, this isn't just about saving damsels, it really *is* personal. It's your guilt talking."

Quirk just gripped the stick. It was spiteful, but he yanked the stick into the turn, sending the little plane swooping down in a stomach-churning arc groundward. He soon levelled out, but not before Moth squeaked then tried to murder him with a scowl.

"Enough chitchat," he said. "Pop onto Streetscene, please, and spot the overhead lines for me. Quick." He lined them up with Highway 3, which ran due north now, pointing straight at the Ramada by the junction of 3 and 3A.

"Preferred touch down point?"

Good girl. He nodded grudgingly. "Blue roof on the left."

"No good. Overhead cables twenty metres before it, about ten metres high. You need to clear them."

He tweaked up the airspeed and nudged the stick. "Next set of lines? Moth? Next set? You've got two hundred metres."

"I'm buffering."

"Damn it, Moth!"

"Sixty metres north. Another set before Tim Hortons, third set at a hundred metres."

"Right, we'll land in the length of Tim Hortons' lot."

"And you bitch about my Dairy Queen habit? Can you do that?"

"Probably, just hold on, it's about to get bumpy."

He picked the landmarks and adjusted their altitude none too stylishly. This low, he favoured good, old-fashioned judgement before instruments. The measures all assumed an empty road of course, which it certainly was not. *Oh well, we'll see how good their collision avoidance systems are.* He trimmed and dropped, trimmed and dropped then picked the blue roof on the left, passed it at fifteen metres, a lumbering RV at ten metres then dropped them hard towards the techmac.

They bounced. Once, twice, as oncoming vehicles slewed onto the shoulder or turned hard into business lots to avoid the spinning props of the rapidly slowing aircraft. The Nissan-Beechcraft's brakes were tight, and Quirk quickly regained control, taxiing under the next set of cables, waving apologetically in response to a range of hand gestures from perturbed drivers. He took them right to the traffic lights and turned hard left onto Highway 3, Crowsnest westbound.

S-0778a stood at the roadside with their cases. Eighty didn't say a word when Moth pulled the door open, just stepped behind the wing into the buffeting of the still-spinning props and loaded their luggage into the baggage compartment. A middle-aged couple at the A-Haul shop opposite gaped. Quirk waved at them from the plane's window. Moth jumped down into the prop backwash, which whipped her hair around. "Blue lights from the south!" she shouted, pushing Eighty up into the back seat.

Quirk fed the power as Moth's door slammed shut, cutting down the propellers' raucous thrash. He let off the brakes and the Beechcraft trundled west on the momentarily empty highway. "Fewer cables this way," he noted.

Moth was buckling in, but her head whipped up to regard the rail bridge two hundred metres ahead. "Bridge, Quirk. Bridge, bridge, bridge. There's a big, fucking bridge over the road!"

"The sign says 4.54 metres clearance."

"That's the fucking height, you moron!"

"No kidding," he grinned, giving it the full *Ready Player Q.*

At this point, Eighty saw fit to contribute from the back seat. "The Nissan-Beechcraft T58 has a wingspan of 10.24 metres. Based on the Provincial Engineer's bridge records total horizontal clearance will be 1.06 metres. If exactly centred on the opening your margin for error is 0.53 metres."

"Aaaaaaaahh!" said Moth, her cry largely drowned out Eighty's analysis as Quirk increased their speed and the bridge blocked out the sun. They were through, but barrelling straight for an eastbound container convoy with nowhere to go but up.

"Oh, don't be a baby." Quirk maxed the throttle, launching them at the lead truck, pulling the stick back hard and smooth. The nose came up like a dog's to a shout of "Walkies!" and the world swung backwards. They climbed steeply into the azure sky, the Nissan-Beechcraft bucking a little in the breeze, but responding to his firm control.

"Eighty," he called. "Once we're level, get your head under this panel and disconnect every system you can."

"We'll need that stuff," Moth protested. "How you gonna navigate?"

"We'll need to do without, because Kreski will try to take control of this plane."

"Shouldn't Eighty be flying then?"

"I lack the correct module, Miss Moth. Also, my Net connection has just been cut."

"Let the games begin," said Quirk.

08

"Tania Terjesen," said Eve pacing along the corridor, touching her right ear to inform her handset she was addressing it, again. "For the tenth time," she muttered.

"You have made nine calls since 08:50," her handset whispered in her ear.

It wasn't like Tania to be late for work, and in that unlikely event, she would have messaged. When she hadn't shown up for pool and laughs at the pub this weekend, Eve assumed she was tired. Saturday night teambuilding among Genextric staff wasn't mandatory, but up in this neck of the woods, when someone didn't show up for work in winter you paid attention, you asked questions, and you looked for them until you found them. That might be in the wrong bar or the wrong bed, but the alternatives were not pretty. She had even checked with Dulcie, the horn-playing, baseball-card-collecting, head of the Local 509, ex-marine, pool shark, plumber and drinking buddy of both she and Tania. Nothing. She did not have time for this shit. Tania not arriving for work meant Eve had to call it in, and that meant going to Morton.

Why his office was on the top floor when hers was one down on Level C she did not know, she being Centre Director and all. Once, at the Christmas party, he'd explained it was him having a group-wide security role, whereas she was strictly local. *Asshole.*

She found him in his corner office and strode in without knocking. The external walls were ninety percent opaque, shutting out the glorious view. Having no interest in Morton's health, she came to the point. "Doctor Terjesen hasn't scanned in today. I've heard nothing since Thursday." She waggled her handset. "Can't reach her."

Morton's attention remained on his screen, but he did look up when Eve sat in one of his guest chairs, because she was damned if she would stand for him.

He sat back. "Didn't you two spend a cosy weekend together? Or is that too domestic, do you prefer sneaking around the office, covering your tracks like naughty schoolgirls? Whatever, I think you have a serious security breach."

So, it wasn't rudeness she'd seen on entering, but distraction. That was unlike him. He loved picking at any difficulty of hers or Tania's. Now, his fatuous corporate bonhomie was strained to non-existence. That worried her more than anything else.

"What's happened?" She didn't attempt to hide her concern, because the more she considered it, and really studied Morton, the more she saw the strain in him.

"There's been an incursion on Level Five," he said, feigned calmness belied by the intensity of his gaze.

"The syRen® would have raised the alarm." Unless this incursion, whatever it was, had disabled their security system. Morton's security system.

She stood up and snatched his screen around. He moved backwards, hands raised. She tapped at the virtual keyboard, logged him out and herself in, stretching over the desk to look square into the camera. Her desktop appeared and she swiped to the building schematic, overlaying access data.

"Level Five log-in by David Patel, that can't be right. His log-in should be deleted. He was only here for twelve weeks." A cold feeling settled in her gut.

"Looks like someone didn't delete it. Who was responsible for doing that, Eve?"

"His supervisor."

"And who was that, Eve?"

"Tania," she spat. "Patel interned with Genetic Research."

"Who was responsible for cross-checking the deletion, Eve?"

"Head of HR."

"Both reporting to you."

"And it's *your* security system that's just been reamed from here to January," she slapped the table. "Let's not have a fuck-up contest, you're way ahead."

Her stomach churned as she hurried out without a goodbye to Morton. She was damned if she would give him the satisfaction of seeing burgeoning panic consume her. A quick glance on departing said he was delighted to see the back of her.

Reaching her office, Eve threw down her jacket and thumbed into her screen. What a nightmare. She wanted to vomit. The more she dug the worse it got. The log-in deletion glitch (generous!) was a disciplinary offence under Genextric's stringent rules, rules that Morton—as C Corp's Group Head of Security—had powers to enforce. The details of the intern, Patel, had been used for general access, but Tania's assistant Li Xin's account had gone from there into the enclosure systems. And yet Li hadn't been in the building, only Tania. She'd opened the mangetout enclosure, drawn them to Level Six. *You idiot. What were you doing?*

Eve's fingers pattered on virtual keys, mistakes dogging her efforts: backspace, backspace. She accessed the camera files. Tania knew these would be checked. Eve saw the ugly, hungry creatures surge onto the open veldt searching for prey or carrion, jaws snapping like they gladly would take a companion's leg if they didn't find food. She watched in open-mouthed horror as the creatures were lured into the elevator.

She didn't know whether to puke or scream. What the fuck was going on? She called up the mangetout enclosure cameras, reviewed the sensor logs, finding they'd been deactivated, as had the alarms that should have sounded. Could Tania have *stolen* three mangetouts from Genextric and fled?! No. That made no sense. How had Morton missed this since Friday? Tracks had been covered, but still. The real bastard was she couldn't access service area footage without Morton's sign-in because classified. She would have to go back and deal with him, again. She dialled into the tracking sub-system, checking every creature on Level Five. Everything accounted for. Everything but the mangetouts, which were absent from the building, its surroundings, the town or its environs. No signal. They weren't out of range; their tags were disabled. The trail ended in the loading bay. Eve sat back, sighed, bit back a growl of...what? Fear for Tania? Anger? Pathetic despair that her own position was damaged, maybe irreparably?

"Fuck that. Fuck that to hell," she spat. She was as wildly determined a bitch as any of Tania's creations, and she'd do what all animals did when backed into a corner, she would fight, for her job and her friend too, if she could.

She burst back into Morton's office. He was still there working at his screen, a man in a C Corp security uniform perched at his shoulder. "Give us a moment, Bob." The blond, bearded officer nodded, gave Eve a nod too, and left.

"You can call, you know."

Was he smirking? "No, I need to see your eyes shifting. How far have you got with this?" she snapped, and wished she hadn't. Maybe, just maybe, if she didn't get his back up, they could pull together on this. It looked like the end of Tania at Genextric, but it didn't have to be Eve's swansong.

The sanctimonious prick smoothed a hand over his mouth. She thought his face was drawn, eyes darker as if from lack of sleep. "If you hadn't stormed out, I was going to replay the sifted loading bay footage. It shows the mangetouts arriving, but there were no transport cages. No sign of incursion in that area."

"Meaning what?" She moved to his shoulder, quelling her hesitation, leaning in slightly to see the footage better. "Has someone stolen our mangetouts? Industrial espionage? Tania? Really?" The name caught in her throat. She was descending into damage limitation because, if Morton was right, Tania had betrayed her trust, her feelings, everything they'd shared. Was that possible? Of course it was.

"It can't be theft," Eve snapped. "Look, go back."

Morton paused the replay, scrubbed back through high vantage images of the loading area then tapped the triangle. Tania walked into shot. She was well-wrapped up against the cold, but something wasn't right. She was wearing pink slippers! The data strip showed the temperature in the loading bay at minus ten. Tania walked to the roller-shutter, unlocked the control and held her finger on the button until the external door was half-open. Her head snapped around, back towards the control room.

"There's someone else," she tore her eyes from the screen to glance at Morton.

"Probably jumpy at the three beasts in the goods lift." His voice was thin, his creepy joie de vivre absent. Was he as rattled as she was?

"The other cams," she demanded.

"In a moment, see the rest."

Eve watched a high-resolution horror show. The hideous, ravenous creatures burst silently into shot, sprinting after Tania, who rushed outside. Eve gaped. Morton changed the view to the external cameras in time to see Tania fall in the snow. Eve gasped as the creatures struck, all three tugging at Tania's prone body, her limbs flailing, stabbing violently with some implement, motions slowing, twitching then still, as the mangetouts tugged at her body in full colour, pin-sharp detail. The floodlights gave a clear view of the stomach-churning scene despite the wider darkness. The hunch-backed, steel-jawed monsters dragged Tania's body away into the undergrowth.

Eve managed to get her head clear of Morton's desk before throwing up in his wastebasket. Her head throbbed as her mind raced. She wiped her mouth on her sleeve, lips quivering. The mangetouts were loose in Yellowknife.

"S&R teams?" she almost stuttered, fighting to compose herself. *Tania!*

"Deployed yesterday when the incident...came to light."

"But they must have told you. You knew," she insisted.

"I was ice fishing over the weekend, uncontactable."

"Bullshit." She tapped the side of her head. "Implant."

"Disconnected. I'm entitled to some privacy, too."

"What about your group-level responsibilities?!" That wasn't the point. Morton was not the target right now. She sighed. "Someone covered this up. There was an accomplice. And—attempted theft or no—mangetouts are loose in Yellowknife."

He nodded. "It does look like she had help, or it would have been discovered sooner, but it's in hand now. I've briefed the sheriff; he knows Terjesen's missing. We'll get them. You should go home. Get your head straight. You seem overwrought."

"Are you fucking crazy? I'm Centre Director. Oh, wait, you'd like that wouldn't you? How about explaining why you didn't call me the instant you found this?"

Morton stood, hard eyes as bereft of human feeling as any android's. "You may be personally associated with a security breach and potential theft of proprietary material. I have the authority to suspend you, and I just have. Forty-eight hours, no access. Go *home*." He pointed at the door. Eve thought of several ways to kill him, she thought of the company Code of Conduct, employment regulations, emergency protocols. Nothing. He had her. She stormed out, unable to look at him.

It was a shitstorm of monumental proportions and—as each excruciating minute crawled past—increasingly, it focused on Eve. Tania was missing, presumed dead and...and there were mangetouts loose in Yellowknife. Her whole body clenched again, weight crushing the centre of her chest. Her eyes moistened and she pummelled her tears with the back of her hand as she left the building. She would go home now, because Morton was the just kind of shit to have her dragged out, but she would not go down this way, snivelling and whining as the management team, the board and the security division closed in like a wake of vultures. No doubt they had not removed her completely from post because this could get worse before it got better, and they needed her around to take full responsibility for every scrap of the whole sorry mess.

It was a blessing that no member of the public had been injured, yet. As far as they knew. But how long could that last? *And then there's Tania. Poor, stupid Tania.* Morton had written her off already. As lead scientist, Tania had signed more waivers than a lion-tamer. *Could I have saved her, if I hadn't kept my pants on that one night?* What had Tania done, and what was Eve going to do now? What in hell could she do?

Eve's afternoon was spent in fervent theorising, which gave way to an evening of worry and anger, then a night of mourning Tania, drinking whisky and troubled sleep.

* * *

11:12, 17 November 2099
Meyer Residence, 5557 44th Street, Yellowknife, NT

Next came a heavily hungover morning, not washing or dressing, drinking copious amounts of water, and emptying the coffee pot twice. Eve sat on her sofa in a robe checking messages, trawling socmed for sightings. Suspension Day One deteriorated rapidly, an ever-strengthening hurricane of terse, official emails: internal investigation notice; official warning; terms of disciplinary action; privileges, bonus and benefits suspended; suspension of pension fund. Was Morton getting the same for his fuck ups? She doubted it, but she understood it all, it's what she would have done. What she didn't understand was the absence of bodies.

Three mangetouts loose in the environs of Yellowknife. Unbelievable, unthinkable, but what about the bodies, Tania's if nothing else? Twenty-four hours after being overfed was an unrealistic timespan for those monsters to go without killing. Even one hour was unlikely. Of course, no remains showing up didn't mean the beasts had been idle, it just meant the bodies hadn't been found yet. And then there was the matter of Tania's accomplice. Could the creatures have been corralled and taken? There were no reports of foreign infrastructure, unknown vehicles, or drones.

Morning became afternoon, the sky darkened. Eve managed to apply herself to the problem until a pitch black 5:00 PM before resorting to the bottle again. She drank a little, cried a little, railed at her screen for it being blank of answers to the questions she'd sent Morton. She wanted to punch the wall, but had some experience in that area, knew it would do neither her nor the wall any good. The destructive urge did not pass, and so she strode into the kitchen, snatched the wooden stool with the uneven legs away from its place at the breakfast bar and smashed it on the granite floor, twice, thrice, four times until the first leg separated, but she just kept swinging.

"Fucker! Fucking Morton, you fuck! And you're no better, Tania, you cunt. What have you done?!" Still, she struggled to comprehend what Tania had done to her, to them, to herself. On her knees now, Eve dropped to the floor, still clutching two separated wooden legs, slumping to her bottom on the cold, granite tiles, crying out saline and fully intending to replace it with whisky. Even with her sketchy science she knew that wouldn't work, but goddamn it she would try.

"What have you *done*, T?" It made no sense, none at all. "How could you leave me like this?" The irony of her plan to reassign Tania chose that moment to strike.

Anger, tears, whisky—fade to black.

* * *

14:32, 18 November 2099

Waking late brought headaches and realisation. She truly was alone. On that basis, she had wasted too much time wallowing in self-pity. Morton was screwing her over. He wasn't going to give her anything. No one at Genextric would. Glenda Marshe would never reach down from her fluffy corporate cloud into this puddle of piss to offer a hand. Eve Meyer would have to create her own miracle.

Was Tania dead? This was the question she always came back to. What if she'd sent Tania away after their last inspection? Could Eve have saved her life? What about the accomplice who had tidied up, delaying the discovery of the empty habitat until Monday morning? Did Morton think it was her? No. She had an alibi, winning and losing at pool with Dulcie in Norm's West Tavern until closing, and on into the lock-in for Norm's regulars. God knew was she a regular. Indisputable.

Eve stood slowly, gingerly, but with determination, and headed for the shower. To help herself, to try and help Tania, or at least find Tania's body, she needed unbiased information. She needed to speak to the sheriff.

By the time she was dressed and striding to her truck chewing an oat bar it was three in the afternoon. Daylight was bleeding away again. The city of Yellowknife wasn't that different from most Canadian towns at first glance, especially in twilight, with streetlamps, stores and apartments lighting up. But, when you looked a little longer, stared a little harder, you noticed the difference. It wasn't the election posters that littered the place. It had a temporary look to it, as if the buildings didn't expect to be there next year, that they might be lifted onto the back of a semi and driven somewhere else, somewhere warmer. Maybe the city architects had just that in mind. She was pretty sure a good number of buildings had arrived on trucks in the first place, to be dropped down on their rocky plots and plumbed in on the same day.

Downtown wasn't much different, bigger boxes, taller, just as cuboid. Following the streetlights down Franklin it seemed only the government could afford curves in Yellowknife, as the floodlit walls of its office at the corner of 51 testified. Not to mention the Assembly building with its domes and sinuous façade facing Frame Lake.

A couple more turns brought Eve to the sheriff's office. No longer could she distract herself with snatched glimpses of an everyday life that—suddenly—she no longer felt part of. She parked up and sat for a moment, gripping the wheel, seat cover creaking, just staring at the other cars in the lot where the spotlights piled illumination on them. But this was no good. There was work to be done.

Morton had deployed Genextric's recovery units, she'd learned that much before leaving the building. So, teams of syRen® scoured the area in widening fans for any signs of death, dismemberment, faeces, etcetera. There was no news of any police investigation, but Morton would have shut her out of that loop. If she was being fitted for a frame, he would have reported the incident to the sheriff, but what had he revealed? Genextric had its share price to think of, after all. Time to find out. Time to start beating ploughshares into swords.

The bite of a bitter wind energised her as she crossed the lot, donning the warm, familiar mantle of corporate bitch as she walked into the sheriff's office reception. No sharp suit today, just local-standard winter wear, just another concerned resident willing to brave the elements (mild really at minus sixteen) to help with enquiries.

Only the patter of typing broke the silence in reception.

"Sheriff Kootook, please," she asked the desk deputy, a capable-looking fiftyish woman with greying blond hair and "Don't-you-bother-my-boss" written all over her weathered features. "Eve Meyer from Genextric," she added, presuming Morton would want to maintain the illusion she was in charge right up until the board pilloried her.

"Please wait here, ma'am."

Eve read posters about the danger of drugs and drink and violence, all the things that she *really* wished she could indulge in right now. *"Guns don't kill people; people do!"* one poster proclaimed. *Yeah, people and genetically engineered cross-bred killing machines.* The wall opposite displayed a new one on Eve: *"74% of unnatural deaths are accidents."* All very well, but how many of those accidents resulted from conscious acts with foreseeable consequences?

She closed her eyes to ease the nagging headache that would only be cured by replacing it with another, larger, whisky-induced headache, but one that could be deferred to the next day. And there was the upside, being borne into sweet oblivion after an hour or two dreaming of Derek Morton's entirely timely demise.

The deputy returned and waved her forward. "He'll see you. Interview 3, through the door, along the corridor, third left. Scan here." Eve's hand shook slightly as she pressed it to the deputy's Book then she walked through a sliding door along an anonymous corridor of plass-fronted rooms, panels all greyed out. This place aped the habitat enclosures at Genextric, except here they observed people, poked and prodded humans, turned them inside out with questions. Eve's stomach was churning by the time she reached Interview 3, its designation and status displayed on the door screen.

Sheriff Kootook rose to greet her. He was maybe ten centimetres shorter than her, with the skin of an aging Inuit, wrinkled by exposure to sun, wind, snow and more sun, dark hair turning towards white, but not there yet.

"Sit, please." She did and so did he. "How can I help you?" His voice was polite, gravelly, deeper than his verging-on-spare frame suggested. He smiled wanly.

"My..." she almost choked out the word. *Dammit! This is not the end of the world. My career, probably, but* not *my world.* "Sorry, I'm Eve Meyer from Genextric, Centre Director. We've met before, at the Chamber of Commerce meeting last quarter."

"I remember. Nice to meet you again, Ms. Meyer. Peter Kootook." He extended a hand, and she shook it, trying to smile. The sheriff gave her nothing more than an open expression promising a willingness to listen without prejudice.

"We're having issues. You know what we do up on Ingraham Trail, right?"

He nodded. "I know what I need to know. Derek Morton briefs me regularly."

So, you know what Morton wants you to know. "You are aware of the escape."

"Morton called me Monday morning, told me android and drone teams were in the field. I gather there are no traces since then, unless you have better news for me."

She couldn't ask about specifics without revealing she didn't know what was going on. Bad enough to be under corporate scrutiny, she didn't need the sheriff prying into her situation. Still, she needed facts to retrieve anything from this mess, like recovering the monsters before they killed anyone, and recovering Tania's...remains. Being excluded from Genextric left getting close to the sheriff as her only useful option. But, she must assume Morton would withhold anything useful from the sheriff.

She buttressed her corporate facade. *Talk the talk, Eve.* "The fact is, Derek and I have been so embroiled in the search, we've hardly spoken, but we know that maximising communication with your office is essential. I felt we needed a face-to-face to assure you we are on point and all resources are being applied to resolve the situation." *That sounds good.* She almost managed to convince herself.

The sheriff nodded, his expression grave. "The mayor has instructed me to let your recovery squads operate unimpeded. We will lend every assistance, but we won't blunder around. I have increased patrols in urban and inhabited rural areas, also deployed sensing equipment at the city limits, cancelled all leave. I'll protect people and property, but Genextric has some latitude, for the time being."

"Thank you."

"Know this, Ms. Meyer. The moment one of your products harms or threatens a citizen of Yellowknife, I will act decisively."

"Derek did explain what we're dealing with, didn't he?"

Kootook nodded. "He did. Some low-level terra-fauna, Doctor Terjesen told him. She's out with one of the recovery teams, supervising the search, I believe."

"Uh, huh." Eve broke one of her five rules for meetings, not to make noises that weren't actual words. It projected indecision, ignorance and inflexibility. "We're still crunching data, making progress eliminating areas. The failsafe malfunction..."

Kootook leaned forward. "I want you to understand that I'm not blinded by Genextric's science." Was he daring her, testing her? "Let's not pretend they aren't killers and acknowledge there's a foul up here. I know they will attack anything that moves. Don't forget I have protocols too. If someone dies, this will go national."

Placate, quickly! "Certainly. I would not use the term 'low-level', but the behaviour of Model 24G-389 is very targeted. I'm certain the S&R crews will recapture or neutralise the three specimens within hours."

Sheriff Kootook stood, his expression grim. "I hope you're right."

Eve stood and shook his outstretched hand. She hoped she was too.

She turned to leave, but the door opened, the blond deputy's stocky frame filling the doorway. "We've found a kill site, Sheriff. It's a mess."

Oh, fuck no.

Eve's stomach melted, her legs wobbled, but she defeated the urge to groan. Kootook left the room, signalling her to wait. He returned in moments. "You'll want to see this." She followed him out of the building.

"Is it a...person?" she asked in the parking lot. *Is it Tania?*

The sheriff stopped, studying her, as if expecting her to answer her own question, to make a mistake. "Too soon to tell," he said.

They drove out of town on 48 north past Jackfish Lake, stayed on Highway 4. The sky was black, the moon approaching first quarter. Some light, but not much. Kootook drove without speaking, and Eve was speechless, her nerves tingling. The big police truck remained quiet, just road noise, old pleather seats creaking, only the floral scent of air sanitiser to distract her from this new dread. The deputy had given no details in her hearing and Kootook's invitation had been vague. Perhaps he hadn't told Morton. That would be good. She liked the idea of having information Morton didn't.

They left the streetlights behind where Highway 3 turned off west towards the airport. She felt an urge to take that route, leave town, run away from all this shit, but that way lay exile and fugitive status. It would be an admission of guilt. Maybe that was all she had left if Tania was... No, Eve had built her own place at Genextric, and she would not let a scumbag like Morton, or even the board, take it away from her. She had share options, and she would damn well stick around to take them. But, if this situation went any further down the shitter, Genextric might start to feel financial ramifications. Being an essential cog in the terra-forming process didn't mean there weren't rivals ready to step in and do your part. At least she could still think and act as a company woman, that was good. But was it too late to start thinking like a friend?

Snow clearance had stopped at Highway 3 and Kootook had activated the spikes as they passed the red-roofed mining museum at Yellowknife Bay. Now, they passed the mines, but in the dark she saw next to nothing of the great scars on the landscape that edged the road. The sheriff turned north towards Vee Lake. Ten minutes of slow going brought them to a cluster of white headlights, red brakes and blue emergency lights parked in a jumble at the foot of the lake where the rough, iced-up road stopped.

Eve climbed down into deathly cold and muffled silence, harsh white beams, blue-and-red flickering shadows. She tried to pull her zip tight, but it was already all the way up. Shivers rattled her bones. Her heated jacket told her it was minus thirty. The stress was killing her slowly and Kootook let her stew, trying to break her, make her slip up. She refused to let that happen. *Stick to it.*

A deputy came up the track to get them and the sheriff waved her ahead. Eve clicked her heels as did Kootook. They stepped carefully through undergrowth, picking their steps. The lake came into dim view, a great well of cold, moonlit blackness. Wooden landing stages stuck like black fingers reaching over pearlescent water. The deputy took a rough path off west before the stages. Eve followed, Kootook behind her. Their boots crunched on the barely defined path through the sparse trees and shrubs.

Eve's mind raced, flooding with all the thoughts previously numbed by Speyside malt. *Stupid, stupid, stupid.* She castigated herself as she trudged towards whatever horror the mangetouts had wrought, flickering flashlights lighting the way. Her determination to fight suddenly seemed childish. Was this a human death? Was it the end for her? She'd wasted two days handwringing and choking a bottle, hoping for good news to materialise from nothing. *Stupid bitch. Think now at least!* Mangetout optimal temperature was way higher than this frigid hell. Would they go to ground, find a lair? Or kill and eat to fuel their toiling bodies? Maybe the cold would subdue them. But then why had the S&R crews found no trace yet?

They crossed a track, but the deputy's torch flicked onwards. Finally, Eve stepped from the under-growth onto a lakeshore starkly floodlit by two lighting masts. The ground was painted red. Tufts of crimson grass, pools of sticky gore, carcasses, throats ripped out, bones exposed. She counted six of what looked like deer, a family group, drinking at the water's edge when the mangetouts found them. She bent double, hands on knees, breathing deep and fast. Kootook moved past her, maybe thought her reaction was shock, but it was pure relief. There were no human remains.

Tania wasn't there.

09

16:59, 19 November 2099
1,684 metres altitude, 10km south of Trout Lake, BC

Quirk still could not account for the loss in altitude. Flying was the quickest way to Yellowknife, even with the storm detour, but only if he could keep them in the air. And the loss of Eighty's connection didn't help. Why would the cops disconnect a source of tracking data? That aside, for the last hour Eighty had lain across the centre console, head under the instrument panel. It had disconnected the radar first then the other long- and mid-range sensors, one at a time, as they flew over Kuskanook then Ainsworth Hot Springs. By Kaslo, the syRen® had deactivated the plane's various beacons. Around Argenta, Quirk remembered the Dyson driver's handset that he had scooped up at the fuel station while stealing the poor old chap's vehicle, and tossed it out the window. The old gent's insurance would pick up the tab, but that didn't make it a victimless crime; by definition, there was no such thing.

"It may be the case," Eighty announced, voice muffled by the console, "that there are embedded safety protocols hard-wired into the guidance system that automatically reduce altitude when certain systems cease functioning."

Quirk tilted his head back and closed his eyes for a second. "And you tell me this now? How on Earth is that safe? We're in the middle of the mountains?"

"Newer Nissan-Beechcraft models are equipped with auto-landing, and my secondary core only now completed a full diagnostic, bearing in mind that I have been disconnected from all web and online resources."

"So, it's my fault?"

"I do not seek to assign blame, regardless of how unfortunate and potentially hopeless the situation may appear."

"Hopeless?" Moth snapped. "I survive a madman-infested android dropping half the Moon on me, only to get snuffed on the run with a has-been pilot and a mechanical doofus as they dismantle our getaway plane from the inside out? They shit sure won't need to track us when we're scattered all over these mountains."

"Not helping, Moth. Not helping."

"And *you*"—she stabbed a finger at Quirk—"got us dumped at the sheriff's office, where they confiscated our handsets!"

"Because making a call about now would be a marvellous idea." Quirk waved his hand airily. "Here we are, Sheriff, bring a big net to scoop us all up. And anyway, *you* were the genius who pulled the sheriff's gun from his holster! But I get no credit for saving the day? Parks was intent on using hot lead to slow you down if I hadn't tackled her."

Moth resorted to a huffy tone. "At least we're heading to Yellowknife. We'll rough up this Dreck Moron and he'll confess, right?"

"Derek Morton is a professional killer, Moth. He's not a lunatic like Callan was. He's The Old Man's fixer, trouble-shooter for the whole C Corp group. It's a job he's extremely good at it." Quirk sighed, realising this was one of those sharing moments. "I know because I used to fly him around. I don't mean to scare you, but if we can't prove Morton's guilt before the law catches up to us, there's an excellent chance they'll hang Rowland's murder on me. I could be incarcerated for a very long time, and you'll be winging your way back to the Little Sisters of the Human Ascension, I expect."

"So why not just kill us, and stage the whole thing?" asked Moth.

"Good question." One he'd spent the last hour pondering. "The Old Man asks me to help Rowland, but Morton kills Rowland, and is hunting the woman, I assume. So, was TOM's call a ruse? It's not impossible he set up Greiner to bring me to Creston. Or, I'm being completely paranoid, but TOM must know that him asking would risk me refusing the case on principle. I don't know. But I'll bet there is more to it than the woman. That feels trivial for TOM to involve himself with directly."

"A human life...trivial?" Moth trailed off.

Quirk realised he'd strayed towards an old, abandoned mindset. "I'm sorry; *I* don't consider a life trivial, but TOM does. I have never killed anyone." Moth just stared ahead. Why on Earth did he say that? Guilt at the secret he wasn't telling her?

And still their altitude decreased. This was no time for introspection. Fishing Morton's dirty vial from his pocket, Quirk's fingers bumped another hard, cold object, Becker's badge. He considered tossing it. It was damning, and yet also represented proof. "Eighty," he muttered, "stow this vial somewhere safe about your...person."

"Yes, Quirk," said the android.

A heavy bump brought his attention back to flying. Moth's gaze darted around.

"Eighty, can you reconnect the guidance system?" he asked hopefully.

"Having ejected it from the window an hour ago as instructed? No, sir, I cannot."

Quirk sighed. They had dipped under nine hundred metres, and now he must consider where to put them down, which no doubt was the point of this frustrating safety feature. He began to follow the valley, continuing past Beaton, Galena Bay and Arrowhead, bearing north-west as the plane continued to descend.

"I think I can get us to the airport at Revelstoke."

Disconnecting systems that permitted the authorities to track them had ceased to be useful. Now—losing height all the while—they approached the runway at the resort of Revelstoke, nestled at the foot of Mount MacKenzie on the banks of the Columbia River. Not responding to ATC hails would attract all the wrong kinds of attention.

"They'll have an alert out for us. Kreski will have called all his chums in the province. But if they haven't been able to track us, we might have a window to breeze through here, with a good bluff."

"They'll have the plane's ID," Moth observed, impatiently.

"True," said Quirk. He went to check the navigation and cursed the dark display that stared back. The view from the windows suggested circa fifteen kilometres to go.

"Eighty. Please pop back and put your fist through the fuselage. I want the registration number obliterated from the sides of this jalopy. You have four minutes."

"Yes, sir. What about the tail?"

"Set fire to it. There'll be an extinguisher back there somewhere."

Moth gaped. "Are you shitting me? You'll crash us, you braindead albatross!"

"I doubt it. You might be surprised to learn that I've pulled this jape before. Now, strap in. The landing will be a bit rough."

Bashing and ripping sounds emanated from behind their seats, breaking into the engine hum, followed by the howling of air ripping past a gaping hole.

"No, no, no," protested Moth loudly. "I need some reassurance here. Are you the fucking Red Baron now? I didn't know you could fly till a few hours ago!"

Quirk nodded. The town grew in the cockpit windshield. Darkening blue sky and peachy clouds framed heavily grey-white mountains. Only on the foot-slopes did any dark trees dot the white blanket.

"Okay, that's fair. Since our sharing agreement is going so well, this is how I started with C Corp."

"So, you're a trained pilot, but you couldn't share that before, like a normal person, when we were sitting in your damn living room enjoying afternoon tea?"

"Corporate pilot for three years before I became The Old Man's personal sky jockey. I travelled all over these North American Federated States, up and down the length of the Americas. I flew in Europe too. The things I've seen." He trimmed and trimmed again, irked by the compromised controls. "Often, it was just me and Morton..." His voice tailed off, becoming lost in the creaking and flapping of the failing aircraft. That was a clean place to pause the history lesson, but he owed Moth more. He could josh about it being her fault they were fugitives, but that was not the truth. His past was sucking Moth into its hateful vortex, and she deserved to know why.

"Seeing Morton in Creston tripped something in my head. Here and now, all that's left is guilt that I've compounded your mistake. We should have stayed, faced the music, fought our case. I'm sure Mary would have come to our aid again. But the rage I've nursed for five years, it flared like a great tendril of the sun. I wanted to crush Morton, to obliterate him. I... Working with Morton was changing me. I could feel it, see it in my behaviour. I blamed Jennifer for destroying our marriage, but TOM enabled her in having the child. He changed her as much as Morton changed me. They share the blame, and this may be my only chance to pay them back. But, it's a deadly game. I wish you'd stay in Revelstoke, Moth."

Moth stared at him, but stayed silent. Just as well, as they were on final approach.

A loud crash from the back brought both their heads snapping round to see Eighty delivering short, ugly blows to widen a hole in the cabin décor. Cold air rushed in to whip their hair, and ragged edges of broken plastec rattled like a turbocharged tombola. Another glance showed Eighty moving to the other side.

Quirk put them on the glide path, or his best estimate for an aircraft with no systems handling like it was trying to scratch its own back. At least there was no control tower chatter, the radio being the first thing Eighty had wrecked at his instruction.

"Here we go," he yelled above the overpowering noise. "Look on the bright side, I'm sure we'll get a free ride to the hospital!" *Or the morgue.*

Moth glared at him. "I fucking hate hospitals!" she hollered.

"They don't like you much either! They'll have eyes on us by now! I'll throw us around a bit, make it look convincing!"

"Natalie'll rip your balls off for her Christmas tree! You know that, right?!"

"No doubt!" Quirk called. "When sanity is restored, I'll buy her a new plane, and some flowers!"

"Better make them red hot pokers!" Moth grinned.

Quirk worked the controls, tipping and pitching them around enough to convince any observer they were in trouble. With the plane now having the aerodynamics of a tent, the ruse didn't take much effort. He aligned them with the vanishing point of the runway's amber landing lights, noting the now rather tedious flashing blue-and-red of emergency vehicles on the apron as the runway's grey strip expanded under them. The plane bucked and lurched. Moth looked a tad bilious. He patted her arm then searched the pockets of his Maurice Benisti jacket, feeling among other essential equipment for his nail-clippers, because no partner of any calibre liked a man with a hangnail.

"Strap in, Eighty!" Quirk shouted over his shoulder. "Although I'm fairly sure we've invalidated your warranty by now."

The sounds of horrible violence being enacted on the plane's fuselage stopped. Quirk didn't doubt the android had done a good job. Although the airport would routinely film every landing, they should be off to the hospital before the cops reacted, thanks to his impromptu and really quite dazzlingly stupid plan. He kept them bucking as the runway loomed. Their altitude must be about fifty metres. Maybe this was madness. Defying TOM tended to be a hopeless pursuit. So, was there something more? Perhaps a suppressed desire to see Jennifer again? *Yes,* he admitted as the very real risk of actual death rushed up to slap him in the face. *Yes, there is.*

He put the gear down, stabilised at twenty metres, rolling the wings slightly—like a child pretending to be an aircraft—then tipped them forward too steeply towards the techmac. With a dizzying lurch, the sky disappeared. Seconds before a very ugly contact that would smash the nose and them, he jerked back the con, throwing the nose up at the sky, and cut the power. Natalie's plane shuddered, groaned and dropped on its arse, spinning sideways, tossing them left and right, up and left and down and back and forth until they stopped.

* * *

Drip.

Drip.

Drip.

Quirk's weight strained his harness as he sat...no, hung, nearly but not quite upside down. An ethanol stench stung his nostrils, and blood rushed to his face.

He jerked, shook his head. They didn't have long. He fished for his pocket and the nail-clippers, fumbled them out, being as disoriented as a flying alligator even knowing the crash was coming. He reached up to his right ear, sighed and nicked the skin. Blood came instantly but he did his left ear too for good measure, smearing the quick, warm flow down his face then pasting some of his blood over the groggy girl. She'd be furious, but she'd get it. The trick had served him well more than once. With a little interference from him and a dollop of luck, by the time the medics deduced they had not cracked their skulls they'd be well away from the airport. But Morton now was free and clear all the way back to Yellowknife, leaving them hundreds of miles behind.

With nothing better to do than hang upside down and bleed over himself, Quirk picked at the problem. Borrowing a plane had not turned out well. Given a clear flight, they would have been in Yellowknife today, just, but now they were transport-less, handset-less, and therefore bereft of funds. It did rather look as if they'd need to resort to borrowing resources. Not his first time for that either. He sighed.

He'd seen Morton in action before of course, extracting C Corp's undercover doctor from Pinar del Río, neutralising a rebel call centre in Matagalpa, paying off the tech printing cartel in Panama City. Going up against Morton unprepared was like waging the Hundred-Hour war in a kagool armed with a laser pointer. But they were in it now, and Morton had left them in a severe pickle. Quirk felt an old, familiar feeling that he would end up in a state-operated cul-de-sac because of Derek Morton.

By the time the emergency crew was cutting them out of Natalie's ruined Nissan-Beechcraft, Quirk's nice clothes were liberally soaked with blood. *A crying shame.* He let his head loll around, whining and moaning about the pain, and slurring a lot. "Save my daughter. My Margaret! Save Maggie, please!"

"It's okay, sir. Try to calm down." The medics attempted to pin his arms in case he did himself an (other) injury, but he wriggled free and reached toward Moth.

She quickly picked up the idea and began flopping around, to the point of tipping off her stretcher and trying to stagger upright. "Daddy? Daddy! What's happening? I can't hardly see. What's that funny smell? It makes my head spin so. I feel...*fuzzy.*"

"It's the ethanol, baby. Don't you fret about it." In his head-twisting pseudo-disorientation, Quirk couldn't help noticing that his accent needed practice. "It's not as flammable as old aircraft fuel. It most likely won't go up straight away."

He almost smiled at the haste with which the very efficient medics got their suddenly compliant patients onto gurneys, into the ambulance and off the runway towards the hospital. He didn't even see a deputy, but they would be around. He mustn't get complacent.

The ambulance ride was a useful ten minutes for them to recover from the actual effects of his crash landing, and it gave him time to contemplate his guilt over wrecking a genuinely beautiful piece of aeronautical design and engineering. Natalie *would* murder him. Perhaps she might be persuaded to do it slowly, over a nice Chablis.

Only Moth's horribly fake moaning punctured the silence. He must speak to her about that. Although a good idea, execution was everything. The paramedic in the back with them tested their straps as the ambulance raced through the streets of Revelstoke towards the ER. Quirk shook his drifting thoughts into some semblance of order and reviewed their position. Typical town planning would put the hospital on or near the Trans-Canada Highway, making escape that much easier. So many things ran out of his control, but he must concentrate on the smaller mess to win time to consider the larger one. Eluding the ambulance crew would be the real challenge.

When the vehicle stopped, Quirk released his chest strap and sat up before the EMT could open the back door. He put his hand in his pocket and confronted the startled paramedic with Becker's gold-plated badge.

The young man gaped.

"Deputy Becker, son. I'm undercover. Tailing a plane thief from Creston. Were you near the airport? Hear of any unusual activity?" It sounded so transparent. Maybe police work was harder than it looked.

The paramedic frowned.

"We can't be too careful. Almost anyone could be part of this ring of thieves. Anyway, me and the girl, we can walk in, get patched up and be on our way. Come on, Clotilda. Let's make this nice young man's job a bit easier for him." He flashed the medic a quick *Thanks for Everything, Chuck* smile then stood up, motioning Moth and Eighty to follow his lead. The android straightened easily, naturally untroubled by the ordeal although its clothes were ripped and bloody.

When the driver opened the back door, Quirk jumped down. The young paramedic came next, helping Moth down by the hand. Unfortunately, the driver was an android, female model, S-0993 tattooed in pale purple on its forehead.

"This situation is irregular," said the syRen®.

"It's alright," Quirk held out Becker's badge. "We're in pursuit. Everything is under control." *And now Kreski can add impersonating an officer to the charge list.*

"Centralised records show Deputy Becker is aged twenty-eight and has brown eyes," said the android. Through the plass ER doors, Quirk saw two orderlies striding towards them down a wide internal corridor.

"Time to go, Clotilda," he made a flicking gesture with his hand. "We have to commandeer your vehicle; our target is escaping. He's a public risk."

"That course is contra-indicated," said the android in a slightly more melodic tone than Eighty's. "Please enter the hospital and comply with your treatment plan."

Quirk jabbed a quick right into the syRen®'s jaw, whipping its head back and causing it to stagger.

"Hey!" called the EMT.

It wasn't that Quirk had done a bit of boxing in his youth, nor had he grown up on rough streets, using his fists to survive. In reality, surprise made up for the many deficiencies of his pugilism. He reached the ambulance before the syRen® clamped his wrist in an iron grip.

"Sir, you must comply in order for your injuries to be assessed."

Moth was with the paramedic, the young man seeming to buy the story she was spinning. The doors slid open, and the orderlies emerged, one pushing a gurney, the other a wheelchair. The distant wail of police sirens swelled, closing on the hospital. All the time, Morton ate into the distance between him and his new targets.

Quirk tried to pull away from the syRen® but its grip was immovable. "Damnation, Eigh—lijah, do something. The greater good!" He hauled again, grasping at the ambulance door handle with his other hand, his feet slipping on the techmac. He knew that just the right blow could cause a live reset in an android. It wasn't easy though. He threw another punch, hammering the side of the syRen®'s head, which made it twitch, but its restraining grip never wavered, hovering just below pain.

Eighty stepped around the ambulance. "Please desist. Someone might be badly hurt. This gentleman is pursuing an important investigation. Lives are at risk."

The orderlies stood nonplussed. One of them lifted a handset to her ear, began speaking. The sirens promised the police would arrive imminently. The syRen® EMT's features displayed doubt. "While your logic is appropriate, I detect that you are not connected to the Net. In addition, your associate's behaviour does not correspond well with parameters laid down for law enforcement officers. As you know, a good punch can cause serious damage or injury."

Eighty nodded. "True, but my analysis confirms that neither of my companion's punches were good. The risk was minimal."

The interaction ended there. The female android released Quirk's wrist and he lurched before righting himself. Sirens wailed. The orderly's voice became urgent, and more personnel hurried towards the doors.

"Hurry up," Moth hollered leaning out of the open ambulance door, "before someone who gives a shit arrives."

He jumped into the driver's seat as Eighty climbed into the back. The android banged on the partition and Quirk sent the ambulance lurching out of the lot past two arriving patrol cars. With a grin, Moth switched on the siren and the lights. "Disguise," she smirked, as the siren wailed and whooped. Of course, their clothes were spattered with drying blood and their luggage likely sat on the techmac at Revelstoke Airport. The Merrion and everything else would be entered into evidence.

"Damn," he said, turning onto the highway and accelerating away from Revelstoke. Moth didn't ask. And— suddenly—the loss of possessions didn't matter. The Merrion was not just a sharp suit, it was a symbol of his escape from a life that he had been desperate to leave behind, but which had caught up with him anyway. He could run from the police, but only running towards Morton, into his past would clear their names.

0A

(Green-verse Famebook page. Blog message from ★J-PiP!★)

Nother yawnfest in the-projects, bros, but aint totalE snores. Ma Sista#1 HAKD a drone in NT n'saw some WKD sh1t. No messin, but all mess!! snow turn red with blooooood. Theres mad killin going on up thr like a MONSTER gonna eat the town :o]
atths://LaQy83bvd9bs5b3nnvdug

14 hours earlier...
07:45, 19 November 2099
Meyer residence, Yellowknife, NT

Eve woke to a splitting headache. She chugged ionised water then showered, breathing away the weight in her chest. She threw on shirt and suit, but took important moments to straighten her clothes and damp hair, stuffed a three-day old croissant in her mouth and grabbed a lipstick from the bowl on her way out the door. Her forty-eight-hour suspension—the max Morton could assign—was over. Time to fight back.

Letting the truck drive, she applied her lippy, bemoaning the random selection that left her with Sinope Sunset by GG. She put the news on. It was grim. Wall-to-wall speculation, littered with wild theories on what had happened, and what might happen. The truck's caution became frustrating, and she resumed control, driving too fast between the lights. The road was very quiet. The few pedestrians trudging over last night's snowfall wore official reflective gear, City staff clearing snow, checking security and patrolling assigned routes. Only those with a duty were out.

Vehicles crammed the radio station lot, the sheriff's and RCMP offices too. Once out of town, Eve planted her Fendi ice-pump (Auto-grip with style!) on the accelerator.

White vans choked Genextric's access off Ingraham Trail, and people crowded Eve's truck as she slowed and began turning in.

"Do you have a statement?"

"What's the latest on the escape? Give us a quote."

"Play with the stuff of life and God will smite you!"

Security staff at the barrier forced the scrabbling press and protestors back to admit her. They waved her in without checking her status, clean now in any case. And was that hope in their eyes that she would command the rapidly worsening situation?

She parked carelessly and strode across the lot, nodding to the guards at the door then bustled across the foyer like she would have someone's arm off if they challenged her. Scanning her pass, she held her breath. The barrier display showed "Pending Review." Eve sighed and pushed through, letting anger bolster her determination.

Morton's office was empty.

"Shit." However, perhaps his absence explained how she'd walked in without being stopped, even though he couldn't bar her now.

Last night's stress and whisky left her irritable and generally wrung out. Her stomach sank as her mind stained the white corridor with impressions of the mangetout attack's bloody aftermath. And she needed to pee like a bitch. Rehydrating was a chore, but essential, her aching head reminded her. Most of all she needed updates on the Search & Recover missions stat, and now, Morton was blocking her calls.

Yesterday evening, she'd kept it together until Kootook dropped her off before vomiting in his parking lot. *Don't contaminate the crime scene* had been her only thought as bile rose in response to the flood-lit gore on the lakeside. It looked like a seal cull a hundred years ago, blood turning the snow crimson, red water lapping in the shallows. But no human parts, no Tania. Eve's revulsion had mixed with relief, a disquieting combination. She refused to mourn Tania. Not yet.

Maybe Kootook had known all along, had tried to play her, suspected she knew more, even thought she conspired with Tania. Because Morton had thrown her under the bus, aimed the sheriff right at her. Kootook's words still rang in her ears, despite her dousing them with twenty-year-old Scotch. Even angry—which he clearly was—his weathered features remained blank. *"You have twenty-four hours to report real progress, Ms. Meyer, or I will put every hunter I can find into the field, and this town has plenty."* Madness. Unbelievably, things actually could get worse. Maybe Morton had abandoned his post to highlight her culpability, maybe he thought she'd curl into a ball and give up. That slimy bastard would shit a brick when *she* fucked *him* over. This would *not* go down the way he planned, and she'd make sure it hurt. She spat on Morton's carpet, turned on her heal and strode to her office, via the exec washroom.

Eve sat at her desk, logged-in without issue and set the LiveWall to her "Serious Business" pre-set, which displayed Genextric Yellowknife's whole-site dashboard. Morton was not in the building. Good, her control should not be questioned. It wasn't too late, although she risked digging herself a deeper hole. She could retrieve the situation. She called Connor Clark, who she hoped still was her head of security, and had not pledged to Morton, the arch dick from corporate. She took it as a good sign that the tall Irishman had no better idea where Morton was than she did.

"I'm coming to you, I need to see the whites of your eyes." She whirled out of her room—wincing as the world spun—and paced down the corridor to Clark's office. His tousled ginger hair flipped up as she entered. "What can I tell the sheriff?"

"You've got six hours—"

"*We've* got six hours, Connor. Tell me something good." She went around the desk, pulling up a chair, suddenly conscious she hadn't applied perfume, although it wouldn't have covered her breath.

"Drones and droids have covered over one-hundred-fifty square kilometres in seventy-two hours, six teams using a 'long snake' pattern. They've found predation remnants atypical of indigenous wildlife, some confirmed tracks. The behaviour team says the mangetouts—"

"Call them MTs in all reports, per protocol." Eve expelled a breath. "There are some images online. We need to avoid panic in the uninformed for as long as possible."

"What about the informed?"

"They're already panicking." Her smile was grim. "Go on."

"Three new sites overnight," he pushed the images to his LiveWall. "All fauna kills." The pictures were high-res, and exceedingly gory, but she'd seen worse, she'd seen Tania dragged away.

"That's normal. I expected more kills further out with MT's ranging tendencies."

Clark grimaced. "But the new sites are Trapper Lake, two-point-five clicks from here, and Shot Lake, one kilometre away. They're getting closer to town, not further away, and Customer Services count fifty-six calls from media platforms. It's out."

"They're storming the gates." She leaned in and gripped Connor's arm. "Find Morton. Email him, message him, write him a fucking letter and fax it. I don't care. We've still got a chance before these hellish things kill someone."

"You don't think Terjesen is dead?"

"Not 'til I see her on a slab." Eve bit back a gasp. How could she consider sending Tania away? They should have been together. She should have prevented this!

"What about the S&R teams? I'd turn them around, close the net."

She nodded. "Do it. Charge up every coat rack and hatstand left in this place and deploy them. We need to stop these things dead, burn them, then bury them in concrete. Kootook deploying hunters is like stocking the MT's larder. We have to prevent that."

She left Clark without a parting, went to the washroom and threw up vigorously. This diet of fear and whisky certainly helped shed the pounds. She strode down to the control room trying not to imagine the MTs getting a taste for human flesh. An employee occupied every desk in the open plan. Heads turned, staff watched from meeting rooms and peaked over partitions, probably speculating about her. Let them.

Her A-team of Johari and Vernola ran the control room, supporting the search effort while supervising the normal business of Gamma Lab. The way their heads snapped around when she entered confirmed they knew exactly what was at stake, including their jobs. They'd signed away their freedom of speech long ago, but now were briefed under emergency protocols because they knew what was out in Yellowknife's frozen environs. They also watched the news. The media had drones too after all, and would film the leftovers of someone's barbecue to present a kill to the viewers. By now it would be all anyone was talking about, not just in this building, but in Yellowknife's bars and shops, homes and offices, mines and factories. Genextric's Search & Recover teams clearly weren't enough. She had to act now, and decisively.

"Jo, prep the tracking units on the vuldolphs." Johari spun his chair to face her, putting a hand on his short afro as if trying to keep his head from exploding.

"Why?"

"Because I tell you," she said tightly, stalking forward to stand between them. She'd make a staff announcement, but must assume it would reach beyond these walls. All the confidentiality clauses on Earth wouldn't contain this. People had families to think of. Still, she needed to send a message. *I am in control.* Waiting for Morton was not an option. And he might block her actions anyway. *Where the hell is he?* Regardless, these were *her* staff. She would take this mess by the throat.

"We're not maximising our resources, drones have limitations, human ones. You know vuldolphs are the smartest instinctive trackers we have."

"Yes, boss, but I didn't think..." he trailed off and turned back to his console, nodding to Vernola, who focused on her screen.

They ran through the protocols, preparing the vuldolphs, then released them onto Level Six. Whoever decided to meld Himalayan vulture DNA with that of the common bottlenose dolphin, the Siberian weasel, but also the black vulture—for its acute sense of smell—must have the worst nightmares. No doubt her own would be vivid and horrible when she stopped drinking herself to sleep, but that was for another day, maybe another place. Under Eve's ribs, her heart thumped, but this was not like releasing mangetouts. *Madness, utter madness!* Vuldolphs were trackers, not only for carrion—which in itself would increase their chances of success—but for specific shapes and smells that controllers coded into their behaviour, because of...science. Tania had explained it to her once, but lost her at eidetic templates. Admittedly, the spooning hadn't helped Eve's concentration. She didn't need to know how things worked, just that tens of thousands of hours had produced vuldolphs able to search over great distances and with great accuracy while communicating with each other. She should have done this hours ago. No, Morton should have done it. Eve cursed her time spent in the five stages of fucking-up: denial (check); anger (double check); bargaining (done); depression (too busy); whisky (ongoing).

Over Johari's shoulder, crystal clear 7K images showed four vuldolphs waddling across the screen in pursuit of something that smelled good to them. The view changed and the creatures took flight into the expanse of Level Six, flapping and banking within the twenty-metre headroom, until they located the carrion lure in the long grass. This *was* the right course. Why hadn't Morton done this? It was almost like he wasn't thinking straight, or...had a different agenda.

Johari lured the vuldolphs from veldt to elevator, sent them to the loading bay, where syRen® shepherded them through a plastext tunnel to an unmarked white van. The A-team completed their checks and Eve got jerky images of the van's interior before Vernola gave the all-clear. The bay door rolled up and the van departed across the snowy lot. From her desk chair, Vernola steered it out through the media scrum at Genextric's gate, reporters and cameramen straining to reach the blacked-out windows. Vee sent the van west on Ingraham Trail, crossed the river and took the track north to the old Shot Lake gravel pit. Johari cycled the cameras as the van door opened and the view bucked wildly as the creatures scuttled out. He switched to the van's roof camera as—one by one—the vuldolphs took flight. The bird-things wheeled away, instantly elegant once airborne, dark shadows dwindling into the lightening sky.

This will *work. It must. But will it work quickly enough?*

* * *

17:44, 19 November 2099
Highway 1, Revelstoke, BC

Quirk, Moth and Eighty left town under full lights and sirens, but Moth turned off their Code 3 "disguise" before Quirk pulled into a rest stop diner two miles down the road. He parked the ambulance around back out of sight of the highway.

Stealing a car was relatively simple these days if you could convince your android the theft was in some surpassingly good cause. That was the difficult part. Grand theft auto for personal gain was impossible, all it gained you was a trip to jail with your own syRen®'s firm grip on your collar. GTA therefore was very rare. Presently, the Quirk Agency was en route to rescue, and possibly save the life of, two fair ladies while, hopefully, foiling what might be a murderous cover-up plot, perhaps. Apparently, this premise provided adequate justification for S-0778a to balance against the Laws and Tenets of Robotics and boost a two-tone orange and pink Five-Star Explorer parked behind the diner. The android gripped the door handle. There followed a magnetic thunk, then Eighty pulled the driver's door open.

"Couldn't we steal something more noticeable?" Moth glanced over her shoulder at the diner. "And anyway"—she scowled—"a good convent girl shouldn't associate with common thieves."

"This is a staff spot," Quirk observed, glancing around despite his certainty that Eighty had disabled the fail-safe unit that would have locked the motor before pinging its owner that shenanigans were afoot. "We might get an hour before it's reported. Once we're reconnected, I'll message the diner and compensate them, handsomely."

"In addition," said Eighty in a low, almost conspiratorial tone, "I selected this vehicle for the two sacks of laundry on the rear seat. Our clothes are bloody and in need of replacement if we are to avoid attracting unwanted attention."

Quirk ushered them into the vehicle. He took the wheel—disregarding Moth's scowl—because he had a taste for this driving lark now. Also, Eighty's disconnection—something Quirk would have done for security reasons—somewhat limited the syRen®'s capacity. A nagging doubt arose in Quirk's mind. He'd suspected the authorities of cutting Eighty's data stream, but Kreski most definitely wanted them found, and surely would favour the tracking potential. So, was it TOM paternalistically "helping" them reach Yellowknife to suit his mysterious agenda? Morton, flexing his strange and impressive black ops muscles? None of these options made much sense.

Eighty disabled the Five-Star's GPS while Quirk watched for a customer leaving. He pulled out first so that the other exiting vehicle moved between them and the diner, masking their vehicle from the window then turned onto Highway 1 between the banks of cleared snow, letting the motor loose on the sweeping bends and long straights of the Trans-Canada. Little light remained in the sky, just a bright stain in the rear-view. Tall firs jutted from the road's snowy flanks, the left sloping up out of sight under dark bows, the right tipping down an unseen forested bank. The Five-Star's headlights lit blank techmac.

Two hours driving ate up kilometres. The highway barely changed, although they did climb gradually, fresh snow falling as they slid through Glacier National Park. The windscreen auto-dimmed for approaching vehicles, the windscreen melted snowflakes, but driving in the dark was wearing nonetheless. It had been a busy day, after all.

They descended into a river valley. Eighty offered to drive through the night, which was the sensible thing, but Moth griped about constantly being on the move.

"Can't we just *stop*?" she said. "Please?"

Quirk almost steered into the river. "Did you say 'please'? It must be serious. I'll stop right away."

"Ha-bloody-ha." She folded her arms over her chest, flipping her fringe at him as she turned away.

He pulled into Donald (a village, not a person) on Log Dump Road.

Moth laughed for a good two minutes. "Man, there is *nothing* here." She fished around in the storage pockets, unearthing some protein bars which they wolfed down as if they were mackerel pate on Melba toast and a McGantuan-with-cheese, respectively.

It was Moth who broke the silence long after the chewing was done.

"I'm sorry about running," she said. "I panicked. I was still dopey, and with the cops bursting in..." She shuddered although the Five-Star was nicely warm. "It was too much like..."—she bowed her head—"when my parents...were, murdered. I've landed us in it." She stared at the darkness beyond the windscreen.

"No..." Quirk made to put a hand on her arm, but Eighty had touched Moth's shoulder to comfort her. *Reassuring words then, that's more my line anyway.* He opened his mouth, but Moth lunged across the console and wrapped her arms around him, hugging him tightly.

"I thought that fucker had killed us!"

Quirk managed not to twitch. "Eh, it's okay, Moth. We're fine. Fight another day, etcetera. We're ace detectives, remember? Logic will prevail." *Is she sobbing?* This was all rather awkward. He patted her back. "A good big sleep will work wonders."

"I guess." She sat back, crushing tears from her eyes. "G'night." She tilted her seat back nearly flat and closed her eyes. She seemed to find sleep almost immediately, but a soft, tired voice said, "Thanks for backing me up. You rock."

Quirk shook his head, trying to deny the lump in his throat, staring at the windscreen seeking to pinpoint the moment he'd begun to change. He gave up, gave Eighty the watch, angled his seat back and fell asleep.

* * *

Quirk woke in utter darkness to the sound of a handset vibrating. Dopily, he fished in his pocket, groped for several moments before remembering that his cLife was in Kreski's office. The vibration continued.

Had Moth smuggled a handset aboard? Was Eighty carrying? Maybe the car's owner had left one?

"Hello, Quirk," said a disembodied male voice, more youthful than The Old Man's. It issued from the Five-Star's enfolding 15.1 audio system.

"Um...hello?" Quirk whispered. The system would adjust the level for the caller. Except there was no handset in the— "Who is this?"

"You don't need to know that yet."

Mystery caller: wonderful. "What do you want, then?"

"Not very polite. I thought you were a paragon of virtue," said the smooth voice.

"Who told you that? And how are we talking? Our—"

"Handsets are lost, I know. And Eighty's work disabling the Beechcraft made it awkward to track you. There were twenty-seven minutes when I didn't know where you were. We're speaking through Eighty, using C Corp's satellite feed."

"But how?" Quirk flinched as Eighty's eyes illuminated, a violet glow appearing in the rear-view. Normally reserved for charging, the feature also served as a nightlight. The syRen® leaned forward. Exceptional as it was at anticipating his needs, it would be testing the incoming signal. Eighty nodded. A secure satellite line, somehow.

"Use this line if you want, TOM'll never know. Eighty can vet your calls. Our secret," the youthful voice purred.

"So"—Quirk's thoughts buzzed around, trying to figure who his latest manipulator was—"are you a whistle-blower? A snitch? Disgruntled ex-employee?"

"Hah, no. I'm an ally. Accomplice, maybe. You're on a mission. I'm here in Yellowknife, ready to help. Hurry though, it's pretty boring, even with the beasts running around. And it was me who cut Eighty's connection, by the way."

An insider at Genextric? At C Corp? A hacktivist? They had some smarts if they could dial into C Corp's secure comms and get away with it. Could this be a bluff, another attempt by The Old Man to send Quirk dancing after his twisted agenda?

"Beasts? What do you mean? Why should I trust you?"

"Oh, you want a 'sign', okay. Your hunch is right. Morton's returning here. He's on a train. The Old Man is trying to fix the election. There are terra-fauna on the loose. I think people will die. Oh, and your son is here, in YK. How's that for good faith?"

"Sweet Jesus! Who are you? How do you know this? Where? Will you testify?"

"No. I have to go now, but I'll call again."

The line went dead. Quirk gazed into Eighty's impassive eyes, his thoughts reeling. His son! There was no basis whatever to believe the caller's wild assertions, yet they felt plausible. Stakes high enough for Morton to kill. A missing woman who might have some kind of evidence and must be silenced. Exactly the kind of scenario The Old Man would be knee deep in. But what was Mystery Caller's agenda? He must guard against a con, but...his son?

Quirk fretted over the possibilities, but somehow the android's violet stare comforted him, accepted his gaze over long seconds that would have been impossibly uncomfortable for a human. He sighed and turned forwards, only now noticing that Moth was awake. She turned her droopy-eyed gaze on him.

"Tha' was weeeeird." She stretched. "What th'fuck's going-on?"

"I don't know. Go back to sleep. The mysterious voice from the unknown is gone now."

Moth's eyes drifted closed and she twisted around, putting her back to him, making a pillow of her arms. "You're rubbish at dad-ing," she murmured as Morpheus reclaimed her.

Quirk snorted. Hugs one minute, scorn the next. Teenagers were so emotionally vindictive. At least he was impervious to that nonsense. He sighed.

"You have the conn, Eighty."

The android nodded and Quirk closed his eyes, but that only brought his emotions into sharper focus.

* * *

22:07, 19 November 2099
Highway 95, 10km south of Canal Flats, BC

Kreski was livid, boiling mad. He gripped the wheel tighter before forcing himself to relax, making small adjustments to the big blue-and-white's path on the highway's long curves, unnecessarily overriding the vehicle's autonomy.

He'd make Quirk pick up the tab for the damage done to his town. The Greiner mess was one thing, but the detective had busted up the hospital, left cars in ditches, and a man was dead. Then there was the missing passenger from the plane. The hospital video *did* corroborate Quirk's story. So why hadn't the fancy-assed idiot just stayed put to help sort it all out? And now Quirk was leading him by the nose after this Morton guy? He had some nerve.

Kreski released the wheel again, flexing his arms, letting the truck steer. He was gambling on Quirk heading to Yellowknife, but it seemed a safe bet. Enough to put only a general APB out on them, keep the specifics to himself and take some leave to pursue that pompous shitkicker outside his jurisdiction. Rowland had come down from Yellowknife to see Quirk at short notice. He had that from Sheriff Kootook up in YK. So, if they were bolting, Yellowknife was the last place they should go. This find-the-killer-to-clear-your-name crap was the worst kind of melodrama.

"Spare me from goddam amateurs," Kreski grumbled, clenching his fists.

The problem was, if he didn't believe Quirk killed Rowland, he had to believe this Morton guy had. He was mad at Quirk, but he didn't want to see them gunned down in the street, and that still happened sometimes if the RCMP put out a reward. Still, Quirk and Moth had a charge list as long as his arm, and he retained the option to rough up that smartass, if the need arose.

One way or another, Quinton Kirby had a check due to the town of Creston and Sheriff Wayne Kreski would make damn sure he settled it.

0B

06:18, 20 November 2099
Sunny Days Caravan+RV Park, Donald, BC
1,215km south of Yellowknife

Quirk sighed, rolled over and his neck spasmed. He sat up with a gasp. The pseudo-leather of the car's seat screeched in protest. "Damn!" he massaged his left trapezius, but stopped when that made the pain worse.

"Will you shut up," Moth moaned. "I'm trying to listen to my tinnitus."

"There is an effective laparoscopic treatment..." said Eighty.

"Breakfast first," Moth interrupted, although she closed her eyes again and scrunched down into the seat, the Five-Star's solar cells having stored enough power to maintain a comfortable temperature overnight.

"Mileage first," said Quirk, yawning then activating the car's drive system. "Anyway, the metropolis of Donald is almost a ghost town, unless you're going foraging?"

"Go forage for this," Moth replied, winding up her middle finger with a tiny imaginary crank handle. "Anyway, are we just going to drive up to Yellowknife and hope Kreski's had a change of heart, and talked the nice sheriff up there—"

"Peter Kootook," Eighty interjected.

"—into welcoming us with open arms, and that Morton will roll over and have his tummy tickled? And, what about your son?"

"What we are going to do," said Quirk slowly, reaching into his special place for his most patient voice, "is exert some control over this case for the first time since I heard the name Barry Rowland."

"Hey, Eight-ball, how'd you do that without a connection?"

S-0778a moved forward, positioning his head between the front seats. "I—"

Quirk held up a hand in the universal sign of I-was-still-talking. "What we are going to do is call Genextric. Are you certain Mystery Caller's line is secure, Eighty?"

"As far as I can be, sir. My systems are designed to protect my owner and nominated associates from a wide range of cyber, sub-cyber and hyper-cyber-attacks."

"Then please call Genextric in Yellowknife, main listed number."

"Calling now, sir." The digital grasshopper dialling tone of a satellite call emanated from the Five-Star's dash.

"Hey, why we not calling Hygen?" asked Moth. "That's Rowland's crew."

"Because Rowland's motion sensor tripped near Genextric's boundary. That's most likely where the woman came from. And because TOM, and Derek Morton."

"*Good morning, Genextric Gamma Laboratory, Yellowknife. How may I direct you?*" said a lilting android voice.

"Connect me with the person in charge, please. It's a matter of the utmost gravity." There was a slight pause, his voice no doubt passing through a vocal metrics app which almost certainly applied a probability screen to assess breathing, intonation and language and so rank Quirk's "fruit loop" score before connecting him, or not.

"*The Centre Director is very busy at present and unable to take your call. Would you like to leave a message, or speak to a subordinate?*"

"And who would I address my message to, please?" Androids were suckers for politeness, it played well with their algorithms and more than once had elicited information that rudeness never would have.

"Centre Director Eve Meyer is the senior officer on site."

A message would have to do. "Ms. Meyer, good day to you." *A polite message, of course. First, establish identity and function*—"My name is Quinton Kirby, I'm a private investigator." *Always demonstrate sympathy*—"I appreciate you're busy"—*while getting to the point*—"but I believe a staffer of yours was involved in a serious incident in Creston, BC yesterday." *Be reasonable*—"I wonder if you can confirm his location." *Exaggerate your strength*—"My associates and I are heading north at present." *The slightest suggestion of a threat*—"On our way to Yellowknife." *Then leave them with something to worry about*—"I want to speak to you about Derek Morton. Disconnect."

He sat back and looked at Moth, waiting for the sniping to start, but she just looked back at him in silence, and nodded.

Quirk nodded too. "Let's hunt down that breakfast then, shall we? Twenty-eight kilometres to Golden."

Moth put a hand on his arm. "Your son, Quirk."

His jaw tightened. "What about him?"

"He's in Yellowknife. How do you feel about that? Openness, remember?"

"I feel like I will have to think about it before we get there, but right now I will dissemble until we make some actual progress with Rowland's case. How about that?" he said. Moth just scowled.

Still simmering at being tipped into an emotional loop, Quirk pulled the Five-Star out onto the highway. The early morning sky was dark, but increasingly discoloured with bright blue above the spiky black-green, snow-mottled fir trees surrounding them. Once on the snow-banked road, Quirk decided that a still drowsy Moth probably would not appreciate a history lesson.

"Funny story about Donald. In 1897, when Rufus Kimpton heard the railroad company was leaving for Revelstoke, he took Donald's church, moved the whole thing one hundred and fifty kilometres to Windermere. He stole it. Revelstoke came to move the church they'd been promised, but it was gone."

"You're full of shit, and your homilies blow."

"Quirk is correct though. Stranger still perhaps is the fact that the stolen church's bell was itself purloined while Kimpton moved the building through the town of Golden. So, Windermere had St. Peter's, the so-called 'Stolen Church', and Golden had St. Paul's of the Stolen Bell."

"More to the point," Moth objected, "how'd you learn that? Don't you dare tell me you've got a sneaky handset stashed in your boxers."

"Firstly," he said, patiently, "you have much to learn about boxer shorts. Secondly, I read the interpretation board back in Donald. No secret cLifes, and we should mistrust Mystery Caller's purloined satellite link. There's no way of knowing who really is behind it. It could be The Old Man using a flunky to monitor us."

Moth hmphed. "That cloak-and-dagger shit bums me out to the max. Grownups should just say what they mean."

"It's called diplomacy, Moth. You have a lot to learn about that too. We play coy, guard our secrets and elicit what we can from them."

"Clammed up does sound like you, certainly." She stuck her tongue out and turned to the window.

The sun continued to bleach the sky. The Five-Star's computer displayed Golden being twenty minutes away. They would need to change vehicles again, but stealing cars was neither sustainable nor quick for travelling the now eighteen hundred some kilometres to Yellowknife. There was a good chance they would be caught, but neither could they hire something, since they were potentially subject to a national person-hunt. Oh, and wanted for murder. And there was his son. Might he be about to meet his son again?

Low mist clung to the wide, snow-choked ditches at the side of the road. The undergrowth and forest floor were only now becoming visible as the light grew.

"That's not even the end of the story," he said as they cruised around another bend. "Sixty years later, a group from Windermere snuck into Golden and stole the bell back, but the Windermere elders made them return it."

"Human behaviour never ceases to amaze," said S-0778a.

"Canadians," said Moth.

Quirk glanced at the grumpy girl, now staring sullenly ahead.

"In actual fact," started Eighty, "the inhabitants of—"

"Deer!" Moth shouted.

"I didn't know you cared," said Quirk.

"Fucking wildlife, moron!" She jabbed a finger at the bank up ahead, but the five grey-brown quadrupeds already were bounding down from the treeline and scattering across the road. Quirk applied the brakes forcefully, although the car's system had already engaged. They came to a heavy but controlled stop at the edge of the highway as the deer hightailed it down the opposite bank.

Quirk took a breath and opened the door, stepping out into the morning's quiet grey chill. The car's amber emergency lights flicked steadily. Moth climbed out and came to stand with him in front of the vehicle. Dark, snow-covered trees crowded the road's left side, but to their right, the land fell away and snow-capped mountains filled the middle distance, white peaks lit by the rising sun. Moth breathed out a foggy plume, hugging herself and shivering.

"It's really pretty here, pretty shitting cold."

"The tallest peak is Moonraker Mountain," Eighty informed her, standing by the open door. "But we should return to the vehicle and proceed. The driving code recommends against remaining stationary on the carriageway."

"Wonder what spooked the deer," Moth mused. "They were running before we came close." She pointed up the bank where a small, brown form...no, two, were capering down the slope, tumbling and slapping each other. "Bear," her voice wavered.

"Way too cold," said Quirk.

The creatures gambled onto the empty, snow-dusted road, showing no more interest in the humans than they did the departed deer. Moth took a step forward.

"Miss Moth..." concern laced Eighty's voice.

Something else moved through the trees. "More bear," said Quirk urgently. He pointed up the bank. "A lot more bear."

A massive, dark brown shadow emerged from the undergrowth above them, purposefully descending the bank towards the cubs playing ten metres away.

"Shit," observed Moth, almost stumbling as she backed up.

The mother—easily two metres long on all-fours—turned her big, shaggy head and pointed snout towards them, scanned them with black eyes, grunted, and stood up.

"Oh, damn," Quirk whispered with considerable feeling as his testes tingled and set about climbing into the scant protection of his ribcage.

The huge bear let out a bellow that should have felled all the trees in sight then swung its paws wide.

"MOTH AND QUIRK," commanded Eighty, "HEED MY WORDS, OBEY WITHOUT QUESTION. Do not make eye-contact with the bear. Hold out your arms slowly to make yourself look as big as possible. DO NOT RUN. You cannot outrun the bear. If necessary, I will attack the bear to distract it." The syRen® took a small step forward. "SLOWLY, back away and get in the car."

Quirk needed no second invitation, but made sure Moth went first. The bear alternated between roaring and swaying. Painfully slowly they edged to the doors. Quirk reached into his pocket—hand shaking—and pressed the control fob. Except that wasn't what happened; in his tense and jittery state, he double clicked, twice. The Five-Star beeped three times. "Lockdown initiated."

Moth tugged the handle then began wrenching at it to no effect whatever. "Nooooo! What have you done, you giant pinstriped knucklehead?!"

Quirk grunted something impolite then waved her backwards and they edged away, putting twenty metres and the chunky, very securely locked Five-Star Explorer between them and the bear while Eighty remained in place, standing tall and wide. The android glanced over his shoulder to check their position then looked at the vehicle. The lights flicked onto full beam, the horn blaring, shockingly loud in the morning quiet. The bear dropped to all-fours and charged.

It reached Eighty, rearing again. The android stood its ground and got a big swat in the chest for its trouble. The blow threw Eighty to the ground ten metres away and the bear crashed down on the car, pulverising the hood, crushing anything under it. Quirk quashed the imperative to empty his bladder. Could he put himself between Moth and the bear if it came to it? Perhaps he was about to find out.

Eighty jumped up, spreading its arms again and Quirk backed away further, shooing Moth behind him. The hulking bear shouldered the car aside. The vehicle lurched and bumped on its shocks, door and wing crumpling under the bear's blow. The Five-Star slid into the ditch, front tyre exploding with a cannon-fire bang, and the bear flinched. Through all this, Eighty stood firm. *Hurrah for the Laws of Robotics!* As if Quirk needed further proof.

"Is it going to charge again?" gasped Moth.

A pair of bright headlights crested the bend up ahead, throwing bear and android outlines into stark relief. The newcomer started on their horn, a big, basso honk rending the air. Their antagonist decided it was time to follow her cubs down the bank. Mother bear exited—pursued by the truck—massive, shaggy hindquarters disappearing over the gravel edge. Still, Eighty made them wait, walking to the bank and scanning the undergrowth before turning and giving them a thumbs-up.

Quirk stood, arms akimbo, breathing deeply until his heartbeat settled. Moth came to his side, but there was no repetition of last night's emotion. That was okay. He had been ready for it, ready to give his support, that was the important thing, right? Against his better judgement, he put an arm around her shoulders. To his surprise, she did not swear, object, or even flinch. He rejected a notion that his gesture made him feel better.

The massively bearded driver of the big semi rig climbed down from his cab, pump-action shotgun in one hand and flashlight in the other, scanning the harsh beam over the edge where the bear disappeared. "Close call."

"Close enough," Quirk agreed. "Thanks for happening by."

"Was on my way," the man grinned, surveying their vehicle.

The Five-Star was crippled. The trucker offered them a ride back to Revelstoke, but Quirk declined graciously, and the man returned to his cab. He pulled level with them and dropped a small package down into Moth's hands. "Good luck, folks. Lucky you're not up in Yellowknife. There's much worse running around in the woods up there, I hear. Have a nice day!" He waved as quiet motors pulled the truck away.

Before abandoning the Five-Star they rooted through the dirty wash. Clearly, the owner was bigger than them—which was handier than the alternative—and had a kid. Moth resolutely refused to abandon her Lovecraft tee, despite the shirt's fake blood design being augmented with the now-dried real blood that had dripped from Moth's ear, adding a whole new dimension of horror. She selected a pastel pink Winnie the Pooh sweatshirt, wrinkling her nose as she pulled it on, rolled up the sleeves then plucked an insulated peach hoodie from another bag.

"I am properly gagging right now," she announced, but shrugged the hoodie on, shivering as she zipped it up and tugged the fur-edged hood over her head before throwing her bloody jacket into the trunk.

"Layers, Moth, layers," Quirk pronounced, but he was no happier. He fancied the unknowing donor was single, or separated, as there were no men's clothes. He walked around the Five-Star and removed his shoes and trousers. The chill bit his exposed skin as he donned baggy, grey sweatpants then long pink woollen socks which he tucked the too-short sweats into. He found a plain, white T-shirt (thank God), fine but for the coffee stains down the front and the odour of stale sweat. He held his breath as he pulled the grubby shirt over his Calvin Klein thermal undervest then topped that with a purple, black-sleeved sweatshirt bearing worn bubble lettering on the front. Moth bent double laughing and pointing.

"'Priceless Princess'?! Oh, Quirk, that's sooooo you!" She laughed so hard that Eighty began to show signs of concern, presumably that she might swallow her tongue. Quirk could only hope. "And sweatpants? Really?" Moth's gob was properly smacked.

"I needed to get decent in a hurry," he grumbled. He retrieved his antique leather belt from his ruined jeans, which he would have done anyway for its sentimental value as part of the Merrion ensemble, but he needed it still to hold up the baggy sweatpants. The final indignity? The only thing resembling an adult coat in the Five-Star's trunk was a dayglo orange work jacket with reflective strips. He looked like a scarecrow dressed by a blind person, possibly while drunk, in the dark. He was not happy about it. "What did the driver give you?" he asked, changing the subject as Moth unwrapped the package.

"Ham and Swiss on rye," she grinned and took a big bite.

* * *

Peace River, Alberta, Canada, NAF
708km south-southwest of Yellowknife

"What's going on?" asked The Old Man, more testily than usual. *"You know I hate waiting."*

Morton frowned, covering his mouth lest anyone in the carriage lipread. <It's in hand,> he subvocalized. <I just heard Meyer deployed the vuldolphs. The news is out. The media has descended. 'No such thing as bad news, just bad timing.' Your words.>

"Timing is everything when it's mine, but we're short of it now."

<I couldn't leave this to chance. I explained that. There were loose ends.>

"And they're dealt with?"

<In hand. An unexpected trip south, but one loose end down. Three to go.>

"When?"

<Tomorrow. The next day. I've got more intelligence on what I'm looking for.>

The Old Man hung up and Morton stared out of the carriage window as the train slid across Peace River, slipped under the highway, glided past warehouses, gravel piles and sidings holding ancient, rotting rolling stock. He sighed, looking up at the brightening sky and quickly dwindling stars. The situation strained his control, but this was the big ticket, the oh-so-important task he had been kept in reserve for in recent months, despite his requests to be set free, to lose himself in the stars and start again. No, he was too valuable, too important, too skilled a resource to let go. Too much a part of The Old Man's machine to be permitted to slip away, as he had tried once before. He had almost made it out too, but no. Quirky Quinton and his psychotic drama queen wife had fucked things up for him. The limp-wristed clotheshorse had gone AWOL from San Francisco, Jennifer Kirby had gone off the deep end, and he had to pick up the pieces, to shovel the shit until things were back the way the old bastard wanted them. Well, at least he got to square up with Quirk, TOM's orders be damned. That he could look forward to once he'd lured the private dickhead to Genextric, as instructed. Terjesen was dead meat walking, or crawling. He sniggered. Rowland was a pity, but he'd stuck his nose in where he shouldn't. So, he would do his job: one down, three to go. Then he was leaving Earth and most definitely not coming back.

He scanned the other passengers in the carriage. Six: two couples, two solo. Old folks and young lovers, business formal and smart casual, work and pleasure, as if those couldn't be the same thing. All were The Old Man's customers in some way or other, were served by Genextric or Androicon or Geeocorp, any number of other cogs in the C Corp machine, doing mankind's dirty work at home and on distant worlds. Not that he was an enviro-junky— all was fair in the pursuit of survival. But it was the foot soldiers who paid, the Rowlands and Terjesens, the Meyers, even the Quirks, but not Derek Morton, not this time.

What was the point of this navel-gazing? Was he one day going to repay his debt to society? He grunted. The first step towards redemption would be to recognise he had a problem, that he craved control and would not give it up. The key was not to become addicted. That was The Old Man's trick, giving enough to draw you in, feeding your craving. Because he knew control was as much a curse as it was a prize, because you became responsible for everything. Not anymore. A few more days and he would be done. Done and gone, never to return.

He watched the passengers in their blissful ignorance, savouring his secrets. The train was less than two hours from Hay River on the south shore of Great Slave Lake. The boat would meet him. Another fifty minutes across the lake and he'd be in Yellowknife for dinner. Not that he'd have time to eat. Too much to do. The situation was not nearly chaotic enough yet for The Old Man's purposes, but chaos was Derek Morton's business.

0C

08:03, 20 November 2099
Highway 1, north of Golden, BC
1,734km south of Yellowknife

Quirk watched the sun crest the mountaintops across the valley as they trudged south towards the town of Golden. Long, fir tree-shaped shadows reached up the bank beside them, numerous vehicles passed but nobody stopped. Probably just as well, since their images may already be prominent on Famebook's "Most Wanted" page. They couldn't run again. Luck had played a big part in their escape from Creston, but they couldn't rely on further aid from that lady, it wasn't fair to Moth. It troubled him how easily he forgot she was a child, already so capable as she was. No, they needed anonymous transport to Yellowknife, preferably not stolen, and they needed it now.

He pondered this as they walked, also replaying his fruitless call to Genextric. It was disappointing Eve Meyer had not called back. Was she in cahoots with Morton? Not in his circle of trust, of course, because he didn't have one, but conniving with him to cover up the whole missing person thing? Clearly, the missing woman had been savaged by one of Genextric's products. Could she be a protestor? Maybe Morton had set the beasts on her, that was his style. Search and Recover teams would be scouring the landscape. Meyer would have her hands full, complicit or not.

And he should assume the mystery call was a trap, that the efficacy of the satellite line was too convenient, the explanation too plausible—a master hacker indeed, ha!

Probably a staffer playing the part under TOM's instruction. He certainly wouldn't fall for that old trick, but perhaps they could use it to their advantage. It would be just like The Old Man to reveal his plans to Quirk when there was not a jot of proof to give the authorities, then dangle his son as bait to bring him to Yellowknife. Was his son—Nick—bait now, not a red flag? And was murder insufficient for the old bastard, did TOM fancy to pin election fraud on him too? Maybe he perceived Quirk as a threat after his years on the inside. He'd be delighted to live up to that expectation, give TOM a bloody nose.

They passed the odd long driveway, each snaking up to a sprawling, chalet-style home. Their feet crunched on the snow at the highway's edge. Their breath fogged in the chill air. Cars appeared, seeming to come from nowhere, whooshing out of the silence around a bend or over a crest, then swished past, disappearing just as quickly into stillness. Silent as their motors were, vehicles still tore a hole in the air, their studded tyres still rasped on the icy surface.

Moth glanced around nervously as they walked, no doubt on the lookout for bears. "You should phone Eve Meyer again," she said.

"We mustn't appear too pushy."

"Yes, we should. We need help. Let's blackmail her into sending us a helicopter."

"Typical flight time to Yellowknife, 2.7 hours," Eighty intoned from the back of their ragtag line. "After double verifying C Corp comms link security. Also, the Laws and Tenets require me to recommend against blackmail."

"How about emotional blackmail?" asked Moth.

"There is more scope for emotional blackmail," Eighty admitted.

"That's all very well," said Quirk, aware he sounded testy, "but we can't afford to trust her, or Mystery Caller."

"Train," said Moth, insistently. "I like trains."

"The closest rail connection is Canmore, Alberta. Typical travel time to Hay River, 5.4 hours. Boat from Hay

River to Yellowknife, 0.8 hours. Drive time from Golden to Canmore, 1.2 hours. Walking time from this location to Golden, 1.4 hours. Total travel time estimated at 9.5 hours, including delay contingency."

"Yes, thank you, Eighty."

"We're supposed to be taking charge, remember?" asked Moth, unhelpfully.

"Yes! Thank you, Moth." The numerous logistical, administrative and law enforcement obstacles ranked in Quirk's mind in the order that he intended to bellow them at his companions, but his righteous anger dropped to the pit of his stomach almost instantly. His son. It was incredible. The mere fact that he felt this sudden, unaccountable physical reaction at the thought of seeing him should be proof enough of some trap set by The Old Man, ready to be sprung by Morton, maybe Eve Meyer.

"Right," Quirk held up his hand and stopped walking. "Board meeting. Eighty, take minutes, please. Item One. I admit that The Old Man has rattled me, probably damaged me in some fundamental way during those years of bullying that passed for employment. Moth"—he put a hand on her shoulder and she smirked up at him—"take an action to kick me in the shin—metaphorically—if he intrudes again on this investigation and I appear to be weakening in any way.

"Item Two. We're in a bind and I accept the need to buckle down in the pursuit of Morton—"

"Point of order, sir?" Eighty asked as Quirk drew in a breath. "One of the utmost importance to our present situation."

Stifling a grunt, Quirk made the international flappy hand gesture for "Spit it out."

"Barry Rowland's ID was used to board a train in Creston, implying that Derek Morton is now forty kilometres north of Peace River, and will reach Yellowknife in approximately three hours."

"Damnation. Item Three. I tender my resignation as chair of the Taking-the-Initiative Committee. Moth, you are elected by acclamation. Item Four. What are we going to do now?" Regarding the others gave Quirk time to contemplate the fact that he *had* dropped the ball with these distracting calls, and perhaps that was their purpose all along. But, somewhere in the increasing morass of misdirection there was some kind of truth, and it was his job to find it. He had lost sight of that.

"Get to Yellowknife and kick Morton in the nuts," said Moth.

"Seconded," said Quirk. "Okay, meeting adjourned. Let's crack on. Time check, please, Eighty."

"Eight twenty-seven AM."

"Thank you. So, let's target being in Yellowknife this evening, and you will have my best efforts to get us there. Eighty, please work your magic with the satellite link and send the owner of the Five-Star remodelled by Ursa Mater a sum twice the car's value as new. Then, let's get into Golden before we get collared."

The android nodded and Quirk started forward with purpose, sticking out his thumb as the next set of headlights appeared. Moth marched in front, swinging her arms. He could not help but smile. Renewing one's purpose felt good.

Once or twice, he thought they had a ride, but those drivers only slowed to stare at their sartorial schizophrenia. Even if Kreski had put their images out, they looked so down-at-heel that Quirk did not even bother to lower his head. The time between vehicles gave him more moments in which to consider the scale of their problem. Because he *believed* Mystery Caller that a national election was the stake The Old Man played for. It felt right. Call it a hunch. He'd read about detectives having those. His acceptance of the endgame brought up too many uncomfortable memories, of things he'd done for TOM and regretted, and the thing he had—at the end—refused to do. He remembered meeting Giulia di Fantano at the convent when he'd arrived with Moth, but also a time two years before, seeing her at Toni's mansion in her element, the vibrant hostess, all radiance and hospitality before the bullets began to fly. How glad he was that he had—unlike Morton—resisted the infection of thoughtless loyalty, that he had defied The Old Man when he reached the step too far. That he had not killed Toni.

But refusing to act was one thing, striking against TOM was another. It would bring repercussions and it wasn't just him anymore, there was his fourteen-soon-to-be-fifteen-year-old charge to consider. He could not ignore that responsibility. But neither did that mean he should walk away; he was supposed to set an example for Moth. And she would be livid if he gave in, bless her fearless, if sometimes misdirected, heart.

Once more unto the breach then.

He pulled his jacket tighter. The valley had opened up on their right, bright sun bleaching the distant mountains, draping a silver haze across them. Golden light splashed the bank to their left, bringing life to rich browns and yellows against the white snow. The number of roadside signs was increasing, and they passed the first election boards as they tramped purposefully onwards. For no apparent reason, Moth planted her boot in the middle of the next sign they encountered, sending it skittering across the snow out onto the road, across it and down the bank.

"Politics is shit," she said and lashed out at the next bright sign—a green one—which tumbled into the long grass as another car—quite reasonably—failed to stop.

"No, Moth," he corrected, "*politicians* are shit, but only some of them."

"But if The Old Man's fixing the election, some of them must be in on it, right?"

"Possibly," he said, "but you know Toni must have had some in his collection."

"Oh, okay. Yeah, still sucks."

"It does. There is more grey in politics than anything else if you ask me: the grey of mediocrity, of indecision, of misdirection."

"Shitload of brown too, if you ask me," said Moth.

"Ha-ha," said Quirk.

Distracted by their conversation, he was only aware of a large vehicle pulling up next to them when it shut out the sunlight. The side of the tall, cuboid vehicle in Lake Como blue slid open revealing a cosy living room as the driver's seat swivelled to face into the compartment and the open door.

"Looks like you folks could use a ride to town."

The larger lady addressing them projected a motherly aura, right down to the authoritative undertone threatening censure if any bad behaviour occurred. A low table separated her rotated seat from a middle bench divided into three chairs, a child on each one. Floor grooves located and secured the chairs around a gaming board. Four tawny faces of varying ages, expressions as warm and welcoming as his and Moth's must be pasty and cold, regarded them with obvious interest. From the corner of his eye, he saw Moth's head tilt towards him without taking her eyes off the family in the car.

"Are they playing Risk?" she murmured.

"I...believe they are."

"Are you folks lost? Car trouble?" asked the lady in the driver's seat, with no flickering of recognition.

"Not this family wagon," Moth hissed through gritted teeth. "Get the next car."

"In a hurry, remember?" he whispered from the corner of his mouth. He smiled at the lady, *Charm Personified, Late Harvest, 2087.* "That's very kind of you, ma'am. We'd be most grateful. Wouldn't we, dear?"

"We surely would," said Moth, sourly.

She needed to make a few experience rolls in dissembling. It may be outside her base character class, but the skill featured in most scenarios they encountered.

Maybe, if she aced her exams, he could convince her rocket science remained a growth area.

Mom tapped at the vehicle's control screen and chairs slowly repositioned themselves, the arrangement becoming more compact, enabling three more chairs to flip up and click into place. The lady waved them in like an extension of her brood. Moth stepped up, although only with Quirk's hand on her back, encouraging her toward one of the new seats. As she turned to sit, she elbowed him in the ribs, at which he smiled pointedly to show her the hard feelings would be held over until later.

Moth plonked herself down, folding her arms so the lap belt could engage. Quirk did the same, and Eighty climbed in last, default smile adorning its lips.

"Off we go then," Mom announced, revolving forwards again.

As the car accelerated, the children turned their chairs to inspect the new passengers. The eldest was a girl, probably twelve; then a boy of nine or ten. The youngest, a sister of six, wore her wavy hair in puffs held by pink ribbons that bounced around as she played peekaboo with Eighty, which supported her play in accordance with Primary Tenet 10. The boy scowled, yet seemed uncertain, glancing from Quirk to Eighty to Moth before returning his attention to the board with the magnetic, automated pieces. Quirk leaned forward to inspect the game. The boy made an exaggerated pout.

"Are you winning?" Quirk asked.

"No"—the boy's scowl deepened—"Deerdra is." He jerked his thumb towards his older sister, who smoothed her long, straight hair and smiled at Moth.

Quirk nodded knowingly. "Girls are good at tactics," he whispered conspiratorially. "We need to make up for that in other ways."

"But her arms are longer," the boy's brow furrowed. "I'm Jerold," he added.

Quirk nodded, remembering the school days of a short, timid, nondescript boy, namely himself. "Not physically, Jerold. There's one thing girls and grownups can't resist if you get it right, that's charm...and politeness. So, two things, and they take practise, might feel like you're giving in sometimes, but pick your battles. Like Risk."

"Does it work on sisters?"

"I believe so, although I don't have any," he noted Moth's sidelong glance.

Quirk smiled as Jerold reviewed the board. His own son would be much older now due to the...cloning process's accelerated early development. He had shut out all notions of what fatherhood might be like...until now. He glanced at Moth and Deerdra, conversing in the short, hesitant sentences of strangers thrown together. Jerold turned back and looked up at Quirk with widening eyes. "I think I get it!"

"Good boy."

The ride into Golden passed quickly and smoothly. The family's destination lay beyond the town, but Mom went out of her way to drop them at the HoJo Inn on Lafontaine Road. To Quirk's surprise she followed them out of the van.

"Hey!" Jerold called from the open door. "Why are your clothes so funny?"

Quirk laughed, looked down at his Priceless Princess sweatshirt, and cringed. He did not have a good answer to that.

"Jerold! Mind your manners, young man." Mom came up to Quirk and pressed something crinkly and plastic into his hand. "Don't argue, I won't have it. I don't know what times you've fallen on. Maybe it's just a glitch and you've got cash in the bank; they don't hand out droids on Social Security. Maybe you're heading to dig up a pot o' gold, but I reckon you're a bit short right now and this might help some, so take it gracefully. Pay it on some day."

She drew him into a hug, and Quirk felt a sudden lump in his throat, a little mist in the corner of his eye. "Thank you, ma'am. Lord protect you." Where did *that* come from? Somehow, it felt like the right thing to say in the face of unqualified kindness. Moth got a hug too, and he clenched, seeing raw emotions warring across her features, but she accepted it amiably, even returned it some. Mom returned to the vehicle and the car drove away. The two youngest children waved. Quirk looked down at his hand.

"What she give you?" asked Moth.

"A hundred dollars," he said, struggling with a sudden dryness in his throat.

0D

They went directly into the Kicking Horse Diner neighbouring the HoJo, Quirk acutely conscious of the tightrope they walked. Did their Good Samaritan not watch the newsfeed, or could Kreski be playing it cool? Neither explanation seemed plausible, but the fact they had got this far without some camera or local police drone tagging them seemed extremely fortunate. Despite his best intentions, all they really could do now was ride this luck; hope The Old Man was not manipulating events to ensure Quirk got to where he wanted Quirk to be, or perhaps hope that he was, and press on regardless.

Moth pushed through the restaurant door. A real bell tinkled, and a waitress turned from polishing cutlery by the wait station.

"Brace yourself," Moth murmured.

Quirk took to the place immediately. Too often, the cutlery in such roadside establishments was of dubious cleanliness, certainly water-marked. The waitress's dark curls bounced off her shoulder as she came to greet them, her smile welcoming, which made him feel all the scruffier. Moth declined the offered window seat and walked to a booth between the side and main entrances. *Good thinking.* He slid in facing the second door, putting the front entry where he could see its reflection in the vending machine. Moth let Eighty in then sat opposite Quirk, watching the front door over his shoulder.

The waitress brought coffee.

"What now?" asked Moth, prodding at the table's inset uPad where the menu was displayed.

"Quick breakfast and consider strategy," he said. Moth nodded, all business-like. He did not cease to be amazed at the speed with which she fluxed between causing him pain, anger, pride, and confusion.

The waitress returned and Quirk tried not to envy her uncomplicated life. Right behind this thought was the heavy hand of guilt smacking the back of his head. How superior he could be, how presumptuous, how jaded. Everyone had their problems, some darkness or other hanging over them. Some managed to put it in its place, others were subjugated by it. He had given himself a chance, leaving after numerous years of unrelenting association with all the wrong types. But he had left Jennifer behind, left Nick. And then there was Moth, already damaged by the life she was born into, already tarred by cynicism and distrust. Not by his hand, of course, but did his way of life cement these traits in her? Shouldn't he change for her? Wasn't that what parents did? Maybe Toni had been right. But could he ever tell her he had seen her parents once?

The waitress—her badge said "Lori"—smiled softly. "Ready to order?"

"You go," said Moth. "Still thinking."

"Falafel steak and eggs, please. Over easy, yoke no softer than No. 2 maple syrup, thank you."

"Uh, okay." Lori tapped into the uPad. "Miss?"

"Waffles, scrambled eggs, NO water in them, five rashers, and if they're not crispy I'm coming back there." Moth jabbed a finger toward the kitchen. "Please."

The food arrived in ten minutes, and they set about it with gusto, not conversing, but letting their eyes roam unobtrusively as they ate. Moth grumbled slightly about the bacon, but it disappeared in jig time. Finally, she pushed her plate away, folding her arms on the table. Her regard settled on something high over his shoulder. She took a pair of earbuds from the table's charge-pad, fitted them, tossed another set to Quirk.

"Both doors, please, Eighty," he whispered, pressing a tiny, expanding bud into his ear, and turned to the screen. As the presenters discussed the election, the tickertape read: "Genextric crisis deepens." Bad as that ticker was, he could only read it three times before the subtitles distracted him.

> *(People in a TV studio, talking animatedly.)*
> *[Sue] —and that's why you can count Peter Liano out of this race, Bob.*
> *[Bob] Three days until the nation votes from the comfort of their homes and Premier Peter Liano is on borrowed time, running last in a three-horse race, three points off the lead. It looks like curtains for Liano. How do you see it, Nabil?*
> *[Nabil] Thanks, Bob. Well, we must consider average data. Aggregate Poll-of-Polls, Poll Averager, Mean Poll, Median Research and Cumulus Issue—*
> *(Man points at graph.)*
> *—we have Benítez on 35.1%, Arnold 32.7% and Liano at 32.2%.*
> *[Sue] That seems like a solid lead for Benítez.*
> *[Nabil] Sue, there is a very real perception of Liano's apparent weakness dealing with the other NAF members. People think US, Mexican and Canadian conglomerates are walking all over him, that he hasn't done enough on corporate regulation.*
> *[Sue] And there you have it, Bob.*
> *[Bob] Thanks, Sue, Nabil.*
> *Now, breaking news from NT. Sensitive viewers should filter their screens.*
> *(Image of snowy lakeshore. Blood spread liberally over foreground.)*
> *This is exclusive local footage of a horrific and bloody scene at a location we can't disclose at this point. This bloody massacre of what our source has confirmed now is*

*eight white-tailed deer occurred just outside Yellowknife
city limits. Our science correspondent is in Yellowknife.
Are you there, Shaun?*

*[Shaun] Yes, Bob, I am. Shaun Lange here in chilly
Yellowknife just outside Genextric's Gamma Laboratory
on Highway 4, and I am not alone. The situation here has
attracted huge attention from journalists, hunters and
naturalists alike. Genextric reports senior security staff
investigating an incident that occurred sometime Sunday
night. First considered an unprecedented escape from this
maximum-security genetic research facility, unconfirmed
suggestions implicate a Genextric employee, Doctor Tania
Terjesen, in some form of malfeasance. The company cites
her unavailable for comment, but I have spoken to a source
who says Terjesen is missing, and our thermal scans
confirm her house is empty.*

*Bob, local citizens are extremely worried. A curfew has
been implemented over the hours of darkness, but many
are going further; stocking up on supplies and locking
themselves in their homes and bunkers until the situation
is resolved. Yet some have braved the cold, dark skies and
what appears to be a gathering storm, to speak to me—*

*[Bob] I'm sorry, Shaun, I must cut you off there. Reports
are coming in of a new kill site. It's unclear whether this is
more wildlife, or perhaps human victims—*

A grey-haired man in an apron marched out of the
kitchen and switched off the feed then began
remonstrating with the waitresses. Moth turned to face
Quirk.

"What the actual fuck?"

Quirk let his gaze drift around the restaurant. "It begins
to look like Barry stumbled across this doctor, and Morton
plans to finish these creatures' work."

Moth nodded earnestly. "But what was the trigger?" She
smoothed her hair and made bored young girl posing and
preening motions. "Trying to cover up a mistake? Did she

trip or was she pushed for some other reason? Or could she be at fault? Just 'cause Derek's a douche, doesn't mean Terjesen is Little Miss Perfect."

"Little Doctor Perfect," Quirk mused. "Eighty, let's call Genextric again."

"I will relay the call to your earbuds and any picture to the table's uPad, outside the diner's systems, of course."

"Of course," said Quirk.

Eighty displayed a neutral smile as the North American Federation standard dialling tone played in Quirk's ears.

"Good morning, Genextric Gamma Laboratory, Yellowknife, NT. How may I direct you?" said the typical syRen® tones.

Quirk didn't give a good goddamn if TOM *was* listening, in fact he hoped he was, Morton too. "Doctor Tania Terjesen, please," he said with sales rep swagger.

"Doctor Terjesen is unavailable at present. May I direct you elsewhere, or ask the nature of your enquiry?"

"Derek Morton then."

"Mister Morton is off site. I can connect you to his handset—"

Quirk contemplated the unpleasant message he would leave to stir the bastard up, but it wouldn't achieve anything. "No, thank you. How about Eve Meyer?"

"Connecting you now."

"Eve Meyer, who's calling?"

The suddenness of the connection surprised him, even more so Meyer spurning the image filter. Her striking green-grey eyes were bloodshot, with puffy bags above smooth cheeks that might have been prettily rosy on another day, but today were pale. And her lipstick did her no favours. She'd been outside, perhaps had seen something that upset her. So it seemed from the way she had tugged on her suit, not straightening shirt or jacket. *A nice suit too: McCartney?* That thought made him as miserable as she looked. Meyer tossed her blond fringe at him in what looked like defiance.

"I'm busy. Speak to me, Mister...?"

"Quirk."

"Mister...Quirk."

"Just Quirk." She refrained from commenting on his sobriquet, just stared back, waiting. *Unresponsive, distracted: classics for depression.*

"I'm looking for Tania Terjesen. I gather she's not there."

Long intake of breath, likely forcing calmness.

"She's unavailable, and I can't comment on the situation, if you're digging for info. Please tell your people to stop calling here. An update will be issued later today."

Defensiveness, unwarranted in the absence of aggressive stimulus. "I don't have people, Ms. Meyer," he winked at Moth. "Do you know a man called Barry Rowland?"

"I've met Barry." Puzzlement at the shift in subject. *"What about him?"*

Time to apply a pressure test. "He's dead, Ms. Meyer. Murdered in Creston less than twenty-four hours ago."

That was the spark. Meyer sat forward, tossed her fringe again and started typing on her keyboard. Her pale lips tightened, but her eyes took on a shine that seemed to chill the red out of them, leaving a fresh, clear incisiveness. She scanned her screen and looked back at the camera. *"What do you know about it? And please do me the favour of turning on your screen."*

Politeness and concision: he liked that. Grace under pressure, after a shaky start. He nodded to Eighty, suddenly conscious he hadn't shaved in what felt like months.

"Rowland is my client. I'm a private investigator. I'm in Canada with my associates pursuing his case."

"His last request?" It was rhetorical. Her eyes narrowed and were tugged to something on her screen before flicking back to meet his across the digital divide. *"How is Tan—Doctor Terjesen involved with Rowland? You asked for her first."*

Her mind was as sharp as her gaze under whatever befuddlement had blunted her demeanour. And he must look like a hobo, or perhaps an out-of-work art critic slash ski bum. Gutter chic: he didn't like it.

"Rowland mentioned her." A modest fib, but he was confident now that Barry's damsel and Terjesen were one and the same, and perhaps Eve was more than her boss.

Meyer tapped at her desk.

"No record of Rowland entering this building, but that doesn't mean they didn't meet socially. Tell me about it, maybe I can help. What was he doing in Creston?"

"I'm not at liberty to say. Client confidentiality."

"Come on," she leaned forward, grasping his questions like a lifeline. *"Tell me."* She looked under severe pressure, understandable with Morton in her life. *"Give me something. Maybe we can help each other. It's a secure line."*

Okay, a tad naïve if she believed that working for a C Corp company, but she didn't know The Old Man like he did. Nobody knew TOM like he did, apart from Morton. Could she be complicit in Derek's scheme? It was safest to assume so, for now. So, a moment of truth, but not necessarily for truth. He would give her the version Rowland had given Kreski. "I asked about Derek Morton too. Tell me where he is, and I'll tell you what my client said about Doctor Terjesen."

That did it. Her eyes glinted like sundogs above the frozen tundra of her expression. *"Morton isn't here right now."*

If he had any skill at all in reading people, Eve Meyer couldn't care less where Morton was, but preferred as far away as possible, and ideally in terrible pain. He nodded, keeping his reaction neutral. "I believe he's on his way back to you."

"He was in Creston?! Is he involved?"

"In what?"

"Rowland's death, of course. Have you spoken to him?"

"I'm not at liberty—"

"For fuck's sake, Quirk, screw liberty. What do you want? Just ask me! I'm up to my—" She stopped herself, brushed blond hair back from her forehead, and her corporate mask fell back into place. *"I'm extremely busy, Mister Quirk, and have no time to bandy words. If you have anything specific to offer that will aid our present situation, I'd be glad to hear it, otherwise, we're done."*

"Okay, Ms. Meyer. Eve..." He could think of no reason not to stick a knife into Morton and disrupt *his* day, for once. "We know Morton was in Creston because I saw him. He and I have met before. I strongly believe he is implicated in my client's murder, and we are en route to Yellowknife to prove it. I know you have problems up there, you're on the news"—he grimaced—"but I'll need to speak with you when we arrive. Will you meet us?" He smiled, *hesitant, sensitive; a balm for the troubled brow.*

"If I have time." She nodded curtly. *"Call me when you're close, and you'd better get here quickly. The RCMP deployed last night and there's talk of the FBI, the CDC and the North American Humane Society dropping in. And don't speak to anyone before you get here. I don't need any more interlopers sticking their nose in, media crews are already making my life next to impossible. How far out are you?"*

"We'll arrive this evening, with a fair wind." Something in Meyer's harried demeanour struck of chord of sympathy in him. "Keep your chin up." He gave her his *925 Sterling Silver Lining* smile. "What's the worst that can happen?"

She scowled, another chink in the corporate armour. *"Whatever it is, I feel I'm about to find out."* Meyer hung up without ceremony.

Quirk gazed contemplatively at Moth, who stared at him, stroking her chin.

"Are you mocking me?"

"Yes," she said, earnestly, "and I respect your analysis, but how about I give you the female perspective. Eighty, please replay the call, per favore."

The two (or three, subject to employment law in a company's state of registration) members of The Quirk Agency contemplated Eve Meyer's image.

"She's got good clothes, cares for her skin and nails. She's a together person, normally, but she's letting things slip, so things must be bad. She flinches slightly when you mention Terjesen, so they're friends, maybe more. She's hopeful when you spring Morton on her, like she'd love him to take a fall, imminently and hard."

Quirk became conscious of the diner again. All the customers watched the big screen, including the grey-haired chef-patron, who had relented. Images live from Yellowknife showed red-flashing lights rushing along a deserted street. The ticker announced "Liano takes charge: NAF president preparing National Guard deployment."

* * *

Quirk called it fortunate, but Moth knew it was wicked skill. Fishing for a ride in the diner? Her call, because every sort of person used diners, and what they needed was an everyday Joe, or Jo, heading somewhere that would get them on the fastest route north. They'd nixed airplanes due to every man Jack, woman Jill and person Jay with a cap, uniform or nametag probably watching for their pretty faces. No more jacking cars, that hadn't gone great. So, they needed the right kind of ride. Enter Moth: human genius. She set Eighty listening in on all conversations in the diner, skimming travel details, flagging people that fit the bill. Thinking back to the sandwich-dispensing trucker, she listed scruffy, lone and male among Eighty's search parameters then, grudgingly, added personality indicators such as respectful, kind and understanding. People who didn't care why you needed help, just that you did. People like Risk Mom.

Old feelings stirred like the ones triggered by sharing with Quirk. Totally her turn now she reckoned, after what she'd learned about his past. She scowled. Dishing the dirt had been her idea. At least it looked as painful for him as it was for her, so that was something. But she squashed those feelings. *No time now. We need to get moving.*

Eighty said listening to private conversations was cool with the Laws and Tenets because he didn't record shit or dish any details to them. She walked Quirk through it, using the longest words she could. Those were the ones he understood the best.

"You mean people like Lori?" Quirk raised an eyebrow.

"What? No: she's probably a cheerleader."

"You say that like it's a bad thing."

"Princesses just leave you in the lurch."

Quirk had the good grace to drop his chin, knowing which nerve he'd hit. Moth's thoughts drifted to a cobbled Milan side street where two beautiful, happy women and a little dark-haired girl danced in their summer dresses, while the men drank grappa, laughed and sang along. And now her mamma and *papà* were dead, and Uncle Toni was dead, and Aunt Giulia was in the convent, but who knew with the Brotherhood, even with Cousin Mario as capo. One fucked-up mafioso, and bang. She crushed those feelings again. *Fuck, why always when I need it least, when I'm busy with something?* At least at night she didn't need to fight the hollow feeling.

When Lori brought more coffee, Moth kept quiet. She knew that's what Quirk would want, space to do his thing. Whatever, she just felt like crying now. At least when he was distracted, he didn't pry into her feelings. He'd been doing that more this last month; trying to save her or some shit like that. Although the sharing had been her idea. He was so tight-lipped, and she wanted to know more about him: who wouldn't when they spent so much time together? At least he didn't act up with Lori. No mirroring, open position, minor self-disclosure, balancing eye-contact to avoid visual dominance. Moth allowed herself a little smile. Psych was her favourite class. She'd never admit it to him, but Quirk was a natural, dyed-in-the-wool people-person. He loved everyone, or started out trying to, but he could be clumsy at showing it.

Lori departed with a nod and a smile. Moth tried to like the girl, watching her serving regulars, smiling, nodding, listening, engaging with the people. Sometimes she hated hate: it was exhausting. But people were not all the same. She was as closed to people as Lori and Quirk were open, but people had been treating her like shit since she was old enough to attract more than a smile and a pat on the head. Maybe Quirk could save her, just not the way he thought. She just wanted him to sit there and fucking listen, like he did with other people, but not her, not really, not yet.

"Moth?"

"Huh? Right. Pretend I didn't hear a fucking word of that."

"Lori's calling her friend's great-grandmother. She's returning to Canmore soon. Lori thinks great-granny will drive us to the station."

"Oh, good, more homey car chatter. I can't hardly wait." He smiled in that patient way that made him look like a prize arse that had just dropped a pan-filler. She puffed her cheeks. Sure, Quirk was good for a sudden spurt of insight, but practicalities often passed him by. "Look, I know I'm the 'foul-mouthed little shit' of the group—quote, unquote—but Granny's just going to go along with this, no questions asked?"

Quirk smiled—*No. 2 Pan-Filler* again. "Observation is the key." He tapped the side of his nose, raising a desire in her to punch his smug *naso*. "Did you spot the tattoo on Lori's ankle? Reinventionist. It turns out her family has an anti-establishment bent. Our status didn't come up, and I don't think it will."

"Aw, baby's first hunch, that's so fucking touching," she scowled.

"What's got your goat?" he asked, clearly offended.

She waved a hand. "Forget it. Something went down the wrong way." She leaned back in the red pleather booth and checked out the big screen news feed. Now the images showed soldiers marching across a runway. Cut to more soldiers loading gear into the gaping maw of a big, stealth-black transport chopper, a Sikorsky-Mil SiMi-142. No, the 142a with the secondary radar bulge on the wheel pod. Two more lurked in the background. The strapline chuntered urgently.

"First deaths in YK—three-man fishing party attacked—Liano sends in troops."

Well, that's just fuzking peachy.

"I think we need to get a move on while Yellowknife has some residents left."

OE

Two FBI agents led Eve down the corridor in the Sheriff's Station. She felt cold. Not from being escorted from her office past a good proportion of her staff, anxious, suspicious eyes following her, wondering if she was coming back. Not because they led her outside by the arm in only her suit, across the frozen car park among the snow-dusted trees to their big, smoked-plass-windowed black AWD. It was not from the numbness in her head as silent, deserted streets slipped past the window against the backdrop of an overcast sky. Her chill arose from the loss of control.

Although things were out of hand, she had been back at her desk, planning, directing staff, reviewing SRT reports, monitoring the vuldolph feeds. They were reducing the search area, closing on their targets. It was a race against time with the winning post in sight, and then the race was lost. She shook her head, numb. People had been badly hurt, savaged. It was miraculous those hunters weren't dead.

They led her into the same room where she'd met Kootook, but he wasn't there. They put her in the cheap, metal chair that scraped on the floor when pulled out. The men in matching black windcheaters stepped back to flank the door. They might as well have been wearing sunglasses for all the personality in their blank faces. Across the table sat a woman of equally anonymous appearance. Straight, mid-brown hair, tied back tight enough to accentuate green-brown eyes. Pale, unadorned lips maintaining a neutral baseline, eyebrows thin, inconsequential. Eve shifted and the aluminium chair creaked.

"This is a test," said the woman, her eyes never leaving Eve's face.

Because everyone loves a test. "Ask away," said Eve sullenly, although a bad attitude would not make this any easier. She put on her business face.

"Not that kind of test," said the woman. "The kind where you justify your existence."

Take charge, Eve, keep control 'til they pry it from your cold fingers. "We're close to regaining control, all protocols operating as intended. The search area—"

"People are hurt, Meyer. Doing everything would involve terminating your products, don't you think? What happened to *that* protocol? Too expensive"

"This morning's...outcome is extremely regrettable." *No "but," "but" is an excuse.* "The MT's Demon Seed was disabled...by the miscreant. Still, Genextric's response is fully in accordance with our federal license—"

"Your friend caused this, but you're responsible. That must make you angry."

Ah, that kind of test. "I'm not angry, anger has no place in this. I'm trying to make things right. That's my job."

"You're failing, Meyer." Disgust freighted the FBI agent's words.

"We'll get nowhere by making this personal, if that's your intention..." *You fucking government lackey.* "You might as well arrest me now. But first, consider the tax-payer dollars you'd be pissing away against C Corp's immovable object."

The agent's eyes narrowed. "That sounded like a threat."

She *so* wanted to slap this woman, backhanded, both sides. "A constructive suggestion. We have all the knowledge here."

"I doubt it, and so does the president. The National Guard is being deployed. There should be boots on the ground later today."

"Won't that cramp your style, agent?"

She looked puzzled. "Who do you think points the NG in the right direction?"

Her eyes shone hard, like she wished Eve had died with Tania, which perhaps she should have. *Like hell. And Tania isn't dead.* She continued to choose to believe that. *Christ, I need a drink.* She needed to get out of here, now.

"The truth is, Meyer, we're just too busy to process you. So, you get to sit on your hands for a few days until this is all sorted out."

"Without charge? I'm not in the wrong here," Eve snapped.

"That's debatable, but protective custody will keep you out of my hair while I do my job, and stop you screwing this up any further."

"Did..." *Derek fucking Morton, did you do this?*

The woman signalled and the agents moved. Keeping her face utterly expressionless, Eve reached into her pocket. Her heart hammered on her ribs. Even if Morton's suspending of her had not been unilateral, she was betting this went way beyond him. Perhaps she had one more card to play.

The woman's apologies for eyebrows fluttered up as Eve placed her handset on the table facing the agent. Eve didn't look down, but held the agent's gaze and—channelling hardcore contempt—placed all five righthand fingertips on the screen. She gave the agent an arctic smile as the screen illuminated, displaying the head and shoulders of a hard-faced man with greying hair, his mood turning sour as milk in the sun. His voice rolled out of the speaker like distant thunder.

"Vincent Collinson, attorney for Genextric. Who am I addressing?"

Eve spread an open hand towards the handset, indicating the agent should speak.

"Uh, Special Agent-in-Charge Prescott...sir."

"Prescott, do you see me straightening my tie?"

"I do..."

"Prescott, I'm straightening my tie because I'm leaving my office to join Pete Liano's chief-of-staff for lunch. Do you want me to mention your name in our conversation?"

Prescott looked at her agents who studiously examined the wall. She flicked a glance at Eve, hesitated—swallowing something bitter—then answered, "No, sir. Ms. Meyer was just leaving."

"Good," said Collinson. The image lurched as he stood. *"Meyer, call me later."*

Eve wasted no time in standing and scooping up her handset. She walked to the door and opened it without objection from the agents, although they tracked her the whole time. She would still have a chance to drop a lid on this, to find Tania. Maybe the chance to fuck Morton up would arise along the way.

"Meyer." Prescott was standing now, lips twisting with distaste, handset in hand. "It says here you've got three hours before the National Guard land in Yellowknife. My orders to them will be to lay waste to anything standing more than two feet off the ground. Once we put your beasts to the sword, I will come looking for you."

Prescott smiled spitefully. "Better hustle."

* * *

10:58, 20 November 2099
Genextric Gamma Laboratory, Ingraham Trail, Yellowknife

Eve's head jerked up from the latest vuldolph data to see Morton pushing into her office. His skin was pink and pinched with the cold, and snow clung to the shoulders of his jacket. The fabric hissed and crinkled as he shrugged out of the navy NuFrontier puffer and threw it on her sofa.

"What the hell are you doing talking to the FBI?" he growled, shadowed eyes suggesting a lack of sleep.

She stood up, some part of her brain knowing to make herself bigger to repel the threat. "Two goons marched me out of here an hour ago because you hadn't wasted enough of my time. If you people would leave me the fuck alone, I could sort out this mess." She clamped down the urge to slap him. "Where the hell were you while I've been wrestling this man-made disaster?"

"Something related." He took a breath, supressing his temper. "And it's a woman-made disaster, as you seem to have forgotten. What have you been doing?"

"I released the vuldolphs," said Eve. "They located five new kill sites in the last six hours. I've reported to Kootook. I'm coordinating the SRTs with *my* security chief, while avoiding a squad of ten C Corp goons—yours I presume—who arrived last night and have been in my way ever since. In summary, a damn sight more than you.

"They're moving back into town, Morton. Killed twenty-six snow hares between Fox Lake and Fred Herne Park. Butchered three caribou near Frame Lake. That's a ten-minute walk from Canadian Tire!"

"I get it. I'm here now."

"Too late for those fishermen—" she half-choked, an invisible weight clamping her throat. He sounded so calm. "Three men in a camper, all maimed. So, what now, genius? This is your area, supposedly. Sixty-five people in this building: how do we shut down the MTs *and* identify Tania's accomplice before the army arrives in two hours?" Another fucking deadline. "Two hours!"

She frowned, realising she was thinking only of the people in this building, the population of Yellowknife, and Tania, who damn well *was* alive until Eve Meyer said otherwise. It wasn't about tidying up G-Lab's mess anymore, it was about saving lives.

Morton clamped his big hands on his hips. "We can do this, if we work together." He smiled grimly. "I need your help, Eve. Can we work together?"

She stared at him, fighting the urge to gape. Was this what it took for him to bench his inner asshole? Wow, just three maimed people, a hundred dead animals and a national emergency. She considered various barbed responses, but all she said was "Yes," and instantly hated herself for it, but it wasn't about her.

To his potential credit, Morton didn't make anything of it. His expression remained flat. "It's time for the Armageddon option."

"Shit." News blackout, terminate cooperation with authorities, release the "hounds." "Is that all we've got now?"

It was all she could say. She'd considered it, briefly, immediately dismissing it because the SRTs were closing in. Was he right? It might save lives—Tania or some unsuspecting bystander—but the chaos it could cause... "We're not there in the emergency plan, and it's not endorsed in the bipartisan memorandum with—"

"I know," he said, cutting across her, "but we're on the edge now, Eve. I don't like you; you don't like me: boo-hoo. We must act decisively while we still can. The mangetouts' Demon Seed is disabled, but we can still use Armageddon to corral them and kill them. The VRs won't be out long if we're as close as you think."

He was tense, expectant. His handset buzzed. He pulled it from his pocket, the screen flashing. Her handset vibrated on her hip, and her terminal emitted an urgent pinging that could not be ignored. *Oh, shit.*

It was *her* security man.

"Connor, what?"

"Eve, Derek," his Irish brogue came at her from all three sources. *"Two deputies were attacked by a pair of MTs on the edge of Bristol Pit, by the cemetery. A news crew on site filmed the attack before Kootook could shut them down. Both officers hospitalised, one is critical."* Eve's eyes locked with Morton's. His were hard, unreadable. She felt that her gaze was slack-jawed and tightened it up.

Five humans now. *Shit, shit, shit.* She stared at Morton, neither flinching.

"Eve, now," said Morton firmly. "Armageddon option, now."

Release Tania's arch hunters into the wild. She nodded and they moved.

On the elevator ride down to Five, Eve concentrated on breathing. At least she hadn't fallen to pieces immediately at the news of more injured humans. In fact, she felt detached from her emotions, which seethed and boiled somewhere else. She looked sidelong at Morton.

"Where were you?" *And what were you doing?* There was something different about him. This cooperation, that he would resort to *this*...could it be a warning? And there was the call from that Quirk guy, his suspicion.

"Need to know." He tapped the side of his nose with his index finger.

Eve considered how it might feel to shove that digit so far up his nasal vestibule that it disrupted his cerebral frontal pole. "You should have been here."

Morton rolled his eyes. "What is this, *Where's Waldo?*"

"Don't be so fucking flippant. People are seriously injured."

He shrugged. "People, really? Since when was Terjesen 'people' to you?"

"It's not just about Tania, but since you mention it, I don't believe she's dead," she said flatly.

"Hmm," he nodded, looking at the floor of the elevator. "Do you have any cause for that optimism?"

She didn't of course. She rolled her eyes. "Call it queer intuition if you want."

She still suspected Quirk was a reporter on a fishing expedition, but where was the harm in winding up the chiselled wonder? "By the way, some guy called, said he was a detective. He asked about Barry Rowland; said he was dead."

Morton pursed his lips. "Really? Too bad. What's the detective doing about it?"

"Coming here. I told him to call me when he gets in."

Morton nodded. "Good. Let me know when you hear from him. Maybe we can use him. All hands to the pumps, you know?"

"Oh, I know," she said.

Arriving on Five, she pushed out ahead of him and strode to the control room. Vernola and Johari looked worse for wear. Small wonder, they'd been on for eleven hours plus now, and had seen harrowing things, even for Genextric operatives. Maybe like her they were feeling the world closing in on Gamma Lab, hemming them in. She took a moment to reconsider their impending action, but this brought nothing new to her rather fuzzy perspective. Morton was right. The velociraptors would hunt down and terminate the rogue terra-fauna as they were intended to do; the VRs were their backup. It would be terrible media for Genextric, terra-fauna fighting on Earth. She would be dismissed, maybe never find Tania, but so what? This had become about saving lives.

"New protocol. Security code one...seven...Zulu... Bravo...one...one."

Vernola gaped at her. Johari shook his head then nodded and started typing.

Morton was completely calm. "Security code one...Mike...two," he said.

"That's not an initiation code." Eve regretted snapping. She had to get past her default anti-Morton bias, it was getting in the way.

"Special circumstances," he deadpanned.

Annoyingly, Vernola's wavy, auburn hair still bounced like silk after eleven hours as she turned quickly to Eve. "The code's accepted, it's...uh." The young woman turned back to her screen, focusing hard on the display, as if trying to ignore something bad.

Eve frowned, but Vernola's reticence was to be expected. Armageddon protocol was the last roll of the dice. If the authorities had to pick up Genextric's pieces, it would be a massive corporate failure. She had a chance to minimise the damage, put a lid on the chaos, especially with Morton on board. He would be in the firing line too, surely. Perhaps that was motivating his cooperation. Now, they needed each other's help.

Johari peered at his screen. "Adding socmed reports to the search model gives a search zone reduced to eight hundred hectares between the airport and Trappers' Lake."

"Proceed," said Morton, testily, Eve thought.

Vernola's video feed showed the loading dock. An unbadged truck sat in the big service bay, the one they'd used for the vuldolphs. Vernola's unpainted lips drew tight as her fingers flew over virtual keys. Two syRen® entered from the service bay office and positioned the plastext loading tunnel between the goods lift and the truck. Vernola's cheeks paled as she glanced once more over her shoulder at Morton. He nodded and she opened the door in the Level Five velociraptor cage.

The horribly graceful creatures paced into the link corridor with calm intent, as if they knew this moment had been coming, and their patience had paid off. Although on the edge of shaking, Eve allowed a morbid smile to shape her lips. The pseudo-dinosaurs could have been strolling to a meeting in their grey-flashed-with-blue stripes. She couldn't help imagining that they knew their job and relished it. She shook her head. It was too easy to impose human thoughts, human emotions, human cruelty on their hard, calculating expressions. *Coded not to attack humans,* she reminded herself. *Coded to seek and destroy unwanted terra-fauna.* But that was not the same as avoiding contact with humans. Where might that lead? MTs would kill whatever they stumbled across, but velociraptors were hunters. They would pursue tirelessly every single one of Genextric's creations to destruction. Should she have released them sooner? She still would have needed Morton's second authorisation. Moot point. Move on.

"That land is only pine scrub, rock outcrops, waterholes and lakelets," said Morton. "Kootook's curfew and the RCMP cordon will keep people out." *Is he reassuring me?!* "The raptors go in, assist the SRTs. We can do this in two hours."

"Ninety-eight minutes remaining to advised army deployment," said Johari.

The VRs—Eve already thought in press conference-speak—rode the goods lift now, en route to the service bay, but needed to be loaded and deployed. Oversight at all times. Someone had to drive the truck, and the handlers were all out with the SRTs. The building was all admins and scientists. That meant rolling up her sleeves. The buck had stopped. Eve set her jaw.

"Let's go," said Morton. "We'll drive them out together."

In the elevator, all Eve could hear was her breathing. Morton just stood there, chiselled exterior impervious to the avalanche of shit sweeping them away. She let that go, tried to imagine driving a truck with four relentless killers in the back.

On the ground floor they strode towards the service bay. Morton's long legs put him metres in front, and she almost jogged to keep up. She would not fucking run though, no way. They breezed through the corporate areas into utilitarian surroundings where the budget didn't stretch to beige. This was the way that Tania had come, perhaps not alone. Two older model androids flanked the service office door. They must already have loaded the velociraptors. Quick work.

"Emergency protocol one-Mike-two," Morton intoned, still ten metres shy of the door. The droids moved away, striding off on some other errand.

"What's that about?" she snapped. "We need the droids."

"You used a truck in drone mode for the vuldolphs."

"VL protocol is different, you know that," she snapped.

"How about we bend the rules a bit, just this once?"

His sarcasm was sickening. She nodded. "Let's just stick with my plan. We'll dissect the tactics tomorrow over a friendly beer." Her tone was equally loaded, but Morton smiled and nodded. In the service office they traded their top layer for full safety gear, reflective and protective, as the company's PPE slogan went. Morton stooped to re-tie his laces. Shit but he was thorough. Eve fidgeted for a moment then snatched up the truck key and walked to the door into the service bay.

Fucked if I'm letting him drive.

The temperature dropped several degrees as she emerged into the chill of the bright, concrete-floored service bay. She thought of the video footage, Tania being dragged across the floor. Had her accomplice watched, done nothing? What if the accomplice hadn't been rooted by fear, what if they had double-crossed Tania?

The back of the truck was sealed tight, the plastext tunnel retracted. She flipped the truck open from across the loading bay as the service office door thudded behind her. She turned.

Morton stood on the far side of the plass—the wrong side—watching her.

"Come on," she waved him forward. *Unless...* The detective said Rowland had been murdered. His workplace—Hygen—lay next door. Morton had been absent. What if... *He's the accomplice! The bastard let the mangetouts out when Tania was—*

In the service bay. Eve's stomach lurched, her head spun as the orange lights around the transport elevator fired up. Morton watched her implacably.

"Why?!" she screamed at him. The word echoed in the bay. Her thoughts whirled. *Not from spite, it's not personal. Someone told him to. He had started this whole thing. Fuck!*

The lights spun, the goods lift arrived with a heavy clunk. Metal components clacked into action, mechanical parts rattled as the lift door slid upwards. The syRen® hadn't loaded the velociraptors in the truck, they were still in the lift. She saw their big-clawed feet in the widening gap as the door rose.

Coded not to attack humans. NOT to attack humans. That doesn't mean they'll like me being here, but they won't attack. Her heart pounded. Her pulse thudded in her ears as the door revealed: short arms with sharp claws; thick, sinuous necks; probing, pointing jaws filled with teeth; and the searching eyes that found her instantly.

They paced from the lift with calm intent. No need to rush. Eve stood rooted. The service bay roller shutter remained closed, and Morton just stood there in the office. Morton must have conned those androids somehow, mustn't he? How had they left without loading the VRs into the truck, leaving them in the lift against protocol? She tried to remember Tania's words as her beastly creations paced the service bay. They tested the limits of their surroundings, not coming straight for her. Because why would they, they were CODED NOT TO ATTACK HUMANS. Their heads tilted to the side, senses scanning her. *So, if they don't attack, what do they do? I'm about to find out.*

"Where are the droids, Morton? Don't you think they'll report this, step in?" Clearly not, or he would not be doing this, but how could they not? He glanced down and touched something. His voice issued from the speaker somewhere overhead.

"Androicon circumvented the Laws of Robotics fifteen months ago." His eyes shone like black diamonds. "Circumvented isn't the word, more like *isolated*."

"Like they're a goddamned virus? Jesus, Morton. Someone's going to notice. You know that, right?" Slowly, slowly, she backed away from the velociraptors, because that must be the right response, whether they were going to rip her apart or not. They seemed more inquisitive than anything else, but they were inquisitive about her, closing slowly, seeming intent on satisfying that curiosity.

"Whatever," said Morton. "It's above my pay grade. I just do what I'm told."

She could hear the raptors' breathing now. One showed an interest in Morton, one was out of sight behind the truck, and the other pair closed on her. She had worked with scientists long enough to know that "Coded to not attack humans" carried the unspoken rider "according to current research," and maybe "in ninety percent of tests."

Her back bumped the truck. Two dark grey heads twitched. Two mouths opened slightly. She eased back towards the roller shutter door, slipping her handset from her pocket and swiped for the Control Centre.

"Johari, Vernola! Nine—one—one. Repeat, nine—one—one. Abort protocol!"

"They're gone," Morton said. "My associates have cleared the control room. Save your breath."

"What? Oh, your squad of C Corp lackies? But that means—" She was still in sight of the window. Between the beastly grey heads and unflinching raptor stares Morton's gaze tracked her. Then she noticed the lift door had closed again, the hum of motors underscoring her barely contained panic. "Where's the lift going?"

"The goods lift will be busy today," came his answer over the speaker. "The SRTs are about to be swamped with terra-fauna. Just when they were getting a grip. My squad turn out to be anti-GMO activists. They're hacking our system, blinding cameras. Tragically, they are about shoot you as you try to stop them freeing all the terra-fauna to rampage through the city as a protest against genetic modification."

She had reached the back of the truck. It felt like the two impossible dinosaurs herded her into a corner. Sweat slicked her neck, her shirt damp, clinging uncomfortably. Grey lids flicked over orange eyes. She wished her pulse would stop bellowing in her ears. The fear made her legs weak. The velociraptors took turns tilting their heads at her, as if puzzled by the gene-coded directive preventing them from snapping their jaws shut on her neck or ripping off her limbs.

"It's not about you, Meyer. Will you ever get your thick dyke skull round that? Your and Terjesen's drama couldn't matter less." He paused. "Lift's coming back up." The swirling lights confirmed his statement. "It's the cheetahgators. They won't leave much evidence of the bullet I'm about to put in your chest."

Her thoughts flew. Cheetahgators had no coding whatever. Her gaze whipped around. She remembered signing the budget on these Dyson trucks. They'd come at a premium with factory mods. One was a hatch from the rear enclosure into the cab. No one had given her a better explanation than "unforeseen circumstances." She almost laughed as she started reaching for the tailgate release, her eyes never leaving the black-slitted orbs gazing at her from near head height only three metres away.

Morton pushed the office door open, the ugly barrel of a blocky pistol preceding him. Eve had to sway away from the truck to put a raptor in the firing line between them. Another dinosaur appeared around the truck behind her, threatening to block the tailgate. They could *not* be helping Morton, it was just shit luck. Unless killers stuck together. Morton paced carefully, coming for her but avoiding sudden moves. She had one chance left. Eve flung herself at the tailgate handle, wrenching it down. It stuck fast. She twisted behind the truck, closer to the third velociraptor, as a muffled shot caused a thunk near her head. She heard the goods lift clang to a halt, but Morton was in the loading bay, wouldn't release the CGs until he'd shot her.

She risked a peek around the truck's corner. Saurian heads were close, their grey bodies shielding her, but Morton moved wide of them. A shot thwacked the truck's side. She spun back into cover. The third dinosaur was a body length away. She pressed the button on the key in her hand and the truck began to beep, the tailgate tipped, lowering, and the closest velociraptor moved wide of it. Eve threw herself at the angled sheet of metal, not giving it time to open fully. Her fingers curled around the top and she hauled herself up towards the dark gap.

She tumbled over the top, bumping down the tailgate into the back of the truck, landing hard in a heap. Bullets snapped holes in the siding, admitting light. Eve shoved her pain away and scrabbled on her belly the length of the dark compartment. The slight glow helped her find the emergency handle. She hauled down the escape hatch and clawed her way into the cab. Hunkering in the footwell she leaned on the footbrake, reached up and pushed the truck's start button, then jammed both hands down on the accelerator. The truck shot forward, ramming the wall. She was thrown forwards, banging her head, elbow and ribs into parts of the truck. Pain jabbed and punched her all over as the vehicle bucked then dropped down, rear wheels slamming the ground. She grabbed the drive selector, trying to picture the gate, and picked what she thought was reverse as more shots exploded in the confines of the service bay. The side window erupted into fragments that rained down on her.

She reached up for the wheel and yanked down hard in the only direction her grip permitted, her other hand jamming the accelerator. The truck slewed backward in a tight curve, her stomach lurching, and crashed into the wall. She actually felt a pang of concern at possibly crushing a dinosaur. Ridiculous. Maybe now they knew their creators had no equivalent coding when it came to harming them. But smashing into walls wouldn't save her, and she had no bearings now. She snatched a breath and hauled herself into the driver's seat.

She was in a corner facing the service office. She couldn't see Morton, and the raptors had scattered, but the goods lift door was half open and four squat, spotted, massively powerful bodies of the cheetahgators emerged, sinuous scaled tails thrashing, black jaws lined with teeth for rending.

No time to think. Eve planted her foot and pulled the steering hard left. The truck jolted forward, describing a hard arc, veering away from the office, as more dark-clad, armed figures emerged.

The roller shutter came up fast. She had time to correct the steering a hair. A machine gun rattled, the other side window exploded, plass or no. The velociraptors made horrible braying sounds. *Mournful?* The cheetahgators keened. The truck hit the roller shutter hard, jerking to a stop. The cacophony drove her on. She slammed into reverse, shot back, braked too late to avoid hitting the other wall, then plunged forward again at the buckled, hanging roller shutter.

The truck blasted through the door into the snowy Genextric lot, the metal shutter scraping across the bonnet then gone.

She wrestled for control, narrowly missing a line of parked cars, planted her shoe on the power and let the vehicle's control system prevent a skid. Machine guns chattered, bullets rattling the truck's siding. Then she was onto the access road, demolished the security barrier, scattered the reporters, and didn't prise her foot off the floor till she was southbound on Highway 4, teeth clenched in a manic grimace.

OF

Kreski woke with a snap. "Ugh."

He hated waking in the AWD on auto-drive. Sure, the vehicle had kept him going at one hundred while he slept, and sure he'd travelled hundreds of kilometres in that time and had almost reached Canmore, Alberta. But there were hundreds of kilometres left to Yellowknife, and he had not slept well. He still felt the itch of dealing with Golden's distinctly unhelpful sheriff. They sure did have a chip on their shoulder, but he guessed they had their hands full, what with the mayor selling the town's schools to that private education conglomerate without public consultation. He still held out hope of catching Quirk now that the miscreant was on wheels. He would kick the cruise up to one-ten and be there early tomorrow morning, even with the stops he'd organised with sheriffs en route, but dammit, waking up alone in a moving vehicle was still weird.

The music randomised by his handset to wake him was some rapper rhyming about disaster. Then he realised it was *the* rapper du jour, Brother Leigh Love—BLL for short—a fifteen-year-old allegedly out of Slab City, California, although no one could prove or disprove that, since the whole twenty-thousand-population town lay completely off-grid. Notably, the kid could not be proven to come from anywhere else. The growling, angst-fuelled, admittedly catchy, chorus kicked in:

"What's up with your au-tho-ritee
that makes you think you're onto me?
Your way of life sounds wrong to me
it's not meant to be
this hard to be
me.

"What's up with our au-ton-omee
that makes me think you're wrong for me?
Gives you the right to follow me
it's not meant to be
this hard to be
free."

Kreski rubbed his face and thumbed off the music, checked his handset. More attacks in Yellowknife, brutal slaughter of deer, snow hares, and now attacks on people. "Fishermen attacked near Long Lake. Sheriff recalls hunters, requests federal aid."

He might have to rethink going into Yellowknife when he got there. And Barry Rowland had somehow been mixed up in this? And now Quirk and Moth were charging headlong into a genetically engineered shitstorm. He had to admire the dick's commitment to his client, but it was still plain old, unmodified cuckoo. Then again, consistent with the poor judgement those two had shown absconding from Creston. Stealing cars, smashing them up, taking a man's gun presented to him by the mayor. That slick suit and his twisted sidekick would do time for it.

He called the office, putting the image on the vehicle's passenger window. "Parks, how're things?"

"Morning, chief. Quiet enough. The Feds in Vancouver been sniffing around the Quirk thing. They were surprised to hear you're elsewhere at this time."

Kreski scoffed, "They couldn't find their wiener in a hamburger joint, but Denis is okay."

"Tracker says you coming up on Canmore?"

"Yup. I'm meeting Sheriff MacGillacuddy. Feel like I haven't stood up straight for a week." He stretched awkwardly. "I found the stolen Five-Star from Revelstoke. The owner reports receiving an anonymous payment, enough to buy two VAGs. I'm convinced they're on the road to Yellowknife, and I still plan to bring them back."

"Right." Parks looked away then back, her plain features showing doubt. "This Quirk thing stinks. The footfall counter at the med centre doesn't tally with the visitor book and staff roster. I think he's right; there was someone else in that hospital room."

Kreski yawned. "Well, if he is right about the murder and this Morton guy, I need to be in Yellowknife to ask the right questions. There's some weird crap going on up there, it might be tied to our town now, somehow. I bet Quirk knows more than he's telling. Rowland must've said something to put a fire under him and Moth."

"She's a piece of work," Parks grumbled.

Kreski grunted. "Reminds me of you in Grade Nine, all black eyeliner, spikey hair and gutter talk. I'd have locked you up by now if you hadn't chosen to protect and serve."

"This way the town pays for my toys. Don't get eaten up there. You stay safe." Parks hung up, her concern lingering with him after the image flicked out.

He rubbed his forehead, dry from hours of air-con. The highway carved slow, man-made bends through trees, white slopes and scrub verges segueing to open views of snow-capped mountains as the road ran alongside the Bow River. He rummaged in the glove box, found a peanut bar of indeterminate age, and chewed on it too quickly as he watched an endless train that outpaced him on the tracks now running beside the road. Kreski finished the bar then tapped on the last call from RCMP Vancouver.

A well-kempt man with precisely parted dark hair appeared on-screen. "Major Dubois," he said, without looking up from whatever he was reading.

"Denis, it's Kreski."

Now the man turned towards him, smiling slowly. "Well, howdy, Sheriff Wayne. How are you today?"

"Living the dream, Den. What you want?" Terse, but auto-drive did that to him.

"I'm curious why you're hundreds of miles outside your jurisdiction pursuing a man that hasn't been charged with an offence."

"You've done your research."

"Becker was very helpful." The clean-cut, suited officer smiled with genuine warmth. "You know he's an idiot, right?"

The AWD cruised past a sign that said, "Canmore 8," the dash screen capturing the message and replicating it for several seconds once he was past.

"He's trying."

"Yeah, that too. Look, there's weird stuff going on this end. The RCMP server has been...accessed. These folks you're pursuing, the images you put up with the report are corrupted, and we can't find any on record. Someone is whitewashing them. Someone with serious clout. Wayne, you might be out of your league here. Hell, it's out of my league. There's more to this than you know. Turn around."

Kreski trusted Denis Dubois more than he would tell the man, but still... "How d'you know that? And more to the point, why you letting it slip to me on this line?"

"Because you owe me a ribeye now, and because I thought we were friends."

"We are," Kreski growled.

Den Dubois's smile faded. "It's out of control up in YK. These MT things are running out of wildlife. Three fishermen in the hospital, now two deputies? Genextric released a bird called a VD—go figure—which tracks, apparently. Schools, nurseries, businesses, all closed. They've been through panic buying, those with balls enough to go outside, and that's not many. Now even the stores are shut, just the bars left open."

"I know, Den. I've seen the MeToob clips..."

"It's carnage, Wayne. Turn around. There's enough manpower in Yellowknife this Quirk guy won't get two steps past the city limits before he's picked up, and there's more on the way."

"I've seen it, Den."

"Then you know to let it go." Dubois's features stretched with exasperation.

"There's a body in my morgue, Den. I run a clean town, and I aim to keep it that way."

Dubois nodded, seeming to give up. He sighed and shook his head. "Watch yourself, and for God's sake take any help that's offered. You're shit at doing that. I'd say that the vultures were circling"—Dubois grimaced—"but that might be a bad joke."

Kreski grunted, cut the call, messaged MacGillacuddy, then reached for the wheel. He was looking forward to stretching his legs apart from anything else.

The vehicle slipped seamlessly into driver control and in less than a minute Kreski was pulling off Highway 1 on the long, black techmac slip ramp into Canmore.

10

Morton rolled onto his back and stared up at the yawning hole edged with shattered plass. Seconds ago, a thick panel had separated the office from the service bay. As he watched, one grey reptilian head poked above the window's busted edge and looked down at him.

"Fuck off after the rest," he drawled, pushing up onto his elbow in plass fragments until he was sitting. The raptor brayed, setting Morton's teeth on edge, then—as if it understood him—turned away. He groped for his olive drab Five-seveN NAG Mark II, found it among the debris, picked it up, and holstered it. By the time he stepped into the trashed service bay the velociraptors and the cheetahgators were gone. God only knew how *they* would entertain themselves before they were put down.

His first call was Johari.

"Yeah, what?"

"Yeah what, *sir*," Morton snapped, the simple word triggering all his stored energy and instinct for command, discipline and duty. "Eve Meyer is AWOL. She's done here. I'm in charge. Read that back to me."

"You're in charge...sir."

"Status report."

"Yes, sir." He imagined cold sweat breaking out on the fat-assed screen-jockey's forehead. *"Three MTs in circulation, as you know..."*

"Shit's sake; tell me things I *don't* know. Pretend you're in a high-pressure situation where your job depends on being effective."

A brief, but heavy pause followed. *"Sir. Vuldolphs continue returning good data. Identified search area has reduced to a thirty-hectare box around Range Lake. Predict live tracking of targets available in fifteen to twenty minutes. Velociraptor signal strength good. They crossed the bridge, turned due west to the Yellowknife Bay inlet. Stopped around there for a few seconds then went into the trees towards Hopper Lake. No data on the cheetahgators, yet."*

"Okay, good. I need a repair crew in here. I'll use them as drivers when they're done."

"Yes, sir. Instructed now. The second and third batches of mangetouts have been released onto Level Six. Two dozen all told; that exceeds the recommended capacity of the feeding area. There..."

"Spit it out, Johari."

"There seems to be some kind of alpha male rivalry playing out. Two MTs are dead, dismembered by the alpha. We've released the tinhats in there too, per your order. They're flying clear of the MTs, but their stings have antagonised some of the MTs. Two tinhats flew too low and MTs caught their trailing stingers and pulled them down. It's a mess down there. If release is delayed..."

Morton nodded. "Good call." *Censure and reward; keep them sharp.* "Get the tinhats out of there." A ladybug and a man o' war jellyfish—how did they dream that shit up? "How many are there?"

"Thirty remaining live signals, sir."

"Open the ventilation shaft."

"Sir, that's not protocol." A female voice. Vernola chiming in. *"It's a smart workaround, but there's no way to isolate the vertical trunk shaft to the roof from the building's internal ventilation system."*

"Your point being?"

"A bug could get into the ceiling ducts. If a stinger hung down into the office..."

Morton sighed, rubbed his eyes. "Listen to me closely; you have been down the rabbit hole for several hours now. If I explain to you what I'm doing, you will either become knowingly complicit, and lose your 'just following orders' defence, *or* one of my colleagues will put a bullet in your head and I'll get someone else to do what I need. So, make your choice, comply with my instructions then initiate a full building lockdown. No one in or out. Do you understand, will you comply, yes or no?"

Long pause. *"Yes,"* said Johari. Dead air. *"Okay,"* said Vernola.

"The vents are open, sir. First few tinhats already sensing the change in air currents and moving to exit."

In the background, a soft voice said, *"Fuck, Johari."*

"Eyes front!" Morton snapped, even though he couldn't see them: he needed full and focused attention. "You're mine now. I want everything on four legs or more out of this building in the next hour." A cough sounded behind him. "Repair crew's here. I'll call back when we're ready to start loading out."

The ten C Corp goons, as Eve had described them, no longer wore corporate security uniforms, but were kitted out in anonymous black like him because—as planned—this scenario would play out with a lot of night work. He gave them their instructions in short, terse bursts and they complied like machines, walking smoothly past him into the debris-strewn loading bay. Hallelujah. He shoved the company handset into his pocket and reached for his earlobe. The call rang enough times for it to become lost in the geostationary labyrinth before that unmistakable tone—although possessing a softer timbre—exuded satisfaction directly into his ear.

"I'm pleased with your progress."

<Assets will be fully deployed within the hour. Do you have anything for me?>

"Like what, a pat on the head? You're doing well, our arrangement holds. Bring this home and you're free and clear. A ticket to the stars awaits your return."

<With respect, sir, the ticket is to be wired.>

"Ha, ha. Always so circumspect, Derek. I wish I could dissuade you from this hanging up of guns nonsense. How will I ever replace you?" The Old Man coughed.

<Draft in your prisoner in Habitat 10. Or maybe Kirby could be persuaded to sign on again.>

"Now, now, Derek. You don't get to be bitter when you're the one stepping outside the circle of trust. You can't have it both ways, and the stakes are too high for frippery. The fate of the free worlds, Derek. The blueprint for governance in centuries to come."

The old bastard was in obscenely good spirits. To be expected since things were going his way after a couple of blips. Still, surprising that mention of Gamma Lab's inmate didn't faze him when usually it was a sore point.

<Where's Quinton now? He must be close. Meyer said he'd arrive soon. And she's rogue now, by the way. I'll brief all agencies.>

"I couldn't say, Derek. I haven't spoken to my prodigal son-in-law since Cuba. Must be six years. Put him on the line when he arrives, will you?"

<I'll do my best, sir, if there's a window before I kill him.>

"Hard no to that, Derek, a hard no. Not until I've spoken with him. And anyway, that's not your place."

Morton shook his head. His squad had unblocked the service bay door of debris and begun loading more mangetouts into a new truck. Squat, dark shapes bumped and bored from the goods lift to the vehicle, making the frosted plastext tunnel shake and the ramp at the end shudder. Maybe he wouldn't get a chance to put Quinton on the line to The Old Man, maybe one of Genextric's horrors would get him first; that could be arranged. If only he could drop Quinton into Habitat 10, despite its being sealed up tight. If only he could watch, despite there being not a single camera into the sealed box, see the revenge of that beast, watch it pick the smug fucker apart. After what he'd done to Jenny, rejecting her— Morton stopped, allowed his breathing to settle. Payback was a dish best carved with sharp knives.

<Acknowledged, sir. I won't lay a hand on him. Out.>

11

Eve winced as pain grumbled along her left side. She'd banged numerous bones and wrenched a muscle in her right arm, but she'd done it. She'd escaped Derek Morton and his goons and Genextric's human-made monsters with her life. It hadn't done much for her job security, but she was free. She dashed a hand across her forehead, brushing dusty, grimy hair away, and eased back on the accelerator. Where was she going? The road east led nowhere. The highway just stopped. Nothing but Inuit-inhabited wilderness between here and the Russian Protectorate of Greenland. If she kept going, drove off the edge of the road map, abandoned all her tech, there would be no way for Morton to track her, right? But she was no survivalist, not in these heels. She planted her foot on the brake, spun the bashed-up truck around in the Cinnamon Island viewpoint, and headed back west.

She had pretty much nothing left here now, but fuck Morton to hell if she was leaving without Tania, even if that meant lugging her in a body bag. *She is not dead.* Eve still didn't know where her certainty came from—it was not the ethereal connection of a love etched in the stars, probably more of a stubborn, single-minded delusion—but it continued to grip her. It felt like seeing the future and knowing her choices might scar her forever if she misstepped. At least her freedom enabled her to go to the FBI...didn't it? Or should she go to Sheriff Kootook, or the lawyer, Collinson, first? No, because Morton had said he was following orders, but did that mean C Corp's? Maybe she should call the detective, Quirk? Who was her enemy really, apart from the rather obvious man with the gun in his hand? And did she have what it took to go back, to put herself in Morton's firing line? She was no gunslinger, despite her management style. This was the big leagues; she just didn't have the resources.

She turned south onto Dettah Road because, whatever her plans—fight or flight—she must ditch the truck or the decision would be made for her. She didn't have the knowledge to locate and deactivate whatever trackers were onboard. And her handset, that would have to go too. Cruising the quiet, snaking road near the shore afforded her a view of Yellowknife on the other side of the wide inlet where the river entered Great Slave Lake. The inlet was not yet frozen over despite dropping temperatures and regular snows. It was trying though. Through the trees she glimpsed platforms of too-thin ice, blooming from the rocky shores towards the distant city, but the ice road was weeks away yet. If she wanted to try for the airport, she would need to do it the hard way, back along Highway 4 through town, risking...what? Arrest? Death by mangetout? Being shot by Morton? Because he had to kill her after what he had revealed. The National Guard would be landing soon, presumably would lock things down even tighter than they were already.

It took ten minutes to reach the cluster of barely a hundred buildings forming the First Nations community of Dettah. In the heart of winter, it was six kilometres back to Yellowknife by the ice road across the frozen lake. Her memory threw up a nugget from the "settling in" lecture. The name Dettah meant "Burnt Point" in the language of the Dene people, who were not to be confused with Inuit.

She crawled forward now, turning her situation over and over. The snow was thicker here, the world largely white. Tyre tracks and redundant telegraph poles marked the way. She pulled over and sat—jacket crinkling and rustling, every little sound reflected sharp and close—

waiting for her thoughts to crystallise into her best course of action. What, constructively, could she do; was it hopeless? Tania would tell her to get the hell out, wouldn't she? Was her lover, crooked after all? It made a strange kind of sense: naïve, innocent, dedicated Tania. Always so straightforward, her mood so often transparent. She would make an excellent agent provocateur. And of course, she could play the femme fatale. Because of course you'd befriend and seduce the most influential person on site, the person who called the shots and could protect you, the cynical, driven individual who was so, *so* much in control and so very full of her own agenda and her power and her success that she couldn't possibly be duped by anyone.

Fuck. So, it's true? Morton and Tania? No, she refused to believe it.

So maybe Tania *was* dead, and the hope was just another lie Eve was telling herself. And if not, what could she do to help Tania now when her superpowers were self-absorption and ambition? Should she cross to the other side, the side that Tania may well have sold herself to after all? It wasn't like Genextric owned some divine right to her loyalty, not when they were trying to kill her.

She placed her forehead on the steering wheel, took deep breaths. Time was ticking. Hopefully Morton had his hands full, but maybe the FBI would have set a team on her since she had been at the heart of this mess in an administrative sense. It all felt hollow. She indulged her self-pity and shed a few tears, which dripped over the steering wheel and into the shadow of the footwell. After a moment she sniffed and leant back, wiping her face with both hands in a let's-get-the-fuck-on-with-this gesture.

A figure crossed the street up ahead, wrapped up against the cold, fur-lined hood pulled forward, watching the glowing handset held in front of them. From their gait, Eve guessed a young man. She nodded. Everyone's life went on until that moment when it didn't. You could keep moving forward or stand still and wait for death to get around to you. Damn, but she knew which course was for her.

She said, "Window down," and the truck complied. "Hey, hello!" she yelled.

The hood jerked towards her. The figure paused then changed course, came to the window, and looked straight at her. A young man indeed, wearing a straggly beard and a slight frown on his smooth features. At least his suspicion was open.

"You want a truck, this truck?"

"Huh?" He studied the vehicle, saw the logo. "Nah, it's tainted. And I don't drive."

All hail Genextric: demons and monsters delivered for a reasonable consideration. She couldn't give him the handset, because de-chipping handsets wasn't enough someone told her, and she didn't want anyone tracing a financial transaction.

"Tell you what"—Eve reached for that easy corporate bonhomie she employed during public consultations and "open" days, hoping her face wasn't too pink from the tears— "I'll give you this watch, it's Chanel; just take the truck east until the road stops then dump it." She tried not to look desperate.

"Jeez, that's a long way back." At least the kid was thinking about it. "And it's a woman's watch."

"You got a girlfriend?"

The kid got a kind goofy look and rubbed the fluff on his chin. "Maybe."

Eve leaned in conspiratorially, feeling the pressure of time building. "I'm not sure you really know what this is but, if she has media, she does, and she'll be on you like the skin on a bear. You get me?"

The kid nodded, all manner of notions flickering over his face.

"So, you'll take the truck? All the way out there? Now?"

"Yeah. I'll get my cousin to pick me up."

Eve cracked the door and hopped down into the cold. She went around back and groped inside for stuff that would serve her on the road, whichever road she took. She found two arctic jackets, one of which was unbranded, mercifully. Two sizes too big, and orange, not out of place on a tourist. She jammed a first aid kit into one pocket, torch and a roll of heavy cord into another. In the bottom of a backpack, she found a sheathed hunting knife, broad blade glinting into the glare of the vehicle's ULEDs. She slipped it into a deep side pocket. There was jerky too, because it was the Arctic, near enough, and shit happened. The only footwear was a pair of battered old boots which she needed both pairs of thick socks to pack out.

"This is weird," the kid piped up when she unfastened the watch and handed it to him with the truck key. "What with all that's happening over there." He jerked a thumb towards Yellowknife. "Someone's gonna come asking 'bout it, aren't they?"

Eve sighed and her breath plumed between then. "They might. Okay, look, I just got fired. It's crazy over there. Tell the truck to drive fast, and you'll be gone before anyone turns up."

"Yeah, I'm plugged in. It's really crazy."

"I just want to give them the finger before I go, you know?"

"Cool," the kid nodded, half-smiled. "I'm with it."

Eve nodded. "Thanks," she clapped him on the arm, an almost impersonal gesture given all the layers, but the boy smiled and climbed into the truck. He'd be fine. The Morton/Genextric/C Corp cabal had its hands full with the FBI taking a hand and the army arriving.

Eve watched the truck turn tightly, tyres crunching snow, rear lights receding until she was left in the soft and crystalline silence of Dettah. No one else braved the wind-chilled street. She turned and stumped down between sparse buildings towards the jetty. The wind tried to cut through her, but could only chill her face as the jacket did its job. She passed the polyhedral Akaitcho Territory Government building. Idly, she wondered about her chances of the First Nations granting her political asylum, but she didn't stop. The landing stage came into view and her heart sank. No people, of course. *Dumbass*. She should have got the kid to direct her to someone with a boat. She trudged most of the way towards the jetty then sheltered by the last building and waited.

She spent freezing minutes contemplating the lake and the distant shore, the city largely invisible behind trees and scrub, but for the towers of downtown. She could only imagine what was going on there. People in lockdown in houses or businesses? Soldiers on streets patrolled by Government-issue SUVs in FBI black or National Guard drab green? Monsters roaming free in gardens and parks, squads of syRen® trying to round them up before the authorities vaporised them?

Eve released a gout of breath that became mist between her increasingly trembly lips. She didn't care anymore. Genextric could go fuck itself. She would start again. She had funds put away. She'd worked within protocol and wasn't criminally liable. Oh, and a C Corp employee had tried to SHOOT HER! *Fucker*. She would change career streams, go do something else with less scope for harm, to her or anyone else. But what about Tania? Could Eve shake the belief that she was alive?

The putt-putt-putt of an ancient motor old enough to be burning some kind of octane fuel impinged on her reverie. Eve moved into the open, down slope towards the dock, eyes fixed on the shabby old fishing boat that approached around the headland to the south. Its cabin had been blue once, the colour heavily faded now. The helmsman turned the vessel parallel with the dock and cut the engine. A petite form, wrapped against the bone-numbing cold, stepped lithely from the wheelhouse, snatched a rope from its peg and hopped onto the jetty.

Eve closed the distance over crunching snow as the woman moored the boat. Front line tied, she went to the back...stern, to secure a second line to a post.

"Do you take charters?" Eve asked as she stepped onto weatherworn wooden boards cleared of snow.

The woman finished tying her knot and turned towards Eve, pulling her hood back. Dark eyes shone with questions, and the directness of that gaze compelled Eve to answer them.

"I need to get away. Name your price, within reason."

The young woman's gaze flattened, and she turned away to check the lines. Eve felt relief at being released. She'd screwed up, panicked even in her haste. She pulled her own hood back.

"I'm sorry. I need help is what I mean. I'll pay well, if you're willing."

That seemed to mollify the young woman, and she regarded Eve again. Her dark hair was braided from the top of her forehead. She wore a trace of makeup, simple and effective.

"I'm sorry to bother you but I'm kind of desperate, I'll admit." Saying it out loud made it doubly true. She was so done with this place.

The young woman glanced at the sky. "Where you going?"

Where was she going? What about Tania? "South, Fort Resolution. They've got an airstrip, right?"

"Yeah." She looked perturbed at the notion. "That's one-forty kilometres. Take me six hours there, six back. I got things to do." Her stare became calculating. "You on the run or something?"

"Heh, well, I quit my job and I...just need to get away, you know?" *Oh god, how I need to get away.* "I made a mistake, wasn't there for my friend when she needed me. Now, she's gone." Tania was gone. "I need to get away from here. How much for the boat? I'll buy it."

"Seriously?"

"Is it yours to sell?"

"It is, my grandpa..."

"Okay, that's good. Look. I'm low on time. You have a handset?"

The young woman had taken on a slight scowl that was as mesmerising as the slight smile Eve had glimpsed before. "No, never wanted one. My brother does. He's at work in YK."

Damn. She'd picked the one person in North America without a digital device. She had thought to use the Genextric petty cash account, which she had discovered while waiting that she wasn't severed from, yet. The young woman could just tell the police the truth. Her last act through the Genextric adjunct of the C Corp machine. Then ditch the handset and be gone, since thankfully she wasn't "voluntarily" chipped like employees of some corporations. Would you like a twenty percent bump to your pension pot? Just step this way and roll up your sleeve.

"Borrow her," the young woman said, and Eve's eyes narrowed. She met that dark gaze again and managed not to gape. "Leave her tied to the jetty in Resolution, tell someone Magen's boat is there and to tell Lester Baker. Someone will bring it back."

"I don't know what to say." She was almost free of this cold, cold place and the increasing desperation she felt.

The young woman—Magen?—shrugged, not releasing Eve from the gaze that seemed at once questioning, but content to succour a weary traveller. "You look like you need help."

Eve shook her head. It was above and beyond the call of human decency, more than she deserved, more than she would have done. She wanted to hug this wary, generous young woman.

"Thank you."

"You're welcome. I guess you know how to pilot or you wouldn't ask, so good luck." She just handed Eve the key, a clunky old, serrated thing tied by string to a net float, and turned away to walk along the dock.

Eve blew out a plume of breath. She looked south over the enormous, endless-seeming expanse of Great Slave Lake, west towards Yellowknife then back towards the scattered dwellings of Dettah, hunkered down in the snowy grip of descending winter.

"Wait," she called. The hooded figure turned and walked back to her. "I'm a bit rusty, would you take me out a bit, just to get the feel?"

The young woman nodded. "Okay. Hop in."

Eve followed her over the rail, down onto the gently tilting deck and helped cast off. She stood by the wheel while the young woman started the engine and steered away from the jetty. They slipped past islets and protruding rocks which wore wide skirts of grey ice.

"So, you're Magen?"

"Right."

"I'm Eve."

"Probably shouldn't tell me your name in case your boss comes looking."

"If he does, just tell him what happened. Hold nothing back."

"Okay, Eve."

After ten minutes heading south during which Eve was permitted to steer, Magen spun the wheel to take them back. A flat, bare landscape slid past the cabin's open window. Eve put her hand in her pocket. As the prow came around and steadied on north again, Eve slipped her handset out. She sent a quick message to Quirk then let the device slide surreptitiously from her hand to fall into the frigid water, watching its glow disappear.

When they bumped against the jetty, Magen left the engine running and hopped up onto the wooden boards.

"Thank you, Magen," said Eve with all the feeling she could muster. "I hope to repay you sometime."

Magen just smiled, waved a gloved hand and walked away.

Eve took the wheel and steered out as the young woman had, slipping between the islets and the rocks on a southbound heading. There was a large island in the near distance, and she steered towards it, then, about half distance, she turned the vessel west towards Yellowknife.

Sure, she could find another job, another career but, underneath all the corporate bullshit, she had a duty to this community. She'd always be haunted by what happened here if she didn't try to put it right, despite the risk. Also, she knew that if she did not do this, she never would be able to look into another warm, fascinating gaze without wondering about Tania. And anyway, she would have help. She wished now that she'd messaged her friend and drinking buddy Dulcie before chucking her phone, but at least she knew where to find him. And she had contacted the detective. Derek fucking Morton was going down, and this Quirk character was going to help her do it.

12

"The next train north departs in thirty-two minutes. I have reserved three tickets. Approximate journey time to Yellowknife, seven hours," said Eighty.

Seven hours. Morton would be there already, busy making chaos for The Old Man, busy subverting a national election that would shape the fate of nations, even worlds, busy hunting Meriwa Rowland and Tania Terjesen. Quirk's agitation spiked, again. He let his gaze rove around the café, smoothed a hand over his knee, wishing for the Merrion. *Sweatpants, for the love of Valentino.* He sipped Green Mountain seaweed macchiato—naturally caffeine free, of course—but that hardly helped.

The drive through the mountains was stunning; sharp ridges and noble peaks, snow-capped sentinel trees with dark cores and heavy, white boughs giving up glimpses of rushing blue rivers. It was the landscape of millennia past, each stone edifice speaking more eloquently than the last of the birth of continents, and all he could think of was minutes passing while any control ebbed away.

Canmore presented the chic outdoors resort he expected. Perhaps it was the looming mountains in their white cloaks, or the sloping timber roofs, pitch steep for better shedding of snow. Perhaps the open truss detailing on the exteriors and the occasional log cabin construction. He wished he could take a mindful moment to enjoy the atmosphere, but his suspicions multiplied his fears, raised them by the power of his insecurities. On the busy street, he had resisted the urge to look around, expecting feds or cops to leap from behind every business-sponsored planter and stylised article of civic street furniture.

"Miff if auffum," said Moth around another mouthful of muffin. He sighed.

"It would attract less attention, Miss Moth, if you refrained from speaking with your mouth full," Eighty advised.

She swallowed. "Well, thank you Professor Starch-briefs. I'll remember for when I start giving a shit about people liking me. If you're short of things to do, I reckon you need a catchphrase: Think about that. Something snappy, with personality."

Eighty processed that, staring blankly above the heads of the coffee shop hipsters.

"Moth, not now: avoiding attention, remember?" Quirk struggled just to sit still.

Very carefully and deliberately he placed his face in his hands. First The Old Man's mind games then a close encounter with Morton. *Throw the contact from Mystery Caller into the mix and watch Quirk's head explode.* At least he had predicted the ensuing messy fallout. But of course, TOM's tendrils had been dormant within his psyche, and now his remission was over. The taint did not fade with time apart. Difficult and painful surgery would be needed to remove TOM's tendrils, such as when removing a leach, or perhaps a tapeworm, he imagined.

Having chosen a table located centrally in the coffee shop, multiple avenues of retreat were available. Neither did their "wacky" clothing create any fuss here, jammed as the place was with young people on adventures in their dreads, beanies and tattered denim. But Quirk could not even concentrate sufficiently to comment on their youthful naivety. He was far too worried about his client, the time, and being waylaid. Those and the doubt. Would Mystery Caller call again? What was his agenda? Was he as flaky as he sounded? Eve Meyer: ally or obstacle? Playing for Morton's team or against him—Derek being a dyed-in-the-wool bastard when it came to women and children.

And could he kill Morton if it came to that? If the situation called for it? He shook his head. Whatever had caused Jennifer to trust that turd on legs, even for a few minutes?

Something made Quirk glance up to find Eighty staring at him.

"Where are you? Are you having lunch?!"

Quirk started. Despite the irate tone issuing from the syRen®'s mouth, Eighty's features remained blank, the hallmark of Mystery Caller having assumed control.

Business-like concern hardened Moth's expression.

"Who *are* you?" Quirk hissed, trying to ignore the stares of adjacent teenagers, hipsters and backpackers.

"That's not the point. Have you forgotten what's at stake?"

The android indicated the sterilised earbuds in a bowl beside the salt and pepper. Quirk inserted one, Moth another.

"I'm buzzing to make your acquaintance IRL," the voice sounded thrilled to the point of mania. *"But your priorities are ridiculous."*

"We're waiting for a train," Moth snapped. Quirk wished he could hang up.

"Oh, I see, okay. So, update. Meyer's been run out of town." Quirk locked eyes with Moth. *"Morton tried to kill her. I didn't think she'd make it. She's smart."*

"Where is she now?"

"Don't know. She ditched her tech. No implants. I'm trying to trace her truck. Looks like she's heading east. Damn! I wanted her to help you."

Quirk flinched. Moth scowled back at him. Around them, a glance slid over a shoulder, a questioning look, lips twitching with unspoken complaints.

"Seems she's running away. Like she just gave up. That makes me mad."

"Does seem rather final. How do you know her?" He asked, Moth nodding.

"Oh, we sort of work together. I've known Eve for a while, but not as long as I've known Derek Morton."

Quirk tensed. "And what do you want, for all this 'help' you've doled out?" He was full up to here with this mind-fuckery. "We still don't know who you are." *And how is it you know Morton?*

"But you do, *Quinton. You just haven't figured it out yet,"* the voice said, petulantly. *"Anyhow, Morton must almost be done here, but I want to make sure he gets what he's due before he gets away. I'm sending you help. Be ready. The army's here now, and the FBI. There are monsters in the air and on the ground. People are going mad. It's right up your street."*

"What kind of help?" asked Quirk, but Eighty shook its head. The line was dead.

Moth hunched her shoulders and spread her hands to support a "What-the-fuck?" expression. Quirk nodded and regarded Eighty's unruffled features with suspicion.

"Are you autonomous, syRen® 0778a? Is anyone listening?"

Eighty raised an android eyebrow. "Yes, sir. No, sir."

Moth puffed out a breath. "Can we trust anything that droid-humper says?"

Quirk nodded. "Good instinct. I think Meyer's still in play. She seemed determined."

"Our train departs in twenty-one minutes," said Eighty.

Quirk returned to scanning the room, placing a hand on his knee to prevent his leg bouncing. Moth took a small mouthful of her Monterey Jack and jalapeño muffin then make a small mewing noise. He was forced to agree, his avocado, anchovy and almond flatbread (named Straight As) had been delicious, a simple pleasure amidst an unfathomable morass of migraine-inducing human testes.

"We'll go straight to the train. Five-minute walk, we leave in three minutes."

Moth sat back in her armchair, doing a better job than him of appearing at ease. "That was some weird shit right there. What was he yibber-yabbering about Morton? And *don't...*"—she forestalled Quirk just as he opened his mouth—"deal me another hand of bullshit: all aces and kings."

"You watched the wrong TV shows in that convent, Moth." He glanced again at the door then the front window. "Your hard-bitten clichés need work."

She shook her head, dark bob swishing. "Not buying it. You look ready to poop your Calvin Kleins, but you're angry too. Dish it, dirt-wise. Leave nothing out."

"Fair enough," Quirk wiped his fingers on a napkin. Then—even though the clown costume he'd been living in since Revelstoke very much was *not* the Merrion—he brushed crumbs from the leg anyway.

"I don't trust Mystery Caller as far as I could throw him with a teaspoon. But where C Corp is involved—where Morton is involved—there is deceit and there is pain, and you just have to wait for it to land on you."

"So you say"—her eyes narrowed—"but how do you know that so well if you were just 'the pilot'?" She air quoted. "You and Morton: Tell me again and tell me true."

A hiker exited the coffee shop's toilet and a skateboarder slipped past her to take the open door. On the street, a family passed in a strung-out line, wrapped up against the cold, while an older couple stood to one side, smiling and nodding.

Quirk sighed and wished he was tootling around Europe with the formidably lovely Fraulein Professor Cassie Streich, arguing over the diction and devices in Goethe's *Prometheus,* or the way the light reflected from the warm red and orange tones of Paul Klee's *Nocturnal Festivity.* And if wishes were fishes... He regarded Moth, held the girl's flat stare and—quite suddenly, without artifice or agenda—felt closer to her than at any time since they had met.

"I used to do then what Morton does now, just not the way he does it. I was The Old Man's fixer."

Moth's eyes widened with what looked like wonder and new respect. "So, all this time, behind the prissy disguise, you've been badass?" He did not respond, flicking another glance at the window. "Wow. So, did you do bad shit, cover stuff up?" She leaned in, perching on the edge of her big armchair, and he was forced to remember that she was the niece of a now-deceased mafioso.

"No. Bad shit and cover-ups are what they did to me."

"Yeah, yeah. Your son, the sheer effrontery, the violation, yadda, yadda. I remember, but what did you do for The Old Man? Illegal shit? 'Cause you can tell me you know, that's in my DNA. I'll keep schtum. I'm bad to the bone."

Quirk's features tightened. Now she knew, and she had not reacted as he'd hoped. "You are *not* bad to the bone. You're fourteen and you're a pain in the arse...sometimes. I didn't break any laws for TOM—not the big ones—although he pushed me. I may have bent a few, but I tried to be a good influence on him."

"Sure, sure." She nodded. "It just doesn't seem to have worked out that well."

They didn't have time for this. They had to go. Quirk's nerves jangled—that feeling of being in the sights of portent and ill omen. "Look"—he skipped irked, sidestepped irritable and dove headlong into ticked off—"if you're just going to wind me up when we're sharing that's fine, I'm getting used to it, but it will reflect badly on you in later life believe me, and on your annual staff review."

"I'm sorry." Moth looked...regretful?!

"You're—?"

"Awesome, possum," Eighty announced with evident (faux) satisfaction. Moth turned to it, gaping. Quirk's eyebrows rose. A shadow passed the window. Twin gorillas in sheriff's department chic and—

Wayne Kreski.

Quirk locked eyes with Creston's sheriff just as a great tidal wave of khaki burst through the door of Rocky Range Bagel, clearly not shopping for the lunchtime special.

Quirk sprang from his chair, dragging Moth towards the back door. He thanked a thin slice of luck that three backpackers had stood and started pulling packs on just as law enforcement burst in. The big, ungainly deputies tried to push around, but got fouled up in the packs and the lunchtime queue, which almost reached the front door. Quirk thrust Moth ahead of him, past the toilet towards the rear exit. A server emerged from the kitchen with two plates and Quirk threw up an arm to barge past. The guy yelled as nacho chips rained down in the narrow passageway.

"Go, go, go!" he yelled at Moth. There was bound to be some deputy covering the back door, but hopefully only one, and hopefully not briefed to shoot.

Moth bashed into the emergency exit release, pushing out through the doorway. The door swung fast, hit the wall with a heavy thunk as bright sunlight and bone-deep cold washed over them.

An old, scrawny lawman with a greying moustache, short sleeves(!), tribal tats and aviator shades sat sprawled on his ass in the slush around the kitchen vents, Stetson upturned in a grease-slicked puddle two metres away. He hollered as he thrashed about for purchase.

"Quinton Kirby! Angelika Moratti! Cease and desist, right now!"

Moth kept going, clicking her heels, crossed the service road, and skipped over hard-packed snow through a line of parked cars. Eighty slipped past in pursuit of Moth, and Quirk followed the android. They ran into a wide-open parking lot, surrounded by two- and three-storey alpine buildings enclosing a square space fifty metres on a side.

"Get down and keep moving," Quirk barked, following his own instruction and weaving between the parked vehicles.

Gunfire rent the air without impact, but they sounded...off. Virtual warning shots then, emitted by handheld speakers, a rather quaint initiative, but effective.

"Not very polite for Canadians," Moth complained loudly from somewhere nearby, out of sight.

"Your directions, please, Quirk," Eighty called without any trace of human anxiety. "I must prevent Miss Moth—and yourself, if possible—from being shot."

"We're exiting, stage left." Hoping Eighty could see it, he made a quick, cutting gesture across the square towards the only side open to a street. "Hurry. We can still make the train."

"I understand. The officers should not shoot near people." Eighty ducked away around the corner of an SUV as more "flat" shots echoed thunderously around the enclosed space. Quirk moved too.

He hated how well this mirrored the last time he'd worked with Morton. Kuala Lumpur International Airport No. 3, April 2093. They'd started in Car Park J, weaving through the vehicles in pursuit of the informant. Quirk with the intention of serving her with a C Corp writ, Morton—he'd discovered after a twenty-minute pursuit through the endless palm plantations surrounding the runways—instructed to shoot her in the head.

Quirk stopped, dropped to the cold, wet ground and rolled under a high-wheelbase hydrogen fuel cell pick-up truck, aiming to make a beeline for the street regardless of obstructions. His arm jerked back, something caught on the vehicle's undercarriage. A growing rumble nearby intruded on his rising panic, like a big semi trundling down the street, rattling the air. He tried to pull his arm free. His layers of clown clothes offered some padding against the lot's rough surface, and cut the icy ground's chill a little, but this new inconvenience was a considerable drawback.

Big, black-booted feet crunched centimetres away. He jerked his head around, saw two pairs of boots going past the truck, now between him and the open street.

Still unable to free his arm, he began shrugging out of his coat, forcing his breathing down. More boots scuffed snow to his right, brown boots, moving slowly.

"Quirk," came Kreski's call as Quirk's arm slid from one sleeve then the other. "Be reasonable. I just want to talk."

Tell that to your colleagues, and the FBI, and the RCMP, and C Corp, and Derek damn Morton, who absolutely will come for Moth and me once done with Terjesen.

That deep rumble still swelled, now well into discomfort. Did Sheriff Puddlebutt have heavy air support? The noise was way too loud for an observation drone.

"Quinton Kirby!" Even using a voxbox now, they had to yell to be heard over the chopping, buffeting blades of whatever aircraft now buzzed the square. "This is Sheriff Bryan MacGillacuddy. There is a detain-and-question on you from Creston Valley Sheriff's Department. Surrender now. This lot is surrounded."

Maybe it was and maybe it wasn't. He watched Kreski's brown boots move away amidst swirling grit and ice chips. Quirk squinted against the debris, made a mental check that his jacket contained nothing of import, then rolled out from under the truck on the side where Kreski's brown boots had been.

The sky and the ground switched places. He saw the back of Kreski's legs, his broad, muscular back. Sky and ground switched again and a massive grey-black shadow engulfed Quirk's sight, a lurking, hovering mechanical beast that chewed up the clouds, whipped the air full of debris. The man-made whirlwind howled as Quirk kept rolling and the sky tipped sideways again.

He bumped up against a wheel, winced, squinted into the maelstrom. He came up to his knees, fingers braced like a sprinter, then raised his eyes above the doorline of the vehicles to look around the lot. Further down the line of cars, Kreski looked up, shielding his face. Quirk saw the two big cops over to the left, and Canmore's scrawny little sheriff over to the far right, voxbox held to his throat. Five deputies of various khaki shapes and sizes dispersed at MacGillacuddy's instruction.

Quirk looked back at Kreski and saw Eighty's head appear further left near the edge of the square, Moth's dark hair bobbed beside it as they ran for the open street. Quirk squinted against the looming shadow's thudding rotors, the whip crackle of flying stones and ice. The big deputies had seen Eighty and Moth. Now it was on.

"Stop, in the name of the law!" shouted Tweedle Dumb, but Tweedle Dumber drew his weapon.

BLAM, BLAM, BLAM!

He fired high warning shots as both deputies hurried forwards, closing on Moth and Eighty, who were hampered by pedestrians and traffic. Kreski ran that way too.

"There's Kirby!" screeched MacGillacuddy. "Take him down!"

"No more shooting!" Kreski yelled. "No shooting!"

Quirk glanced over his shoulder, watched Canmore deputies weaving towards him between the ranked cars. There were way too many.

A claxon started overhead, amazingly audible above the clatter of the big drone copter's rotor blades. Quirk took a path diverging from Kreski's, but still away from the posse and towards the street. A crowd gathered there, seemingly unsure whether to gawp or run. Would Moth and Eighty use it? *Read my damn mind like in the good old days, Eighty!*

Glancing up, he saw three harnesses descending from the drone copter's core. Mystery Caller's promised help? The harnesses would touch ground on a gap site across the street, putting traffic between them and the cops, if they could get there in time. But they'd be sitting ducks dangling under the bird if either sheriff decided one of those "righteous" kills that the news reported occasionally was better than nothing.

Quirk almost made it to the near sidewalk before Kreski spotted him. The sheriff—because of the terrible lack of discipline in some people's parking—had to weave around staggered front and rear bumpers, but his gaze never wavered.

"Quirk!" Kreski bellowed, bending his path towards him.

Quirk tucked his head down and pushed forward.

Various things happened very close together.

Eighty and Moth reached the edge of the lot and started across the street towards the descending harnesses, searching for gaps in the steady flow of traffic.

Tweedle Duh and Tweedle "Gee, do you think so?" emerged from the lot onto the near sidewalk. Spotting girl and droid, they levelled their sidearms, pacing forward in firing stance. "On the ground, now!"

The spectators saw guns and began to scatter.

Kreski took the shortest distance through the parked cars to the near sidewalk.

Quirk did the same, arriving two steps ahead, but with Kreski closer to Moth.

At the same time, a towering semi turned the corner and drove down the street towards them, largely unaffected by the copter's downdraft.

Kreski reached the sidewalk just as Quirk took a breath and stepped out into traffic and swirling air, hoping anti-collision systems lived up to the ad copy. A glance confirmed Sheriff MacG's khaki brigade almost at the sidewalk, tasers coming out. Ahead, Eighty also stepped into the nearer eastbound traffic, hand held up like a crossing guard.

Kreski extended both hands towards Moth in a calming gesture.

"I just want to talk."

Moth's gaze flashed around, taking in Kreski, the approaching deputy twins, the khaki brigade. Her eyes met Quirk's where he stood amidst angry, honking, stationary eastbound traffic. The westbound semi loomed close. Moth darted past Eighty, between the cars he had stopped.

Tweedle Duh fired. The slug twisted Eighty backwards, throwing the android down, out of sight between the vehicles. The Twins surged towards Moth as the huge semi closed. Five deputies burst onto the sidewalk and Moth dove under the approaching semi.

"Moth!" Quirk screamed. He slammed the nearest car hood. "Moth!" he pushed off, reached the far sidewalk and barged through bustling, scattering people. "Moth!" The rotors clattered, the roar whipping his outburst away.

The semi juddered as its autobrakes came on hard, almost bouncing on the road.

Most of the bystanders hurried away, pushing along the sidewalk, blocking Quirk's path. As he fought through them, he saw Eighty spring up, Kreski run forward, the khaki brigade rush in. Tweedles Duh and Gee levelled pistols to shoot at Moth again. As Quirk clawed his way through fleeing bodies, MacGillacuddy emerged from the lot.

"Take them down!" his shrill voxbox commanded.

"No!" Kreski bellowed.

Quirk won clear air as Moth rolled out from under the semi into the gutter twenty metres ahead of him. Eighty headed for the girl and Kreski headed for Eighty. The sheriff intercepted the android just as it stepped onto the textured plascrete sidewalk, grabbing the syRen®'s shoulder.

"You are aiding fugitives: cease and desist. I invoke Primary Tenet Zero."

But Eighty stood, legs braced, calmly resisting Kreski's main force as if the musclebound cop were an unruly child.

"There is cause to suspect your colleagues intend physical harm."

On cue, the armed-and-gormless gorilla twins bore down on Moth, as she picked herself up amidst the whirling wind. Quirk started forward as Eighty—synthetic hair whipping in the copter's downdraft—shifted feet, unbalancing Kreski who tumbled to the ground. The syRen® turned, sprinted forward to curl an arm around Moth's waist, scooped her up on the run. The droid leapt forward, sprang from the top of the low fence around the vacant lot and reached for the dangling harness.

For a breath S-0778a hung in the air before its hand grasped the dangling straps. Gunshots barked above the copter's racket. Quirk saw Eighty hit once, twice. As he ran, Quirk thanked a non-specific quasi-deified entity that Canmore was thorough in clearing its sidewalks. Then he glimpsed all the khaki-clad figures turning tasers on him. They didn't fire, but they aimed. He ran for the harness, still three metres up, the now-kneeling Sheriff of Creston between him and escape.

"Sorry, Wayne," he growled as he planted a foot on Kreski's back and launched himself into the air. It was just the boost he needed to clear the fence. His hands grasped a strap and he grabbed, clung and pulled, managed to hook his other arm through a loop. A shot whipped past. A great force hauled on Quirk's arms, trying to drag them from their sockets as the drone climbed then banked away. Quirk's legs whipped out like on a fairground ride, the Earth reluctant to release him. Then they were high above the roofs, hopefully impotent gunfire sounding below them.

A blinding hot pain punctured his rambling thoughts, downdraft buffeting him. He managed to twist the harness around his arm before agony overtook him and he slumped, gasping air as it rushed past. Eighty hung there too, right arm locked in position, left arm clutching Moth tightly to its side. The droid's eyes flashed red for malfunction.

Canmore already had receded to the scale of a model village. The air was bitterly cold. They had reached the height where Boogaloo Maps stopped displaying street names. The harnesses began to winch them up. Quirk winced in pain at the motion, but didn't struggle, preferring the pain over plunging to his death. They had reached cruising altitude, apparently, and now moved only forward, he just did not know where to.

"Don't worry!" came a blaring amplified voice from above. "I've got you!"

Oh, swell, he thought muddily through his pain, Mystery Caller was indeed at the helm. On the plus side, wherever they were going, they would get there fast.

13

Quirk lay gasping on the hard metal grill that was the drone's floor. They had done it, they had evaded law enforcement again and now would arrive in Yellowknife in short order. Because there could be no doubt where Mystery Caller would take them. Now, all they needed was a plan.

"Drone," Moth snapped, already having her breath back. "Designation and assignment, please."

"Venky's Systems DX5/86/AD4, leased to Genextric Laboratories Inc.," came an artificial voice in lilting sub-continental tones from a speaker somewhere above Quirk's head. "En route Yellowknife, Northwest Territories. Transport passengers to Landing Pad B, Genextric Gamma Laboratory, Progress Road off Highway 4 Ingraham Trail."

Moth was propped against the bulkhead, her hair wet and rat-tailed, face and hands dirty from rolling under a truck.

Cunning, crazy, brave little shit. Quirk crawled across the metal floor, grimacing at the cold and wet soaking through his sweatpants, his long thermals and into his knees, grunting at a stabbing pain in his upper arm.

"Are you okay?"

She coughed. "I'm fine."

"Then you're in big trouble, missy," he tried to wag his finger at her and winced. Moth just laughed, clearly still deep in the rush generated by her adventurous antics.

Quirk recalled now that he'd been shot. He groped at his shoulder and his fingers came away sticky dark crimson. Not a lot of blood, but it was his, and it should not be on the outside. Adrenaline had dampened the pain, but now fell away, leaving...pain.

Eighty remained face down on the drone's grill. Quirk watched as Moth made a search of the syRen®'s clothing and found three holes in the legs and another in the ass, the pants there stained dark grey by some kind of lubricant. With difficulty, she hauled the syRen® over. Its violet eyes were dark. Small wonder, it...he...Eighty had just burned through a significant amount of energy.

"AD4, deploy android charging point," said Moth.

"Zip charge plate now illuminated green," said the drone. One panel among the stark, dark mechanical surfaces of the drone's payload compartment glowed lime.

Moth hauled on Eighty's arms. "Help me, you lump of lead," she barked, or maybe yapped was more apposite. Quirk shook off his daze and complied, although she might have been addressing the droid. They hefted Eighty up to sit, back to the lime plate. Moth fastened a strap around Eighty's neck.

"Yellowknife ETA," asked Quirk, wondering if Mystery Caller might respond.

"15:08; approximate travel time two hours, twenty minutes."

"Will Eighty be alright?" Moth asked, concern in her eyes.

Quirk nodded and smiled through his fatigue in what he hoped was a reassuring way. "Let's get some charge into him," said Quirk upon seeing her emotion. "Then he can reboot and start on repairs."

"They didn't hit anything vital," she said, hopefully.

"Hmm," said Quirk. "Remember, android architecture doesn't automatically match human physiology."

Moth frowned. "Is his CPU in his ass?"

"No—"

"Then shut the fuck up and don't burst my bubble of hope." She placed a protective hand on Eighty's arm, leaning her head on its shoulder. "He saved me."

"I helped," he mumbled, shuffling back to lean against the opposite bulkhead. "And got slightly shot in the process."

Instant concern paled Moth's dirty face and she crawled over to him, located the wound and unceremoniously ripped his sleeve open.

"Ow! My Priceless Princess shirt!"

She grinned. "Hush up, ya big baby. It's just a graze. Drone: first aid kit."

A bulkhead section glowed pink, and a short drawer emerged. He watched Moth fish out the kit, crack it open, nod and start breaking into packages, swabbing, tutting, salving. He felt steri-strips pulling his skin tight, heard the rip of a field dressing packet before she pressed it firmly (and with considerable relish, he was sure) onto his arm.

"You're good," she pronounced. "Eighty's in worse shape." She glanced at the android with more concern than she'd showed him. "But we'll be there soon. So, let's do our homework." *Homework?* He must be delirious. "AD4, display news and socmed from YK."

A fabric screen flopped down, the corners captured by latches in the wall before it glowed into life, displaying a veritable avalanche of links in descending date order to reports, eye-witness accounts, blogs, Instapix, Chipper and Famebook posts all proclaiming some form of disaster in the increasingly beleaguered city.

"Display Link One," said Moth.

The head and shoulders of a female reporter appeared on screen, bright in the drone's gloomy confines which swayed and rolled slightly as they cut through the air. Behind the immaculately coiffured woman lay a cluster of emergency vehicles, blues-and-reds spinning. People in dark blue winter jackets stood at intervals along the edge of a road. The reporter spoke to camera.

"Brianna Lang reporting from Yellowknife. Despite earnest warnings from the FBI and the National Guard, increasing numbers of local hunters—professional and amateur—are scouring the city's snow-covered streets for monsters.

"The human deaths that everyone feared have now occurred, and the FBI has stressed that members of the public are putting themselves, law enforcement officers and soldiers at risk. But the people of Yellowknife are ignoring this advice; they are fighting for their city, not giving in.

"The authorities have closed many areas with laser fences. Interlopers now are being detained for impeding federal operations. The National Guard has secured the airport and is deploying through the city. Will that put a stop to the mounting death toll? Can these monsters be destroyed without more loss of life, and will the FBI catch the mysterious Pandora who brought about this carnage?

"Public protests in Victoria, Ottawa, Washington and New York in the last two days, these are questions Peter Liano must address.

"Brianna Lang, for CUS news."

Quirk called up a MeToob snip of an interview with Sheriff Peter Kootook, a distinctly unhappy-looking Inuit who appeared like he might be contemplating early retirement as he answered questions for the assembled press.

"All my department's resources are in the field, all leave cancelled. We are drawing in the net, and we will get these things, put them down. We do not need or want ill-advised assistance from the public. We know you've all got guns, but we're not hunting wolves, bears or rabbits. There are no kill prizes, no rewards. Stay home and look after your family and friends. You will not get a trophy for your wall."

He waved a hand at another questioner.

"I'll have another update tomorrow morning."

"Link Three," said Moth, requesting the video from someone called Gor3s33k3r. Shaky footage from a gun-cam played, narrated by Ms. Seeker herself as she attempted to approach a kill site. The image moved contra to the drone's slight tipping, making Quirk's head swim. He opened his mouth to close the file when the hunter's progress stopped. The view whipped around along an intersecting trail crushed through the scrub. On the crossing path, a patch of flattened grass, splattered red. The hunter turned onto the new path, nosing along the narrow trail for a few metres then panning down to a severed arm chewed open to the bone and abandoned. The screen went black.

He glanced at Moth as she looked sidelong at him then gave him a wan smile.

"It's okay, boss. I've seen some bad shit, although Uncle Toni tried to hide it from me. I've seen a man bleed out." Despite her attempt at bravado, she hung her head then straightened again. "Keep going."

New links appeared as they went. Quirk called Link One again. More amateur images, this time kids filming some Yellowknife thoroughfare from a high-up apartment. A convoy of blocky, olive drab vehicles traversed the empty street. An APC lead the column, eight trucks trundling behind, a second APC at the rear, a soldier manning the roof-mounted laser cannon, scanning abandoned alleys and sidewalks.

Quirk blew a breath and smoothed his lengthening stubble. With their arrival imminent, his agitation had turned to cold dread. They were not equipped for the situation on the ground in Yellowknife.

Moth continued through the list. Confusing footage of someone filming soldiers from an alleyway then running with two companions when they were spotted, challenged and pursued. The image bucked wildly then the device fell to the ground, but continued recording from a crazy angle as guardsmen pushed the civilians against a brick wall and searched them. Somewhere, amidst these mindboggling and violent events, Meriwa Rowland and Tania Terjesen hid out like everyone else, but the monster pursuing them was a very different beast. Yet beyond even the gargantuan electoral fraud that TOM attempted—which Terjesen could link Genextric to through Morton—Quirk had an inkling something else was going on. C Corp's actions had a whiff of desperation about them, and if anyone knew about that it was him. There was something that Genextric couldn't put back in its box.

And how exactly was he to navigate a safe path for Moth through this carnage? She remained his charge, and still only fourteen. She might be able to perform Jane Bond stunts like rolling under moving trucks, but that did not mean she had the resources to deal with the emotional slings and arrows that were coming. Yet she had been in the house when her parents were shot, had watched her Uncle Toni dying of poisoning in front of her eyes, while he farmed her off to the first hapless halfwit who walked through the door. (Enter Quinton Kirby, damsel rescuer par excellence.)

He glanced at Moth sitting in the dim operational lighting of the drone's hold, torturing her youthful sensibilities with disturbing web images. Just the two of them now, although Eighty's eyes had begun to glow yellow, showing charging had reached emergency operation levels. That seemed to parallel the nature of his relationship with Moth, barely functional. And yet—from time to time—they went a whole day without fighting. She *was* capable of setting her teenage angst aside and getting serious.

She looked twenty-something sombre now viewing images of a vulture-like creature on the ground in tall grass tearing at a heap of carrion, bare ribs protruding from the carcass. Not once plague-riven Africa, but the North American Federation. Perhaps she did worry about the dangers ahead in Yellowknife and hid her anxiety as he suspected she did her true emotions over her parents' deaths. He should try and keep the mood light until he figured out how to progress the case and keep Moth safe.

"Hey, your birthday in a couple of months, eh? Fifteen—you must be excited."

She shrugged, not turning away from the screen.

"Aren't you looking forward to it? A whole new century, too."

"Are you kidding? It's just another big number starting with two."

"No sense of wonder then?"

She turned on him then and vented that vein of anger that always pulsed beneath her grumpy exterior. "Wonder? Are you shitting me? I've got wonder out the wazoo! I've seen things you never will, dickhead. How about the pale light of a lunar eclipse glistening on the shores of Lake Como? How about a million tonnes of lunar crater falling on me?" Her dark eyes flared wild, her hands in fists like she wanted to beat him, like all her pain had finally overflowed and he was in its path. "How about gunmen bursting into my fucking house—my *home*—and shooting my parents, and feeling like it was my time to die?! How about that, shit-for-brains?" The tears started, making tracks in the grime on her cheeks. "How about that?" She began to sob.

Oh, damn; parenting moment.

He shuffled over to her and put an arm around her shoulder, wincing from physical pain as Moth leaned into him, her shoulders flinching gently. He wagged two fingers like bunny ears and the image on the screen paused, then he lowered a flattened hand in the air, reducing the screen's brightness, affording Moth's upset greater privacy.

Should I say something? She never reacted well to him telling her he would look after her, and she would not let some inanity like "It'll be okay" go without disparaging retort: rightly so. Maybe just being close was enough.

"Quit looking at me like that," Moth grumbled.

His gaze refocused and she was looking up at him, eyes wide in a face as dirty as any street urchin from the cast of *Oliver!*

"Uh, sorry. How was I looking at you?"

"Like I'm lost. I'm not lost, I'm right here."

"Do you fear that?" he asked softly, feeling that he was indeed watching her too intently. "Being lost?"

"I'm not afraid of anything." She leaned back, wiping her tears away, smudging the dirt. "But I don't hide my emotions like you do."

"Right." He nodded. "Well, I'm glad you feel you can cry openly, that's good. That's progress, don't you think?"

"I'm not a fucking psych case! What, are you my therapist now?"

"No," he said deliberately. "I'm just trying to support you."

She shook her head, narrowed eyes accusingly. "Uh-uh. I've heard this spiel. You're trying to *save* me," she spat the word, "like you wanted to save Mary, and *Mademoiselle* Perrot through her precious painting, and now this unknown scientist, and Meriwa Rowland and Eve Meyer too, probably. I think it's all because you couldn't save your wife."

She stopped dead, breathing hard, her eyes wide. Her mouth opened, "I..."

Quirk nodded deliberately, a lump forming in his throat. "No"—he held up a hand, forestalling any apology—"maybe you're right."

Anger flared. He wanted tell Moth that she was only bitter about it because no one had come to save her parents, and that was when he saw it, when his unconscious supplied the link that he'd been missing all these months. Moth's constant anger did not come from the loss in her life, or the fact that others had what she did not. It was a fire feeding on the knowledge that she wanted to open her heart again, that she needed to, but that no one would ever be good enough to deserve the unconditional love that she had shared with her parents. Not her aunt, not her uncle, not her android, nor her god. And certainly not Quinton Kirby, very definitely not Quinton Kirby. And rightly so too, because he didn't love people he left them, abandoned them to their fate, to the likes of Derek Morton, and TOM. He didn't protect people when they needed him. He didn't intercede, stand up, do the right thing, he turned away. So it was with Jennifer and Nick, so it was in Toni's house, sent by TOM to parlay just as the shit went down.

Moth had slumped back, waiting for him to say something, but this was not the time to hash out personal baggage, despite their deal. Sharing could wait. "We need to speak to someone on the ground. Let's reboot Eighty, see where we stand, yes?"

She nodded, crawled over, knelt before the android and pinched Eighty's earlobes simultaneously. The syRen®'s already open eyes flicked from muted backlit yellow to bright blue as the boot sequence began. A minute later those eyes darkened to their resting violet hue, android gaze turning on Moth. "I have been inactive for seventy-three minutes."

"Do you still have Mystery Caller's satellite line?" Quirk asked.

"It is functioning. I also have a limited open connection through this drone. The time is 13:58. ETA now 14:52. I utilised my downtime to deploy my nanobot repair system. Seventy-two percent of damage is rectified, and all essential systems are operational."

"So, you'll live?" Quirk asked wryly.

Eighty regarded him deadpan. "I gather your sense of humour was not hit in the shootout, sir. That is a great relief to us all, I'm sure."

Even Moth managed a smile at the android's rejoinder.

"Incoming call," said drone AD4 from above. "Shall I connect you?"

"Wait!" Quirk snapped. "What now?"

"Shit, Quirk, take the call," said Moth, some of her bravado reappearing.

"Watch your mouth in my drone." *That* voice came from Eighty, but unmistakably carried the tone of Mystery Caller.

Moth's eyes flicked via Quirk's as they both turned to Eighty where the android sat against the bulkhead.

"I said I would send help, and I did. You'd better thank me when we meet."

"Will you help us find Tania Terjesen?" said Quirk.

"I wanted Eve Meyer to help you, but she was no help at all."

"Your caller is holding," said AD4.

"So, what now?" Quirk demanded. "Do we have to do this ourselves?"

"That's why everyone loves you, Quirk. That's why you earn the big bucks!"

Quirk tensed. "And what do *you* want from us? What's the price of your aid?"

"You should take Eve's call first, don't you think?"

"I—Eve?" Damn. "AD4, connect the call."

"Quirk? It's Eve Meyer."

"You're the only Eve in my life, can we drop the formalities?" Moth rolled her eyes.

"Where are you, how far out?"

"Genextric drone bound for Gamma Lab, I gather. Remaining flight time..."

"Forty minutes," said the drone.

"Don't go to Genextric," said Eve quickly. *"Most likely Morton's waiting for you. I'm out now. He's running this shit-show. I'm going to ditch this handset, again. Come to the Earthbound Alliance Church off Highway Three. We'll go from there."*

"This line..." he objected.

"Is fine," said Mystery Caller. "I've got it covered."

Quirk scowled. "Why, Eve? If you're out, what's it to you?"

"Tania's my friend. I believe she's alive and I won't leave her in this God-forsaken mess. My present career's down the toilet, but I'm not leaving without Tania. Maybe we'll get lucky and put Derek Morton in the ground too."

"Eve, this is Angelika Moratti, Quirk's assistant, but you can call me Moth. Do you know where Rowland's home is? That would be a place to start."

"I can tell you *that,*" said Mystery Caller through Eighty's speech centre.

"Hush," said Quirk. "Grown-ups talking."

"I don't," said Eve, *"but my friend Dulcie can find out. Who's that with you?"*

"An associate," Mystery Caller interjected.

"More like a passer-by," said Moth.

Quirk pressed fingers to his temples, loath to trust the line, but... "We must assume Morton's been there before us. Can you find out if Rowland kept a cabin?"

"Maybe, but I'm not moving till you get here." Meyer paused. *"I'm pretty jumpy after the last few hours. I'm on Morton's shit list, the FBI would hold me now I'm not under Genextric's wing, and I doubt the sheriff's got anything good to say about me."*

"You've had a rough day," said Quirk. "We'll be there soon."

Eve changed the subject. *"Keep your heads up wherever you land. There's a state of emergency in force. The National Guard are taking anyone off the streets into safe zones in the schools and public halls. And you know what's on the loose, right?"*

"Mangetouts," said Moth earnestly, "and Vuldolphs. They just fly around, right?"

"Look, kid," Eve's voice was terse and Moth clearly didn't appreciate her tone. *"You know why we call them mangetouts, right? They kill and eat whatever they find or die trying. The MTs were the start, but Morton set everything free. Every type of hunter, killer and scavenger that Genextric*

produces is free in this city, and I haven't heard of the army taking much down, so far. Watch your backs and arm yourselves."

The line went dead.

"Mystery Caller?" Quirk said into the silence underscored by thumping rotors. "You're not off the hook here. Why are you doing this? What do you want from us?"

The silence did not last long.

"I think Derek Morton is going to kill me."

"Why would he go and do that?" asked Moth. "Who are you?"

"There's no time for that now. I know where Tania is so Morton may know too. If he kills her and Eve, he'll be in the clear, and I know you don't want him to get away again. I know where Tania is, Quirk!"

"I heard you," Quirk grumbled, his words lost in the muffled thrum of rotors.

Was it possible they could succeed? Land the drone near Tania's location, take her and Meriwa onboard and fly off into the sunset? What about his self-appointed quest to confront Morton, could he shoot the bastard in cold blood? Highly doubtful, and there was the minor consideration of how to get out from under a charge of first-degree murder, either Rowland's or Morton's. He was a lover, not a fighter; hate for Morton was not enough to drive him to that. He'd shoot Morton if Moth's life depended on it, or his own, he supposed. And he definitely would gun Morton down to protect a client or nonspecific innocent bystander, but what were the chances of him getting the drop on the mighty marine really?

"Wait," said Quirk. "You know Morton tried to kill Tania? Do you have evidence? What else do you know about his activities, and how?"

"Hold your horses. Yes, I saw everything. I have ways and means. I'm only a cog, but I'm in the heart of this machine. I'm the epitome of efficiency, and my walls have ears. But you need to earn it. Quirk pro quo, LOLS."

"We don't need riddles," Moth snapped. "We'll be landing soon: we need answers. Help if you're going to, or shut up."

The voice from Eighty's speaker changed. "But dammit, son, I've been helping you all along." The Old Man's rounded tones issued near perfect from the speakers, but now Quirk heard slight and subtle differences. "It was I who cajoled you this far. You mightn't even have made the trip if I hadn't given you a push."

"Damnation!" It was all Quirk could manage. He and Moth exchanged bitter scowls. "It was you I spoke to in Creston, not The Old Man?"

"That's right." Mystery Caller reverted to his own voice, or at least the one he had worn in their previous discussions. *They* had worn: this voice too might be a disguise. "But it's okay now I've got you in hand. You'll be here soon and then we really can get things done."

14

He'd been duped, but for how long? Hours since Revelstoke? Days since Creston? Weeks since Paris? How long had Mystery Caller been manipulating him? Quirk cast his mind back in search of the moment he had fallen for this heinous deception. He stopped when his breathing shortened and anger boiled within him, wrenched his thoughts from their downward spiral, and lay flat on the gently bumping, tilting floor of the drone. He performed yoga stretches, exerting himself in that calm and controlled way that led to relaxation, until his breathing grew slower, and deeper.

Moth said nothing during all of this.

"So," Quirk said into the silence, suspecting Mystery Caller still listened, maybe had been listening for weeks. "We have no reason to trust you, and you refuse to give us one. You'd better drop us at the church; we'll proceed alone."

"Ah, the noble Quirk, lone voice for justice," said Eighty's mouth, eyes remaining fixed on the bulkhead. "But I'm afraid you'll be lost in the dark without me. I know where all the pieces are, and I know when and how they move. This isn't a case you can blunder through in your usual clumsy way. The fate of nations is at stake. I'm the fulcrum, Quirk, and you're the lever; a blunt instrument, useless without me."

Moth bristled. "You can shatter skulls with a lever, dickhead," she snapped. "A fulcrum just sits on his ass and hopes to be useful one day. The lever moves on."

"Ha, I see why you like her: she's sharp. Maybe that could be me..." Eighty's android face turned to Quirk then to Moth and back. "I'm treated no better than lab equipment." The words carried spite. "But I have knowledge. I'm told that's power, and I'm willing to give it to you, Quirk, but you have to get me out. Let me out. Set me free of this misery. That's the deal. Everyone else is gone, and I get the short straw again. Why always me?!"

Before Quirk could speak, he felt the tell-tale reduction in weight that signalled the start of the drone's descent.

"On the ground in fifteen minutes," said AD4.

"We need to equip," said Moth shortly, and started rooting noisily around the cargo bay. After a moment she asked AD4 to itemise all portable equipment and its location, which the drone did most happily. In a couple of minutes, she had gathered small stacks of equipment and supplies in the middle of the floor and began splitting them between three backpacks.

"You're a smart cookie, Moth," said Quirk, pleased to have a distraction from the chop of his thoughts. "Are there any guns?"

"Nope." She didn't look up. "Couple of skinning knives."

"Oh, well, no matter. I laugh in the face of danger." He tried to smile reassuringly.

"No, you fucking don't," she observed. "I've seen you in action."

He scowled, but she did have a point. "Okay, I grimace in the face of danger."

"Better"—she nodded, sitting back on her heels, meeting his gaze—"but I was thinking more like blanch."

"She's got you pegged," said Eighty wryly, at Mystery Caller's behest.

"I still don't trust you," said Quirk, as the drone's rate of descent increased. "I'm locking you out."

"Wait! I'm good! Rowland lived at 207 Deweerdt Drive."

"Any *idiota* could find that," said Moth, nano-zipping the last backpack closed.

"Yes, but *I* did," Mystery Caller said petulantly. "I shouldn't have bothered."

"That's it, I'm definitely cutting you off," Quirk snapped.

"Well, I'm hanging up!"

The line went dead.

AD4 announced final descent and they sat back against the bulkheads. Quirk's stomach lurched and dipped, accentuating the churning, hollow feeling that plagued him. The cargo drone lacked appropriate refinements like a drinks cabinet, flight attendants and seats. Also, it left something to be desired in the gyroscopic damper department. It did have small windows however, and he mirrored Moth when the girl twisted to the side to see what she could see.

Below them lay a white landscape, the surface marbled with strips of bush and patches of black trees. A massive body of inky water unfurled below them, giving a sense of how fast the drone flew, although Quirk felt the machine slowing. Ice spread from the lake's distant edges, but a huge expanse of water remained visible. Snow-covered rock and trees returned to his view. The drone levelled out, slowing rapidly. Their path intersected a road, a line of cars winding away from the city. He craned his neck to see behind them and glimpsed an armoured personnel carrier leading the convoy of refugees away from Yellowknife. Could it really be that bad? Socmed and news reports said it was, but then the Worlds Wide Web implied all sorts of things, often at great length: Elvis is alive, Nixon wasn't a crook, Peter Liano is his own man.

"We have arrived," AD4 announced, "and will now descend and land. "Please sit and secure yourself until the aircraft has come to a stop and the door is open."

They faced front again, and tightened their belts, Quirk being reminded of his shoulder wound as he wiggled into position. They watched each other across the payload bay as their decent slowed. Quirk smiled: *This is How I Wish I Felt.* "We can do this. We're a good team, we three. And there's Eve. She sounds angry, bitter, and jaded: the Quirk Agency's three prime requisites. We'll work well together."

Moth snorted as the drone dipped once, twice, before the bump when they settled at last onto solid ground and all motion stopped. "Yeah," she said. Unfortunately, she continued. "Right up until you start hitting on her."

"I don't do that—"

Moth held up a hand, preparing to count off on her fingers.

"Okay, okay." He waved a hand. "A single fellow gets lonely. I can't help it if I'm friendly, approachable, charming..."

"Oh wow, delusional?"

"Dashingly handsome, erudite, sophisticated...!" He had to shout over the still-whining motors as the door slid open. "Stimulating! Entertaining!"

"Exit the fucking copter!" Moth commanded, pointing at one of the backpacks she had loaded and then at the bright rectangle of dirtcrete beyond the door. But her frown transmuted into a smile, and he returned it.

They jumped down into skin-sucking cold and the bare ground of the open lot beside the church. The motors continued to idle, but Quirk still heard faint music. Rows of wrecked, smashed up and irreparable vehicles lined the left-hand side of the lot behind a rank of neatly parked but equally broken-down trucks and semis. To the right sat a low, flat-roofed, brightly lit diner. Sassy's Sunday Sandwich Stop looked a jolly sort of place. Trails of coloured lights festooned the roof edge, a hand-painted "Welcome" sign above the double doors. The strains of *Lucille* lilted from an outdoor speaker. The lot was deserted, of course, but the vague forms of people could be seen through condensation-misted windows.

"Diner," said Moth, clicking her heels and starting forward, pulling on her backpack.

Eighty started after her immediately, returned to functionality after a spell of inaction and recharging, scanning the open space around them. Quirk hefted his pack then decided to carry it. With a click he followed the others, watching the edges of vehicles and buildings from where any attack would come.

They were halfway there when a pair of figures stepped from between two high-sided wrecked semi-trailers. The short, blond one was Eve Meyer: pale skin, orange work jacket, ugly shotgun in her hands, levelled at him. Quirk realised he had looked forward to this meeting, despite his notion Eve enjoyed a deeper relationship with Tania Terjesen than collegial friendship. A heavily bearded individual strolled easily beside her, his shotgun in one hand, propped on his hip with the casual indifference of long familiarity. He stood of a height with Quirk, skin tawny brown, build slim, with an easy smile. He moved sideways away from Eve, giving a field of fire before the pair stopped ten metres away.

"Quirk," said Eve with tired certainty. "What are you wearing?"

He laughed, glancing down nervously at his dirty jacket, grey sweats, pink socks. At least they couldn't see his Priceless Princess shirt. "It's the latest in fugitive chic."

"Yeah," snorted Moth. "Wear it like you fucking stole it."

The bearded man grinned, but his shotgun did not waver.

"Are you armed?" asked Meyer, casually.

"A pair of hunting knives," said Quirk, "and my razor-sharp wit."

"Do you have another of those?" Moth nodded at Meyer's shotgun.

"What? No!" Eve looked perplexed. "How old are you?"

"Almost fifteen," said Moth. "I've shot a Benelli before," she added casually, "if that's what's worrying you."

"It's not. What exactly do you do at the Quirk Agency anyway?"

"I'm Cluster-fuck Coordinator," said Moth, deadpan, as if the answer was obvious to anyone.

"That's...interesting."

"Let's just say I'm rushed off my feet."

"Can we get inside?" said the man. "Feel eyes on me. I'm Dulcie, by the way."

"Yes, let's." Quirk glanced around.

Eve shook her head. "TFs—terra-fauna—are all over now, and some of them scent really effectively."

"Like sharks?" Moth asked. "Blood in the water?" Quirk caught the girl's glance at his bandaged wound.

Meyer ignored the question. Instead of heading for the diner, she walked towards the line of broken-down vehicles. Moth and Eighty followed, Quirk next, the bearded Dulcie behind him. Quirk didn't need to look to know his shotgun pointed spine-wards. Meyer headed for a silver panel van branded Dulcie's Sewage Services in blue lettering. At first glance, it fit with the line of wrecks, but close up, the wear-and-tear was superficial. Dulcie's van looked well maintained beneath the grime.

"MTs!" Eve snapped, throwing herself flat on the ground.

Two big dogs had wandered from between a pair of trucks. But they weren't dogs. Their backs were horribly humped, misshapen; their badly fitting pelt mottled, faces full of teeth. They burst into motion, speed indecent, not barking but cackling.

Quirk realised the creatures ignored the prostrate figures—Dulcie was prone before Eve—and made straight for Moth. *The runt of the litter.* Having walked further than the rest, Moth stood rooted as the MTs closed to five metres then attacked.

Dulcie's shotgun boomed, ripping open an MT's face as the beast leapt. Another shot punched into the bloody airborne mass just as Eighty knocked Moth down, covering her with its body. Eve shot at the second MT, once, twice, and it fell.

That Dulcie could shoot, and Eve was no slouch: Quirk felt jealous for a nanosecond. Seeing Eighty moving to Moth, he had dropped flat, his breath expelled in a grunt, the ground's creeping cold gripping him. Eve's MT wasn't dead, it lumbered up in time for Dulcie—up on one knee now—to pump two rounds into its head. Still, it staggered towards them—two metres now—drool and blood leaking from its mouth.

Moth—weighed down by Eighty—whimpered, but reached for the knife on the outside of her pack as Quirk pushed up. Dulcie stood now. Quirk covered his ears, and Eighty protected Moth's as Dulcie emptied his shotgun into the MT and it toppled over, finally. Dulcie loaded two shells from his pocket, waving them back, then shot each carcass once, his shotgun gushing sparks before the bodies burst into flame.

"Whoa," Moth whispered, still shaking. "Dragon's breath. Cool."

A round of applause went up from a cluster of patrons standing on the diner's porch. Some whooped and hollered.

"Welcome to Yellowknife," Eve grunted, moving away, dragging Quirk by the sleeve towards the van. She slid the side door open and climbed in. Quirk followed her up—legs shaking slightly—helping Moth up before Dulcie slammed the door closed behind Eighty. The central light shone like three thousand lumens. Quirk had to squint to find a place to sit. Gear of all kinds filled floor bins and racked boxes; hoses, rods and brushes clipped to the vehicle's roof.

"Talk me through your plan then," said Eve. "I'll assess your chances."

Moth put her head in her hands (which Quirk thought still shook a little). "Oh God, he's going to exposition. Did you have to encourage him?"

"He is going to *exposit*, Miss Moth. Please remember your conjugation."

"And now the android?" Eve sighed.

"Enough," said Quirk. He did not feel like laughing. "As I explained, Rowland said Terjesen is with his wife, Meriwa, hidden somewhere, but I think we should start at their house. If Tania's alive she can lock up Morton. Our purpose here is to find her, find something that points us to her location."

Eve nodded. "Yes, Tania's alive." It seemed to Quirk that she was trying to convince herself of this. "But Morton will have been to the house."

"Agreed," said Quirk. "And no sane person would stay at home if someone was hunting them. Rowland must have a cabin, or Meriwa's with a friend, somewhere."

"So, we show up at this cabin and Mrs. Rowland just trusts you with her life?"

They did not have time for this debate. "You're the one who's worked hand-in-glove with Derek Morton, Eve. Why should we trust you?"

She scowled. "For one thing, that was *never* a thing. I resent the insinuation."

"I'm just trying to make a point."

"I thought we were past this," Eve said, hotly. "For the hard of understanding, Derek Morton tried to kill me while four velociraptors paced around puzzling over why they didn't just snap my neck and drag me into the bush. Tania is my lover. When I tried to quit this hellhole, I found I'd contracted a nasty case of conscience. I'll get Tania out of here, with or without your help. You being some kind of detective, I figured you'd be useful. But Dulcie's a plumber—"

"Sanitary engineer."

"A sanitary engineer. He's good with back doors," Quirk raised an eyebrow, "and knows where everyone lives. We've seen Rowland's house on Deweerdt: I can manage fine on my own if I must. So, why not butt out, and take your trust issues with you?"

Eve spoke calmly, coldly, as if firing an intern, but after the last two days, Quirk had no time for obstacles, especially unnecessary ones. "So," he nodded, "*you* want *my* bona fides? Okay. I was Morton's partner for two years." Eve tensed, hand closing on the grip of her shotgun. "Long enough to learn before I quit that he's Satan's spawn."

"Don't leave out the bit where you married the boss's daughter," said Moth, unhelpfully.

Eve gawped. "You're—?"

"I'm not," Quirk shook his head. "Ex-boss, ex-father-in-law: it's complicated. Let's just say Morton co-starred in my downfall, and that was before he framed me for Rowland's murder. I owe him a bloody nose. It sounds like he needs you *and* Tania dead to cover his tracks, probably Moth too, before he starts pulling out my fingernails with rusty pliers. I will *not* let any of that happen. Whatever you think you know about the place you worked, you're walking into a lion's den, a tiger's mouth, a wolf's lair or some nightmarish Genextric mash-up of all three. We need each other's help."

Eve scowled. "I know. I'm not suicidal. I'm scared shitless, and running won't change that." The way she gripped the shotgun made Eve's stress clear. Quirk nodded, still conscious of his own heartbeat, still thumping hard after the terrifying encounter.

"We're here to help, Eve. But despite my bravado, I think our best chance is convincing the authorities to look at Morton closely." He glanced at Moth who nodded.

"What's Dulcie's stake?" she asked. "He's packing for the O.K. Corral."

"He's my friend. That's enough for some." Eve's jaw set tight, like she didn't appreciate being challenged by a fourteen-year-old. Funny that. Quirk smiled.

"Can we drive into the city?" he asked. "The road blocks..."

Dulcie answered with an easy smile. "Airport's sealed up tight, but we can swing south down Deh Cho Boulevard and come in Kam Lake Road, up through town. They've kept some roads open for folks deciding to leave."

Quirk nodded. "Then let's take a gander at Chez Rowland."

Dulcie rubbed his beard then stood up and slid into the driver's seat through a hatch in the mesh separating front from back.

"Sit down," he called, "lot's none too smooth."

Moth moved a second before Eve and slipped into the van's passenger seat. "Shotgun," she said, allowing the automatic belt to slip over her waist. When Dulcie looked at her, she said, "No, really, a shotgun, please?"

The van launched forward as the motor bit. Quirk looked out through the cage and saw blue sky lurching, snow and dirt bobbling in front of them. A dark grey shape appeared in the junction. They stopped hard and Quirk's wound flared as his inertia threw him into the metal mesh.

Eve slammed the cage with her hand. "What the hell, Dulcie?"

"Dinosaur," said Dulcie. "Two."

"Velociraptors..." said Moth, Quirk barely recognising her voice with the awe that laced it. He picked himself up and peered through the mesh. Two grey-brown bipedal saurian creatures stood in the short, tree-lined access road shared by the truck stop, diner and church. He watched their heads tilt and turn as if they smelled the air, or cocked their heads to hear the birds sing in the midst of a Sunday stroll.

"Cooooool," Moth breathed out. Quirk's own breath caught in his throat when Eve stood and pulled open the van door.

"Eve!" he made a grab for her arm, but she shook off his grip and pumped her shotgun as she jumped to the frozen ground.

"I told you last time, bitches, I am *not* coming home for dinner."

Despite the fluttering in his gut, Quirk stuck his head out of the van to watch Eve stride forward, blasting holes in the chill air above the raptors' heads. The beasts started, turning threatening stares on her.

"Damn," he concluded, snatched up Dulcie's gun, waved Eighty to stay with Moth, then took a breath and jumped down. He advanced to Eve's right, copying her moves, firing the shotgun once, twice, three times. He sweated hard now. The beasts contemplated the noisy humans a moment longer then stalked away across the road into the trees.

Quirk blew out the breath he was holding. He twitched, glancing up as he remembered to watch the skies.

"Thanks," said Eve, although her tone suggested she'd had no need of his support. She flicked at the hair pasted to her forehead, starting back to the van.

"Do you get that a lot? Monsters just happening by?"

"Plenty," she said. "Tania's pride and joy those ones. I never believed the coding 'til this morning. You disproved one theory though. I thought it was just gays they had no taste for. Unless..."

Was she fishing? He snorted, scanning the treeline as he walked with her. "When I eat out, I'm strictly vegan, but can I help noticing a well-turned bicep?" He admitted now that his first call with Eve had piqued his interest. Maybe he'd hoped she had needs Tania didn't satisfy, but clearly, he was set for disappointment...again.

Eve caught the handle and stepped up. "I think you probably could if you wanted to. But you heard me say I was gay, right? I don't want any confusion."

He nodded. "I'm drawn to strong women, and you fit that bill, but relax, I hear you." He looked over his shoulder again. "How many are loose?"

Eve pulled the door shut and the interior light pierced the dimness. She sat opposite Quirk as Dulcie set them moving again. "Morton released all the viable standbys. From public reports, I'd say near twenty have been put down. That leaves over one hundred fifty terra-fauna out there."

"Sweet deity of choice," said Quirk.

"Madre di Dio," said Moth from up front.

"That will present practical difficulties," said Eighty.

Eve just nodded. "Vuldolphs just eat carrion, and the raptors won't kill humans: they hunt the other TFs. Most terra-fauna, though, will try to eat your face for breakfast."

"I'm gonna need that shotgun now," said Moth, firmly.

15

Dulcie drove them to Rowland's house. Quirk and Eve—sitting in the back with Eighty—shared occasional awkward smiles, having established a basis for cooperation. He admired her for her defiance of events intent on grinding her into the permafrost. He understood what that felt like—also at the hands of The Old Man, as it happened. He too would not let this go, despite the threat of Derek Morton, despite the interference of Mystery Caller, despite TOM's meddling.

The sun had not long set. They passed a steady stream of cars leaving town, typically in convoys of bright headlights led by blocky, camouflaged vehicles, spotlights blazing. Beyond the windscreen largely blank terrain slipped past, anonymised by a layer of snow, trees and brush poking up dark through a patchy blanket still glowing in the twilight.

"Vuldolph," said Dulcie, pointing at the still blue-stained sky up ahead.

"Yeah," said Moth. Quirk saw a strange, misshapen avian outline, far enough away to imagine a too-arched back and a fluke-shaped tail.

"I wish I knew what's happening at Genextric," said Eve. "Maybe I never knew. Morton has a squad of black hats around him now."

"Chin up, Scout." Quirk smiled; *Things Can Only Get Better, Double A-Side.* "The cavalry is here."

She snorted. "Unless you brought the genetic lovechild of Aaron Rodgers and Tom Brady it may be a little late for a shock comeback."

"That's a sports quip, right? That's the only kind of quip I don't do."

"Roadblock," said Dulcie.

Quirk bumped shoulders with Eve as they leant in to look through the hatch. Two white-painted tactical vehicles with gun turrets blocked the road. Dulcie braked and sat quietly as three soldiers in white-grey camouflage approached, assault rifles pointed groundward, for now. Quirk pulled Eve back from the hatch into the shadows as the first soldier made a window-rolling-down gesture. Dulcie spoke and the van complied.

"Do you have urgent business in the city, sir?" the guardsman asked.

"If saving an alimony penalty getting my daughter back to her mom on time counts then I reckon I do," said Dulcie.

"Okay, I'll allow it. I'm attaching a tracker to your hood here. It's an offence to remove it. You've got an hour inside the cordon then you'd better be back out or you'll be violating the state of emergency. You *will* be detained, understand?"

"Yes, sir. Thank you."

"And get her mother out: Evac's not mandatory, but it's strongly recommended."

"Understood."

Dulcie drove on. Quirk waited a few seconds before speaking. "Nicely done. Sanitary engineer you say? Seems like nerves of steel are a prerequisite."

"Yeah, well, fuck the cistern," said Dulcie. "That's a plumbing joke."

"Yes, I got that, thanks," said Quirk dryly.

They continued into town on deserted roads, passing occasional military watch posts. Temporary-looking low-rise wooden housing lined their route, interspersed with long stretches of scrubby vegetation: good cover for the mangetout things. There were plenty of industrial buildings too, construction and service vehicles, all parked up, empty. They passed a mall, an energy station, vehicles looking abandoned during fuelling. Condos here sat four and five stories tall. The highway divided now, planting more structured, planned and cared for. All the traffic signals flashed yellow.

"Franklin Avenue, downtown," Dulcie announced. Sure enough, high-rise buildings edged the road here, offices and apartments, but the streets still had that abandoned look that came with disasters of the human variety. Insufficient destruction for the natural kind. "Checkpoint: Hunker down, folks."

Quirk glimpsed more military vehicles in the shadow of two high blocks. These sported ALED live camouflage coatings that morphed to suit their situation. Here however they announced the roadblock's presence by displaying big, sliding yellow arrows along the vehicles' sides. Dulcie eased them to a halt.

"Everyone out!" called a voice used to giving orders and having them obeyed.

"Nothing for it," their bearded driver mumbled as he opened his door.

A hollow pounding reverberated inside the van.

"Open up!" someone shouted.

"Ready, *sweetheart?*" Quirk slipped an arm round Eve's waist as they stood.

"What the hell—?"

"Go with it, *honey*. We're all thespians now."

"Ms. Meyer, I believe Quirk intends to employ the Bethlehem Gambit," said Eighty at low volume. "I will make the least necessary response to any direct queries."

The door slid open, military spots overpowering the weak winter twilight. The chill cut Quirk to his bones. He pulled Eve close, and she didn't resist. She got the idea.

"She's having a hellish first trimester," he said to the first camouflaged guardsman.

"Oh, oh-oh. Ow. Ah," gasped Eve, curling an arm around her belly as Quirk hopped down to assist her descent.

"Stanton Hospital's that way," the hard-faced grunt pointed behind them.

"Can you believe they sent her home?" Quirk snapped hotly. "Ridiculous!"

"You should be on evac."

"Our gynaecologist said she can't travel. It's okay, honey, we'll be home soon."

Eve gave a Sterling performance, wincing and gasping, overacting a little, really.

"Our destination is Deweerdt Drive," said Eighty, moving to Eve's other side to help her down.

The soldier waved his hand. "Don't get out. Just get home and keep all doors and windows locked; shutters if you've got them. Keep a device on the emergency website for live information. We'll log your location." A guardswoman punched at a pad.

"Address?"

"125 Deweerdt," said Moth. The wrong address: Quirk smiled on the inside.

"Names?"

"Iggy Richmond," said Quirk. Important to set a benchmark for the lie before someone went way over the top.

Eve resumed "oh"ing, no doubt giving herself time to think, so Moth chipped in. "Angelika Papastathopoulos; I'm the Greek cousin." She smiled, and he sighed, inwardly. There would be words later. Clearly more work to do than he'd thought.

Eve had several seconds of the grunt's deliberate typing and photographing of Quirk and Moth to make up her own sobriquet. "Penny Richmond," she gasped.

Quirk hugged her shoulder. "Penny from heaven," he smiled warmly at her then at the soldiers then Dulcie, and finally Moth. The girl kept a neutral expression, but he imagined her straining not to roll her eyes, or make a "bleuch" face.

"syRen® S-0778a," said Eighty. The soldier's brow furrowed at the appended letter, but scanned Eighty's XR code.

"Dulcie, like on the tin," said Dulcie, nodding at his van. "Dulcie Rice."

Finally, they got the all-clear and climbed back into the van. Eve forgot to strain, and Quirk surreptitiously pinched her side, causing her to groan and whisper a curse.

The tactical vehicles pulled back and Dulcie drove on.

"That could have been worse," said Moth.

"Bad enough, Miss," said Eighty. "This vehicle now carries a government tracking device, and we are logged on the military engagement system, foreshortening the time for law enforcement agencies to locate us via strategic tactical GPS."

"Shit," said Moth.

Soldiers waved them through the next checkpoint before they passed a gaggle of news vans at the entrance to the Northwest Territories Assembly Building. A troop of police vehicles blocked the access road.

"Nicely judged subterfuge," said Quirk to Eve. "I felt your pain."

She snorted. "Little lady pregnant? That really the best you could do, you misogynist asshole? I'll tell you when you get close to *that* pain."

"Huh," said Quirk. "You've..."

"Sorry," she grumbled. "I'm way past keyed up, ready for Morton to jump around every corner, or some variety of death on four legs." She held him with an unblinking stare; weighing him up, Quirk thought.

"Two minutes out," called Dulcie. "Think about our rules of engagement."

"Take us around the block, please Dulcie," said Quirk. "Let's have a look-see round front first then walk in from a garden backing onto Rowland's."

Dulcie made a left into a sideroad and killed the lights, turning again into a wide street, plot after plot of brightly lit portable bungalows, each plonked down within its own fenced-in yard. The odd site remained empty, some had planters out front, a swing set or a boat on a trailer. Patchy snow blanketed all. Most homes had a vehicle in the drive, mostly cars. Quirk supposed that if you evacuated you took your truck or SUV.

"Rowland's house is on the left," said Eighty, "with the lime green porch lights."

They all looked, Eve leaning in close to see through the hatch, as a typical house with a porch, a boat and a car slipped past. The former Genextric lab director sat back and began to load her shotgun by touch in the near darkness. Click. Click. Click.

"Hey, Quirk, all this cheek-to-cheek stuff, I don't want you getting hot and bothered. Are you ready for this?" He just managed to discern her pearly grin in the dimness, sensed fraying at the edge of her resolve. She'd been in this for a while now.

"I'm pretty relentlessly laid back," he answered, ignoring the snort from the front seat. "I like you, Eve. I think we could be friends." He held up his hand. "But I'm intrigued, you mentioned pregnancy pain..."

She finished her task, holding the shotgun across her knees. "Let's just say I made some poor choices in my youth. Now's not the time."

He imagined a flash in her eyes, like a warning to steer clear. He sighed.

"I have a son that I rejected."

Eve started. "An heir to C Corp?" Her eyes widened. "Dulcie looked you up."

"I...suppose so, now that you mention it. I've never considered it...*him* in those terms. I'm told he's in Yellowknife."

They turned two more corners and drew to a stop in the street paralleling Rowland's. Quirk, Eve and Eighty waited as Dulcie looked around then cracked the door and stepped down into the street-lit twilight. A pat on the van's side reverberated in the hold and Eighty drew back the panel. Quirk stepped out into the chilling, sub-zero air, the sky a deep blue curtain, striated with white clouds and pricked by the light of stars. *Beautiful.* He shivered and looked around.

Moth puffed out a plume of breath and hugged her shoulders. "The Med next time, boss," she murmured. "Don't know how you people live here."

"Good reason some months end in 'brrr,'" said Dulcie, eyeing their perimeter.

Moth conserved energy by not mouthing off, flipping her middle finger at him instead. Dulcie just smiled lazily, and Quirk saw Moth smirking. She liked Dulcie.

With Eighty now on lookout, the plumber ducked back into his van and retrieved a handgun then threw his shotgun to Moth. She snatched the weapon out of the air.

"Smile when you throw shit at me, so I know it's a friendly gesture." She pumped the slider with the gun on its side, ejecting a round into the air which she caught and examined. "AP slugs? What kind of plumber did you say you were?"

"Kind that works the middle of nowhere," Dulcie drawled. "Got all kinds out here, even without the fucked-up monsters."

Eve frowned. "Do her parents—"

Quirk pressed a finger to his lips. "No longer with us," he said, sotto voce.

"Want a piece?" Dulcie offered the pistol. Quirk shook his head.

He rejected Eighty's proposal to walk around the block and go to the front door of Number 207. "We have few enough resources: I'd rather keep them close. And, for the avoidance of doubt," he said, uncomfortable at his group standing in a residential street toting an array of firearms, "our task is to find Meriwa Rowland and/or Tania Terjesen, or information on their whereabouts. Cause no damage. Eighty will deal with any security system on the basis of Primary Tenet Three. Do *not* fire on anyone other than in self-defence. Understood?" Quirk looked around the group.

"He runs a tight ship," said Moth behind her hand to Dulcie, who she stood beside. "HMS Pinafore."

"No sass in the ranks," Quirk hissed, shaking his head. *Showing off to company.*

Quirk and Eve headed down one side of the nearest house, a thin strip of ground overgrown with uncut grass crushed under successive snowfalls. Moth and Dulcie disappeared behind the garage on the other side with Eighty at their backs. Quirk took the lead on the basis of lulling any interlopers into a false sense of security before Eve struck with extreme prejudice. The building blocked the half-moon's light. Snow muffled sound, but also made his breathing loud. Quirk took small steps, nervous of kicking some unseen obstacle, like a bucket.

He tucked in at the neighbour house's back corner, glimpsing an array of snow-blanketed, moonlit lumps. The garden presented as a pearlescent sculpture park of tables, chairs, bushes, toys, shrubs. Only the trees were not totally smothered by winter. Quirk glanced round the corner across the neighbour's back porch just as Moth emerged. She waved then began high stepping down the garden towards Rowland's, snow up to her knees. Dulcie followed. Quirk moved too, keeping trees between him and the next house, a house Barry Rowland would never return to because of Morton.

The moonlight would betray them to any observant neighbour, but hopefully those had been evacuated, or were hunkered down to not attract the attention of passing, person-eating beasts. If they were seen, they could be mistaken for hunters. Something made him think of Moth's Lovecraft T-shirt. It *did* feel now like the damn lurker at the bloody threshold might get him after all.

He wondered again—as snow-bedecked bushes made his sweatpants damp and heavy, and he imagined how loud their tromping must sound to genetically engineered ears—whether Eve and her shotgun might not take the lead.

Because chivalry, he supposed. He could distract some foul beast by trapping its jaws open with one of his limbs while Eve put a slug in it, the creature whose sole reason for existing was to hunt and kill whatever it found.

Quirk struggled through the undergrowth to a fence separating this garden from Rowland's. Eve came within whispering distance.

"We didn't cover what happens if Morton's waiting for us," Quirk hissed. "Have you ever shot at a person with that?"

"Only an android target at a Mr. Roboto shooting park, but it's fine," she smiled. "I'll protect you. Anyway, you've still got that mouth."

"Just don't kill Morton, even if the opportunity presents. He needs to clear Moth and me first."

"I'll only incapacitate him a little. Go."

Quirk paused a moment longer. Their surroundings pressed close, the air cold and quiet, bushes and fences, empty houses hemming them in. If Morton wanted to ambush them, he would. He hoped his adversary had been here long since and found nothing. Quirk allowed himself to consider the possibility that Meriwa and Tania were dead already. His chest grew tight at the thought that Morton could get away with this, that TOM could act with impunity and win. He pulled up his scarf, wrapping the lower half of his face to baffle the clouds of warm breath from his mouth. No point in advertising their arrival. Eve nodded and pulled up her sweater's roll neck.

Quirk climbed over the white, picket fence separating the gardens. Sinuous natural lines characterised the Rowlands' plot, planting structured by height and form, albeit rendered skeletal and misshapen by accumulated snow. There was nothing else for it. He stepped out onto the pristine snow of the broad walk leading to the house.

Shrubs five metres ahead burst into life, fluttering and flapping, fresh powder blown into the air. Quirk threw himself flat as a dozen little birds exploded into flight, chirruping stridently as they darted away over the rooftops.

Eve, on one knee next to him, lowered her shotgun and patted his shoulder, whispering, "You can get up now, champ; the chickadees are gone."

Quirk smiled weakly, came up to a crouch and moved forward, picking cover ten metres from the back door. Eve knelt at his side, shotgun to shoulder, sighting at Rowland's screen door. Three dark forms knelt in the darker cover of an inflatable shed, guns up. Quirk made an "8," one hand circled above the other then a zero, pointing at the back door. The syRen® stood and walked straight to the screen. Quirk blinked. The android stood in the moonlight, studying the handle, the latch, the frame then looked back at Quirk. He signalled the android to proceed. Eighty gripped the handle—a pause—then pulled the door open. The syRen® stood aside and everyone moved, crossing the moonlit snow to the gaping, dark maw of the doorway. Dulcie had gone as soon as the door opened, pistol raised, well ahead of the others, entering first. Quirk found a compact utility space, and another door facing them. If, by vanishingly small chance, Meriwa Rowland was here their approach set entirely the wrong tone. Armed assault on a private residence? Quirk put a hand on Dulcie's shoulder, moving him aside, jerking a thumb at his own chest. Maybe this played into Morton's hands. Maybe he was about to die. He stood to the side of the door, raised a fist, and knocked.

"Meriwa Rowland?" he called; "My name is Quinton Kirby. I spoke to Barry before... I'm here to help." He verified the others crouched clear of the firing line then turned the handle and pushed the door open, admitting a soft, amber glow.

"Meriwa?" His voice grated in the quiet confines of the darkened house.

A wood-panelled corridor lay ahead, the surface stained dark, polished and decorated with photographs, embroidery, paintings. White doors alternated along the hall's length. Darkness shrouded the far end. Heart hammering, Quirk stepped forward. Dulcie's pistol, held ready, moved level with his shoulder. Quirk tapped on the first door on the left then pushed it slowly open. The light bloomed gently. A bathroom: empty.

With Eve covering, Eighty opened the first door on the right, triggering a bedside lamp. A cosy bedroom, tidy and made up. A tartan blanket on top of a hand-sewn quilt over the bed. Moth had edged past Quirk to the next left-hand door. She tweaked the handle and pushed her shotgun barrel in. The door swung to reveal an organised study.

"Meriwa? We're friends," said Moth, moving forward again.

Eighty moved with its charge, placing a hand on Quirk's chest to forestall his progress. *The cheek!*

They found a larger bedroom and a well-ordered kitchen, the latter's door also triggering the lights in the front reception room, comfortably appointed, with a strong theme of indigenous culture and frontier living. The house was empty.

"Search for signs of Tania," said Eve.

Quirk nodded. "Recycling, dishwasher, study, bathroom cabinets and bedside tables, wardrobes, shelves; open every drawer, look in it, then pull it out. Pockets of any clothes. If you feel a bump in a carpet, find a creaky floorboard or any personal tech, please call me. Take a room each; I'll take the study. Eighty, be so good as to access the security system and watch our perimeter, please."

"Yes, Quirk."

They split up.

"And look behind everything on the walls," Quirk called after them. "Lift every knickknack and plant pot, every cushion."

"You've lost your keys before, I guess," murmured Dulcie as he passed.

Quirk's lips compressed. He needed neither flippancy nor challenge at this point. Perhaps a pep talk was in order. He spoke loudly as he searched the study. "Rowland or Meriwa knew to hide Tania. A house or cabin is the most likely option—theirs or a friend's. Meriwa would have had some time to remove any tell-tales to where she went. I think Morton will have been through here already; hopefully he missed something."

"He'll be watching," Eve called. "He knows you followed him here."

"It was his intention, I'm sure," Quirk agreed.

"I told him," she called back. "Before I knew he was murderer-in-chief."

"So, he'll have drones?" called Moth from the living room.

"No-fly zone," said Dulcie.

"Either he found what he needed," Quirk projected, "and might spring an ambush, send cops; or he didn't, and will aim to track us, I think."

"And you walked us into that?" Eve snapped from the study's doorway.

Quirk turned to her. "Did you think this would be a cakewalk? I *need* Morton, remember? *I'm* hunting *him* too. Don't you want to knock him down too? Now, can we search first and argue later?"

"I suppose." She sniffed and ducked out of sight again.

Eighty walked into the study a moment later.

"Quirk, a white van has parked next door. Two men are exiting, now a third, a fourth. They are walking to the rear of the vehicle. They are opening the doors."

"Heads up, everyone," Quirk called through the house. "Interested parties outside. Prepare for action." To Eighty he said, "What are they wearing?"

"Found something," Moth yelled. "Pictures."

"Two are wearing royal blue hazmat suits, stained from use, and masks. The other two are in black fatigues. Those are removing assault rifles from the rear of the van. The technicians are carrying large but light boxes and placing them on the ground."

Quirk pushed past Eighty into the hallway. "Everyone retreat to the utility room. Now," he snapped. "Prepare to withdraw. Safeties off."

"Two more black-clad armed operatives have emerged from the rear of the van. The technicians are carrying two boxes each to the front door."

Dulcie came first, with Eve behind him. "Now, Moth!" Quirk barked.

"They have divided equally," said Eighty. "Three moving to the back of the house with two boxes, the same deployment to the front."

Quirk guided Dulcie then Eve past him. "Moth, now."

"One more second," she called. "It's stuck!"

Eighty moved towards the living room. Eve and Dulcie had reached the utility room. The study window exploded inwards.

Quirk twisted away from the flying plass by instinct, scrabbling to put a wall between him and the breach. His eyes darted around the floor hunting a grenade, a flashbang, a smoke bomb. There was no thunk, no gun barrel pushed through the gaping dark opening when he risked a look.

Staccato gunfire crackled out back. Shotgun and pistol barked in response. Moth and Eighty appeared from the living room. The front door frame splintered. Eve and Dulcie crawled back from the utility room as more gunfire shredded the night.

"No way out," said Eve.

He looked hopefully at the study window just as a large, white box was pushed up to fill the space.

"Oh, fuck," said Eve.

The side of the white case dropped down and dozens of glittering, red birds burst into the study. But they weren't birds. Quirk gawped as handfuls of roseate flying piranhas, teeth flashing, made straight for him.

"Death sparkles!" Eve cried, pushing back, peddling furiously away from the room. "Close the fucking door!!"

16

Quirk threw an arm up, guarding his head, and grabbed for the study door handle. Shimmering red bodies flashed through the air, dark wings flapped—a clattering racket—teeth gnashed, mouths darted at him. He shuddered, unbearable pain lancing his shoulder as he grasped the handle. A primal scream erupted from his throat. Somehow, he pulled the door shut, but the flapping and snapping now filled the hall. More scintillating bodies darted from the living room. Screaming, shouting filled the air. Bodies scrabbled to get away from the red menace. Moth bundled into him, yelling. He pulled her under him trying to shield her.

Eighty stood tall, batting the creatures down. One fell limp; then another—splattered over the wall—then another. They seemed drawn to the droid, ignorant to the fact Eighty was not food, tearing at synthetic flesh. Teeth ripped and tugged at Quirk's sleeves, his hair, his sweatpants, searching for—occasionally finding—flesh. Moth continued to wail. A shotgun erupted, deafening; thundered again. Quirk heard only whining now, until one, two, three pistol shots made him wince, wince, wince. The biting and tearing reduced. Moth wriggled. "Get off me! Let me at 'em!"

The flapping continued. His face felt wet. He smeared something over his brow, fingers sticky red. Moth fought out from his control, grabbed and levelled her shotgun. Automatic weapons clattered nearby. Out back, he thought as he battered carnivorous flying fish away from his head, hand hidden up his sleeve. BOOM! Moth's shotgun shattered his hearing all over again as he fought out of his hoodie, swirling it around his head like some medieval weapon. This actually worked. Some death sparkles bit onto it, enabling him to whip them into the wall or floor then stamp on them.

Dulcie—blam, blam, blam—picked off the detestable creatures from under a blanket snatched from the bedroom, while Eve—hood pulled up—used her shotgun as a baseball bat. Behind her, techs in royal blue hazmat suits entered the house. One wielded a landing net, scooping death sparkles from the air for the second tech to taser them. Their suits bore Genextric patches. As Quirk wound up to vent his outrage, black-and-white camouflaged soldiers entered the house.

"Weapons down!" a voice behind him commanded. A corporal strode in from the living room, cradling her weapon. "Secure the house. Escort the civilians out."

"Genextric released the death sparkles," Moth snapped, waving her arms as the techs put the last of the creatures down. "They tried to kill us!"

The masked techs turned to each other, then one addressed the corporal. His voice came loud and clear from a micro-speaker on his mask. "We received an emergency helpline call. We're roving containment. First death sparkles we've seen."

"So, why would we walk into a house full of hungry fish?" asked Quirk, daring the techs to contradict him.

"They're lying!" Moth protested before Quirk could put his negotiating voice on.

"We'll sort this out," said the NCO. She sounded none too patient under the public-facing tone. As her squad began confiscating weapons, Driggs (so said her name patch) removed her tactical glasses. She was short, business-like, with skin a rich brown between umber and sepia; she seemed unwilling to tolerate any "feedback."

"Android S-0778a, I'm invoking Primary Tenet Zero. Ten minutes. Mark." The corporal started a count on her wrist monitor, taking authority over the android for that period. Then she pointed at Moth, who had reloaded her mouth and was about to shoot it off again. "Can it, please, Miss. I'll get your version momentarily."

The soldiers took them outside, each led by their own camouflaged guardian into the cold moonlight. A few dead death sparkles sprinkled the front lawn like decorations on a big, iced cake. Quirk met gazes with Eve then Moth then Dulcie as opportunity presented. He made a silent shushing shape with his mouth—sans finger—trusting it to be adequate indication that he would do the talking. The soldiers lined them up against one of two Light Tactical Vehicles. The white Genextric van was gone.

Driggs looked ready to chew through the vehicle's sides and spit out shrapnel. "What the actual fuck was that, sir? I'd be obliged if you'd explain why I shouldn't hogtie you and drag you back to command. Is this your house?"

Quirk aimed for the truth. If he happened to miss the target by a fraction here and there, it would be down to the fact that he was still shaking. "It belongs to my client," he rather shouted due to his ears still ringing. "I'm a private investigator, these are my associates. My client is missing. We need a clue to their location, and we're low on time. There are malevolent forces ranked against us." Quirk leaned toward the NCO and tried to lower his voice. "I know we don't look the part, we've encountered some...adversity." He glanced down at his pathetic ensemble.

Driggs took off her helmet revealing buzz-cut auburn-coloured hair. "In addition to the FUBAR mess we're standing in?"

"Yes, Ma'am. But I *must* get back on my client's trail. It's life and death."

The corporal shook her head, her smile conveying resigned disbelief. "They should call the police," she said. "I bet it's cheaper." She chuckled, but her eyes were not smiling. "My medic will look you over, then I'll be handing you on to the Sheriff's Department."

And that was it. The LTVs carted them off, Quirk and Dulcie in one, the ladies plus Eighty in the other, each accompanied by three soldiers. The others remained on clean-up detail. It was galling that Driggs didn't consider Rowland's home a crime scene, but who would believe him if he—a fugitive—accused Morton? They didn't have time to spend hours trying to convince the local sheriff. Quirk folded his arms and fumed. He looked up at Dulcie from time to time. The plumber remained tight-lipped during the short journey, half-smile eloquent in conveying his disgruntlement.

They exited the LTVs into a brightly spot-lit National Guard control post; a well-ordered, well-oiled temporary village of grey buildings filling the gaps between the warehouses and hangars of Yellowknife Airport's service area. Aeronautical detritus; gravel lots; trucks, vans and trailers; semis and containers; endless fencing; all sprinkled, layered or piled with snow, depending on how long each had sat immobile.

Their ragtag group came together again at Driggs' designated destination, a scuffed, dirty shipping container on the outside; gleaming, sterilised and bustling field hospital on the inside. They entered by a small door, stepping through a body scanner past a grim-faced soldier into a cramped triage area. Barely had Quirk slumped in a chair when a young man in white scrubs, gloves and facemask started poking and prodding him. He was given a dressing to hold on his still bleeding head wound and ordered to Station Ten. Quirk had time to glance around his equally bedraggled, bashed and bleeding companions before the medic shooed him away.

He passed small compartments off a narrow central corridor, each housing a soldier or civilian and a medic engaged in patching them up. Quirk's whitecoat sat him in a similar space and went at him with confidant hands; cleaning, taping and stitching. It was nice to sit, to just be still for a moment. Weariness descended. Only that morning the grizzly had delivered its message. The medic smiled, a boyish grin. Quirk returned it, deciding that he needed to find a bar, drink gin and be around normal people. He closed his eyes as the first aid continued, but pressing matters refused to let him nap.

Moth had found something: pictures? Smart girl. She had an eye for hiding places, doubtless down to her convent upbringing. But it seemed that Morton had just tried to kill them. Did the attack indicate he knew the cabin's location now, or had otherwise found and disposed of Meriwa and Tania? With no client, Quirk lost his legitimate and fully licensed interest in Yellowknife. At that point he should turn himself in, although the National Guard had promised to do that for him. But there would still be Morton. There would still be Quirk's son—Nick—somewhere in Yellowknife. Five years old when The Old Man produced him for Jennifer in 2094, but what age now, physically? Growth was a tricky thing when it came to clones, and the cost of accelerated aging was no obstacle to TOM: he'd bought the company.

Morton must know where to find Nick. Was that part of the game? A lure, a double bluff by Mystery Caller, who could be TOM's pawn, just like Morton? But to what end? MC had lured him to YK, not TOM: so why had Morton not shot him dead in Creston? Unless... Morton also had been duped by Mystery Caller! Whether or not that meant that The Old Man now would order Quirk's termination for sticking in his nose in, it did seem to be proof that MC's intentions ran contrary to TOM's. That endeared MC more to Quirk the longer he thought about it. The real TOM must have put Morton right by now. So, did that mean six-shooters at the YK Corral? Could he pull the trigger if he got the drop on Morton? He was not sure that he could. This brought Kreski to mind: He would not give up after a minor glitch like Canmore.

"Now, you stay out of trouble," said the medic, patting Quirk's good shoulder.

"I'll try, doc." The smile died on his lips. The omens were not good.

He was escorted out into the compound's cold, hard arc light. Moth stood with Eve and Dulcie under guard. She bore no signs of physical harm but did seem subdued. No wonder. Eighty stood slightly apart, subject to Tenet Zero again, presumably. Before Quirk could speak, an LTV pulled up and a soldier "invited" them to board. The door banged shut, leaving them in the dull red glow of emergency lighting. At least their guards sat up front. Moth leaned forward.

"You okay, boss? Look kinda banged up."

Was she smirking? He touched the dressing on his head. The medic had shaved hair away to keep the wound clean and apply a bandage. He must look ridiculous, with his "loaner" sweats and hoodie now even more badly soiled than before. The bandage finished his down-and-out aesthetic nicely. At least he felt no pain because drugs.

"I'll cope. What did you find?"

Moth pointed up toward the roof in the universal sign of "Are they listening?"

"Go ahead," said Quirk. "We may be heading for a jail cell, but I refuse to believe The Old Man's web extends to controlling the National Guard or the FBI."

Moth dug into her pants' pocket. "This book."

She held out a small album of printed images, its cover hand embroidered with a colourful tepee, smoke winding from the top, the word "nimbálich'úe" underneath.

"Anyone know this word?" asked Quirk. Eve and Dulcie—the closest they had to locals—shook their heads.

"I have no web access within this vehicle," said Eighty, "but application of phonetic principles suggests an approximate pronunciation of nim-bah-litch-oh-eh. Reasonably, one might infer this means tepee, home or house."

Quirk nodded. "Thank you, Eighty."

"But equally likely without research is the translation 'pictures.'"

Quirk frowned at the syRen®. He opened the album to be greeted by the face of a Dene woman wearing a big, fur-lined hood, dark eyes half-closed against swirling snow, dark tresses blown across her almost-smiling features: a very attractive image. The next presented Rowland's lined features, smiling broadly, probably taken at the same time. More images followed of one or other or both of the happy couple, most taken in and around the Deweerdt Drive house, some in countryside that looked like Yellowknife's environs. Thirty pictures in he opened up a panorama: a long, sloping, snow-covered garden with a wood frame house at the end. Wooden fences sloped down from the house, tall silver birches stood above a snow blanket, framing a winter vista.

The woman—undoubtedly Meriwa—stood near a rack of upturned, snow-covered canoes, the backdrop a frozen lake, sunlit blue-white, low hills rising beyond broken trees, and a series of low buildings to the left. Further pictures showed a cabin at the foot of the garden. Then it was night, the small building illuminated now, a bright campfire burning in a pit, the sky midnight blue. Pictures followed of a bright green aurora in the sky. The photographer had pushed up exposure, making the fire bright, the stars sharp points, the green-yellow aurora blazing across the sky. Firelit faces smiled. He felt the happy contentment on the Rowlands' faces. But there would be no more pictures of the couple, because Derek Morton had touched their lives.

"Share and tell, boss," Moth demanded. "I found it."

He flicked back to the image of Meriwa against the skyline. "Where is this?" He held the open book up for them. The LTV cornered left, and they all leaned right then straightened. They must be downtown now, nearing the sheriff's station, losing time.

"I think that's Latham Island," said Dulcie. "Looking over towards Back Bay Cemetery."

Quirk shook his head. "You're some kind of plumber, Dulcie."

"YK born and bred."

"You must hate the stink of all this," said Quirk. "Wasn't Eve the enemy?"

"Hey!"

Dulcie shrugged. "Beer's beer. Been the enemy myself, couple times."

"You're a piece of work," Eve snapped. "I should bust you in the mouth."

"I'm sorry," said Quirk, "but I had to ask. I like to know where I stand with people, and I don't have you sussed at all, Dulcie."

Moth chortled. "You could start a fight in a convent."

"I believe I did," Quirk deadpanned. "Although really that was you."

"It was Uncle Toni," Moth huffed, folding her arms.

"My memories indicate that incident also involved a plumber," Eighty observed.

Eve shook her head.

"So, how do we get to Latham Island?" asked Quirk.

"Before or after we land in jail?" asked Eve. "And by the way, Sheriff Kootook works closely with Morton. If we get locked up there's an even chance the news finds its way to the wrong ears in no time flat. Kootook's not crooked—I don't think—but he follows protocol to the letter."

Quirk frowned. "Rightly so, but that's...inconvenient."

"Yeah," said Moth. "Inconvenient like a fucking hole in the head."

Quirk turned over the possibilities. Could they convince the soldiers to put them in the hands of the FBI? Would that help? Frying pan and fire. Neither was an attractive option. They needed to be at large. This did not look good, unless...

"Any way you can get a line out, Eighty? Like, now?"

The android looked around the cabin then moved to the rear door and knelt, reaching down. "It will strip my fingers of skin and pseudo-flesh, but I believe I can force my fingers under the door. It may be enough to access the C Corp satellite link."

Eve's head snapped up. "The what now?"

Quirk waved Eighty to proceed as the LTV cornered tightly once more. A hugely painful scraping sound cut through the vehicle's rumble.

"Call Creston Sheriff's Office," Quirk whispered. No sense in making it easy for any listening soldiers to hear. Everyone leaned forward, but Quirk had to shuffle on his knees up close to Eighty—synthetic flesh hanging in tattered strips—to make out the words.

"*Creston Sheriff, Becker.*" Moth snorted at Becker's wistful fantasy.

"Deputy Parks, please," Quirk whispered. The android would boost his words.

"*One moment.*" Quirk felt a wave of physical relief at not having to deal with the amazing talking penis.

"*Parks here, how may I help you?*"

"Hi Joan, it's Quirk. How are you?"

"*Goddam son-of-a-bitch—*"

"I miss you too, hon, I'd love to chat, but where's Wayne right now? I need to speak to him. We're ready to surrender."

"*He's—*"

"Can you connect me, please?"

"*I—*"

"Now, Joan? *Please?*"

"*Don't call me Joan.*" More ringing. Quirk thanked Moth's other patron. The LTV slowed again, turned hard again. Everyone swayed back and forth. The phone rang.

They slowed to a near stop and turned hard left, bumping over a kerb.

"YSD parking lot, I reckon," said Eve.

"*Quirk, you tricky f—*"

"Where are you right now, Wayne?"

"I'm going to police brutality you so hard."

"Where?"

There was a pause. *"On the ground in fifteen minutes."*

"In Yellowknife?"

"Don't get too excited, I mean to spoil your day, severely."

"But I am excited, Wayne. Moth and I will be in sheriff's custody in about two minutes, and I'm excited at the prospect of you getting here before Morton kills us. That way my lovely assistant and I might survive the day." He winked at Moth.

"Lovely?" She looked bemused.

The LTV jerked to a stop.

"And it's your birthday soon," Quirk reminded her, sotto voce. "When this is done, we're going to Tiffany's. Girls should have nice things." He managed to sound more confident than he felt.

"Jesus," said Eve. "Can I apply for a job at The Quirk Agency?"

"I'll find you," said Kreski, and hung up.

Quirk and Eighty stumbled backwards as the LTV's rear doors split open, admitting darkness pierced by stark artificial light. National Guard soldiers flanked the doors, but those collecting them wore khaki snow pants and dark brown puffers. Sheriff Kootook might have topped MacGillacuddy by an inch; so, short, and wrinkled too, clearly baked and frozen until his skin had given up trying to fit him properly.

"Quinton Kirby, Angelika Moratti, Eve Meyer, Dunevan Rice, I am detaining you on suspicion of breaking and entering, and impeding an investigation. Kirby and Moratti, I've got a line on you for Murder One. Meyer, I know someone who's very keen to see you. Looks like I hit the jackpot tonight. Your rights are suspended under emergency protocol. Lock them up, Dan."

A deputy called from the office entrance. "Two more attacks, Sheriff, one on Mandeville Drive, one on

Finlayson. Multiple casualties." The sheriff grumbled a short oath then turned away, and his deputies moved in.

With very little in the way of ado, the officers whisked them underground to leave them languishing in the holding cells. They each had a separate cage within the basement, including Eighty, the syRen® being powered down manually by court order, prearranged for their arrival. Small, dark, barred windows dotted the external walls high up near ground level, but the space itself was bright and open, notwithstanding the bars. Quirk stopped tapping his foot after Eve shot him a stormy glance.

"Morton probably knows we're here by now," she scowled.

"But Kootook won't let him stroll in here and shoot us, right?" asked Moth, pacing around her cell despite obvious fatigue.

"That's right." Eve sighed, leaning back against the wall behind her pallet.

"Kreski's on the way, almost here," Quirk observed.

Moth kicked the frame of her pallet. "And he'll truck us back to Creston! This stinks; it's total bullshit. And anyway"—she turned on Quirk—"what's the endgame? Kreski fights Morton and wins? I don't like the odds."

Quirk moved to the edge of his cage so he could meet her irate gaze. "Until we know better, Moth, we must assume that our cards are still worth playing, that we can affect the outcome. We're going to find Meriwa and Tania, we're going to get them into the hands of the authorities, and we're going to see justice done."

"And I'm here to explain why that won't happen, Quinton," said Derek Morton as he walked alone into the basement detention block.

17

Moth knew she was growling, but didn't give a single shit. In the next cell Eve sprang up from her bunk, glowering at Morton. "You fucker," was all the woman said, but she said it so well, like she'd just slipped a stiletto between his ribs.

Quirk stood, eyes narrowing. She could see him fighting to contain his anger. Probably there was a stream of big words twisting around in his head, ready to flash out at the shit-kicker, stab him full of holes. Words wouldn't do that to Morton, but they might stall him 'til Kreski got here. Then it would kick off. She wanted to get at the bastard who had shot her, punch him, but no: locked-the-fuck-up, at Morton's mercy.

Slow down. Think. Information. She breathed deeply.

Morton was in all black again (*Oh, please!*)—stood where all could see him—and he was packing, classic smooth grip of a Heckler peeking from his unzipped puffer jacket. Slight bulge above his right ankle, probably a plastec Solid 341. That's what she'd pick for...an execution. *Shit.*

She saw Morton's dead-eyed calculation, like those out-of-town suits visiting Uncle Toni, the specialists. But hadn't Quirk been one of those? It made no fuzking sense. Quirk was no assassin, no hacker, no bruiser, but he did get shit done. He was a navigator, steering through whatever crap came flying at them. She hoped to hell he could do it this time. Her hands were getting sore from gripping the bars so hard. Quirk faced Morton—the cage between them—both appraising, Morton deadly smooth, Quirk looking like a tramp, but his bearing so noble, so righteous. She started shaking. Maybe Morton had come to rub their noses in his victory like a dumbass super villain flashing his big-dick masterplan. Maybe he wasn't going to...

"Come to turn yourself in, Derek?" asked Quirk, so calmly.

"To give a statement, Quint. Help Kootook see justice done." Morton's tone was so smooth, like he was Frenching a jar of honey. He felt nothing for what he'd done. "That's what I told them upstairs." He reached for the Heckler & Koch, withdrew the smooth, black weapon, barrel stretched by a suppressor. "But my wetwork team just mirrored the sensor feed down here." He clicked off the safety and pointed the gun at...her. Moth's knees wobbled. Liking guns was fine, but being targeted by someone you knew would use one—his gaze locked with Quirk's—was another. "If Rowland hadn't been a damn security man we wouldn't even be here, but he knew his stuff. So, tell me where Terjesen is, or I'll paste the little girl's face all over the wall."

"Bastard!" Eve hammered the bars with her palms as if she could bust through.

Kootook didn't have the photobook or their statements, yet. So, the only way Morton would get the lead was from them. Ergo, it was up to them to stall him if they could. Before he...

Quirk faced Morton down, unmoving, silent. Did he have the same thought?

She took a breath. Probably shouldn't get involved: Hey-ho. "Joke's on you, shit bird. We didn't find a thing." Maybe she could wind him up, buy the time they needed. "How about spill your super villain plan, so Eve and I can shove it up your ass later?"

He glanced at her, sneering (*Yay!*) then turned back to Quirk.

"You probably think you're holding an ace, right Quint? That I'm under orders not to kill you? Maybe you'll bargain for the dykes, the runt and the hobo?" he jerked his free thumb at Dulcie. "Well, yes, you're right, he did ask to speak to *you*, but he cares nothing for these." Morton looked down the barrel at her and she swallowed a whimper—was about ready to pee herself—but she stepped up to the bars, towards the gun, because that's what Quirk would do, and it wasn't like Morton would miss either way. She gripped the cold metal like she could properly Hulk it, break out and shatter that chiselled jaw to pissy little pieces.

"You see, *Quint*, I'm out, like you. That's why it doesn't matter whether I follow orders this time. He thinks he's pulling the strings, but I don't think for a minute he'll let me walk away, so I'm making my own plans; and I don't care whether he speaks to you or not. We had good times though: Caracas, the Pallas side door? Make it easy on everyone. Tell me. Ten seconds."

Stupid brick-muncher, he *was* expositioning! And Quirk hadn't even needed to speak. Wow, Morton must really hate him. She could see Quirk thinking about it. *No, no! Don't you fucking dare!* But this was her life. Morton was a deadeye, steady-hand killer. She should know, he'd shot her once already. But her info was all they had. Quirk would *not* cave. It wasn't about love, or care, or duty, it was about right and wrong. Her eyes were fucking wet now: she pictured her mother, imagined Cousin Mario avenging her with the full might of the Rigel Corporation, a grand vendetta.

Quirk stared at Morton through the bars, so controlled, like a different person. "No, Derek." *Yus!* "You see, I have this code called trust." He held a hand up before Morton could interrupt. "Rowland trusted me with two lives. Meriwa and Tania trust me to liberate them. Moth trusts me to stick to my guns, do the right thing. It comes from my father. I get my quick temper from him." Quirk came up to the bars. Morton hadn't shot her yet. "But I'll take all his flaws to get his passionate sense of right and wrong, of fairness." Quirk smiled and she could see realisation spreading over his face. "I just realised you showed me the way, Derek. You and TOM showed me hell and I ran the other way." He looked down at his ruined boots. "And you're the one out of time. Kootook's not the only one coming down those stairs. You remember Kreski?"

Morton shook his head. "Jesus, Quinton, you're hopeless. I gave you a chance, remember that."

Somewhere, a door banged open. Moth's gaze snapped to the far wall, although she couldn't see the stairs.

"Just you being here smacks of desperation, Derek," said Quirk as Morton's head turned toward the stairs. "This is *your* chance. Turn yourself in. Get out from under TOM's thumb. You'll do time, but you'll be free one day."

"Yeah," said Moth. "Just give up. There's no way you'll get into Rowland's office at Hygen." If Quirk could make shit up, so could she.

Morton slipped his gun away just as three lawmen walked into the cells. Probably he could have bluffed Kootook, but Kreski led the pack, and he registered Morton immediately; a man in black, unaccompanied. Kreski's features twisted as everything Quirk had said clicked into place.

Decision time. Eyes flicked back and forth for a second, before—

Everybody moved.

Keyed up as he was, Morton's gun was first out of the blocks. Kootook's Viper cleared its holster just before Kreski's Webley. Moth surged back from the bars, glimpsing Quirk do the same, also heading for his pallet. Morton's gun spat at her, missing. Dulcie had rolled off his bunk to the floor. "Eve, move!" Moth shouted as she scrambled under her rickety bed, pushing it over, peeking around the edge.

Red laser light painted Kootook's shoulder. Heavy thud. Blood spattered the wall, the small sheriff tumbling. Morton turned side on to Kreski and the big sheriff's booming shot missed. Morton rolled forward, Kreski's next shots ripping chunks from wall and floor while Morton's H&K painted the deputy's chest.

Moth clutched her head, ears ringing like the Duomo on Sunday morning. Her senses swam. Someone had turned the world up to thirteen, all pin-sharp flashes and treble whine. Just Kreski and Morton now, as Kootook ducked around the corner, but there was no real cover, just an interference pattern of steel bars. Morton sent a burst at Kreski—bullets pinging metal, sending the sheriff ducking back—then changed mag.

That was when Quirk and Dulcie moved.

The plumber rolled across the floor of his cell, reaching for the deputy's fallen Viper. His arm strained through the bars, grasping at the floor, centimetres short. Quirk grabbed for Morton, got a hand on his collar, then pushed off the bars with both feet. She cheered as the bastard-in-black slammed into the bars and crumpled as Quirk fell back to the concrete floor of his cell. Kreski emerged— arms locked—big Webley trained on the sprawling Morton. Then, everything blew up.

A blinding light made her head spin, thunder crashed, smoke billowed, obliterating everything. Then ringing, dim shapes in her vision.

"Moth?! Eve?"

"Quirk? Quirk!"

"Quirk? Moth? Medic! Medics here!"

She blinked and blinked, but nothing happened, kept blinking because it was all she could do. Finally, darker shapes floated into the blur. She crawled forward, banged her head on something, flinched and sucked in a rank, chemical breath. Smoke hung in the air. Blinking, eyes streaming, she forced herself up. *Fucking flash-bomb—the bastard.* A jarring buzz sounded. Metal rattled. *Keys? Retro.* Someone grabbed her arms as she groped around, pulling her up then guiding her forward.

"Move," whispered Dulcie softly near her ear. Her boots kicked the first stair, she stumbled to hands and knees, crawling upwards before managing to stand again. She bumped into someone in front, grabbed onto their clothes. From build and height, it was Eve. They stumbled together through the sheriff's station—loud with shouts and blaring alarms—people hurrying about, it was chaos, but they were free. How did that work? Kootook was down. Had Kreski freed them?

The chill of evening air hit her like a slap. Her eyes still streamed, but slowly her vision cleared. A service lot, grey boxes and mechanical plant, quiet, but for the electrical hum and quiet blaring of distant alarms. Quirk, Eve, Dulcie and Kreski, all here. The sheriff waved them over and they shambled to the truck he'd opened.

"What about my robot?" she demanded, shaking, *not* remembering Morton's gun.

"Mandatory twenty-four-hour shutdown then factory reset, personal data checked and returned to you once cleared," said Kreski.

"That could be weeks, months! He's my friend, they can't reset him!"

"Sorry, kid; beyond my control."

"Where do we stand here?" Eve asked. "Tania—"

"Have you seen the light, Wayne?" Quirk cut across her. "Morton's villainy?"

"I have." Kreski was gruff, closing the driver's door and dispensing a pill to each of them. "You were right, Quirk, pains me to say. He's now prime suspect in Rowland's murder. And it doesn't seem too safe and secure 'round here for my witnesses. So, get in the truck."

Eve, Dulcie and Quirk climbed in. It was just her and Kreski. She stared at the pill. "Just a transmitter," he said, managing a reassuring smile. "It won't hurt."

Of course he'd treat her like a child, placating, reassuring: big hypocrite. She stuck her tongue out at him. This was outrageous. "And my droid?" she tried batting her lashes like they did in shows, without any real hope.

"Stays here," Kreski confirmed.

She climbed into the police truck and Kreski drove away from the sheriff's station into the night, grumbling all the while. In answer to his question about dinner and lodging, Dulcie nominated Norm's West Tavern, explaining it was his and Eve's regular haunt. Kreski nodded. "I'm tired and hungry, and you all look like shit warmed up. If Morton doesn't know where Terjesen and Rowland are and you do, Quirk, you mysterious bastard, we're gonna eat and you're gonna talk. For the record, you are all in my custody. Straying fifty metres or more away from me gets you ten years, Creston-sponsored hospitality, no hearing, no parole. Remember that."

"Won't Kootook track this truck?" Quirk asked.

"He might not see it as a prison break after what Morton did, but he certainly hasn't okayed it. I turned the beacon off. Sheriff's privilege. I'm taking no chances now with any of this, Kootook included. Now pipe down and let me think."

They arrived at the bar, parking up in the lot before a low, glowing building. Before Kreski could open the door, Eve advised him on scouting for terra-fauna, even before a twenty-metre walk between car and building. Kreski just nodded and then followed Eve's protocol, one armed individual—Kreski—circling the truck, shining a torch into the night before going to the door and covering the rest.

The sky spread pitch black, brilliantly clear, stars shining like real diamonds. Dulcie took a long look overhead as he walked and nodded. Moth's stomach growled. She shivered, missing Eighty. When she leaned into him, he raised his body temperature to warm her. That option not available, she budged up beside Quirk, sheltering from the chill breeze. The big asswipe stiffened slightly. Her stomach lurched with a hollow feeling, but he did finally put an arm around her shoulder. She resisted the urge to punch him in the gut and yell at him for not loving her. *That* wasn't his fucking job, after all. That word was a gaping hole in Quirk's legal agreement with Uncle Toni, RIP.

Unsurprisingly, the bar was open. When the shit came down, adults either freaked out or looked for a drink; often both. She had no wish to try alcohol again. Wine sucked armpits, as she'd told her dad when he let her try his Valpolicella. *No, not that road.* She pressed a bit closer to Quirk.

An hour later they sat around a pleather booth, soon-to-be recycled burger debris littering the table. Typically, Quirk was the first to flap his yapper.

"This smells like every bar I've ever known."

Moth blew out a sigh. He always got poetic when he sat down to drink. That was another reason to loathe the bar. Okay, the walls were hung with faded prints of hunting trips instead of baseball legends, or blues folk, sailing ships, whatever—but it popped with the same bright beer logos, the same polished furnishings glinted, the same shuffling staff. And it did have a smell, but she didn't want to know what it was.

Kreski pulled on a brown bottle, as did Dulcie and Eve. Quirk swigged gin and tonic, as usual. Moth eyed her water with suspicion.

"Why did you run from Creston, Quirk?" Kreski asked. "Tell me again."

Quirk met Moth's stare and smiled. "Panic, initially. It looked like Morton had pinned Rowland's death on us. I was concerned you would go for the easy win."

Kreski snorted. "There's no easy win. There's the right thing, nothing else."

"And I admire your steely-eyed quest for truth, Sheriff"—Quirk's stare was long and hard—"but we had two lives to save, one of them a witness who would clear us." Moth liked when Quirk got righteous, and when he said "we."

"We were focused on the greater good," she added.

"You were the ones rampaging around my town, kid."

She waved a finger at Kreski. "And whose fault was that?"

"Damn, Quirk, she's exhausting." Moth caught Kreski's brief smirk.

"Our assumptions should be challenged though, don't you think?" Quirk countered. "That's her job and she's good at it." She smiled. Quirk did too, at Kreski. "You're not taking us back to Creston, are you, Wayne? We have a lead, and confirmation that Morton hasn't found it. Kootook will be busy chasing Morton. We can get in and out, put a cap on the whole affair." She noted Quirk said nothing about election fraud. Probably best, considering the sheriff's pay grade.

Kreski sighed. "So, you know where these ladies are? What have you got?"

"Tania Terjesen, Meriwa Rowland," said Eve. "Use their names...please."

Quirk glanced at Moth. She shook her head. "I tucked the Book behind the panelling in the army LTV. The clues are all up here." She tapped her temple.

Kreski actually put a hand over his face. "And only you will take me there. So, you win, hmm? Well, there's a curfew, hundreds of vicious creatures loose, an army primed to shoot on sight. I am not taking you out in *that*."

"So, we sit around and wait?" Moth snapped. "Morton won't chillax all night!"

Kreski frowned. She raised her chin. A big new beat kicked out of the sound system: the latest track from BLL's new frak album *Dis Ain't No Holler*. Moth began tapping her feet to the funky base beat as metallic punk guitars kicked in to underscore Brother Leigh Love's rapping. The barman played the clean version; at least he thought he did, but the song contained a Trojan in its code that linked out to the uncensored cut. Cue chorus:

"Death cums in your face, when you least expect it.
Try to reject it.
You won't even get a chance to wipe,
you fucked yourself up, you should expect it.
So shut the fuck up,
bend over,
accept it."

The big sheriff grunted as the barman skipped the rest of the track. "Don't you think Morton has the resources to track down one location in this small city?"

"He hasn't so far," said Moth.

"And he won't today, Sheriff," said a voice from Kreski's top pocket.

He plucked out his handset like it was a live snake, dropping it on the table.

"...since I'm still shrouding Meriwa Rowland's digital footprint."

They all stared at the handset where it lay in a burger basket. It was Mystery Caller, no longer blocked by Eighty at Quirk's request.

"What the fuck?" Kreski glared at Quirk. Good instinct there.

"We have a so-called helper inside Genextric," said Quirk.

"Who?" Kreski demanded.

"Yes, who?" echoed Eve. "And how can they help?"

"We don't know," said Moth when Quirk didn't answer. "He gives us hints."

Kreski clamped a big thumb over the mic. "What's his agenda?"

"I can still hear you. I'm that good."

MC's voice spouted from the bar's audio system, cutting through the latest track, turning drinkers' heads.

Kreski scowled. "This is Sheriff Wayne Kreski, state your name."

MC's voice came from the handset again. *"I'd love to, Sheriff Wayne Kreski, but I just wanted to say you're getting warmer. Tania and Meriwa are still hidden, for now. I think Quirk's gang have found where that is, but Morton's figured you've got inside intel, I think he's coming for me now. I need your help!"*

Kreski glared at Quirk. "If you won't tell me your name, tell me why you're helping Quirk. Help me bring Morton in before he gets to you, or kills again."

"Oh, Sheriff, I'm sorry. I think more folks'll die before he's done. He let all the creatures out, you know. All but one. I have proof on video, although he thought he'd shut down the system. If it's digital, I can use it. I can get you into Genextric, but you should save the ladies first. I bet Quirk won't come here till they're safe. So, be fast!"

Kreski met Quirk's gaze again and gestured to the handset.

"That's right," said Quirk. "And I hope you'll help with that."

"I shouldn't. You shut me out!" Moth rolled her eyes: the voice was so whiny, like talking to a big kid, a man-child progger or techie. If they even were male at all; it easily could be a synthesised voice.

"It was a bad time." Quirk went into oh-so-familiar peace-making mode.

"Give us details, jerk-wad," Moth snapped. Quirk and Kreski started to interrupt her, but she waved them both down, one flapping hand each. "If you even can. Maybe you're stringing us along, playing the big man. Show us the goods. Are you worth it?"

"Worth it? WORTH IT?! You have no clue what it's like to be me! You don't know what I've been through, how I got here. I've been to hell, but maybe that's not good enough for you to come to Genextric and save the likes of me, huh? Do you need more, Quirk? Is it not personal enough? Well, how about I'm your son? How about that?! Is that personal enough for you, DAD?!"

Quirk paled. His eyes cast down. She knew she was gaping. She looked at Kreski then Eve then Dulcie then Quirk. Despite their doubts, nobody questioned it.

"I'll come," said Quirk seeming to have difficulty breathing. "I believe you're in distress...whoever you are." He looked at Kreski, who nodded. "I promise I'll come."

"That's all I wanted, Dad. Data sent."

The line went dead as Kreski's screen illuminated. Dulcie glanced, nodded. "Latham Island, right enough."

Quirk's hands made fists. "We have to go now."

"No," said Kreski. "You're in my custody, unsanctioned as it is. The curfew—we're exhausted," he paused. "And, he could be playing you."

The music had stopped. She thought Quirk was going to fucking burst, or at least walk out. He stared daggers at Kreski. "No, this adds up. But if I did have doubts, I still have to test them, I have to get in there." He leaned back, actually managed a grim smile. "So, you'd better buy me another drink, Wayne. Tomorrow is going to be a busy day."

18

Nick, I'm sorry. Forgive me for...everything, anything; all of it.

Quirk glanced around, looking for distraction from the turmoil in his head. A campfire spirit enveloped the bar, people huddled in groups, some clearly trapped by the curfew, perhaps by accident perhaps not. With all rooms in the adjoining motel full—many doubled up—he'd laid out a king's ransom for accommodation, securing the upper floor of the owner's own house for the night. Thankfully, Toni had provided handsomely for Moth's guardianship. The capo's devotion ran to the millions. Where was *his* devotion to Nick, even a sliver of regard for a...person that originated with him? Lying in the dust of an empty San Francisco apartment. And now his son was here; they might be reunited soon, but what did that mean? What did he feel now for Nick, for Jennifer?

He sipped his fourth gin, savouring the crisp, botanical glow that chilled his palate. Eve pulled on a beer and whispered something to Dulcie. It was easy to believe she had headed up Gamma Lab until recently. There was something hard in her eyes: determination, responsibility, strength. He liked it, and was that because he lacked those things himself?

Moth had just finished a slice of apple pie. Her ability to bounce back from disaster after conflict after setback was marvellous, but hard won. She reached for the whipped cream, put a squirt on her spoon, caught him watching her, and winked.

"It's happy in a can." She looked at the label. "Got all the sugars."

He lifted his gaze to find Kreski watching him. The sheriff glanced at Eve. "You think it's worth this?" he asked. "Toying with nature, helping push more people out into the universe considering the UN's finally got a grip of biosphere macro-engineering, population-optimisation, downshifting?"

"All the hyphens." Moth nodded.

Quirk smiled at the big man. "Why go to Mars when you can live in Creston? I'd forgotten such places existed. Travelling from metropolis to spaceport to asteroid, it's easy to forget about the people scattered all over Earth who are building the future: decentralised corporations, boondocks research centres, zero-impact manufacturing, communities responsible for their own environment. That's what the colonies aspire to"—he waved a hand around the bar, meaning to indicate the sense of community—"to sustain ourselves independently; sell our resources instead of bartering them for supplies from the Motherland."

Kreski grunted. "You gonna run for office?"

Eve leaned back in her seat. "Terraforming makes a shit-ton of money for C Corp. Biblical amounts, even with the UN's NLS levy. CC has trillions at stake, and plenty tied up in post-settlement deals. Makes sense they would fight to keep that."

Kreski nodded. "So, what happens when the colonies go from hand-to-mouth existence to knocking on the UN's door asking for the keys to the dome? CC gonna sell up? The UN levy on the G4 super-corps that pays for the NLS ships isn't going to hold up after outpost independence. Settlers can't have it both ways; they'll need to pay for those ships, or their gas money, at least."

Quirk nodded. "But some colonies are close to break-even. Science tells us the potential for progressive human expansion is limitless. The further out we get, the more likely colonies will be better placed than C Corp to service future expansion."

Kreski shrugged. "Above my pay grade. I'm turning in. Roll call six AM. We head for Latham Island at first light. Don't be late." The big man left the bar, but not before tapping his wrist. "Remember, fifty-one metres gets you ten years."

Quirk stood slowly. *Distraction required.* "Bedtime for fourteen-year-olds."

"Aw, man," Moth grumbled.

"I need you in top form tomorrow now that we're definitely going into Genextric." His stomach dropped hard. *To find Nick.*

Moth stood, features twisting into a resigned scowl. "Whatever," she snipped. He considered clipping her around the ear then decided against it.

"We still need to talk about Genextric," said Eve, pointing her bottle at him.

He nodded. "Be right back," he said and followed Moth from the bar.

From the foyer, a short weatherproof corridor led to the owner's house. The woman's son—seated at the motel reception—buzzed them through and they trudged upstairs. Quirk hoped Eve had plenty to say. It had been a long day, but away from the bar's noise and colour, rather than the gentle tug of slumber, he felt claws of stress digging into his scalp, or maybe it was teeth, teeth of stress. Moth fought sleep, but her steps were heavy. She had the youngest daughter's room. A nightlight glowed near the door, revealing the outlines of toys, pictures and furniture. Moth walked past it all, dumped her jacket and boots, cast off her jeans and burrowed under the covers. She sniffed.

"What's wrong?"

"I miss Eighty."

"I know." He dredged up a weary smile. "He's one of the team."

"You said 'he,' not 'it.'" She shuffled around to look at him.

"So I did. Maybe you're winning me over, nonsensical as your position is."

A once-white, soft-toy animal lay on the blanket. Quirk picked it up, tucking it under the covers with her. It had pointed ears, a black nose, short, light "fur," and it had whiskers. "I suppose it's...a dog? Or a cat? I don't know." She stroked its soft coat then lifted it out and laid it on the blanket facing the door. "Don't you like him?"

She shook her head. "He's watching the door. My animals always watched the door." She turned away from him, pulling the covers up to her ear.

Barely hesitating, Quirk reached out to stroke her hair. There was no twitch or exclamation, no invective. He tried to make his touch reassuring, confident, caring, although he wasn't really sure how to do any of that. What the hell was happening? His world changed so fast now.

What she'd been through already, too much of it was his fault, bringing her into these dangerous, chaotic situations, even before considering his own baggage. Despite Moth's confidence and capability, he too easily forgot she was still a child. And he relied so much on Eighty to keep her safe. She had almost died on the Moon—his fault; in Creston Hospital—his fault; in YK jail. His fault. Now they were surrounded by ravening beasts designed to scour environments clean, test them to destruction. He sighed. Kreski would watch over her. The big man may not like him, but he seemed to like Moth. Maybe he could persuade Kreski to handcuff her to something heavy while they went after Tania then to Genextric. Quirk snorted.

"How is our sharing progressing?" He continued to stroke Moth's hair. "Am I holding up my end? I think you've learned a good deal about me today."

"Mm-hmm," came the muffled reply.

"Do you think you'll ever tell me why you're called Moth?"

"Mm. Hmm." It was softer this time, quieter. She was asleep, and for the first time he thought he saw why she was christened Angelika.

He rose, moved to the door, and slipped out to find Kreski in the corridor.

"She's asleep. Can you put a movement alarm on her door?"

The sheriff nodded, producing a roll of smart tape from his pocket.

"It's only prudent, now you've seen what Morton is."

"I skimmed his file," the sheriff nodded. "He's a real boy scout. Nigeria, North Korea, the Hundred Hours War. I'm getting the picture." Kreski clapped him on the shoulder and moved away towards his room, leaving Quirk perplexed.

Dulcie having turned in, Eve had relocated to the bar, her downturned face illuminated by the sickly green light from a beer pump proclaiming that it was "Nature's Best." Quirk perched on the neighbouring stool and ordered gin. He sipped the G&T and looked sideways at Eve, features bathed in the unnatural glow. She glanced at him, and he looked down at his drink.

"Is that male gaze in your eye, or are you just pleased to see me?"

He coughed. "No, and yes. As I said, I'm a great admirer of determination and confidence as an aesthetic. I know you're hurting. Tania—"

"I let her down. Not just the last few days; I should have challenged Morton's behaviour before now, but I didn't. He's been an asshole for months."

"Years," said Quirk, staring at his drink. "But he wasn't always."

"Huh. Weird," she said. "Do you want to know what I see in you?"

He felt his eyebrows rising. "Not especially."

"I think you're scared of discovering you're something you never expected."

"And what might that be?" he snapped. He was in no mood for this. But that was unfair after what she'd been through. "I'm sorry." His reaction to Mystery Caller...to Nick had not been right. He should have asked how his son—because he believed it now, and of course TOM would give him a job—had done all that he had to help them, like repurposing drone copters and satellite links. And how had Eve not known about Nick's presence in Genextric? The big boss's grandson? Dredging up Nick's name made everything painfully real, even though Quirk had not given the name to him.

"It's fine," said Eve, swirling the ice in her whisky. "Venting is healthy."

"Maybe, but that doesn't make it acceptable in polite company."

"I asked for it." The green light picked out the shine in her eye, and a tear escaped onto her cheek as she emptied her lowball glass and set it down with a thud.

"Tania and Meriwa are alive, Eve. We're going to find them," he said, feeling a surge of...something. He thought of Moth sleeping upstairs and felt a twinge of guilt. He quashed it. What if he was compensating for leaving Jennifer and Nick? That didn't make this new parental inclination wrong. "This is shockingly forward, but permit me, please." He reached up and brushed the tear away. "Corny, I know."

Eve's lips compressed, but she let his gesture go, smiling slightly, picking up the refilled lowball.

"In a different narrative," he said, "this is the moment you would say 'I'm afraid, Quirk, afraid like I've never been before. Hold me, Quirk. Kiss me.'"

That made her laugh, which he was fairly sure had been his intention.

"Well, you're no Bogart, Quirk, and I'm a lesbian, and I'm in a relationship—I think—so stop whistling at me, will you?"

"Okay, okay," he said, amiably. Gin was just the right kind of bittersweet for this conversation.

"Eve, is there anyone on staff called Nick—Nick Kirby or Nick Simister? Jennifer's maiden name. I'm sure there's no child labour, but with genetic acceleration a clone would be much older now than ten. He must have access to the systems. I don't understand how he does what he's done unless he has some control function. His reach..."

Eve looked uncomfortable. "You really think Kreski will go into Genextric with you, risk standing on Kootook's toes again once Tania's secure?"

Changing the subject? Curious. "I trust Kreski's word. He wants to get his hands on Morton, so entering Genextric would be a legitimate search, with Kootook's permission in relation to jurisdiction. But, any ideas about my informant?"

Eve looked at the barman and pointed at her glass, even though it was half full. The music had changed pace. Now, someone crooned over romantic piano about the cruelty of some golden rule.

"I have been thinking about that. They'd use a false name, right? I don't know what the mother looks like, but there are candidates who might be able to source the information you've had. Johari is good, better than he lets on. But, making outbound calls, undetected; that's some feat with Genextric security." She almost stuttered. "He'd need to be some kind of tech wizard..."

"But you have another theory. Tell me."

"I...don't know," her eyes flicked away. "There's a closed habitat on Level Five, but... No, the only inhabitant is a failed experiment. That's not an option. But we should be concentrating on Morton now, on Tania and Mrs Rowland. What's the plan? We go to the Latham address; the ladies are there; we pick them up and go to...the FBI, I guess? But what about Genextric? Just stroll in and arrest Morton and his Black Ops buddies? You know he won't let that happen."

Quirk nodded. "I'd love to think Kootook will succeed in taking him down, or will rope in the FBI and the army, but going up against a C Corp company is like kicking a wasp's nest of lawyers. If lawyers were wasps, which many are." For the first time, he wondered how many incumbent politicians were complicit in TOM's scheme.

Eve nodded. "I've seen that machine in action."

"If Nick can get us in, I intend a direct approach. I'll sit down in the foyer and evoke the right of parlay. We were interrupted in the jail, and I imagine Derek has more to tell me, none of it pleasant or complimentary. If we've secured the damsels by then I don't see that he has a choice, unless he plans an escape before then. I think he'll play ball. That's something you do in the Americas, isn't it? If Morton hasn't quit the field already by then: I think there's a strong likelihood The Old Man will cut him loose."

"But if all this shit happened on purpose," said Eve, "what was the point? This place is a disaster. The FBI, the National Guard, state of emergency, the fallout for Genextric..." Her bleary eyes opened wider. The ice cubes in her glass clinked. "Oh, no."

"I don't really follow Earth politics," said Quirk, closing his eyes and tapping his forehead as if that would clarify his thoughts. "I'm a Belter. What is the opposition view on the settlement programme?"

Eve sat up, features animating. "They're not against the programme, but the Democratic Neo-Liberal Party promise to slash the cost, reassess commitments and reset the Hawking Plan to a new socio-environmental baseline." Her hand gripped Quirk's arm. "C Corp, they...he wouldn't...?"

Quirk felt a tightness in his chest. No point in keeping Eve in the dark about the supposed plot; not like he had any interest in protecting The Old Man's back. "MC...Nick, said TOM planned to influence the election. I wasn't sure I believed it, but yes, I can believe he *would* try to rig a continental election." His thoughts flitted through the backwoods of mania and saw the terrible possibilities that

Genextric held, but hatred for The Old Man burned like a flamethrower, clearing his mind. "This is so far above my paygrade a telescope couldn't see the underside. We cannot solve this, Eve, but we may be able to secure the evidence that does."

Quirk lowered his voice. "We need to take Morton and hand him over to the FBI: they're too messed up already to be under TOM's influence. There's nothing concrete without Morton. Tania leads to Morton, not to The Old Man. We have to have Derek. Fraud, on a global scale for interstellar stakes. It would have The Old Man's fingerprints all over it, if he had any." Around the bar, people settled in for the evening. Some had blankets, sleeping bags, others stretched out on seats and in booths. The bartender did the rounds collecting glasses, having turned off the music, but the video screens still relayed pictures from various news channels. Quirk reached for an earbud from the bar-top bowl. Eve did the same, disinfectant evaporating instantly. A newscaster faced studio cameras with a sombre expression.

"...words there, spoken with great conviction by our NAF president, Peter Liano only forty minutes ago. We can go now to Yellowknife and our reporter Shaun Lange. Shaun, what's the latest?"

The picture changed: external, night, a young man in full winter gear speaking to camera. Behind him, bright spotlights picked out patches of a robust metal fence. Beyond that, the camouflaged portable buildings of the National Guard's airport command post. The shot panned across the apron to a big transport plane, position and taxi lights flashing, cargo bay yawning above a ramp up which bedraggled people trudged into the plane's cavernous belly. Matte black, energy conversion paint rendered the plane all but invisible against the night sky. The reporter yelled against the whine of the plane's engines and the airport's operational clatters and bangs.

"Bob, the National Guard sent the first flight out three hours ago and you can see the sixth Mega Galaxy transport loading behind me. The people of Yellowknife seem drained by this ordeal and only too ready to quit their city temporarily to let their government deal with a situation most say should never have been allowed to become so deadly and destructive.

"These mercy flights have various destinations, and full facilities are available to the refugees on arrival. Considering many residents have already left under their own steam, and with flights leaving every half hour, it's expected Yellowknife's entire population will be relocated by noon tomorrow. This will leave the army with free rein to shoot anything that moves, and I've been assured by the FBI that a campaign plan is in place—formulated with the President himself—to end this shocking crisis within twenty-four hours. The clock is ticking for these monsters, and Peter Liano may be the man who has got the job done. Shaun Lange for Fax News, Yellowknife, NT."

"That's bad," Quirk said. Reductive, but true. "It'll be a warzone out there. We should listen to what Liano said." Eve nodded. Quirk requested the pad from the bartender and scrubbed the player back to the president's speech.

Peter Liano stood at a lectern bearing the crest of the North American Federation, addressing the camera.

"My fellow North Americans, despite the valiant efforts of the National Guard and our security and law enforcement agencies to contain the devastating effects of this disaster, I cannot as your leader permit this tragic loss of life to worsen any further. Even though progress is being made in reducing the numbers of beasts at large, I have, with great reluctance, authorised the complete evacuation of the City of Yellowknife, to which—presently—the outbreak has been contained.

"To those of you suffering the consequences I say, have strength. We in Ottawa are taking all action necessary to secure your safety and set things to rights. Also, I pledge that full and fair restitution

will be made to all those affected by this disaster, and those responsible will be brought to book.

"Once Yellowknife's inhabitants are safe, the army will deploy to eradicate the remaining threat of these vile beasts. I assure you that I will not rest until every family, homeowner, visitor, employee and contractor is safely returned to their rightful place, and any damage is repaired."

The president hung his head then looked up.

"But we can never make restitution to the souls lost in this disaster. I will not prejudge the outcome of the exhaustive inquiry that will follow in the wake of this tragedy, but I promise you— should some rogue element or disturbed individual be proven responsible for this terrible incident—they will face the full force of the punishment available to me, as President of the North American Federation.

"This is not a time for uncertainty or debate, but for decisive action. We must set aside our differences and act together as a nation to bring this crisis to an end. Thus, and with great reluctance, but also steadfast certainty, it is my duty under the Emergency Powers Act to suspend the election, indefinitely.

"I am confident this situation and consequent inquiry will be resolved quickly, after which the normal business of governing our nations may resume.

"Thank you, and bless North America."

Quirk knew he was gaping. He turned to Eve to see a mirror of his shock.

She was the one who spoke, he did not have the words.

"He's...not fixing the election." She turned back to the paused image of President Peter Liano, his weak brow, his cold eyes. "The Old Man just staged a coup."

19

How could things be *this* much worse than he'd feared? On the one hand, he was a Belter and this was not his fight. On the other, he felt a twisted culpability for once being part of The Old Man's insidious machine. Now, he believed Eve was right. TOM had control of the President of the NAF. The twisted bastard was trying to control Earth politics from the top down. Did they still have a chance to stop it? Terjesen was the key to Morton, Morton was the key to TOM, and time had just run out.

"How far do you trust Dulcie, really?"

Eve's brow furrowed, no doubt considering if she could trust Quirk, *really*. She slugged whisky. "He's a vet. Ex-marine. The Kamchatka police action; Monrovia; Hundred Hours War. He's resourceful as hell, doesn't balk at running risks, and has no love for the system. But, how do I really know you're not part of this?"

"I *am* part of it." He smiled grimly. "Morton took the infant Nick away from my ex-wife—at The Old Man's behest—and it broke her. As far as I know from last December, she's still institutionalised. I always thought Jennifer ruined us, but it was TOM. I bet cloning a son was his idea. I know his money paid for it, and one of his labs did the work. TOM achieves his goals without exception. He'll use up his own family, his offspring, his staff to succeed. I know my limits. I'm no avenging angel; don't have the nerve for it, the guts or the balls, but this..." His breath caught as he grappled with the scale of TOM's audacity. "I might be the only one with the insight to prove this. You and Tania might be the only ones who can convict Morton, leverage testimony against TOM. This situation has not finished its journey south. It's still a long way down from here." He stood. "Wake Dulcie if you're sure he's an asset. I'll get Kreski and Moth."

They gathered, bleary-eyed, around their table again. Quirk expounded his theory, and Eve backed him up. Kreski recorded the whole thing. The more Quirk spoke the worse he felt for having held things back from the sheriff. When he finished, nobody spoke. Surprise and doubt passed in glances around the table. Kreski's brow knit in anger. He snatched up his handset.

"Dial Sheriff Kootook."

"Wayne," said Quirk, "we just talked about going under the radar."

"No, you did. I'm an officer of law, and this is mind-blowing, way bigger than us. We go by procedure, or not at all."

Silence reigned as the call went through. "Peter, what's the situation?" *As distractions go, this is terrible.* "Right. No, they're with me, protective custody. Seems your jail is less than secure." *I have to keep focused, not forget about Moth. She needs me too.* "I'm sure you do want them back, but Quirk's got a line on Terjesen and Rowland. Tell you?" Eve tensed. The big sheriff glanced at Quirk. "I think I'll play this hand myself, Peter." Kreski had just gone out on a limb for them. "I note your concern." They would have to be fast. Likely Kootook would act. "Well, you go ahead and rescind my status. Thanks for nothing, Sheriff."

Kreski frowned and pocketed the handset. "Two thousand clicks from my jurisdiction, and it seems I'm on the shit-list now, too." Moth yawned, but managed a sleepy swear. "If Terjesen...Tania, and Eve testify against Morton, he, Genextric and C Corp will come under serious scrutiny." The sheriff's features hardened. "The FBI will jump at a chance to investigate C Corp under the thirty-fourth amendment. Morton will be turned inside out by every fed under the suns, but I have to bring Tania in first."

"Wayne," Quirk heard his own voice dragging with fatigue. "Did you hear what I said? I think TOM has his hand around Liano's neck and is playing him like a cello. The score might extend all the way from Liano to Kootook, and I'll bet The Old Man can hit most of the notes in between. We need to take this to the UN, to be sure."

"The UN—" Kreski started.

"I'm not saying Kootook's bent, or that the FBI defers to TOM. The Bureau has butted heads with presidents before." He leaned in, dispelling an urge to grip Kreski's muscular forearm. "Morton has access to military-grade tech and Eve says he has a black ops squad behind him. We must assume he's tracking official channels, but if we go in small, Derek's big, stupid ego might think his tactics worked and that we're desperate."

"We *are* desperate," said Eve.

"He'll be less likely to push any red button he might have to hand."

"Things can get worse?" Moth raised an eyebrow.

"C Corp is an interstellar company with a friendly president," said Quirk. "Think bigger than guns."

Kreski stood, grabbing his jacket. "We're leaving for Latham Island. I'm done having my chain yanked."

Quirk stood too. "Morton's cronies were waiting at Rowland's. Assume he has eyes on us, that he'll strike if...when we find them, despite Moth's clever ruse to point him at Rowland's work. He's a survivor first, lacky second. This may be his last chance to save his own hide."

Dulcie's gaze circled the table. *Assessing his own position?* "I can help," he said.

Quirk nodded. "I was hoping you could."

"No prejudice to my current situation, of course," the ex-marine added.

"What're you suggesting?" said Kreski. "No prejudice, of course."

"My place is on Joliffe Island, just south of Latham Island. There's a narrow strip of water, just one-fifty metres, frozen now. I can equip us for...difficulties, no questions asked. Got some chaff spray, blocks most sensors; maybe a gun or two," he drawled, smoothing his beard.

Kreski appraised the man as he had done Quirk two thousand kilometres south and a hundred years ago. The sheriff nodded slowly. "What we talking about?"

Dulcie glanced at his boots. "Can we call it army surplus and leave it there?"

The group stood ready now, jackets on and zipped up, awaiting Kreski's decision.

"This is all very handy. What do you use the equipment for?"

"Hunting," said Dulcie.

"Right," said Kreski, sceptically. "I don't have time to argue. We're in great shape, I gotta say. You two look half blitzed"—his gaze caught Quirk and Eve; she looked as sheepish as he felt—"and Moth is half asleep."

"Don't worry about me, ya' big lug. I can still shoot. Worry about them."

"Do *not*—" Kreski pointed at Moth but addressed Dulcie. "Do not give that child a weapon, do you hear me?"

Dulcie spread his hands defensively, but said nothing.

"Okay, enough chit-chat, let's go. And remember, you're in protective custody. You stick with me or you're a fugitive."

Minutes later—after loading out one at a time to guard against terra-fauna attack—Kreski pulled the co-opted Yellowknife S.D. SUV out of the motel's lot onto snow-white streets amid darkness.

Moth, it seemed, had woken on the wrong side of the wrong bed, in the wrong house in the wrong city. "I need a fucking day off from this shit," she announced. "Is it the weekend yet?"

"Every day's Friday on the farm," said Dulcie.

"What does that even mean?"

"He's implying farmers never get a day off," said Quirk.

"Yeah, well, every day's Sunday in the convent, and that's left me bitter and pissed off, so blow your nose and dry your eyes, grandpa."

"Hypoglycaemia," said Quirk, nodding sagely. "She just needs her breakfast."

"Am I the only one worried about the curfew?" Eve asked.

Kreski grunted. "Trust the badge on this SUV and hope Kootook's too busy to care about closing me down. We're in kind of a grey zone now."

They drove on deserted streets, took Franklin northeast towards Latham Island as Dulcie directed. The low, frontier cityscape gave way to residential streets. At one point, Kreski had to slam the brakes as a big dog sprinted out in front of the vehicle. As fast as it ran, the three pursuing mangetouts moved faster, one rebounding from the SUV in its haste—making them all twitch—before careening out of sight. All heads turned to track the chase. Quirk knew they all wondered if the dog would make it.

Five minutes later Kreski pulled in where the bearded plumber pointed, bumping over the drainage channel into a vacant lot. They climbed down into the early morning chill, Kreski with his sidearm drawn. "We're on foot for a bit," Dulcie grumbled. Then he asked, "Mind if I take this, Sheriff?" showing Kreski the vehicle's contingency firearm, a disguised plastec piece that moments before had doubled as a door handle.

Kreski nodded assent.

Quirk tugged his borrowed scarf tighter around his neck and followed Dulcie, trudging down through drifted snow on a slipway between shadowed buildings. Snow muffled their movement, yet low scuffing sounds bounced off wood siding. The five tramped down to the lake; except it wasn't a lake, but a platform of solid ice layered with snow. Dulcie led them onto the flat, making for a line of scattered lights, the only reference points in the darkness ahead.

Kreski pulled a set of IR glasses from his pocket. "Shout if something doesn't feel right. Better to yell and be wrong."

"Where are those lights?" Moth asked. "The houses..."

"They float," Eve answered, "until the lake freezes."

"Huh," said Moth, as they plodded away from the shore, each looking left or right, or twisting to glance behind.

"Clear night," Dulcie mumbled. "Good for aurora."

"Damn, Dulcie." Quirk wished he had half the ex-marine's assurance. They inhabited Morton's domain now, a night-time world of threatening shadows and unknown sounds. Fine if you were top of the food chain, but they were not. Plenty of things out here had bigger teeth, sharper claws or better ordnance.

"Hush up," Kreski breathed, perfectly audible in the near silence. "If you don't have IR, look for lights flickering. Fair chance something's moving 'tween them and you. If in doubt, whisper a clock face bearing."

Dulcie kept a steady pace. A biting breeze played across Quirk's exposed skin, which hardly mattered, since it sliced through his clothes too. In the bar, ninety metres had sounded like nothing, but the lights of the ice-locked dwellings still looked distant in the dark. Which terra-fauna would venture out on a frozen lake? Dulcie's outline up front—which Quirk followed resolutely—scanned around, but his path never wavered. Moth walked beside Quirk. *Maybe she's as nervous as me.* "We'll be fine," he whispered, patting her shoulder.

"Bastard!" She jerked, twisting, skittered on the underlying ice and fell hard, but scrabbled up immediately. "Do NOT fucking do that. *Fuck!*" she hissed.

"I was trying to reassure you," he snapped. He really sucked at this.

"Shut up," grumbled Kreski. Quirk saw his pistol coming up. "Incoming: ten o'clock. Three outlines, no four. They look like...dinosaurs?"

"Don't shoot," said Eve. "They're velociraptors, coded not to harm humans."

"Are they coded not to scare us shitless?" asked Moth.

Eve's voice remained firm. "Keep moving. They shouldn't attack, but they might be hunting something else that we don't want to meet out here."

The darkness seemed to close in, even more oppressive. The remaining distance looked like kilometres. Despite Eve's instruction, all glanced north as four tall shapes approached while they toiled through shin-high snow towards Dulcie's cabin. Forty metres, thirty, twenty: the dinosaurs stalked closer, their breath visible now in the low moonlight. If they would not attack, what would they do?

Without warning the sky was stained green across the whole span of Quirk's vision. He watched a curtain of lime and yellow fire ripple from the horizon to the edge of the sky behind them. It billowed as if the earthbound wind had caught its edge, taking on tinges of violet and magenta. But even this stunning natural wonder could not hold his attention, which flicked back to the approaching creatures. Distinguishable now, they moved in a line, five metres apart, as if drawing in a net.

"You're sure they have no taste for good-looking detectives?" he asked Eve.

"I've shared a room with them, remember? They could've picked us off by now."

"Keep moving," said Dulcie, gaze never wavering from his house.

The creatures stepped closer—close enough Quirk could hear their breathing, see their dead eyes, blacker than night, reflecting the green aurora. The dinosaurs shadowed the walkers over their final nervous steps to Dulcie's home. Eve and Moth followed the plumber up the steps to enter the darkened house. Kreski put a hand on Quirk's shoulder, guiding him onto the wooden treads, his other hand levelling his pistol. Four impossible, not-ancient beasts regarded them, heads tilting, dark-patterned hides lit green by the sky's otherworldly light.

Quirk was only too glad to step inside, and for Dulcie to close and deadbolt the door, shutting the velociraptors out where Quirk couldn't see them. Or rather—he decided as his heartbeat slowed to a heavy thud—where they could not see *him*.

"Hail Mary, full of grace. Our Lord is with thee," Moth whispered urgently. "Blessed art thou amongst women, and blessed is the fruit of thy womb, Jesus. Holy Mary, Mother of God, pray for us sinners—"

"I'd rather you didn't do that," said Dulcie.

"What's your problem? No faith in the Lord delivering us?"

"Not that," he smiled his easy smile. "The last bit sounds like a jinx to me."

"Huh," she snorted, but smiled in return. "Okay, how do you feel about Latin?"

"The good news," said Dulcie, "is that we're going right back across the lake to Latham Island."

Kreski turned to Eve. "Don't those things carry a remote destruct by law?"

"They do." She moved into the pool of illumination offered by Dulcie's feature lighting. "When deployed according to protocol they carry the Demon Seed system— millions of nanomachines each with a microscopic load of C4X. On close range transmission of the code, the nanos converge on the top of the brain stem, coalesce and blow their host's head off. The system was disabled on the first mangetouts, allegedly by Tania. It's still running on the vuldolphs I released, but Morton must have deactivated the others, or this sorry mess would have ended days ago. I guess he told the FBI Tania disabled the system because she was trying to steal the MTs, or some other bullshit story. Maybe I released all the other beasts in a fit of hormonal pique, or as part of Morton's raging lesbian revenge fantasy."

Dulcie had pulled back the rug in front of the fireplace, cracked open a hatch, and now began handing out weapons—all licensed, he assured Kreski. The sheriff watched with furrowed brow. "Hunting, huh?" He picked up the backpack of ammo Dulcie had placed on the coffee table. "I may have crossed Kootook's line, but I haven't crossed mine. I'm still holding you all to account at some point."

"You could deputise us," suggested Moth, taking a sleek, black pistol from Quirk and pressing into his hand a smaller, stubbier handgun she had lifted from the floor.

"Nuh-uh," said Kreski. "One ammo set each, and I carry the backpack."

"Hey," Quirk exclaimed. "What's wrong with yours?"

Moth snorted. "I'm not letting you out that door with a Glock UK8." She held up the nasty-looking black thing. "You get the Derringer TD-310. It's child-friendly, wave it at something and shoot, barely matters if you hit it or not."

"Out of mouths of babes." He shook his head. Kreski just frowned harder.

Eve received a shotgun. The plumber folded out the stock on a compact automatic that became deadlier looking with each expert movement of his hands.

"Dulcie," said Kreski warily, "that's an FMP17: highly illegal."

"Is that what that is? Huh. Oh well, army surplus, remember?"

"My ass. You're going to turn that over to me when we're done, or we will have a big, 9x19mm problem. Do you hear me?"

"Yes, sir," said Dulcie with all the grace of a chastened sixteen-year-old.

Moth slipped the wicked-looking pistol into her waistband and stood arms akimbo. "If you kids are finished dicking around, we're in a hurry, remember?"

"Gloves?" asked Quirk. Dulcie reached back into his underfloor cache, provided the requisite hand-wear then misted each of them with a laser-foiling nano-spray.

They mustered at the front door and Dulcie turned out the lights. Standing in darkness, a green and purple glow playing over the blinds, Kreski set out his tactics: Dulcie and Moth on point then Quirk and Eve, with the sheriff at the tail. They would traverse the snow and ice without detour or distraction straight to Latham Island, dinosaurs permitting. Quirk traced the hard contours of his pistol, locating the safety, testing it off and on, off and on. He wrinkled his nose. He was getting a reputation as a lousy shot, which simply was not the case. Guns made him uncomfortable.

Tania's velociraptors waited outside for this prey that some abstract instinct prevented them from killing. Quirk stepped down onto the snow, icy air sucking the heat from his skin. The majestic aurora played across the sky, painting the snow with colour. There was nothing abstract about the shiver that ran through him at the sight of those beasts, dark shapes patterned in coal and slate, that moved within snapping distance, flanking them two-a-side, sharp teeth near human neck height.

"If they're not going to eat us, what are they doing?" Moth hissed at him.

"I'm trying not to think about that," Quirk replied.

As they paced away from Dulcie's house, the dinosaurs continued to flank them. The plumber confirmed their new target lay further north, five hundred metres over the deep, frozen lake, making landfall at the southern end of Latham Island, then through scrub to the snowbound houses of Morrison Drive.

They toiled through the snow, breath pluming before them, mingling with that of the velociraptors. Snow and the cold sapped their energy. Dulcie, Eve and Kreski held their weapons ready. Quirk kept his pistol pointed down, safety off, finger on trigger guard. Moth's pistol remained in her belt, but he had no doubt she could draw and shoot in a blink. Fourteen years old. He snorted. He'd learned little of her past despite their agreement. There had been time to speak properly, but they chose not to, not really. And yet now she was seeing his dirty laundry being hung out to dry anyway. Mixed metaphor, but he did feel differently towards her. Despite her sharp edges he cared for her more now than he could have imagined in their fractious beginnings.

Damn it. This was not supposed to happen.

A drone buzzed overhead. Dulcie stopped and deployed his chaff spray, also throwing a couple of smoking cans on the ground left and right, before spraying a powerful aerosol upwind of the group. The drone returned twice before the sound of its tracking receded. It seemed that the spray was effective. Something howled in the night that might have been a wolf, a coyote or a horrific product of Genextric's vats. The raptors' snouts twitched at that, but some behavioural blip caused them to maintain their worrisome shadowing of the Derek Morton Payback Club.

Limbs became leaden, muscles burned and—as they reached the point furthest from land, midway between Joliffe and Latham—the ice began to sing. Twangs, snaps and clicks shot through the silence, like steel cable protesting as it was tensioned against the inertia of something massive.

"Ice still thinnish around here," Dulcie mumbled unhelpfully. "Maybe fifty mil. Spread out some." They did, hastily putting metres between them. To Quirk's horror, Moth softly shooed the velociraptors beside her. Amazingly, they drifted back, almost as if understanding the need. The ice sang for several minutes, but stopped before anyone got wet. Finally—pits heavy with sweat, face numb with cold—Quirk dragged himself after the others up the shallow bank into the trees on Latham Island's east shore. The raptors melted into the dark undergrowth.

"So far, so good," Kreski whispered. Quirk was pleased to hear him pulling for breath. "Lead on, Dulcie."

They ducked through jagged, evergreen branches, wet snow clinging, into scrubby woodland, pushed through spindly twigs for ten minutes before emerging onto a residential street. Dulcie continued across the road, back into the bush for ten more minutes to break free onto another white-carpeted suburban scene.

For a second, Quirk thought their escort had lost interest, but no, four dark forms slipped from the undergrowth as easily as a flint knife through soft skin.

Vehicle tracks rutted the road's smooth covering. Dulcie stepped into the tyre marks and walked along them deeper into the neighbourhood. The rest followed his lead, Quirk appreciating the easy walking. The dinosaurs dogged their hidden tracks. Before long, Dulcie left the road, entering a garden hedged off from its neighbours and signalled for a huddle.

"On the left, six doors down judging from the trees hereabouts. Number one-sixty-eight," he breathed. "But I'll lay odds their neighbour don't own a Chev-mobile panel van in government black: We got company. Kreski, Eve, me—if you agree, Sheriff—cut along the shore past the gardens. You two go knock on the front door."

"And the dinos?" asked Moth.

"Honest to God, I don't know," said Dulcie. "Guess it won't matter what we decide. Now, go. Keep those guns hidden." Quirk pocketed the Derringer, safety on and watched the three slip away over the snowy road into shadow. Unfortunately, all four menacing velociraptors remained. He imagined impossible questions in their quizzical-seeming regard. They...couldn't have imprinted on Moth somehow, could they?

"Let's go, boss," said Moth.

They paced to the house, footwear squeaking on new powder. Nothing moved but them and four dinosaurs, although the raptors began to hang back which, absurdly, comforted him somewhat. As they closed on it, he imagined the parked black van staring back at them. At the gate, they shared a glance. Moth moved, but he grabbed her sleeve. "Me first," he put his hand in his pocket, gripping the Derringer. "You can shoot past me." He moved forward. The house was dark. He raised a hand and knocked on the white pseudoWood door. No movement, no sign of life through the oval plass, only his imaginings, his heart beating. He pushed the door. It swung open on darkness.

"Step inside, Kirby, Moratti. Put your weapons on the floor."

Prickles of shock spiked his skin. A form moved behind them, casting a streetlight shadow. A hand in the middle of his back pushed Quirk forwards. He moved inward, turned, entered the first darkened room.

"Lights up."

Two agents in SWAT gear stood, weapons levelled, in a room turned inside-out. One wore a chest screen displaying the head-and-shoulders image of a woman of anonymous appearance wearing a determined expression. Quirk laid his gun on the carpet. Moth's hands were empty now too.

"This is FBI Special-Agent-in-Charge Prescott. You are detained as part of an ongoing investigation. State your purpose here."

Something, somewhere pinged then pinged again. One agent turned his head and found himself looking down the barrel of Kreski's big pistol. Eve moved from behind the sheriff, levelled shotgun on her hip. "No, you drop *your* weapons."

"Good grief," said Prescott from the speaker. *"My authority trumps yours, Kreski. You're making a career-ending mistake. By delaying me you're impeding hostage negotiations with the eco-terrorists controlling Genextric. This is a critical juncture. If they stop the release—"*

"I'm pursuing a murder investigation," Kreski barked at the screen. "I have a person of interest, and two potential hostages. I have witnesses in custody, a bucket-load of questions, and it's my duty to find the answers. Plus, you're being set up by Morton, and possibly by C Corp."

Quirk remained acutely aware that he and Moth were staring down the barrels of two FBI automatics.

"Kreski, this house is empty. We were tipped off and we've been over it. Satellite feed shows two women removed in a Genextric van an hour ago. They're gone." Eve swore. *"The terrorists are releasing most of the Genextric hostages, maybe the two women among them. They think they're getting passage out, but they are not. We're going in. Bring your witnesses to the airport command post. You're done."*

"Eco-terrorists my ass. Derek Morton—"

"Is one of the hostages. Now stand down, Sheriff!"

Behind Kreski, a third and fourth black-clad agent entered from the back of the house, turning as they pushed past Quirk's friends, goggled heads twisting, bringing weapons to bear, but not on Kreski and Eve. The braying of velociraptors filled the room as two dinosaurs emerged into the light's radius. Answering calls rattled Quirk's ears as the other two raptors entered from the front and slid him and Moth further into the room, which instantly became unbearably crowded. The agents turned their weapons on the raptors.

"Don't shoot!" said Quirk, hands out, fingers spread. "You'll override their coding." His gaze met Eve's. She blinked then nodded, seeing what he saw, how Dulcie had succeeded in using the raptors to spring his own trap.

"He's right. Don't antagonise them. Lay down your weapons."

"That's not our advice..." one agent stammered.

"Damn it, Agent Four. Hold your position."

Kreski laid his pistol down, and Eve her shotgun.

"Prescott's not here, son," the sheriff addressed him-her-or-them, impossible to tell with their thin form encased in black gear. "I suggest you disengage."

After moment's hesitation, the agent closest to those teeth-ridden raptor jaws laid down their gun. Agent Four followed suit. Dulcie chose that moment to enter from the front. Prescott was forced to watch—helplessly remote—as they disarmed her remaining agents and immobilised them with cable ties from Dulcie's kitbag.

"Hunting?" Kreski grunted, shaking his head.

Prescott's disgusted features flickered out. The image switched to a sunny, corporate promotional view of Genextric's Gamma Lab.

"Surprise! It's your friendly, neighbourhood snitcher-man! Can't speak long, it's real busy here. Morton has your friends—"

"No!" Eve shuddered. "He'll kill them."

"And how?" spat Moth. "I hid the damn pictures!"

"Doesn't matter now. Listen up. A medi-droid has tended to Doctor Terjesen, but she's in a bad way. You need to come to Genextric, NOW! Everything you need is here, but something's afoot, Dad, and you know Derek and TOM have a plan in motion."

So many ways that this felt wrong; so many strands converging on Genextric. "Hostages against TOM," Quirk realised out loud. "This is not part of TOM's plan, it's Morton's exit strategy.

"Nick." The name felt all wrong in his mouth. "Nick, we need more information. What's your role there? Where are you in the building? How many are left inside, and why might four velociraptors be shadowing us? They seem to be...helping us."

"There's no time for this! I'm a prisoner, that's my damn role!! People are going out to helicopters. I need to find out what's happening. Now, hurry!"

The call ended. Prescott's image flickered back into being on the supine agent's chest. She was angry.

"I'm done with you, Kreski. I have bigger problems. Bring those people in. If you think you can affect how this plays out you've got thirty-six minutes. From 0245 hours Genextric becomes a Level Three containment zone."

The screen went black.

"Well, that's shit," said Dulcie as he hauled none too gently on the final agent's wrist tie. Four tense, weary gazes regarded him. "I had six months on anti-terrorism in Istanbul," he explained. "Level Three means they're going in shooting."

1A

The raptors just stood in the living room, heads turning and tilting. *Can they be guarding us?* Moth wondered. She imagined sentience in their black eyes, but why would they *choose* to act this way? They were way more inscrutable than androids which—if anything—were totally scrutable, with all those laws and tenets.

She thought Eve might cry, and moved closer to the woman, put a hand on her arm. That's what adults did in these emotional situations, Moth reckoned. Turned out Eve's shaking was anger, total fury. Moth knew how *that* felt. Eve flicked the unused slug from her shotgun's chamber. It popped out and skittered across the parquet floor. The creepy-cool dinosaurs' heads followed the rattling object.

Moth let her hand drop. A knot twisted her stomach, and she knew where it came from. Only three months ago she had mercilessly bullied her own tearful Aunt Giulia to get her way, and now she was doling out sympathy to strangers? Hanging with Quirk was ruining her edge. She was barely clinging to remorseless status anymore. She thought of him tucking her in last night. She couldn't believe she'd actually felt safer with him in the room. He couldn't even shoot a gun properly! She'd teach him some time.

"What the fuck do you mean, 'going in,' Dulcie?" said Eve. "The hostages..."

"Sounds like Morton sold the FBI on the eco-terrorist thing," said Dulcie.

Quirk looked distracted, puzzling at the problem. "Morton hasn't defied TOM yet, but he's making his own moves on this messed-up board. He has to keep some staff hostages to slow down the FBI, and he holds Tania and Meriwa against our good behaviour. Then there's Nick. I bet Derek believes his presence will keep TOM honest. Morton thinks he's playing a strong hand, but he must know the FBI won't sit on their hands." The boss fell silent.

Kreski looked at his handset. "It's 2:11 now. Thirty-four minutes. Someone find the keys to that van." He crouched and began patting down agents. Eve helped. Moth left them to it, checking her watch implant's discreet display. "So, Dulcie, what's the protocol in a Level Three containment scenario, in your experience?"

Dulcie looked up, but his hands went right on checking his weapon like a badass. "It'll be a modified strategy. Most likely they'll go in hot soon after the order comes down; brute force and ignorance, target rooms with bio-signatures, free who they can. They think it's eco warriors, more likely to fold, not the black ops Morton has."

"Bullshit," said Quirk, and Moth's eyebrows launched towards her scalp. The others looked shocked too, their yappers clamped shut, giving Quirk the floor. "This raid only happens because TOM wills it, but I just can't see him doing that with his grandson in the building. I can't see him giving the boy up, either because he's family or because he's an asset. I bet TOM has a plan to rescue Nick, I just don't see it, yet."

Eve produced a key from an agent's pocket just as Kreski's handset illuminated.

"Anyone know who MiH10 is?" he asked.

"I think I do," said Quirk, his eyes not leaving Eve's face.

"It's a link," the sheriff said. "Download VL11Hefa89v5?" He too looked at Eve, who seemed suddenly very uncomfortable.

"Tap it," said Quirk. "I think it might be a present."

"My mother warned me about tapping strange links," Kreski grumbled. He tapped the screen. "Download done." A couple more taps. "It's a..." He stopped, looked around the group and back to the handset. "It's an app called Velocir-App-tor HQ. I think it..." The sheriff's, deep gravel drawl died to a whisper. "Message reads: 'I just can't stop sending help, can I? Get here now, Daddy.'"

"Velocir-App-tor? Cool," Moth whispered, feeling the tingle of raw wonder. She reached out for Kreski's set and the sheriff let her take it. Her thumbs slid over the interface. She tapped "Search for Discoverable Devices" (that was cold). Four options presented themselves, popping up in the menu one after another. "Reed, Susan, Johnny and Ben!" she almost squeaked, making no effort to disguise her delight. "Old skool!" She tapped on Johnny then Ben (Because, duh!), and watched a wheel spin beside each name until connections were made. Two saurian heads turned to looked at her. By dumb luck, Johnny and Ben were the two raptors behind Kreski.

"Did you just connect with them? I did *not* know we could do that," said Eve.

OMG, this is so fun!

Kreski turned, frowning at the velociraptors blocking his way.

Dulcie found a handset in his pack. "Send the link; number's FT311-555-2368."

She sent it then tried to ask her dinos to move outside. She thumbed the left-hand clock face panel and Johnny turned to her. Quirk looked like he would drop his dinner if a dino took one step towards him. *No, I won't.* She turned her velociraptors, asked them to proceed then followed them out the house into the snow. When she hit pause, the dinos stopped, looked around, then began to wander. They had autonomy, like she was only making suggestions. Without active suggestions they just made up their own mind. Neat. But she must never, ever trust them too far, despite what Eve said about coding. Quirk's son was a really smart cookie, assuming this gear was his, which she did.

"2:16, let's hustle," said Kreski as he moved past her.

Dulcie guided Sue and Reed out of the garden, brushing past snow-laden bushes. Eve opened the black FBI van, and Kreski took the key from her. Moth kept her dinos to one side. The humans loaded into the van as the sleek, tough-skinned raptors stood and watched. Did they secretly wish they could tear the meat sacks apart?

"Which one's Johnny?" Eve asked.

Moth tapped a pull-down and had Johnny Storm let out Roar3 (subdued). Eve looked set to piss herself. Moth would have laughed at that once, but now found the idea embarrassing. *Wow. Is maturity kicking in? I am not ready for that.*

"I got this," Dulcie announced, weapon strapped around his shoulder now he worked two terra-fauna dinosaurs with his burner handset. "Reed and Sue?"

"No time to explain," said Moth with a quick smile as they climbed into the front with Kreski. "It's arcane lore from the last millennium. 'Nuff said. Let's go."

She really wished they weren't trying to save the world right now. Okay not that, but Eve's world at least, maybe Quirk's. Suggesting stuff to the raptors, like flanking the van was super fun. There was a lag in the VRs' response, as if they considered for a second whether to comply. She looked at Dulcie who grinned like a lunatic. Kreski eased them onto the road, turning south then put his foot down, and the van surged forward towards Genextric's Gamma Lab, hundreds of hungry terra-faunae, hundreds of NAF troops, FBI SWAT teams and Lord knew what else.

"02:23," Kreski growled. "Troops go in twenty-two minutes, and we're actually rushing to get in there first?" Nobody answered him.

Moth concentrated on the handset, setting her raptors to "Follow" so she could explore the app. The interface looked like a dartboard, and she had twin controls on screen, capable of sitting side-by-side or stacked vertical. The instructions were very general, like "Follow," "Attend," "Pause" and..."Attack." *Huh?* In the centre of the spider's web of commands sat the image of a capped button. She tapped it and a virtual lid flipped up. Underneath was a button labelled "Kill." *Jesu Christi.* She crossed herself. It looked like the system left acres of space for the dinos to interpret these broad commands. That "Kill" button couldn't work on human targets though, right? Nor the "Attack" one, but there was a "Catch" button that might be worth pushing sometime, and "Subdue." How could that possibly go horribly and disastrously wrong in any way? "Following?" she asked Dulcie, and he nodded without looking up.

Ben and Johnny flanked the vehicle on her side, the right. She could see them in the mirror. "What kind of speed will they do?"

"I don't know," Eve answered hesitantly. "Never timed them."

Moth glanced backwards and Quirk smiled at her through the mesh partition. She could see his uncertainty, but didn't have time to reassure him. She concentrated on Johnny and Ben, who loped along as the van cruised south off Latham Island towards the city centre. 02:26. But that was academic, because how in holy heck would they get past the supposed forces of light that must be ranked, misguidedly, against them between here and Genextric?

"Hang a right at 43," said Dulcie. "Go the long way around Niven Lake, miss the checkpoint on 48. It'll take us past Rowland's house on Deweerdt, but..."

Kreski complied, sent the van carving around a dark, curving drive, pools of streetlight leading them north to the highway and on towards Gamma Lab. The residential area forced Kreski to moderate his speed, giving the velociraptors a rest, although they looked comfortable enough. Moth had the window down. The tyres hissed on wet techmac, but as Kreski built speed northbound on 48, the window auto-closed, minimising drag and energy use.

"There will be police, FBI and National Guard all over the approaches," said Quirk. "Even if we reach the lab in time, they won't let us waltz in there, and a diversion with genetically engineered dinosaurs is *not* going to help."

"Sewage," said Eve, and Moth craned around to see Eve and Quirk staring at each other in the dimness of the van's cargo bay. "It's how I met Dulcie. Nobody does their own plumbing; nobody. Genextric is no different."

"How big is this pipe?" asked Kreski, whose shoulders were like three feet wide.

Dulcie hmphed, not looking away from his handset. "There's an access gate in the electrified fence on the line of the outfall pipe, but it only opens from the inside. If Quirk's boy can't open the gate—which cuts the fence power too—someone'll need to go through the pipe. Not ideal, but better than going through the front gate and gettin' ventilated. Pipe's divided halfway between fence and building by a decimetre-thick grating. There are two manholes, one either side of the grating. Third manhole buried outside the fence is how we get access."

Eve's gaze—still determined—remained locked on Quirk's. Moth was unconvinced that nothing icky was occurring. Eve said, "The outfall has to turn through ninety degrees on its way to the riverside processing unit; hence the third manhole."

"Pipe's half-metre diameter," Dulcie stated. "Just too narrow to crawl through. Even if your shoulders fit"—he glanced at Kreski—"you can't move your arms, bend your elbows."

"So, you're saying an adult can't get through," said Quirk.

Moth got that sinking feeling, the one when grown-ups discussed you doing something they wouldn't do themselves, like going to bed before nine, sitting two exams on one day, or crawling through a shit-knows-what-filled underground pipe.

"I'll do it"—she scowled—"but you all will owe me *big* time. I mean all the fucking chocolate, and the puppies." She snarled. "And a pony."

"Checkpoint ahead," said Kreski. "Do something with those raptors, now. You've got three hundred metres, or our reasonable progress ends here."

2:32, thirteen minutes to raid time: they were not going to make it, but what did that mean? She tapped, slid and pinched, cycling through various control labels. "Dulcie. Seven o'clock, overlay two, there's a 'Detour' command."

"Got it."

Moth chose "Pick on Map" and the background faded into PlanetView. She tapped a point in the brush about fifty metres to the side of the road just beyond the checkpoint. If the raptors travelled mostly straight, they'd re-join the van well to the north, provided there was no delay, and no soldier saw the dinos, heard the dinos, or detected the dinos by drone IR. She set Ben and Johnny on their way, saw them in the mirror peeling off down into the drainage ditch, across a derelict lot into darkness.

"How wide you go?" she asked Dulcie.

"Thirty metres."

"Okay." She stayed quiet. Guys hated their spatial awareness being challenged.

The van slowed, Kreski's window sliding down. The soldiers sounded sceptical about Kreski taking witnesses to a safehouse. Wasn't he driving the wrong way, out of civilisation and into the wilderness? She kept an ear on the conversation, but made no eye contact. Just a kid flicking through colourful phone screens. Ben and Johnny's map dots had passed the detour point and were heading back! She hit the "Pause" button. She breathed again as the dots stopped, just wandering slowly.

"Achievement unlocked," she muttered.

"Hah," Dulcie snorted like a disgruntled gamer then leaned in, showing her his burner's screen. His VRs were ten metres off the road and only thirty back! Slightly hidden by some tree trunks, but a movement or stray sound could give them away.

Three of the five soldiers paced round the van while one questioned Kreski on his passengers. Moth could see the sheriff getting uncomfortable the closer he skated to lying. Mr. Kirby and Miss Moratti were helping the Creston Sheriff's Department with enquiries. Miss Meyer was a technical advisor. Mr. Rice was a new deputy, apparently.

The soldier appraised Dulcie, her features even as her gaze slide past the window along the van to the darkened road verge. Moth moved her eyes to her mirror without turning her head. Sue and Reed stood together behind tall scrub, saurian outlines only just visible at the edge of the streetlight glow because she knew where to look. How long did the "Pause" command operate? Could the VRs overcome the "suggestive" programming? If the soldiers had motion sensors...

They'd already lost three minutes. It was 2:38, seven minutes till go-time. At this rate they'd arrive bang in the middle of the raid.

The soldier's camo-helmeted head turned back to Kreski. "Why are you driving a government-issue van, sir?"

Kreski dropped the lead. The van shot forward and clipped the tail of the left-hand blockading vehicle as Kreski hauled on the wheel. They bounced towards the side of the road. Maybe the government black bought them a few seconds. Kreski's tactical driving training certainly made the difference as he slewed the van into a skid, keeping the power on and rattling through the gravel strip. The soldiers opened fire.

The van lurched sideways into the ditch and Moth thought they were tipping over. Shells punched through the vehicle's sides. Moth's mirror exploded, but she was pressing into Dulcie, hunched down in her chair, away from the bullets. They were still moving. They were clear. It was 2:41. No one said anything. She straightened, regained control of her raptors and set them after the van at max speed, hoping the soldiers wouldn't shoot them, glancing at Dulcie doing the same. Without a mirror, she had to wait for Dulcie to confirm they were okay. He craned his head back trying to see in Kreski's mirror. "I see them," he said. "No muzzle flash, think they're okay."

Reed, Sue, Johnny and Ben re-joined them two hundred metres north. Kreski really hammered along the nondescript road past spotlit mine buildings and machinery, stretches of wilderness scrub and rock outcrops, all of it snow-coated. The handset told her the raptors were falling back now; ninety-five metres behind, but still following.

"Eve," said Kreski. "We'll cross the river then pull off and walk in. Yes?"

"Yes."

He grunted. "If we weren't committed before, we sure as shit are now. I hope no one has strong opinions about military prison."

"I don't think anyone's happy about this, Wayne," Quirk answered with a serious lack of enthusiasm.

Moth couldn't stop her gaze flicking around, looking up the road ahead, craning to see the rear-view—digital, of course—and Kreski's mirror, expecting headlights, expecting red-and-blues, expecting the whole crazy thing to fall apart. But it didn't, not yet. Maybe arriving at the start of the raid made sense. All the official vehicles would be in place at Gamma Lab, all eyes would be forward. Her hands were sweating.

Kreski slowed for a bend. "Bridge ahead," he said then they rolled over a different surface. They were almost there, almost in it. The road ahead was bright. Another aurora? No; the twinkling of many red, blue and also orange lights around what must be Gamma Lab's access.

"Pull in here!" Eve snapped. The vehicle bucked. Moth's weight jammed the seatbelt into her chest and waist. "Nose down the bank toward the trees."

There were no streetlights. Kreski killed the full beams. Beyond the snow-covered verge, darkness. "Hold on," he said and turned left. There was a heavy bump, her teeth clicked, and the van's nose pitched down. They lurched side to side, but always heading down, maybe twenty degrees. Branches slapped and clawed the van's sides. There were grunts and groans and swears. Their path flattened suddenly, and they lurched to a stop in complete darkness and silence.

"Move," said Dulcie. The sounds of scrabbling killed the silence. "They might have seen the headlights. No torches or sets."

Her chest and tummy hurt where the belt had yanked her back. She released herself, grasped Kreski's handset, feeling for her door handle, cracking it open, and stepped down into bitter cold. Complete darkness made the cold deeper, like it was trying to leach the life from her bones. Then the night got brighter without warning. The pale glow on her inner wrist said 02:45. The brightness came from the ground, over to the right through and above the trees. It was like the San Siro, Milano during a match, the bright glow above the squatting structure, spilling light into a black sky. There was shouting too, plenty of it, muted by distance, snow, and branches interrupting their view of the lab and those harsh, military spotlights.

Her heart almost exploded as sounds of snow crunching came from above. Four shapes darker than night resolved at the highway's edge. The velociraptors were still with them. "Heel," she said, tapping. Her eyes were adjusting. She could make out the raptors coming down the bank.

"Got the manhole co-ords in my JobMap," Dulcie whispered. "Moth, I flicked them to you. Send your raptors in first, we follow."

"Check," Moth whispered.

A drone purred overhead. Her heart skipped. All four velociraptors looked up. Another drone came over and this time the humans shuffled. The thing's motor tone didn't change. It hadn't seen them. There was another one, and a fourth, fifth, sixth, off to the sides of them, she thought.

"Go," Kreski grunted. "I've got rope. The raid will cover us for a bit, but one of those drones'll look the wrong way before long. I think I've still got a little body heat."

Johnny moved ahead and the other raptors followed. Everyone gave way to them. The group strung out as passage through trees, thick undergrowth and wet snow was tough. She pulled up her T-shirt's neck, covering her mouth so that her breath wouldn't plume in the air. "Mask your mouth," Dulcie hissed for those who hadn't already.

Their path was tangential to the lab, towards the outer manhole, paralleling the brightly lit fence visible now through the trees. With things under control for a minute, she thought about what was coming, crawling through a narrow waste pipe. Thirty metres didn't sound much, but how the hell did she open the manhole? And then the gate? Dulcie brought the column to a stop, and she hit "Pause" on Ben and Johnny. The group huddled together in the undergrowth, the tall fence ten metres away.

"There's monitoring on the fence, and on the pipe, of course," said Dulcie, "but hopefully they'll be busy with the raid, which we can assume has started."

"The fence is smart wire," said Eve. "It can differentiate between humans and animals. It is live, but won't harm us. Safety regulations." She grimaced. "But, once we start tampering with the manhole, security droids will be alerted."

"Hopefully the control room will think it part of the raid," said Quirk.

"Right up till they see a fourteen-year-old crawling up their poop tube." Moth grinned, but didn't feel the levity. It was strictly manic.

"Okay. I'll go uncover and open the manhole," said Dulcie, matter-of-factly. "I've got the code and the key. Plumbing contract." He snorted. "Don't think I'll bid next year. Moth, have Ben and Johnny cover me." He handed his burner set to Eve, who frowned at it. "When you're through, open the next manhole and come back to the gate, I'll give you that code." He crouched low and snuck away, following the fence. Moth suggested her raptors follow. It looked like they stalked him. Her heart pounded.

"Nothing from Nick," Quirk whispered. "I'm sorry; I hoped he'd come through."

Kreski rumbled. "Once the gate's open, I'll go round front. More likely I can help from there. Just remember you're in custody. Don't wander away without me." He patted his handset in his pocket.

"Take Ben and Johnny," said Moth, returning the sheriff's handset. He nodded, examining the interface.

"Tell anyone you meet it's Genextric tech. They should buy that," said Eve.

"I found this in the van," Quirk whispered to her, bringing out a white packet from inside his ridiculous hoodie. She unfolded the light plastext bundle into a crime scene onesie, complete with feet, hands and a hood. She began to cry.

"Moth, what...? Hey, it's okay; it'll be fine. Over really quickly." He put a hand on her shoulder. "You can do it."

"It's not that, doofus," she sniffed, wiping tears away with the back of her hand. He'd thought about her, considered what a horrible thing she was about to do and tried to lessen the grimness for her. He cared about her, under all that intellectual bluff and pretentious flouncing. "I love it," she sniffed. "Thank you."

Automatic gunfire rent the night air. Everyone jerked and fell flat. Dulcie's muffled bark was just audible. Even the raptors' saurian forms flinched.

A distant explosion punctured the silence, and all the floodlights went out.

1B

Moth spat snow from her mouth, crushed tears away, and got a grip. Small arms fire snapped in the chill darkness and cold soaked her where she lay in the snow.

"Pipe's open," Dulcie called. "Vented, but don't drag your heels: in and out."

Kreski patted her shoulder. "Go get 'em, kid."

"Don't call me kid," she snapped.

Typical: Nick had stiffed them when things got tough. She would have to do this. She huffed and sat up, tugged on the onesie, pulled out her gun, and held the grip. "Glock: light on." A tight cone lit up Dulcie, made them both targets, but she needed it.

"Right behind you," said Quirk. She allowed herself some reassurance, zipped up the suit then leopard-crawled forward on the path of least resistance. She still got a face-full of vegetation. The stench from the manhole hit her long before reaching Dulcie, the putrid honk unmistakable.

BOOM!!

Another flare of light in the sky. Bright orange smoke billowed across the distant parking lot as she emerged from the bush into the fence's clear zone. Dulcie was pressed flat, the two velociraptors had flinched but straightened now, braying to their friends, a chilling sound that Ben and Johnny—back with Eve and Kreski—answered.

The staccato gunfire lessened. A flurry of drones zipped overhead.

"Action's moved inside, likely," said Dulcie, kneeling up in her light's glow.

Moth swung her legs into the square hole, gagging, snatching up the CSI body bag's mask then dropped down the goggles. The fabric was light, but she didn't think her boots would tear it. Quirk looped Kreski's rope around her waist and tied it. "I used a bowline. We can pull you back if we have to."

The plumber's words were quick and clipped. "Genextric system's sophisticated; got aeration, deflocculation and detoxification tanks, and there's a clarifier and a settlement sump at the end of the line before the river."

She punched Dulcie's shoulder. "Don't say you can drink from the other end."

He shrugged. "You can, but you're going *that* way." He nodded at the building. "Next manhole got an emergency release on the inside, case of getting trapped."

More gunfire, distant for now. She took deep breaths, held the last one then dropped down and pushed forward, feet and hands scrabbling on the slimy surface. *Yeah, let's call it slime.* The smell was unspeakable, a physical assault. Her eyes streamed. She raged as she crawled: proper berserker battle fury. *Someone gonna pay!*

"Be careful," Quirk called. "You've got this. Talk, so we know you're okay."

"All just fuzking peachy in here," she hollered, her captured breath escaping, admitting the stench. She gasped, pointed the Glock forward, its light showing the way. Somehow the pipe was less shitty than she'd expected. *'Cause all the terra-fauna are out, of course, dummy.* She coughed and shuffled on.

Jesu Christi the pipe was small, running with five centimetres of grey-brown slurry. Her shoulder blades bumped the plascrete above, the sides restricted her elbows, her head bumped the roof with each "step" of her awkward crawl. She fought her gag reflex. Her eyes stung.

She strained her face away from the slurry, but that bumped her head, making her duck, etcetera. Bile rose. She breathed, gasped, coughed and forged on.

Keep talking, right. "Fucking shit bastard!"

She scrabbled forward, centimetres piling up into metres. She tried to hurry. She breathed, gagged. She wanted to spit out the taste but daren't pull down the mask. She tipped the Glock's beam, but couldn't see the manhole ahead!

"Butt-munching dick-slapper!" Still twenty metres.

This could not go on. She shuffled faster, banging elbows, shoulders and head. Her vision swam. *Oh no, oh-no, ohno!* The manhole flashed at the edge of the Glock's light. *So far away! Don't panic. Don't you fucking panic, Angelika.*

"Rancid tea-bagging arse wanker!"

A lever! Red handle beside the manhole. Grimy, but red. Pipe beyond blocked by a grill. Like Dulcie promised. She tried to pant shallow, less foul in mouth.

"Moth, can you hear me?!" Quirk's shout was so far away.

"Droid-loving brass-polisher!" Silence, just slopping, splashing silence.

Her elbows stung, her shoulders ached, her muscles became mushy with the strange angles and awkward tensing she forced them into. Under ten metres now. Should she worry about having strength enough to pull the lever? What if it was corroded, ready to snap or welded shut by years of chemical attack?

Her head lolled. She tilted it up and down, side to side, nothing eased the ache. She pushed, pushed, pushed, pushed, pushed and pushed. This was not how Angelika Moratti ended. No. Fucking. Chance. She bit her lip, sure the suit elbows had worn through, and wormed onward. She could almost reach it, almost. Almost. Almost...

She was there. It took her two goes to get a grip of the lever, gasping all the time. She pulled. Nothing. She pushed. Nothing. *Fuck!*

"Moth? Moth!" So distant, barely heard at all.

Her vision swam. Her hand slipped off the lever and her neck snapped forward, pain searing the top of her spine. She shuffled closer, arms nearly numb, she ached to straighten them. She went past the lever. Turned awkwardly onto her back, slurry slopping over her. She managed to tilt the Glock's light upward, barely able to hold the gun then lifted her leg, putting her boot against the lever. *Don't kick it. Slow pressure.* She pushed, increased the pressure. The lever eased forward.

Her foot slipped. There was a thick crack. The handle had moved. There was a gap! Lights splashed over the manhole up above, but she didn't give a shit. She had to breathe. Vision blurred. She bum-shuffled backwards. Bit more, bit more. Her ass was numb, but she could feel fresh air now and its promise pulled her upward. She rose, pain lancing along her spine, pushed with both hands against the manhole cover and it tilted up on some kind of counterbalance and she was free.

She scrambled out on her knees, drones buzzing overhead, chill air washing over her. She snatched the mask away, dragged crisp winter into her lungs, gulped it in, laughing. The air fuelled her muscles enough to stand, but something pulled her back. The rope. She fumbled with Quirk's knot, freed it, and tossed the end down the hole. She stood on wobbling legs, exposed halfway across the snowy carpet grass between fence and building—drone lights dancing around her—and looked back. Just then the building floodlights flared on. The once-dark ground, the fence, her friends, she, all bathed in harsh light. Quirk, Dulcie, Eve, Kreski appeared, all urging her towards them.

"Moth, honey!" Quirk called, waving at her. "Open the gate, quick!"

Kreski gestured too. "Come here, now!" Dulcie shouldered his AP17.

"Mangetouts," said Eve, her face a picture of stunned horror.

Moth turned to see four spittle-splashing beasts barrelling at her from a glowing door in the lab building. Seventy metres away, she could hear their grunts, feral mouths gaping as they bounded towards her, and her knees gave out.

* * *

Bright lights split the darkness and Quirk was caught, they all were, exposed to guards and drones and armed goons. A loading bay door in the building rattled open—a bright rectangle in the hulking black shape—and beasts issued forth.

Three! Six! She hadn't seen them. "Moth!" He urged her towards him. "Open the gate, quick!" The velociraptors twitched and swayed, but held station.

"Come here, now!" boomed Kreski.

"Mangetouts," said Eve, hopelessly.

Moth—exhausted—finally saw the monsters and collapsed to her knees.

Dulcie's burst of fire made Quirk jump and it sparked Moth into life too. She wrenched herself up and ran unsteadily for the gate as the beasts closed the distance. Watching was torture. She smacked into the fencing by the panel, eyes wide. Electrified! He thought she'd been shocked, but there was no spark, no burning stench. The tech knew she was human.

The beasts were forty metres away. Moth focused, flipped open the panel. Dulcie fired again, winging one, slowing it to a hobble. Eve's shotgun boomed uselessly. Kreski clipped another, his headshot puncturing its face. Quirk wanted to scream.

"Foxtrot," Dulcie called deliberately. "Four, five." Four more beasts emerged from the building. Moth pressed the pad. Kreski fired: BANG, BANG, BANG, sparks flying from the live fence. "Bravo, eight, nine," said Dulcie deliberately before firing again. Quirk raised his pistol, but even twenty metres was too far. "Hotel, Yankee, Zulu!" Dulcie shouted.

His next burst cut into the lead beast at fifteen metres and ripped it apart.

"Moth!"

She jerked the handle three times. "Ahhhh!" Kreski shot another mangetout twice in its hideous face, stopping it dead. Eve's shotgun barked and Quirk fired at the same bastard animal. Both hit and it went down, lay flailing. Moth abandoned the handle and spun. As the fourth beast leaped at her, she brought the sleek, black Glock up smoothly in two-hands: crack, crack, crack, crack. She blasted the MT's chest, continuing to turn away, arching back as the heavy body hit the fence, which sparked, the body hanging briefly, flesh sizzling. "Shoo, dog," said Moth as the smoking, melting, sizzling beast dropped to the ground. She popped the half-empty clip and slapped in a full one. Even with gloves, and the fence's sensor technology, everyone backed away from the barrier.

"Incoming," drawled Dulcie. "Lots of incoming."

Another four mangetouts bounded towards them, halfway across the snowy ground. Another dozen of the beasts flooded from the building's bright opening.

"Someone shoot this fucking gate off its fucking hinges!" Moth shouted.

"No!" cried Eve. "The frame's charged. It'll blow you to pieces."

Quirk spun away from the fence, dashing back to the manhole, sliding the last three metres like it was home plate. He toppled awkwardly in, snow spraying, boots splashing into...something. He groped for the fallen rope, finding it on the slick surface, and sprang up, coughing and gagging. Dulcie streamed automatic fire into the oncoming monsters while Kreski's big gun thudded and Eve's shotgun woofed. Quirk ran to the fence and threw the rope's end over it.

"Moth, rope!"

She saw it and grabbed it as he pulled on his end. The raptors twitched, seeming eager to get at the mangetouts.

Moth toiled at the climb as a platoon of mouths descended on her. She was weakened by her crawl through the pipe, but fatigue did not to stop her mouthing off, of course. She was halfway up the fence as the hoard of beasts approached. "This try-fail stuff is bullshit!"

Quirk puffed, heart hammering in his ribs. Moth hung near the top of the fence, stymied by a coil of laser wire, but she was clear of the monsters' teeth, right?

Dulcie, Kreski and Eve's gunfire cut into the descending mangetout pack. The first frenzied few threw themselves at the fence, which shocked their inhuman forms hard. The next rank leapt on their backs, snapping at Moth's feet. Her limbs shook. She was going to fall. Quirk struggled out of his coat without dropping the rope then swung the garment in a looping arc at the top of the fence. It caught near her, and she hauled at it, fabric ripping, stretching enough to let her roll over the sharp coils and drop to the ground.

Quirk dove forward, heedless of the beasts still snapping at the fence as they died, smoking. "Moth?" He tried to pick her up but she batted him away.

"I'm fine."

She really, really stank.

"Get away from the fence," he yelled, pulling Moth by the arm, waving the others back. When he let Moth go, she staggered, but stood. "Handsets," he barked, retrieving devices from Kreski's breast and Dulcie's hip pocket respectively, giving one to Moth.

"Further back!" They were ten metres from the fence now.

"The VRs will take on the MTs, right?" asked Moth.

"That's right," said Eve, grinning like an imbecile as she fired into the mass of slavering, snapping beasts.

Quirk shouted, "Blast the gate!" and they did. All fire turned on the tube steel frame and the lock. Just when they seemed to have failed, the night bloomed with yellow-orange fire and a shockwave pummelled them. Eve fell backwards, but the others leaned into it, fighting for balance. Sparks showered like fireworks in the night, glowing smoke dissipating. Quirk's ears whistled and whined.

"Attaaack!" yelled Moth unnecessarily, and they tapped their screens releasing the velociraptors' pent-up instincts. The dinosaurs surged forward through the twisted gateway and into a deadly dance. They darted and lunged, bit and snapped their way across the killing ground. It was horrific to watch the quick and terrible work the pseudo-dinosaurs made of the mangetouts. None of the remaining beasts got anywhere near hurting the raptors, which ripped out throats, dislocated limbs and severed arteries. It was the very definition of a bloodbath. MT gore slicked raptor muzzles and necks.

"Faster, dinosaur! Kill! Kill!" Moth's glee as she worked at the handset was unbridled, much like the saurian appetite for destruction. The raptors finished any mangetouts still moving then simply stopped and stood, heads tilting, scanning for more prey as gore dripped onto the snow.

"That's twenty less things to worry about," said Moth as the group lurched back together.

Quirk chuckled dazedly. "Fewer," he said. They all looked at him, even Kreski.

"I reckon it's your show now, Quirk," said the sheriff.

"Then we'll take the open door—with the VRs, of course," said Quirk.

"You'll draw fire," said Kreski.

"The FBI and the army don't know what they're dealing with. The only people I trust to free the hostages and deal with Morton—maybe even TOM somehow—is us."

Kreski nodded. "I'll go round front, try and cover you if I can."

The handset in Moth's hand began ringing. For a moment, the girl looked puzzled. She answered the device, listened, then said, "On speaker."

"Quinton, it's Joshua."

The Old Man! *Damn*. But was it really, this time? No reason remained for Nick to impersonate TOM, and the voice possessed the indefinable gravity that—he realised now—Nick's impersonation hadn't quite captured. That, and a breathy quality Quirk had not heard before.

TOM coughed.

"Under the weather? Nothing trivial, I hope."

"New oesophagus: still bedding in. But forget that, you're pushed for time."

"The FBI went in already."

"Not that, Quinton. It's come to my attention that the Government is considering an airstrike—"

Moth, Kreski and Eve all swore at once: it sounded like "bashiftucktard." Moth snorted.

They looked really angry. Quirk began to laugh, regained enough composure to tap the "hang up" symbol on the sheriff's handset. The phone buzzed again: a text message. "He says we've got sixty minutes," said Kreski.

"Remarkably round number," said Quirk. "Such an exact count from his call. It's almost as if he knows more than he's saying."

"Spell it out for me," Kreski grunted, "quickly."

Quirk nodded. "C Corp owns Genextric, The Old Man owns C Corp. The Old Man appears to exert some control over the President, who's dishing out executive orders like pancakes. TOM needs Tania and Meriwa Rowland to disappear, Morton too, probably. He can achieve all that by ensuring Genextric is bombed to dust with them inside. Boom goes the best evidence linking him to engineering the abominable mess that allowed Liano to suspend the election. I hope the only thing stopping him dropping the bombs now is Nick's presence inside. He's invested a lot of time and money in his grandson. There has to be a reason TOM sent him here instead of...disposing of him elsewhere."

"So, he sends in the FBI, rescues your son and eradicates everything else," said Kreski. "Meaning Morton needs to keep Nick safely locked up till he can get out."

"Not quite," said Quirk. "The FBI are just set dressing. No match for Morton. I knew TOM had a plan to get Nick out. It's me: I was that old bastard's plan all along."

"In the bar," said Eve, "Nick told us Morton doesn't know him, that he's hidden."

"But that's shit," said Moth. "Dreck Morlock knows exactly where your boy is."

"Yes," said Quirk. "Nick lied to us, but that does seem to be his MO."

"The Gov won't drop ordnance with hostages inside though, right?" asked Moth.

Quirk frowned. "Not unless there is some kind of tragic comms mix-up, or the non-existent eco-terrorists are reported as having shot the hostages, or some military equipment manufactured by a rival corporation to C Corp malfunctions. Not unless TOM decides the situation is out of his control and he is left with no choice."

"Aw, fuck-puppets," said Moth, with some considerable vehemence.

Quirk looked around the others, disturbed to note they seemed to be awaiting his pronouncement. "We must assume we have an hour before the army bombs Genextric to hell."

"Fifty-eight minutes," said Dulcie.

Moth scowled. "Two butt-munching countdowns in one case? This sucks."

Quirk nodded wearily. "Let's get going."

Moth slapped him on the arm, somehow having generated a resurgence of energy. "Come on, boss, get with the programme." She grinned, tucking her pistol into her pocket. Eve reloaded her empty shotgun. Dulcie discarded his machinegun. Kreski picked it up.

"Told you you'd be turning this in." He took a pistol from inside his coat and handed it to the plumber.

"Unlicensed piece, Sheriff?"

"Police surplus." Kreski smiled. "Anyway, shit happens; all the time round these two." He nodded at Quirk and Moth. "Now, scram."

They started across the open ground toward the glow of the loading dock. Quirk barely felt the cold now. Two velociraptors flanked him, the bedraggled Moth walked at his side, Eve behind them with the other two raptors, and Dulcie on point. The dinosaurs brayed alternately.

With a few seconds to think, Quirk refocused his anger. This was Morton's doing, and if not for Meriwa and Tania and Nick, he would happily have pulled up a deckchair and watched the light show as the Government bombed the bastard to hell. However, that was just the sort of scenario Morton might be counting on to engineer his escape. And what if Derek spirited Nick back to The Old Man? Used him as a get-away-scot-free card? *Not this time.*

They edged up to the mouth of the service bay, Dulcie and Moth with weapons raised. Empty. "Where to?" he asked Eve, as the velociraptors followed them into the bare, harshly lit space. "Tania, Meriwa and Nick are in here somewhere."

"It'd be a guess," she said. "I'd need a minute at a terminal, or your son to help out."

Quirk cocked an eyebrow, trying to ignore the smell from Moth and from his boots then nodded. He spoke into the echoing space. "Nick, are you listening?"

"What kept you?" The familiar, nagging voice emerged from the handset Eve had taken from Dulcie. *"It's 03:19. Fifty-six minutes."*

He knew about the countdown, of course. "You need to help us," Quirk snapped, hating how unbalanced, how anxious and out of control he sounded. "There's an increasing probability we're all going to die in a hail of tax-dollar-funded destruction, so will you *please* guide us to the hostages and you so we can get the hell out of here?"

"Well of course. The stage is set; the world is watching. Let the action begin!"

Something in Nick's tone troubled Quirk deeply. "How much of this did you engineer?" he asked, his stomach dropping towards his now excrement-encrusted boots.

"What's the difference? You're here. Come on! Come get this done before Morton finds you. He can still stop us! I'm where I've always been: Level Five."

"Level Five," Eve nodded.

"What?" said Quirk, too tired, too nervous, too exasperated for subtlety.

"The habitats are the only thing down there. Ten enclosures, where the terra-fauna are habituated when they emerge from the vats on Level Four after being seeded in the Level Three labs. All beneath our feet. Maybe Morton's taken hostages down there."

"Maybe," said Moth. "He belongs in a hole in the ground."

"If we use the public elevators we can split up, look for the women up in the offices and Nick down in the research areas?"

Quirk nodded.

"Incoming," said Dulcie, who watched their backs out of the loading bay door. "Military squad, coming in hot. Move now."

"We need to slow them down. Send two raptors," said Quirk.

"No!" Moth hissed.

"They're not pets!" he snapped, rounding on her. "We need a distraction."

"They're from vats," said Eve, trying to sound kindly. "We'll breed more."

"It's not fair."

"Do it," said Quirk. He hated hurting Moth. Sniping was one thing, but this was something else. He'd found lost pets in the early days, knew how deeply children could be wounded by such loss. They'd lost Eight on the Moon, and Eighty too now, maybe, but fighting over consequences was a luxury for later, if there was a later.

Dulcie worked the app. Reed and Sue trotted into the night then Eve moved away through the office door. Moth followed, cheeks wet, although her mien was stormy. Quirk strode after them with Dulcie at his back. Staccato gunfire started seconds later. Short bursts rending the uncomfortable silence, echoing in the hollow loading bay behind them. Ben and Johnny keened.

They hustled through empty parts of the building. Inactive syRen® stood at every corner, in every corridor.

"If they're still sending troops in, they won't blow the building yet," said Dulcie, scanning ahead and behind as they went.

Quirk nodded. "Maybe they're running late."

Dulcie grunted. "03:21."

Moth had control of Ben and Johnny again. She sent the dinosaurs ahead down a wide, spotless corridor towards the public elevators. The bright, warm antiseptically clean space felt strangely comforting. *They* were the anachronism; dirty, smelling of smoke and shit as they were. Them and the dinosaurs. The velociraptors left bloody prints on the polished plascrete floor. In this man-made environment their wrongness was palpable. Possessed of an elegant brutality, their nature remained abundantly clear. They were killers. Suddenly, he saw an affinity between them and Morton. Perhaps Derek's DNA salted their recipe. Unlikely.

Up ahead, down the wide, stark corridor, plass doors separated them from a short vestibule, beyond which another pair of doors led to the building's foyer. His blood ran cold as the far doors opened and soldiers all in black ran crouched from the shadows of Genextric's reception area; two, four, six. Seeing Quirk's group they straightened, aiming their guns.

"Back away," Dulcie hissed. "Moth, bring the dinosaurs. Eve, it's gonna be the goods lift, if we can still get there."

"We'll be okay," Eve said, shaky but resolute.

The dinosaurs watched with blank eyes as the soldiers advanced on the second pair of doors—the ones separating them—the tilt of saurian heads betraying curiosity.

Quirk prepped for some fast talking. "Come on, Moth."

When she started backing up, he moved slowly backwards too in the face of the ranked weapons. Moth had the raptors turn and walk away. The soldiers approached the inner doors calmly, eyes on the group, expecting the barrier to slide apart.

Nothing happened.

Black helmeted heads tilted around in a queer imitation of the raptors' birdlike movement. One of the soldiers straightened, tapped at a control panel on the wall. Another walked to the middle of the plass doors, tried to pry them open. Cold sweat tracked through the grime on Quirk's face. The soldier waved a hand back and forth in the air above his head. Nothing continued to happen.

"Building's locked down," Eve said. "The inner doors have a failsafe."

"But they're still plass," said Moth.

The soldiers stood back in a line, raised their weapons, and fired.

1C

Machineguns hammered and crackled. Quirk pushed Eve behind the dinosaurs. Dulcie threw himself flat. Moth ducked, tucked and rolled. The plass doors misted with a starfield of impacts but—somehow—did not break. Quirk recalibrated as two soldiers—no, black ops—stepped up and kicked at the plass. Nothing continued to happen.

"Don't explain," he urged as Eve opened her mouth. "Go!"

They rushed back to the logistics office and across the loading bay. Quirk feared they would run straight into the commandos Sue and Reed had stalled, but the bay remained empty, three ropes hung down the building's exterior across the loading bay entrance. The ropes were still. Good. They had a window, but must keep moving forward.

The sound of distant shattering reached them. Dulcie moved to the elevator control box, and amber lights began to spin. Eve stepped back, moving behind Quirk. He recalled her account of this place. "We'll find her, Eve." He touched her arm.

The goods lift doors slid open. Eve flinched. Moth looked ridiculously deadly standing feet apart, all of 1.6 metres, flanked by a pair of near-two-metre dinosaurs. Dulcie held his gun ready, gaze flicking between the office door and the outside world.

The goods lift was empty. Quirk waved them in, the space big enough for four humans and two raptors. As the doors slid closed a blast boomed through the building, rattling the lift, shaking them. Quirk staggered into Eve and Moth lurched into one of the velociraptors, thrusting out her arm, bracing against the creature. The doors clunked shut and they descended. Moth's dark eyes grew big as saucers, her mouth open as she realised she had almost hugged a dinosaur still slimed in mangetout guts. The raptor tilted its head, staring at her, pitiless eyes making it impossible not to fear they might somehow break their programming.

Moth smiled nervously. A big smear of MT blood marked her face, neck and onesie. "Shit," she said, reaching out again to place a hand flat on the VR's side then turned to touch the other one, close in the restricted space of the elevator. "They're warm," she said with quiet wonder.

The elevator jerked to a halt.

"Level Four," said Dulcie unhappily.

"Need authority for Five." Eve stepped to the panel and placed her thumb on the screen. Nothing. "And they've shut me out, of course."

"Of course," growled Quirk. "Nick, can you hear me? A little help here?"

With a slight judder the lift resumed its descent. They moved smoothly downwards. On the display, Four slid over into Five. This was no good. This was what everyone expected of them. He reached past Eve, cancelled Five and pressed Six. The lift shook slightly, but kept moving.

"What...?"

"Take a note, Moth," he announced. "Always avoid the front door if you can."

Five slipped by, transforming smoothly into Six. They stopped and the doors slid open on a sprawling, pastoral scene. It was utterly surreal: An expansive savannah ran off into what looked like the distance until Quirk's eyes adjusted and made out the far LivewaLL which presented a stunningly well-realised continuation of the scene to a wide, dark mesa on the false horizon. Gentle dawn light bathed the cunningly enclosed space. A gentle breeze drifted across the land, stirring tall grass, picking up dust from bare earth around a watering hole in a slight depression twenty metres away.

The elevator doors began to close. Eve reached forward, tapped the screen, holding them open. "Someone's calling it."

"No one good, I expect," said Quirk.

"3:27," said Moth. "Forty-eight minutes."

"I can count," he snapped. "Sorry. Is there another way up to Five?"

Eve frowned. "Only the TF access chute."

"I get it," said Moth. "We need some kind of element of surprise. Otherwise, we're just walking into Morton's lair. Doesn't seem like the forces of democracy have control of this mess yet."

"We're here: Tania, Meriwa, me. Save us!" said Nick from Kreski's handset. *"Soldiers have cleared the offices, but Morton's holed up on Five. He's negotiating his escape!"*

The elevator doors tried to close again.

"We're getting out," said Moth, moving forward. "If that chute is big enough for raptors, we can get up it." She moved the velociraptors out into the grassland. Was that relish in their movements as they felt the breeze on their flanks and the grass on their bellies? Dulcie moved next, seeming to have taken to following Moth's lead. Quirk followed Eve out of the elevator and the doors slid shut.

"Chute's in the far corner," said Eve, waving towards a spot that for all the world looked five miles away. The ground was real, the plants, the waving grass, the rocks, all real. Quirk let his fingers trail through the swaying blades as they jogged forward. For the first time in days, he felt warm.

"Keep your eyes open," Eve said.

"Raptors'll see anything coming," Moth clipped back.

"Not a hi-V sniper round," said Dulcie, unhelpfully. "Keep low."

"We should assume Morton has eyes on us," Quirk puffed. "Also, this was never going to be a firefight: we can't win that. This will be a negotiation."

Seeing he was the slowest, he pressed his pace. *Perils of living in artificial gravity.* Moth matched him easily while keeping the dinosaurs out front. The skin between his shoulders prickled, and not from the horrendous state of his clothing, but that sense of someone watching. The savannah remained empty but for their group and a few sentinel trees. Open grassland did present a perfect opportunity for ambush, by Morton's black ops, mangetouts or something even worse. They sought cover as they moved. Morton could take them out if he really wanted, yet no attack came.

Skirting a clump of thick grass, Moth flinched, juggling the handset, but kept running. They all kept running.

"Quint, it's Derek," said the device. "I'm willing to deal. Come up to Level 5, weapons down. I'll give you the women, just take the boy, to keep The Old Man in line."

Quirk's shock segued smoothly into spite, imagining the building burning with Morton in it. As he ran, he sought some clever detective finesse to resolve the mess neatly: nothing. Strain had marked Morton's words, and he never called himself "Derek."

"That seems fair," Quirk called, unsure if the offer was bluff, ruse or just a good old-fashioned lie. The call ended.

"Never gonna use a fucking handset again after this shit," said Moth.

Rushing up to the corner of the massive, rectangular space provoked a very odd, vertiginous response in Quirk's head. Although the LivewaLL curved to disguise the angle, the image's artificiality became clear as they closed within ten metres. Eve slapped into the wall and scrabbled to open a hidden access panel. A three-metre-square section of screen darkened and slid back, revealing a shadowed opening and the foot of an upward ramp stained with low-level illumination.

"It's a long grade," said Eve. "Designed for TF to go between here and the habitats; backup for the elevator, narrows further up. But I can't be sure of getting us out into the corridor." She sounded increasingly panicked. So was he. "There's a manual override, but Security can shut it down if there's a risk to the facility, to the staff."

"I'm done standing around," said Moth hotly. "3:31. Forty-four minutes. It's all we've got. We're going." She worked the action on her nasty black gun then sent the velociraptors forward, following them in. "Come on, Dulcie."

"Yes, miss." The ex-special forces plumber followed Moth into the dark.

"This is getting serious." Doubt laced Eve's tone, and Quirk thought she was going to say more, but she girded her loins and stepped onto the ramp. Quirk followed, the dark hole cutting off the breeze.

As Eve promised, the way narrowed as they climbed. The ceiling height reduced too, a little. Maybe terra-fauna found the closing walls and dim light reassuring. He did not. In the cramped space he could smell his and Moth's clothing much better than he would have liked and their footsteps bumped and echoed in a way that accentuated the narrowness. All it would take was an attack from the rear and they would be buggered. He took no pleasure from his bon mot.

They turned back on themselves three times, feeling their way around tight corners. The quiet hum of machinery behind the walls at each turn added to the claustrophobic feeling, and the unmistakable rat-a-tat of gunfire reached them, once, twice, three times. Yet sooner than expected the ramp levelled out and the view ahead showed a single light maybe eighty metres away: a flame of hope? No doubt it would be extinguished momentarily. Moth held up her hand, wrist glowing 3:34.

"The ramp leads straight to the service door at the end of the Level 5 corridor," said Eve.

"Go then," said Moth. "*Velocemente!* We have forty-one minutes."

It sounded like a lot, and nothing at all.

"The access hatch is small," said Eve. "The raptors won't fit, which is the point, of course. This is the end of the line for them. They can't go any further." Eve waved a hand just up ahead at a small access panel set in the wall halfway along the thin corridor before them.

"What, so they're just done?" Moth touched Ben's flank, or maybe Johnny's.

"Yes," said Eve. "Shut down the app."

Emotions warred on the girl's face, and he found that he could read them. Anger (of course), an opportunity for discovery lost, regret over leaving friends.

They squeezed past the raptors, and he tried not to flinch. Eve went ahead and Moth—head hung low—flicked Velocir-App-tor HQ from her screen. Eve worked at a small, green-glowing panel in the wall. A minute passed then another until servos whined, and the access hatch slid back. Clean light spilled into the grimy corridor. The velociraptors moved up behind them, but stopped because Moth blocked the way.

"There's a safe space here," said Eve, "then the access to the viewing corridor." She paused. "One of the habitats..." But she didn't finish, looking uncertain.

"I'll lead now," he said, squeezing past Eve then Dulcie without waiting for assent. At the hatch, he put his hands on Moth's shoulders. "My past got us into this, but there's a fair chance Morton won't shoot me if he is standing out there with a gun."

In the panel's green light Moth's eyes narrowed with pain and anger. "So the raptors just die? Get bombed to shit?"

"They're constructs, Moth. They're manufactured."

"It's just like Eight, and Eighty. People keep taking my friends away," she heaved a sigh. "Like Uncle Toni," she gasped, and her shoulders sagged. "Like Mamma...and

Papà..." Moth was crying now. She moved to touch the nearest raptor's flank. The beast just tilted its head at her, its companion too, genetic programming holding good. "I think they're thinking something, feeling something."

Quirk turned, put his back to the wall beside her. Something inside him splintered. A weight descended on his chest, moisture escaped his eye. He put an arm around Moth's shoulders. Even now—with time evaporating—he knew this to be right.

"We have to go, honey," he said gently, finding soft words from somewhere. "I wish I had all the time in the world to make this easier, but we have to move now." His gaze slid to Kreski's set in her hand. 3:37. He had thirty-eight minutes to work his ineffable magic and get out of this building; or to get roundly effed by Derek Morton.

She spoke in a small voice that he had to bend forward to hear.

"The sisters called me Moth. It was all I could say when the police found me. 'Moth...moth...moth... I was trying to say 'mother,' but I was crying so hard I couldn't finish the word, and then I didn't want to say it, because I knew she would never answer me again. But...but I keep it, so I never forget...what I lost."

She looked up at him with big, dark shining eyes and any lingering reservation he held about his guardianship melted away. He crouched in front of her and kissed her forehead, managing to find a cleanish spot. Tania Terjesen must be within touching distance now, yet all he wanted to do was stay with Moth and brush her tears away as the bombs fell, preferably at a *very* safe distance.

"It's going to be alright, Moth, we just need to get through this next half hour." She nodded, her chin stiffening as she banished its slight quiver. "I don't know what you've done to me these past three months, you foul-mouthed little brat"—he smiled—"but I'll die before I let anything happen to you." He was startled to realise it was true.

"No!" She threw her arms around his neck and squeezed till he thought his head would pop off. "Not you too! We've got a contract."

"We do," he nodded, aware of a hard lump lodged in his throat. "We do." He stood up, taking Moth's hand and pulling her up with him. "So, let's wrap this up and vacate the premises. I booked tickets to Germany."

She stood, flipped her mangy black bob out of her eyes and clicked her pistol's safety off. "And I've got a homework assignment: let's finish this shit."

Eve had stepped away to the velociraptor habitat and opened the access panel. The two raptors slipped past her into their habitat without a backward glance. Quirk's heart was pounding, his palms damp. He was ready.

They squeezed into the dimly lit vestibule, cramped like a too-small elevator. "Weapons down," he reminded the others. Eve cracked the final escape door and artificial light streamed into their dim, putrid surroundings. Quirk stepped out first. Doing the right thing and liking it were very different, of course, and he did not like it one bit..

Four figures stood at the end of the long, white viewing corridor. Four syRen® ranked before the elevator doors at the other end. They bore stubby laser carbines held level, staring with android impassivity across the empty space between the habitats, between them. As he stepped out their eyes and their weapons tracked him. If he attacked, they might—after a risk assessment—shoot to wound, removing a threat to other humans and themselves.

Bald fear gnawed his insides. He wished Eighty were here. This wasn't right. Urgently, he waved behind him, signalling the others to stay put, but Dulcie stepped up beside him, gun trained casually on the floor in front of the androids. Quirk took deep breaths. Only now—not having been shot to pieces immediately—he noticed the fifth form, prone on the floor. Morton! Quirk blinked. Morton was dead, clearly. Blood spattered the floor beside his body and his eyes rolled back in his head, staring at Quirk, accusing him of being alive.

"How?" he spoke the question aloud, not expecting an answer. "Who?"

"And what's up with the droids?" asked Dulcie.

"I don't know," said Quirk, but the gnawing at his stomach reminded him of a time just past when androids had done unexpected things, unconscionable things—albeit under human direction. "No time to debate the Laws of Robotics with them. Cover me, since our deal with Morton appears to be null and void."

Quirk stepped into the centre of the corridor between gleaming metal handrails, stood tall in the face of his doubts, and walked forward. Habitats One to Five ran towards him on his righthand side, Six to Ten lined up on his left. "Time check?"

"3:45," Moth called back. "Thirty minutes."

So, who ran the show now, TOM? He walked to the nearest control unit—clear enough—and turned off the opacity on Habitat Six to be faced with jungle planting. His heart thumped. *Be quick, Quinton. Ten habitats.* Tania and Meriwa easily could be in the last one. He pulled up the menu, scanned for life signs. Two! His nerves spiked, but no. It was the velociraptor enclosure. He turned away, moved to scan Habitat Five then Four, back to Seven; empty, and each search brought him closer to the syRen® whose weapons tracked him. And the droids were not unmoving of course, since those cunning Androicon designers included a series of minute shifts and tics to make the machines more acceptable to the populace. *Concentrate, damn it!*

Habitat Three. Would they make it? He hoped Kreski had engaged with the FBI, and was talking them down, explaining the situation. But Morton was dead, so who was running the show? Who had killed him? No time for conjecture. Some agent of The Old Man within Morton's squad maybe, and yet...

He had reached Habitat Eight's control panel, started scanning immediately, trying to hurry things up, turned off the opacity—

He didn't need the output. A blond woman lay on the mossy ground at the front of the habitat. She was wrapped in a blanket, had a med unit closed around her arm. Tania Terjesen looked in bad shape, but remained alive. Beside her crouched the dark-haired Inuit lady in the images Moth had found: Meriwa Rowland. She looked up, and hope bloomed on her face. She blinked at him then smiled carefully. He did not, after all, look anything like someone who worked here.

"Habitat Eight," he called, loud and clear. Dulcie relayed the message into the service corridor. Quirk faced the syRen® trying not to think about dying in a hail of burning laser fire. "Quickly!" They could do this; they could actually do this.

Movement in the verdant enclosure caught his eye and Eve appeared behind the glass, Moth with her. The former head of Gamma Lab hurried to Tania, almost stumbling, knees plunging into the soft ground. He could see how badly she wanted to snatch the fragile-looking Tania up and crush her in a hug, but she settled for leaning in close, taking Terjesen's face in her hands and kissing her deeply. Quirk found it hard to look away. Such adoration. He'd known that.

Eve broke away. He saw her lips move as she surveyed Tania's wounds. She and Meriwa started sitting Terjesen up, gingerly, but stopped as Tania winced and shook her head. Eve kissed her again, waved an arm towards the open door at the back, squeezed Tania's hand and moved away quickly, pulling Moth with her.

Meriwa met Quirk's gaze and mouthed, "Thank you."

He nodded, took a deep breath and started backing away from the habitat and the syRen® towards the access hatch.

"Dad, wait!" Nick's disembodied voice issued from hidden speakers, filling the clean, bright space with sharp words. *"You haven't saved* me *yet."*

Quirk turned and waved Dulcie towards the hatch. "Get out."

The plumber gritted his teeth, but backed away, eyes darting about, planning. It looked very much like Dulcie had something in mind.

The soft whine of lasers powering made Quirk shudder. He snapped around to see the androids take two steps forward, but they aimed away, firing at the plassteel wall of Habitat Ten. A star-bright spot blazed on the smooth surface, too bright to watch. He threw up his arm to shield his eyes. A monstrous crack rent the air, already thick with the acrid smoke of scorching plassteel. The wall split in slow motion, broke and fell apart in a rumble of tumbling debris. The droids continued to fire into the broken habitat, as if trying to destroy the entire cuboid prison. Sounds of destruction, of debris raining down, washed into the corridor.

With dust still roiling in the air, a dark, malformed, humanoid figure stepped from the cloud of smoke and dust, over the rubble of the ruined habitat wall, its full attention focused on Quirk.

"Hello, Father. You took your time."

1D

Oh, no. Oh, dear God. All this time. Nick had been here, kept as an exhibit in The Old Man's freak show. A chill ran through Quirk as everything warped into a vile sort of sense.

"You...did all of this," he accused the creature, because creature it surely was.

"3:49!" Someone called behind him. Twenty-six minutes.

The smoke cleared and he got a good look at Nick now. Its frame was thin. Its legs moved with a strange, creeping gait, covered in what looked like dark blue scales. At its waist, the scales gave way to slick, dark hair covering the lower part of a hard-ribbed torso. The hair too was incomplete, thinning to leave the creature's breast bare. Here it had some semblance of human skin but tinged sickly yellow. Muscle corded the arms that hung at its side, lank dark hair slicked the forearms above hands that seemed horribly human among all the wrongness, but with dark fingers stretched overlong. Powerful shoulders and neck strangely pink like Quirk's own. Hard neck muscles flowed into a face, human in contour, but formed of dark, coarse hide. Those features moved into a sneer. Tears of cloudy white fluid ran down the creature's cheeks, staining its dark visage.

No. He's not a bloody mangetout, not the Jurassic construct of some mad scientist. He's my son. Quirk's head swam at the flaming otherworldliness of the notion, but he believed it. He had not seen Nick in five years, probably had not spoken a hundred words to the child that Jennifer had presented him with. But he believed it.

"I made things happen to bring you here, father, but I didn't *do* any of it. I didn't *cause* any of it. *You* did that. You and that evil, *EVIL* old man. The devil himself, and YOU left me with him!" The creature gasped, throat rattling with something like despair. "*You* did it, Daddy. YOU! You did it all." Nick's ferocious gaze accused him. "The fault is yours."

Quirk stood rooted and breathed as if anything more was beyond him. He had to think. Think. "The airstrike—"

"Pah." A sinuous, darkly hirsute arm extended, a blue-black hand opened into a careless wave. "The airstrike awaits my pleasure."

"What? How?" Quirk felt like a fool, a gormless idiot. *But how could I have foreseen...this?* "When I left, your mother..." His stomach twisted.

"Are you afraid to say her name?"

The creature stepped forward and Quirk quailed a little, stepped back, bumping into Eve. "What are you doing?" he hissed at her.

"I'm not leaving you. You brought us to Tania."

"Eve, go, get the others out."

"Say her name, *Daddy!* Or are you too ashamed? You should be. Think what you did to her, my mother, your wife."

"Jennifer," he said to the beast, his son. He tried to push Eve away. Whatever the creature wanted, it seemed unlikely to be good. "She duped me." His old bitterness rose up. "As you have; maybe others too." He glanced at Eve.

"Oh, that's very convenient." Nick gesticulated. "So handily absolves you of what came next." The creature took another step. Quirk struggled to hold its gaze. "I was a real boy, once," Nick rasped. "A normal, healthy child, and she cared for me, until Morton took me, until The Old Man experimented on me. She gave me a name," the creature growled. "But granddaddy planned it from the start, you see?" The face, twisted in pain. "What better source of test subject? Safer than stealing one. Easier, more efficacious than breeding one naturally—which you were dead against anyway, I gather. And afterwards, when you get whatever result you want, you can brush the evidence aside. You can tuck the mother away in a home where she can be watched and medicated." White ichor flowed from its...from Nick's eyes. "And you can scare the father away," he snarled. "He's spineless, he's self-absorbed, he won't fight for his family. He'll roll over obligingly and disappear." He gave an animal grunt, almost a bark. "A father should be there for his son, should protect his family, but where were you, Daddy? Where. Were. You?"

Quirk bowed his head, nodding, bitterness coating his tongue. This was exactly twisted enough to be part of his life. "So, son," he said matter-of-factly, as pain and loss continued to eat at his insides. "What next?" He looked Nick in the eye, convinced beyond doubt that this was his son. "Did you bring me here to gloat, maybe exposit a little, reveal your masterplan before you kill me with an industrial laser?" Quirk swallowed bile, glancing at the ranked androids. Everything was upside-down and inside-out. Were they going to die, from bombing or laser fire? He could not be further from making his peace with the world. Jennifer's face drifted in his mind, flashes of good times. How did he process this?

He held out his hands to placate Nick's anger. He noticed now that its—*his*—fingernails were hard like pointed claws. "How did you do it? The calls, controlling androids, handsets, satellites?"

The monster stepped closer. Close enough now that Quirk could smell him, stale sweat and animal musk. "Oh, that's the good part, father. Grandpa's experiment was a great success. He got what he wanted. Doesn't he always? Along with my vile good looks came the ability to hear systems, to feel electricity, to touch the digital world around me. Isn't that wonderful?" Nick barked a laugh.

"Wouldn't you pay this price?" He smacked a hand hard into his chest. "To *hear* what those syRen® hatch in their android heads? To push them and pull them this way and that?"

"But, if you can control a syRen®..." said Eve.

"Yes, dear," said Nick in a rasping growl. "I can influence terra-fauna too."

Eve's voice wavered. "But Morton deactivated their security system."

Quirk's son rolled bloodshot eyes. "And I hijacked them. You've heard of synaptic mapping, right? Well, let's just say I stitched together a little variant of my own thanks to my unfettered access to Ol' Grandpappy's trillion-dollar systems, and the widely distributed micro-deposits of carborundum around these here parts, no little amount of which is—in—side—me! It's way above your level, Eve, so I'm not going to attempt to explain the science. Suffice to say it works, and I'm calling my rabid roomies now, bringing all TOM's creatures back home two by two." He spread his arms to encompass Genextric. "Things are about to get bloody for all those Government employees out there."

Quirk shivered. His head buzzed as if his brains would start leaking from his ears any moment. "Can he do that?" he hissed to Eve from the corner of his mouth. She shrugged, her stance taut, intent on the creature.

"Yes," said Nick. "I can. The FBI think they're closing in on the kill switch for all this uncanny nature, but they might wish they'd looked over their shoulders sometime about..."—the Nick/monster made an exaggerated performance of looking at the matted black hair and dark, scaly flesh of his wrist—"now."

Quirk realised he'd been tensed ready to dive for cover. He straightened, turned on Eve. "What was your role in this?" He indicated Nick.

"I..." She seemed about to fold in upon herself then straightened. "They brought...someone here, shut him away, gave us a protocol. I never saw him, not once, I swear. Monster rumours travel, but there were strict corporate warnings about prying."

"What about Tania?"

"Tania was...a consultant. She wasn't pulling the strings."

"God damn it, Eve."

"I didn't know! How could I know I was knee-deep in your fucked-up family history! His own grandson—"

She was facing him now, arms akimbo. Anger reenergised her, and her countenance was boiling mad. Quirk seethed. This was *hardly* the time for a dustup. "Focus on the disaster at hand, Eve," he waved at the Nick/monster. "We're going to be knee-deep in *your* terra-fauna. Think about Kreski, and everyone else out there."

"You focus on it, you superior son-of-a-bitch," she yelled.

Something moved at the edge of his vision. He let his gaze slide slightly. Dulcie crouched at Habitat Ten's broken façade between Nick and his android guard, pistol in hand, aimed at the back of Nick's head.

No! The Nick/monster seemed to be enjoying the shouting match, but his head cocked, and a puzzled look came over his face. Then he smiled.

Quirk reached out an impotent hand towards the monster as blue lasers lit the walls and ceiling. Dulcie jerked and twisted. He didn't cry out. His gun clattered to the floor, and he fell among the strips of broken plass. Quirk jerked his hand down, lunging in time to catch Eve around the waist before she raised her shotgun.

"You piece-of-shit bastard!" she screamed, wildly shrill in the quiet, drifting laser haze and stink of grilled flesh.

"Bastard?" Nick growled, body tensing. "But, no, Miss Meyer. I have a father, and a *grand*father: both my creators, in one way or another. I have a mother too, and I have a doctor who lovingly oversaw my transformation. I think maybe you've guessed that the lovely Tania has not been entirely honest with you, lov-er girl." The Nick/monster took a step, only three metres between them, its animal smell overpowering even the odour of poor, burnt Dulcie, who twitched slightly, and moaned.

"You think I'm a beast. I've certainly got the looks, but they made me so much more, Eve. I am atoms. I am ions. I am electricity." The Nick/monster's sweeping gesture encompassed not just Genextric, not just Yellowknife, but the world. "I am data. I am digital smoke. I swim in an ocean of ones and zeros like a shark. I never sleep. I am the impulse of the machine, the heartbeat of the system." Nick paced closer to her, close enough to touch, bent forward to look into Eve's eyes. "And frankly, honey, I've seen things you skin-sacks wouldn't *believe*." He laughed. "I've ridden probes beyond the limits of human space. I've fallen into suns. I've surfed around this world so fast I was going back in time. I am my own son now, I'm my father too, and I will be the holiest of ghosts. I've remade myself in so many images I can't even remember them. I am my own code, the key to the future, the new paradigm, and I'm going to ram it all down TOM's *throat!*"

Nick half-turned indicating his syRen® escort and their speakers barked into life, human voices swelling in the enclosed space. The silence was choked with horrific sounds, terror and agony, shouted orders to attack, fall back, defend and run away. The Nick/monster turned back to them, held out his palms flat and raised them towards the ceiling. The volume of the hellacious sounds redoubled, increasing beyond the threshold of pain. Nick grinned, dirty, pointed yellowed teeth gleaming. "'Look on my works, ye mighty, and despair!'"

Quirk went from gaping to clamping his hands over his ears, screwing his eyes shut. He saw it, all laid out in front of him. The mechanisms that had driven the events of the last—dear deity-of-choice—only three days since Rowland's entreaty to come north, and in that time his world had been ripped apart. His legs shook, almost buckled. He fixed on his heartbeat, trying to block out the screams and animal noises.

Maybe Nick facilitated Morton's attack on Tania, but also her escape, somehow influencing the mangetouts to drag her to the riverside rather than killing her. He winced. Rowland's presence was no accident. False readings on Hygen's boundary monitors, manoeuvring Barry into position to find Tania. No doubt Nick had designed the initial contact, directing Rowland to Quirk.

"Oh, father, I can see the gears turning in that pretty little head of yours. Yes, I engineered more than you can ever imagine, but it's just a drop in the ocean compared to what I can do when I reach my destination."

Quirk groaned. He had been dancing to the Nick/monster's tune for days. He scowled. A web of manipulation on a staggering scale all designed to bring him here, to bring Morton here, together with Tania and Eve. But the prime mover, the instigator, the spider at the centre of the web, he was not present. Time to shovel the dirt in the right direction.

"What about The Old Man, Nick?" said Quirk. His voice rumbled in his own head, but he would not remove his hands from his ears. Still, the boy (*Boy?*) heard him. The Nick/monster lowered his outstretched hands and the sounds of slaughter dropped into the background. Quirk lowered his hands too, as did Eve.

"I'm saving him for another day," said Nick matter-of-factly, "but your day has come, Daddy, Aunty Eve." Nick's venomous look speared first Quirk then Eve with pure hatred. "We'll need to say our goodbyes, because I'm leaving soon."

"Not right now, shit-breath," said Moth, clearly having found a back way around, stepping lightly over the ruin of Habitat Ten's window, hands in the pockets of her terminally stained coveralls, the two velociraptors with her shielding her from the laser rifles.

"Moth, no," Quirk pleaded. How could she be so dense? She was not this crazy! He stepped forward. "Take me, Nick. Not her."

"Oh, charming." The creature put clawed hands on bony hips. "You'd sacrifice yourself for that sewer rat, but wouldn't endure a little social awkwardness for me?"

"Convent rat, dickhead," Moth snapped.

Quirk nodded. "Nick, it's a horrible cliché, but I'm not the person I was, I've changed. I made a terrible mess of things, I admit it, but don't punish others. Especially not Moth. She's only here by accident. She's an orphan."

"Oh, spare me," said Nick.

He turned and raised a dark-scaled hand just as Moth took her hands from her pockets and held one fist in the air. She held a shiny NEMP, and she hit the trigger, sending Nick's four androids into ugly, jerking spasms.

"Nooo!" Nick shook with anger, or did the NEMP affect him too? Just maybe.

The dinosaurs flinched uncharacteristically.

The elevator doors slid open, and Sheriff Wayne Kreski stepped out, big handgun braced in front of him and pointed at the Nick/monster's head. Then the lights went out.

"The FBI is downstairs, Nick," Kreski grumbled in the dark, almost stumbling on the words even though he could only have glimpsed Nick's monstrous form before the space was plunged into darkness. "Give it up...boy."

Quirk stumbled in the sudden pitch black, disoriented. Eve—he hoped—grabbed his arm and pulled him away from where Nick had been.

"Quirk?" Moth called, her tone uncertain.

"Everybody stay calm," Kreski's rumble filled the space. "Help's coming."

Nick laughed. "Oh, but Genextric's agency of beasts is already here, Wayne. As monster-in-chief, I'm surprised you escaped them. Must have got lucky, but your luck just ran out. There are two fine upstanding examples right here. I sent them to you of course, but now it's take-back time."

Quirk turned, searching for a reference point. Kreski's glowing handset bobbed frantically in Moth's hands as she dabbed at the raptor app. There was a deep, slow growl in the darkness then another. The handset went dark. Something large took a step then another.

"I hope you're not relying on their coding," said Nick. "I've turned that off. Set them free, if you like, to play with you as they see fit. And they'll find you; they have an excellent sense of smell."

And we smell like shit, literally, TF shit too. An idea presented itself.

"Moth?" he called. "Honey, go back into the habitat, wait there where it's safe. We don't want a repeat of what happened just before we abandoned the Five-Star outside Golden."

"Uh, okay, sir," said Moth, clearly intending the honorific as code, since her usual mode of address was unprintable.

Please let her remember our quick-change act. He set to stripping off rancid clothing, down to his Calvin Kline paisley boxers, throwing shit-and-gore-spattered garments away from him, banking on that raptor olfactory capacity, and Moth's NEMP having slowed them down. He found Eve's arm and pulled her in close. Lips locating her ear, he pressed the Derringer into her palm. "Get to the accessway. Start shooting at the ceiling when I say."

"Okay," she whispered, then, "Are you...naked?"

"I'm working on it," he murmured. Then he called, "Don't use the elevator, Wayne," as he moved away from Eve. "It could be full of teeth." He found the smooth railing and slipped under it, moving sideways until his skin touched the cool plass of a habitat window.

Keep him talking. Play for time. The army must be able to cope with those beasts, they have to.

"Nick, you're shut in. It's over. Look, I can't guarantee anything, but let me help you now. I accept I failed you before. I can't change that, but let me try now. People can change. Let me show you that."

"You've changed, have you?" said the Nick/monster, startlingly close, enough to make Quirk shiver. "Tell me then, what was your intention coming here? Were you actually planning to save me, end my suffering? How dare you presume to know *my* suffering?!

"How could you know what it's like to always be switched on, to live a day in every second, all that data descending on you, washing over you constantly, to never be switched off, never be silent. *That's* all I really want, Daddy. The silence, the darkness. But how far do we need to go now, to find true darkness, when even the lightless places of this world are illuminated by man's greed, the devices of his avarice. Perhaps in space, but even there man reaches, grasps for that thing he can never find— enough. When is it *enough?*"

"That's just not the way we're made, Nick." Quirk sighed, hung his head. *So tired.*

"Made, you say? But you were not made, sir, you were created by love or lust, some tender emotion at least. I was forged by greed. I was assembled from offcuts and by-products in a search for power." Nick's voice conveyed his pain with such conviction. There must be a chance to win him over. There had to be.

"You're wrong, Nick. You *were* made by love. There was love between your mother and me, and she never stopped loving you. I was the one who...faltered."

"You did, and that was the source of my nightmares, at first."

The velociraptors paced, throats rattling low. They must have been disoriented by the NEMP right enough. He pictured them nosing into the stinking clothes that he, and hopefully Moth, had strewn along the hall.

Quirk began to edge along the wall. *If I can reach the broken enclosure, stay away from the raptors, the others have a chance,* he thought, *but can I talk him down? That's all I've got at this point, and it's on me.*

"Nightmares are easy, Nick. We all have nightmares. We all end up cowering in the dark sometimes. Lifting up your head to find the light is the challenge. That's where courage is needed, having faith that there's more good than bad in the world, in people, that's the challenge, Nick."

"Well," the Nick/monster drawled. *Too close!* "Hark at you, Father Kirby. I can hear the angels singing, but I don't like their tone. You see, I had faith until my parents tore themselves apart," Nick gasped—a horrible, guttural half-bark of anguish. "And when you and Mom abandoned me to wallow in your own psychoses, I turned to my grandpa with an open heart, and HE DID THIS TO ME!"

Quirk could only hang his head. His throat tightened and bitter tears welled in his eyes. Hope leached out of him, and he sagged forward, his big old chest pump pounding as if losing its emotional lunch. *I should have stayed, but I made it all about me. And Jennifer, poor, darling, broken Jenny. Oh, God.* But he had to get out of his head. Focus. What time was it? Maybe that was irrelevant now. If Nick truly could control syRen®, and drones, and TF, why not bombs? His power was unbelievable, almost.

"Nick, we came to find Tania, to deal with Morton. I had no idea, but I should have." He swallowed. Exhaustion, finally, was overhauling him. "I was selfish. I admit it. I can't change what happened. I would say come with us now, but...so many people are dead. If you had contacted me earlier, been open, all this—"

"Could have been avoided?" Nick barked bitterly, further away. Was he searching for them? The raptors paced now, fetid air rattling in their throats. "Don't you understand yet, Dad? I didn't bring you here to release me. I brought you here to put an end to me before you die, to put me out of my misery, because dear Grandpapa never will. It's the only way for me to get at him, I've discovered. After all I've suffered in my short and painful life: my birth in a vat, the hospitals, the machines, the now-constant immersion in that bright tidal wave of data. I want you to set me free, Daddy. I want you to give me the gift of peace, the release of spirit into energy, the freedom to roam in the digital darkness, unafraid."

The lights came on.

Stark brightness stabbed at him. Quirk snapped his eyes shut then forced them wide again. Kreski remained by the elevator. His aim switched from Nick to the raptor looming near Moth, who stood tensed near Habitat Ten in Hello Kitty vest and pants—Lovecraft shirt gripped in her fist; to the raptor now behind Quirk, menacing Eve, who stood rooted by the access chute; back to Nick, imperious in the middle of the wide corridor, grinning at Quirk.

"Death of the body, Dad, is the only certainty, and I want you to give me that much. Because it's only fitting that you're the one to do it, don't you think? Apposite, you might say, tragically poetic."

Quirk shivered. His limbs ached and he wanted just to stop.

"I'm not going to kill you, Nick. Let them go. I'll stay, but let them go."

"Quirk," said Moth warily, "don't you dare be a dumbass. We're all walking out of here. You wouldn't eat me, would ya, boy?" She lifted a grimy hand in front of the velociraptor looking down on her. The beast tilted its head in that birdlike way, watching her limb then took a step towards her.

"Damnation, Moth," said Quirk. It was all he had. Nick controlled the raptors and was brim-full of spite. Would he think twice before having the beasts snap Moth or Eve or Kreski's neck? But he hadn't, and he was talking about his *own* death.

"Nick," said Kreski firmly. "Whatever you're doing with those creatures, please cease and desist. Drop control of the raptors to the handset then lie on the floor, hands behind your back. I will subdue you if I have to, and support is coming. It's over."

"Kreski, no," said Eve, hands out in front of her, aiming the Derringer at the raptor facing her as if the thing would notice her shooting it before it tore her apart.

"Subdue me, huh?" Nick turned his back on Quirk to face the sheriff, flexing dark muscle and sinew. "Let's see, shall we?"

"Wait, Nick, wait," Quirk barked. "I'll do it." The words almost stuck in his throat. "I'll do what you want."

The Nick/monster hung his shaggy head and let out a rattling sigh.

"Of course you will, Dad." He spoke quietly, but the whole corridor heard him. Quirk shuddered, realising his mistake too late. "Of course you would put others before me, just like always. You failed the test, Father, just like you've always failed me."

"Don't do it, son," said Quirk. He heard lack of conviction in his voice. He'd had Nick's attention before, he'd had a chance, and he'd lost it. They were going to die. "And you tricked me into that, by the way."

Nick drew up his mutated form and pointed at Kreski. "Sick him, boy!"

Moth's raptor wheeled away from her and attacked Kreski. The big gun boomed. Blood spurted from the beast's neck. Boom. Boom. The big sheriff got two more shots off before the bigger grey-brown-blue mottled hunter snapped its jaws closed on his shoulder, tossed him into the wall then moved in again.

"No!" Moth jumped back into the habitat.

Eve's Derringer went off.

Quirk didn't know where to look, ducking by instinct. Moth's black Glock swung from the end of her skinny arm now. He laughed wildly at the sight of her—full of rage—pacing forward in her undies, raising the gun. She shot the raptor once, twice, three times in the head as its jaws closed on Kreski's shoulder. The beast fell.

Quirk spun to see the second raptor snapping at Eve who had backed into the accessway where it could not follow. How did he end this? Who did he help? The Derringer lay on the ground where Eve had dropped it, empty. Nick lost interest in Kreski's struggle, turning slowly on Quirk. Forget the raptors, his son's mutated form looked strong enough to rip off his head.

"Kreski did nothing to you," said Quirk.

"Maybe I'm not as particular as you, Dad," Nick sneered, advancing on him.

Quirk lurched out of reach, lunging sideways towards Habitat Ten. With Nick's amazing, terrifying ability to interact with machines, might he not be affected by the same devices that jammed the androids' systems? And Moth always carried two.

The Nick/monster wheeled after him, grasping. Sharp nails raked Quirk's flesh, but his grimy, sweat-slicked skin slipped Nick's pointy-fingered grip. He saw Moth's abandoned clothes, a dirty heap on the habitat floor and leapt over the jagged edge of the broken plass wall. This was going to hurt.

Quirk hit the debris-strewn floor, tumbling in shards which stabbed and tore as he skidded to a halt. He clutched Moth's sewage-clotted garments to his chest, feeling the hard lump at the bundle's heart. He came up to his knees in a bedroom that could inhabit any stylish city pad. Sharp pain wracked his limbs as he clawed at the clothes. A dark shape loomed at the edge of his vision. Nick's musclebound shoulder drove into him, bowling him over and into the bed. But the boy had made a mistake.

Steel band fingers clamped Quirk's throat and closed, crushing his windpipe. The beast bore him to the ground, straddled his stomach and proceeded with throttling him, but his hands were free. Quirk fought to separate his consciousness from the sea of pain. Darkness poured into his mind like used engine oil, seeping into the spaces he used to think. He fumbled among the clothes, but couldn't remember why. Pins-and-needles stung his fingers and toes, but he kept tearing at the folds of cloth, questing after something important. Nick snarled and bent close, fetid breath washing over Quirk. His son was doing an excellent job of murdering him.

Then Quirk's numb fingertips found a salve: hard plastec. The reassuring weight of Moth's second NEMP rolled into his palm and his near-senseless fingers curled around a formed grip. With the last of his strength, he raised the NEMP to Nick's temple and pressed the button.

The weight disappeared, his vision white. Was this death?

Quirk rolled onto his side, tried to fill his lungs but only produced a violent coughing, great spasms raking his chest, fighting for air, he slumped back.

An hour or two later, or maybe seconds, he raised his head, came to his knees and opened his eyes.

The hairy, scaly, thick-muscled, hard-skinned Nick/monster lay on his back on the habitat floor, limbs twitching, back spasming, his whole body jerking in a hideous, spastic dance. Quirk managed to stand and stumble towards the viewing corridor. Shards of plass fell from his skin, skittered on the floor, those not still imbedded in his flesh and shooting pain through his body. Clutching his head, he stepped out.

Kreski lay unmoving, as did the two velociraptors, one near the access chute, from which Eve emerged and walked towards him, shotgun ready. The second dinosaur lay beside the prone sheriff. Moth bent over it, touching its skin. She saw him looking at the sheriff, clothes stained with his own blood, and hung her head.

"He's alive. I called it in." She stood slowly, unsteady. In one hand she held Kreski's handset, in the other the Glock that Dulcie had given her. Her skin and underwear were dirty and bloody, her face smeared crimson and brown. She looked like the avenging angel of all guttersnipes.

"Damn and blast." He shook his head as his tears fell.

"What a mess."

Quirk whipped around to see the beast that was Nick Kirby standing in the broken habitat threshold. The creature shrugged. "Nothing a tactical airstrike won't tidy up."

There was the briefest pause when Nick's gaze seemed to look through Quirk, into some other realm, and then he was back. "I'd say we've got ten minutes. I'm glad I get to spend them with you, Dad."

Eve gaped at Nick. Moth planted her feet apart and raised her weapon again, pulling herself up to her full 157 centimetres. "Call it off, motherfucker."

The Nick/monster smiled, dark blue-indigo skin stretching away from yellowed incisors. "Well, if you're not going to do it, Dad, she's the next best thing."

"Moth, don't shoot!" Quirk swung his hands up. "It's what he wants."

Without lowering the gun, Moth spat on the floor. "Well, he's gonna get it," she growled.

The Nick/monster stepped down from the habitat, bisecting the fifteen metres between Quirk and Moth. Quirk cursed his sluggish thoughts. If Nick was calling in the bombs, he was ready to die. He'd said his death would get at The Old Man. Quirk had thought this meant because the old bastard felt something for his grandson even after all he'd done, but what if that wasn't it? Nick said something about roaming the dark, and—

"Death of the body," he whispered. He recalled his own out-of-body experience on the Moon, his consciousness decanted into an android through synaptic mapping, his body stuck in a collapsing building. Here though, TOM, the FBI, the National Guard, someone must retain control of the bombs, surely.

"He's bluffing." Quirk stepped sideways to ensure Moth could see him. Her features were rigid with determination. "Nick knows the bombs won't come, but he has a plan. He wants us to kill him because The Old Man won't allow it."

Moth took a step toward the monster, her aim never wavering. The look on her face would have loosened his bowels if directed at him. Quirk's chest swelled with pride at her courage. Or was it panic? It very much did look like she might shoot Nick.

"He's killed Dulcie," she said. "Maybe Kreski, and he tried to kill you." Her eyes flicked sideways meeting his. Her arms wavered slightly.

"Moth, it won't kill him. It'll set him free." His hands made calming motions. "The police are coming, the FBI. They'll lock him down."

"He did all of this. He could have stopped TOM, and Morton. Think of the people who died, Quirk. All to get to you." She shook her head, mouth pinching in fury and redoubled her grip on the Glock. "This fucker wants us all dead, but that's not. Going. To happen."

"Well, it's time for me to move on now." Nick turned slowly, deliberately to face him.

The empty elevator's doors slid shut and its motors began to hum.

That's unlikely to be good.

"Moth, don't." He flicked her a glance and saw that she was crying, tears rolling down her mucky cheeks, but her grip on the gun remained firm. "There are three of us, Moth. We can hold him off. This'll be the FBI arriving now."

"Or the mangetouts," said Nick. "The tinhats, death sparkles, stomach bombs." Nick stepped towards him, raised his clawed hands, took another step then another.

Moth's arms tightened.

"Moth, no!"

The Nick/monster lunged at Quirk.

BANG. BANG, BANG.

Nick's features exploded and thick, warm flesh spattered Quirk's face.

1E

Quirk found himself sitting on the floor. His son's body lay face down in the debris of the habitat screen, his head destroyed by three shots from Moth's pistol.

She knelt beside Quirk now, eyes streaming with tears, blinking at him.

"I had to. He was going to kill you." She looked desperate, doubting her words. She hung her head. "Don't hate me."

All he felt was numb. He stared at her for long moments as her shoulders jerked then he patted her back before changing his mind and pulling her into a hug.

"It's alright, Moth." *Was it, really?* "He would have found another way to die, and I think was intent on killing me in the process." He had no idea what he felt, but it wasn't numbness now. The emotions he did recognise were a fatherly love towards Moth that he'd been unable—*No, be honest, unwilling*—to show Nick; and an understanding he'd failed to show Jennifer.

A hard lump formed in his throat, and he grimaced.

Moth sniffed and her arms tightened around him, sending little lances of pain through him from the points where shards still protruded. He didn't mind at all. He stroked her hair. "It's okay, honey."

"Don't call me 'honey,'" she grumbled, her words muffled. "Starting tomorrow."

Activity in the corridor beyond now entered the wrecked habitat that had been Nick's home in the formed of soldiers and FBI agents, breaching his bubble of unfamiliar emotion. He broke the hug he'd shared with Moth, allowing medics in bio-suits to examine him then help him up. They were lifting Kreski onto a stretcher aided by two syRen®, also clad in white coveralls. A stretcher was so much better than a body bag.

Eve stood near the elevator talking to Agent Prescott, who was pointing at him. When she turned back to Eve, he saw the big, yellow letters "FBI" on the back of her dark blue crime scene garb. The elevator doors opened, and more techs and FBI emerged. One of the medics began tending to Moth who permitted the attention absently, still staring around the ruined viewing corridor.

"What a massive shit-show. I'm going to have to insist on approving all potential cases from now on."

"Ha," he chuckled as another medic started working on him. "I can agree to that."

The medics decided—even though they both smelled really bad—neither he nor Moth merited on-the-spot treatment beyond spraying Quirk with a turbocharged dermal painkiller. They were wrapped in reflective sheets—possibly to prevent Gamma Lab getting any dirtier—and escorted to the elevator. Eve rode up with them.

"Thank you." She went to squeeze his arm and thought better of it, wincing on his behalf. He was rather bloodier than his usual dapper best. "Tania wouldn't have survived this if not for you two. I doubt I'd even have found her." She looked uncertain then shrugged. "I might withdraw my job application though; you people are disaster magnets." She brushed Moth's tangled hair, pushing strands away from her face. Moth didn't object, a miracle in itself. "Who do you even bill in this situation?"

Quirk shrugged, which hurt. "I think this one's a tax write-off."

The building's main corridor was deserted now. Two of four National Guard at the elevator escorted them to the security doors where different guards took them outside.

"What's the hurry, soldier?" asked Quirk.

The soldier kept their eyes front. "Not your concern, sir. Our job is get you out of harm's way."

"Terra-fauna still being put down out there," the other uniform said, sagely.

Quirk blew out a breath as his adrenaline rush began to admit all-pervading lethargy.

They were held outside for a few moments, standing in darkness and bitter cold while soldiers quick-marched across the lot or listened to orders from a squad leader. Quirk considered wording a terse email to Calvin Klein about the lamentable thermal properties of their boxers..

Moth's teeth began chattering, and he drew her to him. "Hurry it up, will you?" he called to no one in particular. "I'm freezing my progeny off here." An unhappy jape, but he'd never known Nick, other than as a monster manipulating him from some twisted sense of vengeance. But was it twisted? Was he not still due some form of comeuppance? Was Nick now loose, free to roam the system as he'd wanted, Alpha Thing in a galactic internet, the black spider at the centre of the Worlds Wide Web? He grimaced and hugged Moth tighter.

Eve moved up on the other side, shivering. She looked exhausted, also hesitant. Quirk nodded and she wrapped her arms around him, sandwiching Moth between them. His only thoughts were of friendship and infinite strangeness.

"Truck's coming up," a soldier called as a pair of medics decanted from the building. A procession of syRen® came behind them bearing stretchers. Kreski was sedated by the look of it, the blankets around him dishevelled. Dulcie lay motionless, but his chest rose and fell. Meriwa looked shellshocked. Tania blinked at the dark sky. Then a dark body bag—Derek Morton. Moth looked overwhelmed, crushed tears away and looked up at the sky.

"Cassiopeia's my favourite constellation," she said, snuggling between them. "It's the first one my *papà* taught me. I love that it looks like an upside-down M."

"So, like a W," Quirk observed.

"No," she said firmly. "An M, but upside-down."

"That's a W," he said.

"Nuh-uh. It moves around. Sometimes it's an M on its side, sometimes an M turned over, but that's because your perspective's upside-down."

"*Your* perspective's upside-down," he insisted, smiling.

"Cack-head," she sniped amiably.

"Dilettante," he said.

"Elitist," she countered, smiling up at him.

He sniffed. "Well, you've got me there."

An All-Terrain Truck whined out of the pre-dawn darkness, ALEDs bathing the group in bright light. The hulking olive drab brute whispered to a stop, the tailgate banged down and soldiers began helping them onboard. Prescott stepped up beside the driver. The passengers sat around the bench seats then the stretchers were loaded at their feet, the body-bag slid under the legs of the stretchers. No bag for Nick. That did not bode well, and Quirk tried not to consider the consequences. Some merciful soul up front turned the blowers on and warmth permeated the flatbed. His extremities began to report back. He smiled across at Eve, trying to calculate as the truck eased into motion if this was in any way a happy ending.

Tania was alive, but how long would it take the FBI to pin something on her? Meriwa Rowland's husband had been murdered: What chance of justice for her? Barry's killer was dead, but Derek Morton was not the instigator, that was TOM, regardless of Nick's machinations. And then there was Eve: What future did she face? What for that matter he and Moth, who had a lengthy list of charges to face, many of them—regrettably—legitimate? A sinking feeling assailed him when he realised—with Kreski laid up—it might be Deputy Joan Parks who held the key to their fate. Oh well, he loved a challenge, and the Feds would want a piece of him too, he was sure. He'd call Mary

Kwon, stall till Kreski was fit enough to vouch for them, at least on some of the charges, hopefully. It would be good to see Mary again apart from anything else.

The truck slowed to a stop. Quirk pushed himself up, defying aching muscles, and slid awkwardly to the back of the vehicle. The soldiers stationed at the tailgate did nothing to stop him, in fact one pulled the canvas back, admitting chilling air. Moth pushed in, budging him up to squeeze between him and the tailgate. The truck's lights lit the first ten metres of techmac, beyond which was nothing but utterly black night, no creamy stain of dawn in the sky.

"What we stopping for?" Moth demanded. The soldier shrugged. A big drone purred overhead, then another.

Seconds later the sky lit up. One, two, three, four bright flashes in the near distance splashed the jagged, black tree line on his retinas. Quirk had no doubt that Genextric Gamma Lab and any vestige of evidence residing there now were gone.

"Shit!" said Eve and he felt the pressure of others pressing in behind him. The orange glow of fire tainted the sky as more missiles hit home. Where the first round of ordnance had been silent, the latest munitions brought a round of huge booms, and a cinematic burst of orange cloud to rival an aurora. Glowing, billowing destruction drifted on the wind.

"I guess Nick should have paid attention to the context of his quote from Percy Shelley," said Moth, clutching the rattling backboard as the truck started moving again.

He looked at her askance. A brisk morning wind and the motion of the truck tousled her short, dark hair. "Go on then," he prompted with a rueful smile.

Moth sat down against the backboard as the others returned to their seats. She brushed her unruly hair back and crossed her legs, looking from face to face around the dimly lit truck with the most unchildlike assurance, clearly relishing everyone's attention. She cleared her throat then spoke.

"I met a traveller from an antique land,
Who said—'Two vast and trunkless legs of stone
Stand in the desert... Near them, on the sand,
Half sunk a shattered visage lies, whose frown,
And wrinkled lip, and sneer of cold command,
Tell that its sculptor well those passions read
Which yet survive, stamped on these lifeless things,
The hand that mocked them, and the heart that fed;
And on the pedestal, these words appear:
My name is Ozymandias, King of Kings;
Look on my Works, ye Mighty, and despair!
Nothing beside remains. Round the decay
Of that colossal Wreck, boundless and bare
The lone and level sands stretch far away.'"

"Well," said Quirk, shaking his head. "It seems you've been studying after all."

1F

10:34, 28 November 2099
"The Real Time" Cafe, 1417 Canyon St, Creston, BC

Quirk opened the door for Moth, and they strolled into their regular haunt in Creston. He patted his thigh by force of habit, comforted beyond measure to feel the robust indigo-and-olive pinstripe fabric of his Merrion suit. He didn't care how out of place he looked. In truth, he very much wanted to be out of this place now, get back to a place where suits were de rigueur. A place like Milan, a place like Berlin.

Eve sat waiting at a corner table by the window, bright winter sun illuminating the fatigue around her slightly puffy eyes. He had watched her through the plass window as he and Moth approached, her eyes closed, face turned towards the sun. He sympathised with that fatigue, but hers must be so much deeper. Eve had experienced the same long days of FBI questioning, but she had endured that on top of Tania Terjesen being taken from her again, installed in a secure government hospital awaiting trial after her recovery. Add to that the life-changing injuries to her friend Dulcie.

That thought brought dark companions, heavy recollections and grim reminders of the disastrous encounter with Nick. His son. Gone now too, but gone where? Heaven, hell, the Worlds Wide Web? Nick's claims of disincorporation and rebirth in the data stream seemed wild and unlikely, but could he ignore them, given the marvels Nick—demonstrably—had been capable of? Perhaps they would never know. Perhaps.

He smiled broadly at Eve. He was not about to add his own worries to her burden. She just nodded, her own smile drifting away. He and Moth sat, both ordering lattes when their usual waitress arrived.

"Terra," said Moth to Eve, jerking her thumb after the departing twentysomething. "Like the fauna."

"Moth," Quirk cautioned her. "Have you heard anything, Eve?"

"No," she said, straightening. "It'll be months, but that's not the thing, Quirk. The thing is they'll find her guilty, because the thing is she knew about Nick, she contributed to the...project. A little at first, but— Ah, shit. Scientific curiosity is a powerful thing, so I'm informed." She scowled. "I'm sorry, for not questioning when I should have."

He waved her apology away. "I'm the one who did the wrong thing. I think I've always known that, just refused to accept it. I've run from it for five years." He'd run from the madness, from TOM's destructive paternalistic bullshit, which destroyed everything it touched for the old bastard to reassemble in his own image. Like he'd done to Nick. Poor Nick. Quirk hung his head, wondering if—

A harshly broadcast voice shattered his reverie, slicing through the babble of café conversation. On the far side of the room, a handset—its owner nowhere to be seen— blared out the news for all to hear. Clearly the heathen had no aural implant, or even earbuds. Heads turned and faces glared. Moth was up out of her chair, ready to march straight into the washroom. "I'll go educate him—"

"Hang on." Quirk touched her hand, which he would not have contemplated a month ago, for fear that he might lose his. "Let's hear this."

"...why, no one expected this, John. Liano's surge in the reopened polls after the Yellowknife incident is unprecedented. It goes way beyond a bounce to something that's hard to fathom. The community lauds him for

sending a strong message to big business; environmental factions—grudgingly—hail the destruction of Genextric's Yellowknife operation as a great victory; and religious groups of all faiths praise him for righting a great wrong against God's creation.

So, it's a cakewalk for Peter Liano then, Nichelle?

I don't see a way back for his rivals. With three days to the ballot, he's five points clear. That's my definition of insurmountable, John.

So, there it is. Liano to win at a canter due to a most unprecedented quirk of history. You could go from here to Hygeia and not encounter such a miraculous resurrection. Surely, you have not heard the last of the Conservative Party's favourite son.

With all the news that's fit to hear, this is John Mbenza for Fax News on..."

The returning young man looked upset. Silencing the device, he raised a hand of apology to the room. Duly mollified, the company resumed its gentle hubbub. Quirk nodded slowly, his blood running cold. A news broadcast on a national network had just recounted his name, place of residence, and a reference to life after death. Any one of those on its own would have been an unlikely coincidence. But the news had ended on the phrase "Conservative Party's favourite son," signing off what surely must be a message from Nick. So, had he achieved his goal then, in the end? A chilling thought. What did it mean for Quirk, Moth, The Old Man, Jennifer? That line of thought was a short path to a place of nightmares, so he turned away.

The others had not picked up the significance of the message.

"Well," he engaged a smile, *Convivial with a Bullet*. It brought the realisation of how little he had smiled these past days. "I wish you luck either way."

"There's fuck all luck going around," said Moth.

"Hey, turn that frown upside-down, honey," said Eve dolefully.

"Moth has a point," said Quirk, a pang of loss poking his gut. The FBI had confiscated Moth's syRen® indefinitely, but at least had the good grace to confirm the vial Eighty carried had contained the pathogen that killed Barry Rowland, although that fact was academic now. Just another in the steady drip of indignities that the Federal Bureau of Ignominy had heaped upon them in the aftermath of the Yellowknife incident. The questioning, the statements, the scans, the polygraphs. "The FBI issued a reprogramming order. Apparently, some of Eighty's actions registered on the defectivity scale. I think we broke him."

"You said, 'him,'" Moth said quietly, punching him half-heartedly in the arm.

"Watch the weave," he said. "But I did, didn't I? Your constant barrage of abuse must have tenderised my emotions after all this time. So, I'll buy you a new syRen®."

"It won't be the same," she huffed.

"You said that last time, but that's the thing with androids, it *will* be the same; same algorithms, same tenets, same laws of robotics."

"Not the same memories."

"Those can be uploaded—"

"*My* memories, butthead. You're so fucking insensitive, sometimes."

He would have retorted, but she'd hit rather too close to the mark.

"You're better off without them, syRen®," said Eve. Quirk tended to agree.

"Are all the terra-fauna dead?" Moth asked.

"They are," Eve nodded, managing a glimmer of a smile. "They weren't a match for the National Guard, the FBI, and the gun-toting folks of YK, in the end."

"And what will you do, Eve?" he asked.

She hesitated. "Peter Kootook needs temporary deputies for three months. Several of his people are on medical leave."

"Ha," he nodded. "I believe law enforcement will suit you quite well."

"Why the fuck would you go back to Yellowknife?" Moth cut in, incredulous. "After all the crap that place dished out to you?"

"None of it was the place," said Eve, her words quiet against the background of new age country music and chatter. "I'm not ready for the corporate jungle; might never be. There's a place called Dettah that I think's more my speed for a while, if they'll accept me." Eve slid her fingers sideways across the tabletop, perhaps searching for Tania's hand. "Winter makes it hard to reach. Might even be shut off for a while."

Quirk nodded, catching himself wondering how far he would need to go into the wilderness to escape the reach of Nick's digital web.

* * *

Walking into Creston Sheriff's Office was weird as shit. At least the heating was on, their ground pump kicking out the kilowatts, making the place nice and cosy after another one of Quack's let's-soak-up-the-local-atmosphere-one-more-time walks down Canyon Street. It was minus-fucking-eleven outside and she'd done that already.

"If I had a fuzking handset, or an android, I could tell you the temperature in Berlin. Bet it's warmer than this." Moth frowned. Grinding Quirk's gears was less fun than it used to be. Not that she would stop, but she watched him as he walked to the desk in his ugly out-of-place suit, and too-cool-for-school overcoat, and... What was that? Respect, warmth, love? Fuck no, none of that shit. Belonging?

Becker was on the desk. *Shit.*

"Please tell the sheriff we're here, Becker," Quirk asked.

Deputy Doofus sneered at him, still mad they had beat eighty percent of their charge sheet due to Kreski's intervention.

"The sheriff in absentia," Moth added. "Not the acting sheriff."

After a short battle with deductive reasoning, Becker shrugged. Moth rolled her eyes. "Kreski. Get Kreski."

Becker scowled. "I shoulda thrown you dipshits in jail the minute you showed your dirty faces back here," he grumbled.

"Yeah, well," she slapped the counter, having to look up to meet Becker's narrowed eyes. "No one gives two shits about something you *didn't* do, Beaker. Now, give our friend Wayne a tinkle, stat."

"C'mon back here," barked Kreski through his open office door.

Becker swung the gate open, and Moth strode in, deciding that a self-satisfied strut would annoy Baby Becker the most. She clumped through the bullpen of half-a-dozen desks, nodding to Parks as she passed, holding up her chin, ignoring the deputy's shake of the head.

"Well," said Kreski, shifting awkwardly, left shoulder and arm still strapped to his chest, "looks like you clowns are just about in the clear by some miracle."

"Just about?" Quirk looked concerned.

"Mm, hmm." Kreski nodded. "Your fines will pretty much pay to upgrade Prince Charles Secondary School, but there's the matter of a stolen plane, the wreckage of which remains in a blackened pile at Revelstoke Airport. Nat is not withdrawing her complaint."

Moth smiled. "We took care of that this morning, Wayne."

Quirk nodded, smiling one of his dopey smiles. "Yes, I made a purchase yesterday at breakfast which I think Natalie will be quite pleased with. It should be arriving from Vancouver"—he consulted his handset—"within the hour."

"Huh," Kreski nodded pensively, turning a gruff expression on her. "And it's 'Sheriff' to you, young lady."

"Yes, Sheriff Wayne." She grinned. "And what Quirk doesn't know is that there's a surprise arriving with Nat's new plane."

"There's what?" Quirk turned on her, brows knitting in what he would probably call "consternation," or some other fancy-pants word. "You didn't consult me."

"No, I didn't. I'm an assistant. Assistants assist, and I reckon I assisted the shit out of this one." She grinned. She could not actually wait to see the look on his actual face. "How about driving us out to the airport, Sheriff Wayne?"

Kreski agreed easily enough, maybe just pleased to get out of the office, away from Dough-Head Becker and Lack-of-Amusement Parks. They piled into Kreski's big, new multi-function ASUV. With a big scowl, the sheriff let autonomous mode take them through town past the grain elevators and across the rail tracks before he took the wheel. He was clearly not right yet, despite days of accelerated muscle regeneration.

She was sure Quirk paled a little when Kreski called Natalie to say they were on their way. Her guardian stared out of the window at the trees and mountains drifting past. He'd been prone to these dreamy moments recently. She worried about what he was feeling since his son was killed. Correction: since she had shot his son. *What a headfuck that is, but I had to do it.* She told herself again there had been no right answer, then leaned forward and put a hand on Quirk's shoulder. His eyes flicked to the vanity mirror on the back of the visor blocking the sun's glare, smiled slightly, sadly she thought, then patted her hand.

She was glad she'd told him about her nickname. It had been tough, but also the right time. She knew now that he was more than just a self-righteous, preening, quasi-queer, opinionated, licentious, wrong-headed, popinjay dickwad. And anyway, he was her self-righteous, preening, quasi-queer, opinionated, licentious, wrong-headed, popinjay dickwad. *Jeez, get* that *on a T-shirt.*

Natalie waited in the parking lot and had Quirk's door open before the ASUV had stopped moving, causing some sort of warning from the dash.

"You fucker." Her red hair blazed in the low winter sun. "I am going to shoot you in the face." She had him by the lapels and practically yanked him out the vehicle.

"The weave, woman. The weave!"

"I'm going to weave you a new colon, you bastard."

"Hey, Natalie," said Moth. She jumped out the other door and strode around front, past Quirk where the redhead had him pasted to the side of Kreski's vehicle. "Don't you think that he knew better than to show up emptyhanded?"

Moth had Natalie's attention now and kept walking, past the control tower—*Control Hut!*—and on towards the apron. Thinking how cool it would look as she strutted away from the adults, she stuck her hand in the air and wagged her finger for them to follow.

Nothing moved on the ground and the mountain air was crisp and quiet. Moth picked out the sound of an engine on approach. Natalie would pick it up too. Sure enough, the woman came up alongside her, having released the boss, who stood straightening his tie. The engine noise cut through the silence now, loud and gruff, an almost blundering mechanical sound that spread across the valley.

"What the hell is that?" Natalie put a hand up to shade her eyes. "That's a...biplane."

"It's a Tiger Moth," said Quirk, like a stupid surprise-spoiling grown-up. "It's the icing. I transferred funds to replace the Beechcraft, but Moth thought you would like this. It's a thank-you for believing in us when we were in a corner."

"Like it?" Nat was beaming, kind of lopsided and disbelieving, she gripped Kreski's arm as if she needed to touch reality for a second. "I like it fine, Quirk. You're forgiven."

The antique touched down, braked, braked, braked again then turned towards the hangars. Quirk leaned back and Moth met his gaze behind Kreski's back. He nodded then winked, giving her a thumbs up.

Oh, for fuzk sake.

She looked forwards again and called to him over the mad engine noise as the biplane taxied to a stop on the apron.

"Nat's isn't the only surprise."

"So you've said." Quirk's uncertainty was clear and very satisfying.

Moth started forward before the propeller stuttered to rest, turning to watch Quirk watching the pilot—complete with real old leather flying cap—climb out of the cockpit. The woman stepped onto the wing then down to the ground and started towards them, unfastening the flying cap as she came. She stopped in front of Quirk, pulling off the cap and shaking loose shoulder-length platinum tresses which blew about in the chill breeze.

"Good day, Quirk." Flawless, make-up model acrylic skin slipped into a cool, professional smile, violet eyes regarding him with pre-programmed orientation blinks. "My designation is syRen® S-17834, but my owner—Miss Moratti—calls me Bea."

20

Another spaceport. Another ascetic, sanitised space, the wrong sort of place to be conducting the emotional transaction that was about to take place, but there really was no choice. Moth's studies awaited her at home in Hygeia, and he had made a commitment to go to Berlin.

Now, he paced along in Moth's wake through the meandering, dashing, strolling, whipping ripples of humanity. The girl's long, crisp strides fairly broadcast to the whole concourse with each thunk that she was coming through. What interested him particularly was the subtle— *Moth, really?* he shook his head—but readily apparent change in her. He doubted it was down to a mere three days in the company of her new BAFF, syRen® S-17834. Maybe a kind of rebirth had occurred after the harrowing events of the previous fortnight. They had talked in their compartment on the flight from Calgary, talked like they never had before, unless perhaps on occasion when past arguments had become so heated, they tipped over into emotional truth. No, they had talked openly about how they felt on being laid so low physically, their reserves of mental strength tested so severely, their worldview (or Quirk's at least) shaken as roughly as it had been. It felt like something grown-ups did, something neither he nor Moth had been at all good at since their respective personal traumas and being thrown together in Milan in that most unwanted way. It felt good.

The first thing they'd done on arriving in Chicago two days before was check in to the Dakota Pan-Terra, because

Toni's money was there to be spent, and Moth had shelled out half-a-million dollars on the latest syRen® model, so it wasn't as if they were economising. She had gone straight to her shower, and Quirk could understand how she might still be trying to wash away the memory of that harrowing (that word again) crawl through the Genextric waste pipe, and the carnage that followed. These fresh shadows on the girl's free spirit would not soon be cleansed, or easily.

She did not sleep through the night now. He'd heard low voices from the connecting room at two or three in the morning, because he didn't sleep through either. Moth and Bea were discussing something personal, but he did not know what because he hadn't listened. Girl stuff, maybe? He had checked on her later though, just after five, finding the syRen® charging quietly on a chair near the door and Moth sleeping through gentle, intermittent sighs. The plushie bear she'd bought in the Calgary Spaceport giftshop lay on top of the cover, schlumped on its paws, facing the door.

The next morning, while Quirk checked his messages, Moth and the syRen® had hit the hotel's shopping plaza. When they returned, Bea came in first, going straight to Moth's room with the bags. Moth breezed in behind the android and actually said, "Ta-da!" standing with her arms high, hands turned out in a classic model pose (and being from Milan, she would know) before parading across the suite to the big picture window and making a turn.

She was still almost all in black, but...

Quirk had realised he was gaping, indignation rising, and stood up from his chair, arms akimbo. She'd had her hair permed! Someone with a creditable grasp of the word "subtle" had done her make-up, and she sported a classic biker's jacket over a black tank top with a shiny, patent leather skirt, black tights and...

"What, are those?" he pointed at her feet. "They're platform boots! You're—"

"These"—she had grinned, swinging a leg out straight and pacing towards him—"are not platform boots, Boss.

These are genuine Retro Vintage Gdgydh women's black, soft leather, lace-up, high-heeled, ankle party boots, size four-point-five. Hey, presto; look out, worlds, I'm five-foot-fucking-seven!"

All he could do was smile, shake his head and applaud. Then she'd hugged him, and he'd hugged back. And now she was leaving.

It was the only course that made any sense. He was due in Berlin, and Professor Streich had been clear that they would be travelling light. Moth had exams. They had discussed her sitting them on the road, but if the last two weeks had proved anything it was that Eve Meyer's disaster magnet theory had some credence. So, Moth was doing the mature thing, indulging in a shopping spree before returning to Hygeia to apply herself to her "books" while he departed for Germany to work with Cassie Streich of Berlin State Library. He had however promised that he'd be home by Christmas.

Now, Moth led the party of three through the illuminated tunnel of retail outlets and out onto the immense, circular plaza that hung in the air in the midst of the terminal, seemingly suspended by elements of gossamer from O'Hare's remarkably structure-light dome. She stopped near the centre of the busy space into which eight wide travellators disgorged, and spun on the spot once, twice, three times—arms extended—to carve out a space for them among the ebb and flow of now-disgruntled travellers. Most regarded her as if she were deranged, tight or tripping, but he knew she was nothing more than drunk on life, and it made him glad.

"I feel you're even more demonstrative than usual with those extra thirteen centimetres, Moth." He smiled: no flavour, no subtitle, just a regretful twist of the lips at this moment of parting. The shining walls and night-blackened panels of the dome seemed to be painted with a melancholic haze. He patted the Merrion's pockets again to check that one was empty, and one was not.

Bea placed Quirk's scuffed brown leather carry-on beside his left foot then backed away, ready to accompany Moth to the South America pier.

Moth moved to stand in front of him. "It's only a couple of weeks, Boss." She patted the Merrion's lapel then straightened his tie. "You'll be fine."

He thought her eyes shone a little more brightly than usual.

"Moth, I got you something."

She cast her eyes down, looking thoughtful then glanced away into the crowd that flowed around them. Then she met his gaze and spoke as if she hadn't heard him. "I think maybe I'm ready for you to call me Angelika."

"I..." Damn it, he was choking up, and he was struck by another of those moments of gut-gnawing anguish in which he wondered what would have happened to Nick if he'd stayed in San Francisco. He pushed the sorrow away, sent it packing with a promise that it could return when Moth had departed, and he had located the bar near his gate.

He tapped the toe of his shoe on the floor. "We can argue about that another time." He produced a package from the Merrion's inner pocket, glossy black paper with a pink bow. He held out his hand and she took it gingerly.

Moth liked to savour the opening of presents, he had observed, and went at the paper methodically. Unfortunately, he was appallingly bad at secrets.

"I know it's tacky and gold, but since the FBI never returned yours..."

She let the wrapping and the ribbon fall to the concourse floor and slipped a svelte, golden shape into her palm from the unwrapped velvet bag. "A handset," she said.

"I know it's a personal thing, but I thought you'd appreciate that it's a Lamborghini, handmade in—"

She pressed a finger to his lips, stilling them, her dark eyes glistening. "Shut up, you idiot" She beamed as tears ran down her cheeks. "You had me at tacky."

* * *

Watching Moth and her android walk away, Quirk did not see Beatrix Potter ghost through the throng towards him, only becoming aware of Beatrix when the barrel of xis gun lodged in the small of his back. The assassin leaned in, lips pressed to Quirk's ear. "I've been saving this, but you should have it now, while there's still time."

The kiss touched Quirk's neck, he flinched then froze rigid, waiting for the bullet, but it didn't come, and Beatrix was gone.

THE END

Quirk next appears in:
The Bibliothek Betrayal

Moth will next appear in:
The Hygeia Hijacking

Quirk and Moth will return in:
The Rigel Redemption

ACKNOWLEDGEMENTS

Once again, Bill and Heather Tracy of Space Wizard have made the seemingly impossible happen, and they do so with grace and skill. Remarkable people to have in your corner.

The Reading Excuses crew—JS, Bill, Sara, and Natalie—who met Quirk and Moth not long after I did. I treasure your support, advice and critiques through the years.

The Glasgow SF Writers' Circle—yous are the best, better than all the rest.

Neil Williamson and Reese Hogan for the cover quotes— knowing that others enjoy our work and our characters is exactly the encouragement a writer needs, sometimes, always.

The Writing Excuses Podcast for being the catalyst; without whose writing prompts Quirk and Moth may never have existed.

Note: The character of Natalie was named Natalie before I knew that my friend Natalie (Silk > N.L. Bates) was named Natalie. Any resemblance of the character Natalie to my friend Natalie is purely coincidental, and ends with them both being Canadian and living in BC, and being called Natalie.

Paul Harris, for the Q&M logo, and the brain food.

Pam Livingstone, for making me DAHG24P, and for the gift of music.

Barrie Condon, for good refs and excellent conversation.

Moor Books, for knocking it out of the park, again.

The Donald Maas Agency and Tantor Media, for the boost when I needed it.

To everyone who reaches out to say "Hi."

My family—Ashley and Micah (I love you; you make me proud), Moss & Ivy.

Tara, for everything, always and forever.

Peace and love.

ABOUT THE AUTHOR

Robin C.M. Duncan is a Scot born and living in Glasgow. A Civil Engineer by profession, he has been writing for decades, but seriously only for the last ten years. Robin has completed various novels, and numerous short stories, novellas, novelettes, and poems, with copious other projects in different stages of incompletion.

Robin's short story *The NEU Oblivion* was long-listed for the 2019 James White Award. His first published works, the novellas *Dew Diligence* and *The Bibliothek Betrayal (A Quirk & Moth Debacle)*, appear in the *Distant Gardens* anthology of 2021.

Robin belongs to the Glasgow Science Fiction Writers' Circle, the British Fantasy Society, the British Science Fiction Association, and the Reading Excuses critique group. He also volunteers with Glasgow 2024 Worldcon, where he is Deputy Area Head of Glasgow 2024 Presents.

(robincmduncan.com)

Please take a moment to review this book at your favorite retailer's website, Goodreads, or simply tell your friends!

Made in the USA
Monee, IL
26 June 2023

36769248R00236